Emily Forbes is an award-winning author of Medical Romance for Mills & Boon. She has written over twenty-five books and has twice been a finalist in the Australian Romantic Book of the Year Award, which she won in 2013 for her novel *Sydney Harbour Hospital: Bella's Wishlist*. You can get in touch with Emily at emilyforbes@internode.on.net, or visit her website at emily-forbesauthor.com.

Born and raised just outside Toronto, Ontario, **Amy Ruttan** fled the big city to settle down with the country boy of her dreams. After the birth of her second child Amy was lucky enough to realise her lifelong dream of becoming a romance author. When she's not furiously typing away at her computer she's mum to three wonderful children, who use her as a personal taxi and chef.

Withdrawn
Dublin P

D0656697

Leabharlanna Taistil
Mobile Libraries
Tel: 8691415

Also by Emily Forbes

One Night That Changed Her Life
Falling for His Best Friend
Reunited with Her Brooding Surgeon
Rescued by the Single Dad
Taming Her Hollywood Playboy
Reunited by Their Secret Daughter

Also by Amy Ruttan

NY Doc Under the Northern Lights
Carrying the Surgeon's Baby
The Surgeon's Convenient Husband
Royal Doc's Secret Heir
Pregnant with the Paramedic's Baby
Baby Bombshell for the Doctor Prince

Discover more at millsandboon.co.uk.

Withdrawn From Stock
Dublin Public Libraries

Leabharlanna Poiblí
Mobile Libraries
Tel: 8691415

THE ARMY DOC'S SECRET PRINCESS

EMILY FORBES

REUNITED WITH HER HOT-SHOT SURGEON

AMY RUTTAN

MILLS & BOON

All rights reserved including the right of reproduction
in whole or in part in any form. This edition is published
by arrangement with Harlequin Books S.A.

This is a work of fiction. Names, characters, places, locations
and incidents are purely fictional and bear no relationship to
any real life individuals, living or dead, or to any actual places,
business establishments, locations, events or incidents.
Any resemblance is entirely coincidental.

This book is sold subject to the condition that it shall not,
by way of trade or otherwise, be lent, resold, hired out
or otherwise circulated without the prior consent of the publisher
in any form of binding or cover other than that in which it is published
and without a similar condition including this condition
being imposed on the subsequent purchaser.

® and TM are trademarks owned and used by the trademark owner
and/or its licensee. Trademarks marked with ® are registered with the
United Kingdom Patent Office and/or the Office for Harmonisation
in the Internal Market and in other countries.

First Published in Great Britain 2020
by Mills & Boon, an imprint of HarperCollins*Publishers*
1 London Bridge Street, London, SE1 9GF

The Army Doc's Secret Princess © 2020 Emily Forbes

Reunited with Her Hot-Shot Surgeon © 2020 Amy Ruttan

ISBN: 978-0-263-27978-8

MIX
Paper from
responsible sources
FSC® C007454

This book is produced from independently certified FSC™ paper
to ensure responsible forest management.
For more information visit www.harpercollins.co.uk/green.

Printed and bound in Spain
by CPI, Barcelona

THE ARMY DOC'S
SECRET PRINCESS

EMILY FORBES

MILLS & BOON

For dearest Xander and Mel,
Congratulations to you as you celebrate your wedding day
and your commitment to each other.
Xander, make sure you treat Mel like a princess!
Mel, please take care of my nephew.
Wishing you both a lifetime of happily-ever-afters,
with all my love,
Auntie *Emily*

PROLOGUE

Two years ago

CAMPBELL'S HEADPHONES BLOCKED out most of the engine noise, but he could still hear a faint rhythmic thump-thump as the chopper blades beat the air and he could feel the vibrations as they shuddered through his body. After almost six months he thought he'd be used to the overwhelming assault on his senses—the smell of fumes and dust, the incessant noise, the constant jarring and jolting—but he had yet to get used to the tension. He was always on edge when he was in flight, despite knowing that one of the Australian Army's best pilots was in control of the aircraft, and he was looking forward to getting back on the ground.

Cam kept his eyes cast down, focusing on his patient. He kept up a one-sided conversation despite the fact that his patient was heavily sedated, and the engine noise would make conversation almost impossible even if he were conscious. He gave him a rundown of his situation—only the positives though. His IV line was running smoothly and his vital signs had stabilised, he told him. He avoided the specifics of his injuries. The soldier was badly wounded, but he didn't need to be re-minded of that. He'd live, at this stage that was the important information, but he'd be getting sent home for a while. Home to Australia. Where he'd have a chance to recover physically, if not mentally.

Cam knew the soldiers would always be haunted by their experiences fighting a war on the other side of the world. Some would cope better than others. He knew he'd have scars too. Mental, not physical. This war wasn't what he'd anticipated or expected.

Gemma had warned him, but how did you warn someone who had grown up in rural Australia? A land of dust and dirt but safe enough. Hot, and at times desolate, but it had been a different sort of barren. A different sort of danger.

Apart from the snakes and some angry rams or falling off a motorbike or a horse, Cam hadn't really had anything to worry about. Now, every day was a battle. Here, there was always a chance of getting hit by a bullet, being on the wrong side of an IED, being wounded or killed by enemy fire or even by a civilian on a suicide mission. Life here was stressful.

His job as a medical specialist with the Australian Army meant he was responsible for lives in a country where lives were not highly regarded. Lives here were seen as disposable, which went against everything he believed in and made his job difficult and, at times, impossible. He still had access to First World medical facilities but, more often than not, he was trying to save lives in the middle of a dust bowl, trying to do his best while war raged around him. Gemma had tried to explain it to him but, until he'd seen it with his own eyes, until he'd lived through the experiences she had told him about, he knew he hadn't understood.

He glanced towards the cockpit to where Gemma sat

in the pilot's seat. As if she had felt his gaze, his fiancée turned and looked back at him and smiled.

Cam was looking forward to getting back to base. He was looking forward to dinner with Gemma, even if it was just in the mess tent. He could pretend for a moment that they were a normal couple, looking forward to making a life together, planning a family. He needed that idea of his future—it was what kept him going on tough days. Gemma was the bright spot in his world. He loved his job but, if he was asked, he'd have to admit he preferred to do his job in the sterile environment of an Australian medical facility. He didn't mind dust and dirt, he was country born and bred after all, but practising medicine in these conditions was challenging, often unpleasant and definitely not fun.

But no one was interested in his opinion and if he wanted to be with Gemma, this was where she was.

He wondered if he had any chance of convincing her to quit the army and return to Australia. She loved flying but it would be years before she would achieve flight instructor status with the army. Years before she wouldn't have to fly combat missions. Perhaps she could work privately instead.

He wondered when it would be safe to have that discussion. Would it ever? Could he ask her to give up something she loved? How would he feel if she started to tell him how to live his life or run his career?

He knew he wouldn't be happy.

He blew her a kiss just as a bright light burst in his peripheral vision.

The chopper lurched as Gemma's head whipped around and even through the headphones Cam could hear the sound of tearing metal.

The chopper shuddered and he could see Gemma and

her co-pilot fighting to keep control as the bird started to spin.

It took him a few seconds to work out what had happened. It felt like an eternity.

They'd been hit.

There was a second explosion, the burst of light so intense that Cam closed his eyes against the glare.

He could feel the chopper spinning wildly. He opened his eyes and saw the ground rushing towards them as the machine fell from the sky.

Black smoke filled the cabin, making Cam's eyes water. He couldn't see Gemma. He couldn't see anything. He lost all sense of space and time.

He threw himself over his patient as the helicopter plummeted. He knew it was a ridiculous gesture. He wasn't going to be able to protect him. He wasn't going to be able to save him. The situation was completely out of his control.

There was nothing he could do.

Cam's eyes flickered open.

His head was pounding and he closed his eyes again as he fought back a wave of nausea. His ears were ringing and there was a metallic taste in his mouth. Blood.

He licked his lip. It was split and swollen but the blood was still wet. He was dazed, disoriented but he knew then that he hadn't been knocked out for long.

He opened his eyes and looked around the cabin. Acrid smoke still billowed in the air, making his eyes water and obscuring his vision.

He breathed in through his nose, trying to avoid getting a mouthful of smoke. A sharp pain speared through the left side of his chest, making him gasp with pain. His breathing was shallow, restricted.

He lifted one hand to his chest and pressed gently under his armpit. His ribs screamed in protest even as he subconsciously registered that his left arm still functioned. That was good. He had obviously fractured some ribs, but it appeared that he hadn't sustained major damage to his upper spine at least.

He could feel pain in his right hip as well as his ribs, but he knew that sometimes pain was a good thing; it meant his nerve endings were intact. Sometimes even a painful sensation was better than no sensation.

The smoke was acrid but, underlying the smoke, Cam could smell fumes. That focused his attention.

They needed to get out of the chopper.

Would it explode? How long did they have?

Who had fired the missile at them? And where were they? Were they close? Or perhaps far enough away that they hadn't seen the distinctive red cross marking the bird as a medical transport? Or perhaps they didn't care?

The inside of the chopper was dark. The faint glow of green emergency lights gave an eerie aspect, failing to pierce the smoky interior. Visibility was poor but the cabin was also quiet. He couldn't hear a sound. Was everyone else still unconscious? Or worse?

The smoke began to clear, and Cam peered around the cabin. The stretcher that had held his patient was on its side. Crumpled. He was sure he'd thrown himself over his patient, but the force of the impact had thrown him against the opposite wall of the chopper.

He looked to the front of the chopper.

There was a gaping hole where Gemma's seat should be.

'Gemma!'

Pain shot through his chest again. He was out of

breath and his voice was raspy. Hoarse. His tongue felt thick and his swollen lip deformed his words.

'Gemma!'

He had to move but he knew it was going to hurt. He pressed his right hand against his ribs, trying to hold them together as he grabbed the side of the chopper with his left hand. He tried to keep his left elbow pressed against his side, pressing against his right hand, but still his ribs protested and his vision blurred with pain. Little black dots danced in front of his eyes and he blinked, trying to clear them away as he pulled himself to his feet. He made it into a semi-upright position, leaning through his right side, but the moment he put his weight onto his right foot an intense pain shot through his pelvis.

His right leg refused to take his weight. It wouldn't hold.

It gave way beneath him as searing pain tore through him.

He collapsed, Gemma's name still on his lips, as everything went black.

CHAPTER ONE

Present day

CAMPBELL'S LEG ACHED and he fought hard against the urge to stand up. The meeting had been long and he was beginning to get restless. He'd never been good at sitting still and these days it was almost impossible. He needed to stand and stretch; prolonged periods of sitting disagreed with him. Irritated his mind and his body. If he sat still his leg complained and his mind wandered. He needed to be moving, he needed to be busy. He wanted to keep his mind occupied. He didn't want time to dwell. Too much time to think had proven to be difficult.

He stretched his right leg out under the boardroom table as he tried to ease the cramp in his hip. He needed to get in the pool. Swim a few laps. He would prefer to swim a few laps in the ocean, but he knew from experience that he'd fare better in a warm pool. The heated water would ease his aching muscles. It had been two years since the chopper crash and he didn't need ice baths any more.

It had been twenty-four months since the incident, but he was still adjusting to his new life.

A life as a solitary man.

'Any other problems?'

He brought his attention back to the meeting as Douglas began to wrap it up.

Thank goodness it was almost over. Cam hoped no one had any additional items for discussion. He looked around the table at the ten other men and women, trying to gauge if any of them looked like they had something on their mind. He'd had enough experience with meetings, ward rounds as well as military discussion groups, to know that there was always one person who seemed to delight in dragging meetings on for far too long but today, for once, it appeared as though everyone was just as eager to escape as he was.

He stood up the minute Douglas officially closed the meeting. He stretched, knowing that if he didn't take a moment to ease the stiffness in his back and leg his limp would be far more pronounced, and he preferred not to draw attention to himself.

He was used to being noticed but he didn't want to be noticed for the wrong reasons. He knew that was ironic and he'd never say it out loud, not when he was surrounded by so many others with far more severe disabilities and injuries than he had, but he knew that perception was a very personal thing.

'You okay?' Doug was beside him.

Cam knew Doug would have noticed his attempt at surreptitious stretching. Doug was one of his closest friends in the service and had been a good support to him during his rehabilitation and recovery phase. His family and friends had helped get him through the past year. He felt he owed it to them to pull through, although there had been times when it had seemed like too much effort, but he was having better days now.

He knew he'd been difficult. He'd been the sole survivor of the incident that had claimed the lives of five others, including his fiancée. He'd been angry but he'd eventually managed to let go of that anger; however, guilt had continued to eat away at him. It still did. He knew the incident hadn't been his fault but the fact he hadn't been able to save anyone, especially Gemma, was hard to live with and it remained an effort to get through his days with a smile.

Work had been his saviour. Initially he hadn't wanted to listen to other people's problems but gradually he'd found that if he focused on their issues it gave him less time to think about his own. Keeping busy had been the key and now he threw himself into whatever came his way and he had taken on all manner of tasks in the past twelve months since returning to his post as an army medic.

'Yes,' he replied, 'just too many meetings.' His need to keep busy was what had landed him in this situation in the first place. 'When I agreed to be the medical liaison officer on the committee, I didn't expect to spend so much time in discussions. I expected my role to be in an advisory capacity.'

His pain made him grumpy. He knew it. He should take some painkillers, but he needed the strong ones and he needed to keep a clear head. He needed his wits about him; he didn't want to get roped into any more committees or be given any more tasks to do. He had enough on his plate.

'It is.'

'Well, then, I didn't think it was possible to have this many meetings.' Cam had made no secret of the fact that he liked to be busy and when he'd agreed to be on this committee he'd imagined that he'd be doing something practical like overseeing the medical facilities and pro-gramme for the games, not sitting around in meetings.

'We're almost done,' Doug said, making an effort to appease him. He knew full well Cam's opinion about meetings. 'The Games start next week.'

The countdown was on until the Legion's Games began, when hundreds of injured veterans from twenty countries around the world would descend on Sydney to compete in a dozen different events across ten days. The Games were the brainchild of Prince Alfred, an army captain himself, and the Games Committee was responsible for the event but, as the host nation, the Australian defence force was heavily involved. It was a massive exercise and the logistics of the Games fell to the Australians, which was how Cam found himself involved.

'Not much longer and your suffering will all be over,' Doug added with a smile.

Cam doubted that. Sure, he'd have fewer meetings to attend but his current life was still so far removed from what he'd thought it was going to be; he wasn't sure that his suffering was ever going to be over.

He'd hoped the Games would be a good distraction, a way to mark the passing of time. He'd expected to be consulted over the details of the medical facilities, but somehow, he'd found himself dragged along to every damn meeting in existence. He tried to be positive. He'd put his hand up for this project after all, but he'd put his hand up for any work that had been offered to him over the past year. Exhaustion was the only way he could get even a half-decent night's sleep. A few hours when he could shut out the horrors of everything he'd experienced during his tour of duty in the Middle East.

'What are your plans for tonight?' Doug asked as they left the boardroom together, Cam's muscles finally relaxing enough to enable him to walk without a limp. Well, without much of a limp.

'I'm going to head to the pool.'

'You're not seeing that girl from the other night? What was her name?'

'Caroline,' Cam said, before adding, 'no.'

He'd been on a few dates recently, if you could call them that. Dates that had been set up through his friends in the armed forces. Dates with girls who were happy to have a night out. But not one of them had progressed further than a single night. Not one had ended in anything more than a kiss. Cam was scarred, physically and emotionally, and he wasn't ready to expose himself to anyone new. He wasn't ready for those conversations. He wasn't interested in having a relationship.

He wasn't short of female attention; he knew women considered him good-looking, and while the copper crash had shattered his femur and fractured his pelvis his face had remained relatively unscathed. He had a small scar running through his bottom lip but otherwise his facial features were unmarked.

He wasn't lacking female attention, but his heart remained hardened. He wasn't interested in getting to know any of them in detail and he definitely did not want them getting to know him. He didn't want to answer questions about himself. He didn't want to open up, to share his thoughts and feelings. He wanted to lock the pain away.

He disagreed with the psychologists. Talking about what had happened only made the pain worse. It only kept the memory alive. Made it stronger. No one, least of all Cam, needed to be reminded of what had happened.

'Well, before you go, can I have a word with you about tomorrow's schedule?' Doug asked.

'Don't tell me there are more meetings—I'm consulting tomorrow and I know my list is pretty full.'

'I know you're out at the rehab centre tomorrow; that's why I need to speak to you. I have a favour to ask. The Prince's social media manager has arrived in Sydney ahead of the Prince and has asked for a tour of the facilities.'

'Which facilities?'

'All of them. But I thought we could start with the old barracks first.'

One of the old inner-city army bases had been re-purposed as a rehabilitation facility when the site had needed updating. The active units had been reassigned to a new purpose-built base in the outer suburbs of Sydney and the old base had been upgraded and was now home to the medical facilities, including doctors, physiothera-pists, psychologists, exercise physiologists, a purpose-built gym and pool for the injured and returned soldiers, along with outdoor sporting facilities. The repurposed base was going to serve as the venue for the majority of the events in the Legion's Games.

'You're out there tomorrow,' Doug continued. 'Can they go out there with you?'

'You want me to babysit the Prince's—what did you call them—social media manager?'

Doug nodded and sweetened the deal. 'If you can do me this small favour, I promise I won't drag you into any meetings for the rest of the week.'

Cam sighed and ran his hand through his thick, dark hair. A day out of the boardroom was preferable to an-other day of meetings. Even playing tour guide to a stranger would have to be better than that. 'All right,' he agreed.

'Okay, I'll send you the details,' Doug said as he took out his phone and tapped away. 'Can you collect her from her hotel at o-nine hundred hours?'

'Her?' he asked as his phone pinged with the incoming email. Prince Alfred had a military background and Cam had, incorrectly it seemed, assumed his social media manager would be a man.

Cam had met the Prince once while he'd been deployed in the Middle East. Once, in the days before the incident. In the days before his life went down the toilet.

'Yes—' Doug grinned '—see if you can dredge up some of your old charm. Be nice.'

Cam looked at the email on his screen and noted her name, along with the hotel address, with a raised eyebrow. Apparently, Viktoria von Grasburg was staying in one of Sydney's five-star hotels on the Harbour. He wondered who was paying for that.

'Sure,' he said as he sighed and stuck his phone back in his pocket, before massaging his hip subconsciously.

Viktoria woke up well before sunrise as her body clock still hadn't adjusted to the Australian time zone. She rolled over and picked up her phone, knowing she wouldn't get back to sleep. She had plenty of time to kill so she opened her emails and was relieved to find nothing important. Out of habit, she googled her name and then wished she hadn't.

Another name popped up in the feed. Luca Romano. The successful, handsome captain of Italy's national polo team and her ex-fiancé. She knew his name would always be linked to hers—as a princess, she was a popular topic for the European media and her tumultuous love life was considered headline news. And nothing was more interesting in the world of 'entertainment' news than a royal scandal.

She'd thought Luca was her perfect man—strong and handsome with enough confidence to cope with the expectations of the public and the palace. But he'd turned out to be just another person who was more interested in fame and fortune—his fame and her fortune—than in settling down into a monogamous relationship. And loyalty and trust were two things Viktoria was not prepared to compromise on.

Luca had cheated on her and made sure she found out. As a defence he said he'd wanted to save her the embarrassment of being dumped by making it impossible for her to forgive him. He'd *wanted* her to break off their engagement but even though she had been able to end their relationship it had still hurt her. More than she would ever let on. She'd been taught to hold her head high in public but that hadn't lessened the pain she'd felt in private.

Three months later Luca was free now to do as he pleased and, by the look of the woman on his arm, he was enjoying his freedom. She knew she was better off without him in her life; she just wished she had the same freedom. She wished she could do as she pleased.

She closed the browser and put her phone down, sighing as she swung her legs out of bed. In a way Luca was responsible for her ending up here, in Sydney.

She was in Australia to have a break from her royal duties, a break from the tabloids constantly following her disastrous love life, and she was determined to enjoy her anonymity and associated freedom.

Her freedom would end soon enough, once she returned to Berggrun. She accepted that; it was the promise she had made to her parents. Berggrun princes and princesses were expected to marry by the age of thirty—to marry and start producing heirs to the throne. It was a tradition and the only way of ensuring the tiny principality didn't disappear. The timeline had been pushed out by her father but, even so, the deadline was looming for Viktoria. She would turn thirty next year and, while she might not be married, she would be expected to be engaged. She hadn't managed to hold on to her fiancé and she knew her parents had a shortlist of eligible potential husbands. By the time she returned home she expected her fate would have been decided. The next two weeks were her last chance of freedom.

She pressed the button on the remote to open the curtains. She stood up and gazed out of the window, refusing to let her future issues ruin what looked to be another glorious day. The sun had risen in the east and the endless sky was duck-egg-blue, broken only by a few wisps of white cloud. The water of Sydney Harbour sparkled in the early morning light and the Harbour Bridge looked almost close enough to touch, looming large outside the floor-to-ceiling windows of her penthouse suite.

Well, she reminded herself as she watched the boats scurrying across the water, today was the first day of the rest of her life. For the next couple of weeks, she was free from the constraints of being a royal and she was going to make the most of it. She was in Australia to do something worthwhile, something meaningful, and she was damn certain she would give it her best shot. She didn't have time to dwell on ex-fiancés, future husbands or even her life as a royal from the House of von Grasburg. This was her opportunity to be something other than a princess.

She headed for the shower as she thought about the conversation she'd had eight weeks ago with her cousin Freddie, when she'd flown to London to join in his thirtieth birthday celebrations. The two of them, and their siblings, had a close relationship but at that moment in time Viktoria had felt the gap between their lives very strongly. She'd been very aware of the immense divide between their lives and their futures. Freddie and his siblings had grown up in England—his mother was her father's sister—and Viktoria had always envied their more relaxed royal protocols. While they were expected to fill their days with meaningful pursuits—Freddie had served in the British army and had founded a charity he was passionate about—they weren't governed by the same strict traditions. Unlike her, Freddie was not expected to marry by the age of thirty.

'So,' he had said to her two months ago, 'my parents were telling me that yours are busy narrowing down the list of potential husbands for you.'

'Do not remind me,' Viktoria had groaned. 'I cannot believe it has come down to this. I cannot believe I thought Luca and I were going to live happily ever after. I cannot believe I am in this situation.'

'Do you have any idea who the options are?'

'I know my parents have mentioned a count from eastern Europe and also Tomas, the Duke of San Fernando.'

'Do you have a preference?'

'Tomas, I guess. At least I know him.' Part of her still imagined she'd find her true love before she ran out of time, but she knew she wasn't being realistic.

'Let's hope, for your sake, your parents make better decisions than you did. What *are* your plans for your last few months of freedom?'

'I wish I knew. I imagine it will be the usual list of functions. I don't mind the charity work but I am not looking forward to a life of service. I am tired of handing out awards and trophies and making small talk with a smile. All I seem to do is open museums and visit schools and hospitals. I want to feel like I am making a difference, not just decorating an event. I would like a break from being a royal for a while, but I cannot see that happening.'

That was the problem. She was jealous of other people, who could reinvent themselves or do as they pleased. People who could change their mind without having to ask for permission. She'd never been able to make independent decisions about anything ever. And after ten years as an adult that was beginning to get mighty frustrating.

'But, to be honest, I would really rather stay out of the spotlight. It would be nice to think I could experience life as an ordinary person before I am married off. You had your time in the army, when people treated you like a soldier, not a prince. You told me how much that meant to you. I want that. Maybe I should come to Sydney with you.'

Freddie, or Prince Alfred as he was known to most of the world, had been a captain in the armed forces and was the founder and patron of the Legion's Games, which was about to be staged for the third time in Sydney. The event was designed to inspire recovery and aid rehabilitation for service men and women in the armed forces through the healing power of sport. It was Freddie's brainchild and something he was passionate about. Viktoria envied him that passion and was in awe of the fact that he had been able to create something that would have a lasting legacy. She knew her work as a royal was important for the small principality of Berggrun, but she couldn't honestly say she was changing the world. She knew she was unlikely to ever make a significant difference but she'd like the opportunity to find out what she was capable of, rather than being instructed in how to live her life, how to behave, and directed to what tasks she could undertake, which duties were considered suitable for a princess.

She was passionate about horses but that was a personal passion and she had no idea how to make that something she could share with the world. She wasn't sure what she would do if she was given free rein, but she wished she'd have an opportunity to find out.

'Maybe you should,' he replied.

She had made an off-the-cuff comment but Freddie had taken her seriously.

'Really?'

'You could come to Australia as part of my team.'

'And do what?' she asked, tempted by the idea of travelling to Australia. Being on the other side of the planet sounded pretty good to her right now.

'I'm not sure exactly, but surely we could find something that could use that marketing and public relations degree you got at university. Maybe you could run the social media accounts for the Games and liaise with the press? Sort of like a marketing exercise. You could sell the Games to the general public. We could use this as an opportunity to promote the benefits that sport can make to physical and mental health. How does that sound?'

'I want to be anonymous for a while; I do not want to be part of the royal entourage.'

'You could simply be an employee. No one needs to know you're my cousin. Trust me, most Australians don't care about royalty. I swear most of them only make a fuss because they think it's expected. Don't forget I spent a year there at boarding school when I was fifteen. They only cared about my sporting skills, whether I was any good at cricket and rugby, not about whether I lived in a palace. They couldn't have cared less.'

'They know you.'

'That's because they're still part of the Commonwealth so they have a direct connection to me through the Crown, but I doubt many of them would have heard of the Principality of Berggrun. If they ever knew my mother was a Berggruner I'm sure they've forgotten that by now and I bet most Australians would never have heard of you.'

Viktoria laughed for the first time that day. 'You sure know how to make a girl feel special, Freddie.'

'You can't have it both ways, Viktoria,' her cousin teased her. 'You might want to be anonymous, but you know your parents have to give their approval if you want to run away. You need a valid reason to skip off to the other side of the world. This way, I can speak to Uncle Georg and make it sound official. Believe me, you won't regret it. Think about it and let me know. I guarantee you'll love it.'

Viktoria hadn't had to think about it for long. It wasn't as if she had anything better to do. Her parents and brothers could manage any royal engagements for two weeks. Handing out trophies was hardly challenging.

She was on the other side of the world and, she thought as she turned off the shower, she was about to start her first day 'on the job'. One that had nothing to do with her being a royal, a princess. Nothing to do with cutting ribbons, shaking hands or making speeches. She was working for her cousin, the Prince, but no one in Australia actually knew who she was. No one here knew she was a princess. As far as the organisers of the Legion's Games were concerned she was just running the Prince's social media campaign.

Freddie had told her no one would be bothered anyway but she hadn't believed him. She was about to find out.

She wrapped the soft white towelling robe around her and stepped out of the bathroom to find her assistant waiting for her. Viktoria's father had given permission for her to travel to Sydney with the proviso that she was escorted. Brigitta was on hand to attend to her schedule, wardrobe, hair and make-up. They had known each other since they were children—Brigitta's mother worked in the palace too—and Viktoria had to admit she was pleased to have some familiar company. As eager as she'd been to escape the palace, she wasn't accustomed to being alone.

'Can you run me through the plans for the day?' she asked as she noticed the outfit Brigitta had chosen and laid out on the bed for her.

She was confident she knew what was on the agenda, but she knew that plans could change at the last minute and she didn't want to be caught out. It was important to her to give a good first impression.

'One of the Games officials will meet you here at nine o'clock and escort you out to the facilities,' Brigitta told her. 'I gather most of the events will take place at one main venue and you'll tour that first.'

Viktoria planned to take some photographs throughout the day and start tweeting some inspirational messages to get the competitors psyched for the start of the Games and to catch the public's attention too. She looked at the outfit Brigitta had laid out for her again. A dress with a full skirt, wide straps and buttons running down the front was paired with wedge-heeled sandals. The irony that she'd wanted freedom to make her own decisions yet was still happy for Brigitta to select her clothes was not lost on her.

'Do you think I could wear something a little more casual?' she asked. 'It sounds like I could be doing a lot of walking. Flat shoes maybe?' She could tell by Brigitta's raised eyebrows that she had confounded her. Viktoria's mother, the Princess, *never* approved flat shoes but Viktoria wasn't going to let her mother's fashion sense dictate her wardrobe from the other side of the world. 'I imagine I'll be spending the day with a lot of people in uniform,' she argued, before Brigitta could protest, 'I do not want to look overdressed.' Besides, she'd worn flat shoes yesterday when she and Brigitta had played tourists, but she knew that was different. She wasn't pretending to work then.

'What did you have in mind?'

'I am not sure,' she said, realising that she really had no idea but knowing that she wanted the freedom to make the decision, 'but I am definitely thinking flat shoes. What about those trainers I wore yesterday?'

They had spent yesterday morning wandering around the historic Rocks area adjacent the hotel before heading down to the wildlife park on Darling Harbour. They'd been accompanied by Hendrik, a member of her family's security team who doubled as a driver and had also been sent to Australia by Viktoria's father. She wished she and Brigitta had been permitted to venture out alone, but she knew better than to suggest it. Hendrik would never allow it. Instead she'd tried to get Hendrik to blend in, to give the impression that they were three friends travelling together as opposed to a princess, her security guard and her personal assistant. She wasn't sure how successful they'd been, but no one had seemed to recognise her so maybe Freddie was right. Maybe she would get some freedom here in Sydney.

Brigitta disappeared into the walk-in closet and

emerged with a pair of Viktoria's white jeans, white leather sneakers, a navy blazer and a selection of light-weight camisoles. 'Something like this?'

'Perfect,' Viktoria said as she chose a patterned cami-sole and dressed quickly before sitting down to let Brigitta attend to her hair.

'What are you going to do today?' Viktoria asked as Brigitta brushed her thick, pale blonde hair before styling it in a loose plait that fell over one shoulder.

'I think I'll have to go shopping if you're going to insist on changing up your outfits. One pair of flat shoes is not going to see you through the next two weeks,' she said with a smile as she started applying Viktoria's make-up. She kept it simple, applying light foundation to Viktoria's creamy skin, highlighting her cheekbones with blush and using mascara and eyeliner to frame her blue eyes. As she finished coating Viktoria's lips with gloss the hotel telephone rang.

'There's a Dr Campbell Hamilton here to escort you,' Brigitta told Viktoria once she answered. 'I'll message Hendrik, tell him you're ready,' she said as she handed Viktoria a small bag. 'I've put your phone, a credit card, a make-up purse and your sunglasses in there. Your schedule is on your phone.'

Viktoria took a deep breath to calm her nerves, suddenly realising this was it. She was doing this. Going off to work like a regular person, out into the world.

She took the lift down to Reception. She stepped out, wondering how she would know who to look for, before realising the reception staff would advise her. She looked to the front desk and her attention was caught by a man in army uniform standing near the concierge.

'Miss von Grasburg?' he addressed her, and she was momentarily flummoxed. She wasn't used to being addressed so casually. There was no *Your Highness* or even *ma'am*.

No, this was what she wanted, she reminded herself. He knew all he needed to know. She smiled to herself and swallowed her surprise.

She was Miss von Grasburg.

CHAPTER TWO

'PLEASE, CALL ME VIKTORIA,' she said as she nodded and held out her hand to shake his.

'Campbell Hamilton.'

He was tall, over six feet, with thick dark hair which was a little longer than she thought would meet standard army regulations. He looked lean and muscular, fit without being too bulky. He had wide blue-grey eyes and a dimpled chin. He was clean-shaven with a full mouth and she could see a small scar running through his bottom lip. He was handsome. Very handsome.

She wasn't sure who she had been expecting but she had never imagined this.

His handshake was firm, his skin cool, but she wasn't prepared for the heat that spread from his fingertips into her hand and up her arm. She managed to maintain her composure even while her skin tingled and flared under his touch.

She waited for him to say it was a pleasure to meet her, but he didn't. Was that something people only said to be polite?

'I understand you want to see the Games facilities?' he said as he released her hand.

She nodded. The power of speech had deserted her

momentarily. Dr Campbell Hamilton was tall, dark and handsome and made her feel strangely nervous.

She had an odd sensation that this man was the reason she was here. That he was what she'd come for. She had an overpowering sense that he was going to play an important role in her days here. Or was she just getting caught up in the excitement of the day ahead?

'My car is out the front,' he said as he turned and began walking towards the exit. He was quite abrupt, and Viktoria was a little thrown. While she had the sense that he was important, that there was some sort of connection between them, he didn't appear to share her thoughts. She got the impression she had annoyed him. He seemed to wish he was somewhere else. Doing something else. Her bubble of enthusiasm deflated slightly but, refusing to be completely crushed, she followed him outside.

He was standing beside a white SUV, holding the door open for her.

She hesitated.

'Is there a problem?' he asked when she made no move to climb in.

Viktoria looked down the driveway and saw Hendrik pulling to a stop in the driveway.

'I arranged for Hendrik to drive us,' she said.

'Who?'

She gestured towards the black luxury SUV that was now stationary behind Campbell's car. 'Hendrik. My driver.'

'You have a driver?'

'Oui.'

'No one said anything about a driver. This is my car. I will be driving.'

Viktoria made a split decision. She didn't want to irritate him further and she wanted to live like a normal person. She'd let him drive. That would be safe enough, surely? After all, he was a government employee. 'Do you have some identification?' she asked.

'Identification?' He was frowning.

'*Oui.* If you can show Hendrik some identification to verify yourself, I will give him the day off and let you drive me.' She knew Hendrik wouldn't be happy, but she'd deal with him later.

'You'll *let* me drive you?'

His tone was frosty, but Viktoria nodded even as she wished they could begin this conversation again. They were not getting off to a great start.

Cam bit back a sigh and resisted the urge to run his hand through his hair in frustration. He should have taken the meetings. This was going to be a nightmare. They already seemed to be at cross purposes, working off different briefs. He couldn't care less if she came with him or not, but he had gone out of his way to collect her this morning and he didn't appreciate finding out that it hadn't been necessary. He could have easily met her at the barracks and sorted out her credentials and visitor's clearance then. But he knew he had to be polite. This woman worked for the Prince. It wouldn't do to get her offside. He suspected she was going to be demanding. She probably had every right to be, but he wished he wasn't going to be the one who had to meet her demands.

And then she smiled at him.

The photo provided for her clearance documents hadn't done her justice. It had been a flattering photo—she'd looked attractive—but he'd been mistaken. She wasn't just pretty; she was absolutely stunning.

Her smile was like the sun coming out and it burnt through the fog that had surrounded his psyche for the past two years. As the fog lifted, he felt as if he could see clearly for the first time in months…and what he saw made him catch his breath.

She had blonde hair that fell past her shoulders in a long plait, and flawless skin. Her legs were long and looked slim even in a pair of white jeans. About five foot eight, she was trim but athletic. She looked fit and healthy, young and full of energy. Her blue eyes sparkled, and he lost focus as he looked into them. He was well aware that she was the first woman he'd truly noticed in a long time and for a brief moment Gemma was not first and foremost in his mind.

And then the ever-present guilt resurfaced.

Gemma was his responsibility. His burden to bear. This woman, Viktoria, was gorgeous but their relationship was purely professional. It didn't matter what she looked like.

She was still smiling as he dug out his army identification and passed it over. He waited while she inspected it and then showed it to her driver.

He stuck it back in his pocket when she returned it to him and resisted the urge to slam the passenger door when she finally climbed into his car. He might be frustrated but he still had the manners instilled into him not only from the army but from his parents and he remembered Doug's words. *'Be nice.'*

It shouldn't have been a hardship to spend the day with her and it wasn't her fault he was grumpy—that his guilt made him irritable.

He was mollified when his actions were rewarded with another smile.

'*Merci.*'

Her voice was pleasant. Deep for a woman. Her words precise. Her English was scattered with French words and slightly accented.

He resisted the temptation to ask her about it. He told himself he didn't need to know anything personal about her. That he didn't care to. He told himself he was just surprised. Working for the Prince, he'd expected her to be English, but he knew that would say more about him than her if he expressed his surprise. There was no reason why the Prince couldn't have anyone he liked working for him.

He'd keep the conversation generic, he decided as he started the engine. That was the safest option. 'I understand you want a tour of the facilities and competition venues for the Games?'

'Yes.'

'It's a bit of a drive to the old barracks which is where the majority of the events will be staged. Are you familiar with Sydney at all?'

'Not really. From what I have seen, though, it is a stunning city. And I have heard you have amazing beaches. I am looking forward to seeing Bondi Beach.'

'There are much better beaches to visit than Bondi.'

'Oh.'

He didn't think one tiny word could hold so much disappointment and he felt bad that he'd caused that. 'But you should still go there,' he said in an attempt to remedy the situation. He didn't need another thing to feel guilty about.

'I would really like to see the Outback and the Reef too. I want the full Australian experience.'

'You haven't been here before?'

'Never. I am very much looking forward to seeing your country.'

She sounded so eager and Cam couldn't decide if her enthusiasm was endearing or annoying. He couldn't remember the last time he'd been enthusiastic about anything. 'How long are you here for?'

'Fifteen days.'

'Including the Games?'

She nodded. *'Oui.'*

'You know it's a long way to anywhere in Australia, right? There's only so much you'll be able to see.'

'Yes.'

'Where are you from?'

'Berggrun.'

'Berggrun? Is that in Europe?' Cam had never heard of it, but he couldn't admit that. It was one thing for people to think you were ignorant, another to speak and confirm their suspicions and he did *not* want to appear a fool.

'You have heard of it?' she asked but he couldn't tell if she was surprised or pleased.

'No, I haven't,' he had to admit.

'It is in Europe.'

'It's a city?'

'No. A principality. A small one. It is only about the same size as Sydney.'

'Like Monaco?'

'Oui.'

'How did you get from there to working for Prince Alfred?'

'I have a degree in marketing.'

'That doesn't answer the question.'

'What question exactly?'

'The Prince's office asked me to show you around

today. I just wondered what made you so important. Why you and no one else from his office?'

'No one else has arrived in Sydney yet. The Prince and everyone else with him are flying in via New Zealand in a couple of days.'

'Why didn't you come with them?'

'I do not normally work for the Prince. I am just working on this one event.'

He stopped his car at the entrance to the barracks and showed the guard their credentials before driving onto the grounds and, out of habit, parking near the medical centre.

He was going to ask her why she was working on this particular event, but she spoke again before he had a chance to.

'The hotel said you are a doctor,' Viktoria said, looking around as he switched off the engine. 'Did they mean a medical doctor?'

'Of course.'

'Do you enjoy your job?'

He didn't really enjoy much any more but it kept him busy. He made a conscious effort to get through one day at a time. He'd been doing that for two years now, waiting for things to get better.

'It keeps me busy,' he replied.

He was a general surgeon but, when he wasn't deployed, he worked as a GP. He wouldn't be deployed again, he would not see active service again, but she didn't need to know any of that.

'If you are a doctor, why are you being my tour guide?'

That was a good question.

'A friend of mine is second-in-command for the Games and put me in charge of the medical team. I'm on the committee in addition to my day job,' he said as he headed around the medical centre towards the gym, hoping she would stop asking questions and follow his lead. 'This used to be an active army base but now it is a rehabilitation hospital and facility. The sports venues have been revamped and some additions have been made so that most of the events for the Legion's Games can be held here. What exactly is your brief?'

'I have to update the social media sites associated with the Games. I have to engage the competitors, tweet about the events and the results. I also want to promote the idea that physical and mental health have a link, but I am not sure just how I will do that yet.'

'What do you want to see?'

'Can I just wander around the facilities, get a feel for the space?'

'I don't have time to wander around the grounds with you.'

'If you can tell me if there is anywhere that is out of bounds for me, I am happy to wander on my own.'

Maybe he could do that—give her a quick overview and leave her to get on with it. That would give him some much-needed space; he was finding it difficult to concentrate with her around. He suspected she might be demanding but he could handle that; what he was concerned about was whether he could handle his own reaction to her. He was far too aware of her and it was making him edgy.

He was attracted to her and he didn't want to be.

'There's a medical facility and rehabilitation clinic on site. We have doctors, psychologists, physiotherapists, masseurs, exercise physiologists, podiatrists and prosthetists,' he said as he crossed the car park.

Viktoria matched his stride. She wasn't as tall as him

but she moved quickly, her gait smooth and graceful. He wasn't as quick on his feet as he used to be, and he was concentrating hard to disguise his limp. He shouldn't care but he did. He didn't like to appear damaged.

He pushed open a door that led into the gym. There were basketball and volleyball courts overlooking a fifty-metre indoor pool with a traditional weights room and indoor rowing facility at the far end. It was an impressive facility.

'The sports are weightlifting, swimming, rowing, basketball, volleyball, cycling, archery and rugby?' She counted them off on her fingers. 'That is only eight. What have I missed?

'Tennis, athletics—track and field are counted separately—and sailing. Those events are not being held here, neither is the cycling, but the other seven events will be on this site. There's a rugby pitch and archery field outside.'

He walked with her along the pool deck and into the gym. It was a hive of activity, with dozens of people in training. Some were competitors in the upcoming Games, others were taking part in rehabilitation programmes.

'Hey, Doc, do you have a minute?' one of the delisted vets called out as they walked past.

Cam stopped and introduced Viktoria to the soldier. 'Viktoria, this is Lieutenant Andrews.'

'Just Mark these days,' he said as he shook Viktoria's hand.

'Are you competing in the Games?' she asked.

He nodded. 'Archery and swimming.'

'Two sports?'

'Lots of us are doing multiple.'

'You have to get selected, yes? It is not a matter of

simply turning up and putting your name on a list?' She turned to Cam with the question.

'That's correct. There are a thousand athletes registered from around the globe competing across a dozen different sports and most of the Aussies are competing in at least two sports, some three. The Games programme has been arranged to allow this. I haven't seen the final programme yet, but I've heard it's massive. Most of the competitors have multiple events.'

'That was my plan too,' Mark said, 'but I'm getting a pain in my arm when I lift it above shoulder height. It's bad timing; it's affecting my aim in archery and also my stroke in the pool. Have you got time to take a look at it for me, Doc?'

'I'm consulting most of the day,' Cam said as he checked his watch. 'I'm due to start in twenty minutes. Head over to the clinic now and I'll make sure we squeeze you in.'

He turned back to Viktoria. He had work to do and he hadn't thought about the logistics of getting her back to the city. He should have let her driver bring her. 'Do you want to call your driver to collect you when you're done? I'll be busy for the next few hours.'

Her reply was unexpected. 'I am happy to stay. I can wander around until you are free. I can chat to the competitors if they are willing to talk to me. You have my cell phone number if you need to get hold of me.'

'I don't think I want you fraternising with the enemy,' he said, only half joking.

'I am not the enemy. I know there are medals on the line but Berggrun doesn't have any athletes in the Games and, even if we did, the Games are about more than competition. They are about mateship, camaraderie, a sense of belonging.'

'All right, I'll come and find you when I'm finished.' He couldn't be bothered arguing and he knew she was right. It irked him. *She* irked him. But it wasn't her confidence or even her tendency to challenge him that bothered him. It was simply the fact that he was aware of her.

His head was all over the place as he left her to go and tackle his consulting list. She was affecting his equilibrium, leaving him quite unsettled. He felt as though he'd been living in a haze, unaware of the world around him for two years and now, all of a sudden, he was noticing things. He was noticing her.

A pretty face and a foreign accent shouldn't be enough to make her interesting, but he knew he was kidding himself. He was intrigued but he wasn't willing to admit that he found her attractive. That he wanted to impress her.

She was calm, happy and relaxed. He was tense and grumpy. He had never thought that opposites did attract, and he couldn't speak for her but he was certainly attracted.

He focused on his patient list, squeezing Mark into his diary, and tried not to think about Viktoria von Grasburg.

Several of the competitors had aches and pains from training, Mark included. Mark had been medically discharged from the army following a crippling leg injury and multiple surgeries. He was still battling depression but being chosen to compete in the Legion's Games had marked a big turning point in his recovery. Cam knew how important this competition was for him and he reluctantly gave him his diagnosis.

'I think you have sub-acromial bursitis,' he told him after conducting his assessment.

'What's that?'

'Inside the shoulder joint is a bursa, which is a small pouch filled with fluid that helps to reduce the friction of shoulder movements. That has become inflamed and swollen, which is affecting the quality of movement and causing your discomfort.'

'How did that happen?'

'It can present as a result of a fall, but it is most commonly an overuse injury, usually caused by repetitive overhead movements.'

'Like freestyle swimming.'

'Yes.'

'What do I do now?'

'Make an appointment with one of the physios.'

'What can they do?'

'A number of things: treatment, taping, exercises.'

'What about my events?'

'We'll know more once you've seen the physio. With your shoulder taped, archery might be possible; swimming might be more problematic, but don't write it off yet.'

'I'm sure I've heard about people having cortisone injections in their shoulders. Would that work?'

'Possibly, but if we went down that path I'd want you to rest your shoulder following the injection for a couple of weeks, which would mean you'd definitely miss your events. I'll organise an ultrasound scan just to be sure,' Cam said as he wrote a referral, 'but I'm pretty confident my diagnosis is accurate. Make an appointment to see the physio and we'll go from there.'

Cam finished his clinic and went in search of Viktoria. He found her in the gym, chatting to the athletes, just as she'd intimated. He stood inside the doorway for several minutes, observing her interaction with the competitors. It was obvious she had no shortage of people willing to talk to her.

That in itself was unusual. He knew from his own experience that many of the veterans were reluctant to talk to strangers. Many of them were physically or emotionally damaged, or both, and often that made them reticent to talk to people. Their scars went deep but they seemed perfectly happy to talk to Viktoria and she, in turn, seemed perfectly at ease talking to them. He was aware that she was able to draw people out. Or maybe she drew people in. He couldn't deny she had drawn him in.

She did seem very approachable. Despite her looks.

Maybe she was used to people giving her what she wanted, he thought. Beautiful people had a tendency to get away with things that ordinary people didn't.

With that slightly harsh thought, he left the shadows of the doorway and stepped into the gym. She noticed him approaching and smiled and Cam felt as if the sun had come out.

That reaction was unwanted, and he could feel grumpy Cam returning. The best thing he could do now was to drop her back to her hotel.

He needed time.

He needed space.

The smell of her perfume lingered in his car even after he'd dropped her back to her hotel—a floral scent, but not sweet. It was light, feminine, and enveloped him gently. It was pleasant, soothing.

His car suddenly felt too large for just one person. He was aware of a void, a feeling of emptiness.

That was ridiculous. He was used to being by himself. He'd spent a few hours with her; that wasn't long enough for her to make an impression. It shouldn't be long enough for him to notice her absence.

But a few hours in one day was more time than he'd spent with any stranger in the past year and more than he'd spent with many of his colleagues too. He could count on one hand the number of people he spent time with. Probably on three fingers—his sister, her husband and Doug. Not even his 'dates', for want of a better word, lasted more than a couple of hours. He'd become a bit of a recluse. Work, an occasional beer with colleagues, sporadic visits to his sister's farm and an even rarer date night were the sum total of his social activities. Even his exercise regime was solitary. He walked his dog and swam. Neither of which he did with company.

He didn't think he needed interaction with other people, he certainly didn't seek it out, yet he replayed snippets of the day, snatches of his conversation with Viktoria, as he drove home. He was surprised to find he remembered a lot of what she had said and even more about the way she spoke, the way she mixed her languages, the way she walked and smiled.

He let himself into his house, still thinking about Viktoria. That made a pleasant change to where his thoughts usually lay but he found it a little unsettling to be thinking so intently about a woman he'd just met.

He changed his clothes. He'd take his dog for a walk on the beach while he tried to clear his head.

The dog was a border collie, a retired farm dog, given to him by his sister. Skye had insisted that Cam take him when the dog was too old to work with the sheep any more. He wasn't a trained therapy dog, but his influence was the same. Cam always felt some of his stress dissolve when he walked Rex and today was no exception. Just the dog's company was enough to invoke calm; he had the same effect if they were just sitting still. Cam liked to keep one hand resting on Rex's head and that connection to another living, breathing being was always restorative.

He threw a ball for Rex—despite his age, the dog still wasn't truly happy unless he had a purpose—and let his mind wander as the dog ran up and down the small beach.

All his life, Cam had always had a plan. He'd always known what the next thing, the next five things, on his list of goals was. Where he was headed. He'd been certain of his path. Until two years ago.

What was the expression? *Man makes plans and God laughs.* Well, God had more than laughed at him. He'd given up on him altogether and Cam had struggled for the past two years. Since losing Gemma he'd felt rudderless.

The ache in his chest was gradually diminishing; emotionally and physically, he knew he was recovering, but it was a slow process. He knew he'd always hold Gemma in his heart but, even though the pain was no longer as acute, his future still looked bleak. There wasn't a lot he looked forward to. He was still just getting through one day at a time. As best he could. He'd forgotten what it was like to be excited about things.

Meeting Viktoria was possibly the most excited he'd felt about anything in a long time. He wasn't even excited about work. Work was a means to an end, but what end he wasn't sure. It was something to occupy his time.

Doug had tried to persuade him to compete in the Legion's Games. After all, the Games were for injured soldiers, those with both mental and physical wounds, and he knew he fell into both categories, but he'd resisted, hiding behind the apparent need for his services as a medic—using his job as an excuse to keep himself isolated.

He smiled wryly as he scratched behind his dog's ears and threw the ball again. He knew what he would say to any of his patients who were doing the same thing. He knew what he *had* said to them. But he was a firm believer in his patients doing as he said, not as he did. And he wasn't ready to let go of his pain just yet.

He was driven by guilt. Guilt was making him hold on to his pain as a punishment. He blamed himself for Gemma's death. He should have been able to save her.

He knew that if he hadn't been there that day, in the chopper when it went down, he would feel differently. If he hadn't been there the outcome would have been the same but that was different to being there and doing nothing. He knew in his head that she was dead before the chopper hit the ground. He knew there was nothing he could have done, but that didn't stop the guilt.

Survivor's guilt.

But giving it a name didn't make it any easier to live with. He would punish himself for a bit longer. He wasn't ready to let go of it just yet.

He had got used to the fact that Gemma was gone. That he was alone. He'd even got used to the idea that he would be alone for the rest of his life. But he hadn't got over the idea that all of it was somehow his fault.

He'd been through therapy—that had been non-negotiable under army guidelines—but he couldn't honestly say he felt any better for it. He knew all the statistics. He'd heard the spiel, read the research, but the fact of the matter was that nothing was going to make things return to the way they had been before the incident and he just had to get on with it, on with his life.

He was trying but he wasn't finding life very enthralling any more. The joy was gone.

Viktoria had arranged for Hendrik to drop her off at the base and she had spent the morning interviewing Games competitors. The base was busier today; veterans from other countries had arrived in Sydney and many of them were on site, utilising the training facilities ahead of the competition.

There was a lot of camaraderie between the competitors, which Viktoria had not been expecting. But, as they described their involvement, it became clearer. The veterans talked a lot about mateship and survival and the role the Games played in their recovery. While the Games were essentially a competition, Viktoria was realising they were about challenging yourself rather than beating others.

She wandered through the gym, past the stationary rowing machines where a solitary athlete was vigorously training. A Chocolate Labrador lay by her side and it was the dog that initially caught Viktoria's eye. As she got closer the woman's pace slowed.

Viktoria stopped beside the rower's right side and bent down, letting the dog sniff the back of her hand. 'What a gorgeous dog,' she said. 'What is his name?'

The athlete didn't acknowledge her, although the dog's ears pricked up. Viktoria hadn't meant to interrupt, she'd assumed she was finishing her regime, but perhaps she was doing interval training. Viktoria was about to apologise for interrupting and walk on when the athlete turned her head.

'Sorry, were you talking to me?' She pulled headphones out of her left ear as Viktoria spoke.

'Yes, I was just admiring your dog.'

'Would you mind standing on my left side?' the woman asked. Viktoria thought it was an odd request but moved around the machine as the woman explained, 'I've lost the vision in my right eye and I'm deaf in my right ear.'

'I asked what your dog is called.'

'This is Leroy—' the dog turned to look at the woman when he heard his name '—and I'm Fiona.'

'My name is Viktoria.'

'You don't look like you're defence force?' Fiona said as she slid her feet out of the straps and stood up.

Viktoria heard the question. Fiona was obviously curious about why Viktoria was there. 'I am not defence force, but I am working for Prince Alfred.'

'Doing what?'

'I am in charge of updating all the social media around the Games. Prince Alfred wants to keep the athletes connected but he also wants to promote the Games to the general public. He is keen to raise awareness of mental health and the benefits of exercise.'

'I can vouch for the benefits of exercise,' Fiona said as she scratched behind Leroy's ears. 'Exercise and my four-legged mate have made all the difference to me.'

'Is Leroy a guide dog?' Now that Fiona was standing, Viktoria was well aware that she had lost the sight in her right eye.

'Not exactly. He has multiple hats to wear. Technically, he is a service dog and he will assist me with my hearing and vision issues, but he's really been trained as a therapy animal. He does help me when I'm out or when someone stands on the wrong side of me. I had no idea you were there until his ears pricked up, then I knew to look out for something.'

'He is a therapy dog?'

'Yes. I sustained a head injury and lost the sight in one eye and the hearing in one ear on a tour of duty when a roadside bomb exploded under a vehicle I was travelling in, but the thing Leroy helps most with is managing my PTSD. Since the incident I struggle in traffic, big crowds, unfamiliar environments. Leroy helps calm me down.'

'But you are competing in the Games?' Viktoria asked. Sweat was dripping off Fiona; she certainly looked as though she'd been training hard. 'The organisers are expecting large crowds. Is that going to be a problem for you?' Viktoria wondered how Fiona would cope with the crowds and the noise that would come with them.

Fiona nodded. 'I am competing but only in the stationary rowing. That's a controlled environment. Indoors. Only a certain number of people competing, limited by the number of machines. And it's not going to be quite such a popular spectator sport as, say, the basketball or swimming. Fewer spectators, less noise. And Leroy can stay beside me. He couldn't do that in most of the other events.'

'He really helps?'

'Definitely. I don't leave the house without him.'

As Viktoria spoke to Fiona she thought about the tales other athletes had already recounted to her and the role she could play took shape in her mind. There was a bigger story to be told. She could do much more than post pictures on social media. She would write brief articles on the competitors—delve into their stories if they would let her, take their stories to the world. She would use the Games to highlight not only the benefits of exercise but to show what these competitors from all over the globe had in common. Some of the athletes had physical disabilities, others emotional, but they all carried scars and it was those scars that united them. She would showcase their resilience, their mateship and their determination and maybe inspire others through those stories.

She wandered through the gym and out onto the pool deck as she thought about how to get the ball rolling. She wondered if she could ask Cam for help. He hadn't made any plans to meet her today and she had no idea if he was even on the base, but she kept one eye out for him anyway.

As she walked beside the pool, she spied Mark, the ex-soldier she had met yesterday, sitting on the edge. He looked up as she approached and smiled in recognition.

She stopped to say hello. 'Have you been swimming? I thought you were injured?'

'I have a sore shoulder.' He shrugged. 'I've had worse injuries.'

Mark was heavily tattooed across his back and arms but sports tape over his shoulder partially obscured some of the tattoos.

He pushed himself up out of the water to stand on the edge of the pool and Viktoria noticed that his left leg had been amputated below the knee. She hadn't realised yesterday.

He hopped easily over to a chair on the pool deck, where he sat to towel himself dry. A prosthetic leg stood beside the chair.

Viktoria followed him. 'I thought you said swimming aggravated your shoulder?'

'Yes, it does. But until someone tells me I have to stop I'm going to keep swimming. I guess I don't like being told I can't do something,' he said as he slid his prosthesis on.

'And Dr Hamilton did not tell you to stop?'

'No. He sent me to get some scans done of my shoulder, which showed I have an inflamed bursa, and he sent me to the physiotherapist. I'm going back to see her shortly for more treatment.' Mark pulled a pair of trackpants over his bathers and stood up. 'What are you doing here?'

'I came to take some photographs, but I have been talking to some of the competitors and now I am looking for stories.'

'Stories?'

'I want to tell the stories of the competitors. Do you think people would be willing to talk to me?'

'About what?'

'I want to acknowledge the struggles and the sacrifices you have all made. I know not everyone will want to tell their stories publicly, but I'm sure, out of a thousand competitors, some will. What do you think? Could I interview you?'

He hesitated. She could see his deliberation. 'Me?'

She nodded. 'Prince Alfred is keen to showcase the benefits of exercise in promoting recovery, both physical and mental, and I think this is a way we could do that. Will you help me? Can we at least give it a try?'

'I'll think about it.'

Viktoria spent the rest of the afternoon talking to various athletes before making her way to the medical centre. She had dropped in there earlier and asked for a time to catch up with Cam. She hadn't heard from him at all and, after speaking with Freddie about her idea, she wanted Cam's opinion.

'Hello, Viktoria.' Cam stood up as she entered his office. 'What can I do for you?'

'I need your opinion.'

'You didn't need to make an appointment to see me for that,' he said as he repositioned a chair for her.

'I had not heard from you today,' she replied with a shrug, 'and I did not know if I would see you…so…' She sat and Cam perched on the edge of his desk. 'I saw Mark today when I was at the pool. He'd been swimming. I wondered why, when he is injured, you did not tell him to stop.'

'That's what you wanted to see me about?'

'Not only that, but it is related in a way.'

'I can't discuss Mark with you.'

Cam stood and moved around the desk to sit in his chair and Viktoria wasn't sure if he was distancing himself from her or just her line of questioning. She rephrased her question.

'I am not asking you to discuss his injury—he has already explained the problem to me—I am simply asking you to explain why you did not stop him from training.'

'Because it was highly unlikely that he would listen. These men and women who have seen active service aren't likely to let someone like me, or something like this—a relatively minor injury—stop them. It's about managing the problem, not dictating to them what they can and can't do. They're used to taking orders in their job; it's important to give them some control of their bodies.'

Viktoria could respect their need to have some control. She felt the same way.

'Mark is intelligent enough to make his own decisions,' Cam continued. 'You'll see. He's swimming in a relay—if he doesn't pull up well enough I'm sure he'll make the right decision for the team. If there's one thing most soldiers are good at it is being part of a team. But tell me, how is that related to your other question?'

'After speaking to many of the competitors today I also spoke with Prince Alfred and we think that it would be good to do some articles on what soldiers go through emotionally and what families or loved ones can do to support them. Obviously, getting back into physical exercise is a great outcome for a lot of people but it is a challenge for so many. There must be a lot of stress on everyone, the families and the soldiers, when they are dealing with these issues. I wanted to link the benefits of exercise to positive mental health and Prince Alfred and I think this could be a good way to do that. Your insight would be really useful. Would you be prepared to talk to me about your views?'

'My views?'

'*Oui.*'

'On what?'

'To get a professional perspective on what the athletes have gone through.'

She'd noticed his limp and wondered if he had his own personal story to tell but she suspected he wouldn't be very forthcoming. He asked questions of her but had given her nothing personal. She thought she was a master of being able to make conversation with all types of people, but she struggled to get anything much out of Dr Campbell Hamilton. Perhaps a professional opinion piece would build some trust and, if nothing else, she was sure it would be interesting.

'I can't give you any specifics about the athletes and I really don't have the time.'

She had hoped he would agree. It would be a way to spend a bit more time with him. She was attracted to him. He was sexy in a brooding, distant way and she wanted him to like her. She was used to people being excited to meet her, being keen for her attention, but he seemed as if he just wanted to be left alone. If he wasn't so sexy, she'd be inclined to do just that but she was very aware of him and she wanted to get to know him better.

She definitely had a type and Cam fitted into that perfectly. She had always been attracted to tall, dark and handsome men but usually they were charming too. Cam was an enigma. His manners were impeccable, but he seemed to be operating on autopilot.

He was a challenge.

And she was definitely up for the challenge.

'It would not take a lot of time.'

She waited for him to relent but he said nothing. The silence stretched between them.

'Would you think about it?' she asked with a smile. 'You have to admit it would be a good way to raise awareness of the issues surrounding mental health.'

'Do you think you can simply smile at me and get your own way? Hasn't anyone ever said no to you before?'

'Not often,' she admitted. She wasn't used to being told no. She was used to people doing what she asked. She supposed it was one of the perks of being a princess, but it looked as if she had her work cut out for her trying to get favours from Cam. 'Please, think about it. I am happy to go over any concerns you might have. We can discuss it over dinner?'

'Dinner?'

She nodded. 'I am free tonight.'

'Tonight?'

'Yes. Are you busy?' Nothing ventured, nothing gained, she figured.

* * *

Yes, he was busy.

'I'm going for a swim,' he said, perhaps a little too abruptly. His leg was aching, and he knew he needed to exercise to loosen up his hip. He also needed to exercise to clear his head.

He had known Viktoria was on the base today, but he'd deliberately steered clear of her. Even so, she had crept into his thoughts on numerous occasions, making it hard to concentrate on his work. It was a slightly infuriating situation. He liked feeling in control and he was definitely thrown by her. He didn't like feeling off-kilter.

'Are you swimming for exercise or therapy?'

'Pardon?'

'I have seen you limping. You are injured, *non*?'

He hadn't disguised his limp as well as he'd hoped but his limp was none of her business. The rebuke was on the tip of his tongue, but she apologised before he could say anything, defusing his temper.

'No matter. You cannot swim all night, surely?' she asked. 'Shall we meet afterwards?'

Not everyone wants to talk to you.

He bit back another terse reply, knowing it was his own guilt that was making him unsettled. His bad mood was not her fault.

He hadn't wanted her to see his weakness.

He wanted to make a good impression on her and knowing that annoyed him. He hadn't cared about impressing anyone for a long time. He had kept his feelings locked away—he didn't want to share them; he didn't want to let anyone in—and he wasn't about to share his feelings with her. But he also didn't want to appear rude.

He was going to make up an excuse, but he didn't want to lie to her. She hadn't done anything to deserve that.

'Or I could come with you,' she said.

She was persistent. He'd give her that.

He didn't mind a determined personality unless it made his life difficult, and he suspected she would make his life difficult. Not in the sense that she would complain about his behaviour but in the sense that she would complicate his life.

She was obviously used to getting her own way. It should annoy him, but he knew he wanted to give in to her too. But his stubborn streak made it hard to give in gracefully.

After his swim he was supposed to be going to a fundraising function for Doug's cricket club. He'd bought his ticket as a favour to Doug but he'd never intended to go, but somehow the night had arrived and he hadn't begged off yet. He was about to put her off when he realised that she would give him the perfect excuse to get out of attending the fundraiser. He knew Doug had invited him partly to get him out socialising, but he also knew Doug would cut him some slack if he said he had a date. Maybe he was stretching the truth and the friendship, but he'd text Doug anyway—he would never know. He would make sure he gave a big donation instead. He was sure he wouldn't be missed.

So, instead of making his excuses to Viktoria he said, 'Do you have a pair of swimmers with you?'

'*Non.*'

'Are you planning on skinny-dipping then?' If he closed his eyes he knew he'd be able to picture her naked. He shouldn't be able to, but he knew her features were imprinted on his brain already.

'*Quoi? Non!* Where are you swimming? I can buy a swimsuit or you could lend me a T-shirt.'

That conjured up a whole other image, of Viktoria in one of his T-shirts, wet and clinging to her curves.

He fought the urge to close his eyes and said, 'I was planning on swimming at home. Would you like to come with me?' He spoke without thinking, without stopping to consider the consequences.

She smiled in reply and he knew he was in trouble.

She was beautiful, smart and she radiated warmth. The trifecta. And he was fascinated, intrigued, unsettled.

He was in big trouble.

CHAPTER THREE

WHAT WAS HE THINKING?

He wasn't sure. He wasn't thinking clearly, that much was certain. He was unsettled. Viktoria was disturbing his equilibrium and now she was about to step inside his house.

What the hell was he doing?

He didn't know that either.

He actually hadn't thought she would take him up on his offer but when she had nodded and smiled widely he hadn't regretted the invitation.

He hadn't brought a woman home in two years and he'd never brought a woman to this house. Gemma hadn't even seen this house. He'd bought it after the incident, when he'd needed a single storey house with easy access. The pool was a bonus. The privacy even more so.

The only female who had visited him here was his sister. And now Viktoria.

Was he making a mistake?

It was too late now, he thought as he unlocked his front door. The offer had been extended and accepted.

He tried not to feel as if he was cheating on Gemma. Tried to convince himself that the invitation he'd extended to Viktoria was completely innocent, devoid of any attraction. But he knew that wasn't the case.

But that didn't mean he was going to act on his feelings. For all he knew Viktoria had no interest in him. Why would she? He was certain she would have her pick of men. Why would she look twice at him?

He was kidding himself, thinking he was in control of the situation because he had issued the invitation. He knew, very clearly, that she was in charge and he suspected he had just become one in a long line of men who hadn't been able to refuse her requests. Another who had succumbed to her wishes because of an innate need to please her, to see her smile, to feel enveloped in her warmth.

He pushed open the door and held it for Viktoria to enter first, but her way was blocked by a very excited Border collie with a rapidly wagging tail.

'*Bonjour.* What is your name?' Viktoria asked as she bent over and offered the back of her hand for the dog to sniff before rubbing his head.

Cam was treated to a delightful and distracting view of Viktoria's backside as she bent over in front of him. He did his best not to stare, focusing on his dog instead. 'This is Rex and it looks like he's expecting a walk.' He gave two short, low whistles followed by a slightly longer one and Rex left Viktoria and came to his side, allowing Viktoria space to enter his house. She took three steps and came to a halt again as her attention was captured by the view.

'*Oh! Très magnifique!*'

To their right a passage led away to the bedrooms but in front of them the entry hall opened up into a large open-plan kitchen and living space. An expanse of windows stretched across the far wall, making the room seem part of the outdoors. Through the windows the eye was drawn over the infinity pool to the ocean beyond and Cam knew that was what had caught Viktoria's eye. The view was incredible.

His house was stunning, simple and modern with clean lines, but it was the view that captured one's attention. The house was perched on the edge of a cliff overlooking a small private beach which only a handful of houses had access to and the view and the seclusion were the reasons Cam had chosen this property over the other single-level houses he had inspected. He had sunk his inheritance and his compensation from the incident into this house, but it had been worth every dollar.

He'd bought it eighteen months ago. After the incident. Gemma had never seen this house and that was how he liked it. There were no memories here.

The views over the ocean were stunning but the house itself was a clean slate, a blank canvas. Somewhere he could escape to. Somewhere he could forget about the past. Somewhere he could have solitude.

The furnishings were sparse and there were very few personal effects but that didn't bother him; it was the view that captured the attention and furnishings and artwork were never going to be able to compete. It appeared as if the furnishings had been kept deliberately minimalistic but the reality was he had never bothered to furnish it properly. He never entertained and the only visitors were his sister, her husband and Doug.

Rex was weaving circles around his legs and Cam decided that a walk would be a better form of exercise given the circumstances. He didn't trust himself to take Viktoria swimming in one of his old shirts. A walk seemed like the safer option.

He changed out of his army fatigues into a T-shirt and a pair of shorts, long enough to almost cover the scar that ran down the outside of his right thigh. He could just make out the end of it at the edge of his knee but if he walked on Viktoria's right side he didn't think she would notice the mark. He left his feet bare and led her down the wooden steps that led to the beach.

'This is so pretty,' she said as they made their way down to the sand.

The beach was small, only a hundred metres from end to end, curved between two cliffs. The sand was golden and fine, and the water was crystal-clear. For now, they had it to themselves. A little piece of paradise and tranquillity.

He threw the ball for Rex as Viktoria slipped off her shoes. She held her arms out wide and tipped her face up to the sun as she twirled in circles. She was like a bubble of sunshine, a balloon of happiness floating along the beach. If she had a string Cam felt he could grab hold of her and absorb some of her positive energy.

'Are you always this upbeat?' he asked.

She wobbled slightly as she stopped twirling. 'It is impossible not to enjoy this,' she said with a smile. 'It is a beautiful day in a beautiful place. I feel free. Like I am on holiday, far from everything.'

'You mentioned you're only working for Prince Alfred for these games. What do you do for work at home?' Cam asked as he bent down to retrieve Rex's ball.

'I am involved in events.'

'What sort of events?'

'Polo matches, charities, galas.'

'In Berggrun?'

'Yes.'

'Does your population support all those events?'

'We are a tourist hot spot and in Europe there are constantly events. It is not far for people to hop from one country to another if there is an event worth attending.'

They walked the length of the sand while Rex chased the ball until he started to tire. As they turned at the far end of the beach Viktoria stopped and rolled up the bottoms of her wide-leg navy linen trousers and waded into the water. Rex barked and dashed in after her, gently pushing against the backs of her calves, which Cam had to admit were rather shapely, until Viktoria found herself out of the water again.

She was laughing as Rex herded her back to Cam. 'What is he doing?'

'He's rounding you up. Bringing you into line,' Cam said with a smile. He was surprised to feel a smile on his face; he couldn't remember the last time he had smiled spontaneously, the last time he'd felt happy. Viktoria was making him feel things he didn't expect. Her happiness and her delight in the day was rubbing off on him.

'Why?'

'It's in his nature. He's a sheepdog.'

'Why do you have a sheepdog?'

'He's retired, or supposed to be, but it seems he hasn't got the memo yet. He belonged to my sister, but when she retired him she thought he should come and live with me. That was kinder than trying to keep him out of the paddocks,' he told her as Rex proceeded to shake the water from his fur and showered them with the droplets.

Cam hadn't wanted to take responsibility for a dog, but Skye had insisted. Tired of his stubbornness and his refusal to agree to her suggestion, she had arrived on his doorstep one day with the dog in tow, and left him with Cam.

That had been a year ago. Cam had still been on medical leave from the defence force and the days had stretched endlessly before him. With no real reason to get out of bed, it had been all too easy to let the days blur together. Skye had insisted that having a dog would motivate him to get up and she'd been right. Having Rex around had made Cam get out of bed but, even better, the dog was company. He listened without judgement, and hadn't minded Cam's tears, and lay by his side when he cried.

'Are you going to swim?' Viktoria's question brought Cam back to the present.

'I don't think I need to now.' His leg had loosened up with the walk and he didn't want to swim alone. He assumed she wasn't about to join him without bathers. He would swim in his pool later if he needed to.

Viktoria tucked her hand into the crook of his elbow as she walked beside him.

He let himself relax into the moment and it actually felt good to let his thoughts go.

He knew he was wound tight, but he found it hard to take a deep breath, he found it hard to relax. He knew he tended to keep busy, sometimes frantically so, as that didn't give him time to dwell on the past or think about a future that was different to how he'd imagined. But to actually just stop and be in the moment, in the present, was okay. He didn't need to think about the past or the future. He could just be.

Their steps were in sync and left two sets of perfect footprints in the damp sand. Confirmation that he had shared this moment with her. A moment he didn't regret.

'Thank you for bringing me here,' she said. 'It has been a much nicer way to spend the evening than being in my hotel.'

He felt a little guilty that he'd only invited her to join him as it had given him an excuse to get out of Doug's function.

The sun was low in the sky by the time they climbed

the steps back to the house. 'Would you like to go out for dinner?' she asked. 'My treat, in return though I want to pick your brains about the issues facing the athletes.'

'I can throw something on the barbecue,' he said. He was reluctant to go out; he was enjoying her company and he wanted that feeling to last a little longer. If they went out, other people would intrude on their space and he selfishly wanted to keep her to himself.

Viktoria couldn't cook—she'd never needed to learn—but she chopped vegetables for the salad while Cam barbecued lamb fillets.

They ate on the terrace overlooking the ocean and the sparkling lights of the other houses on the clifftops. Their conversation flowed smoothly, and Viktoria was able to get Cam's opinion on what she had discussed with the athletes. She had spoken to several of the Games competitors and they all had similar stories to tell. How the commitment to an exercise regime had helped to get them out of bed or socialising again. How exercise and the Games had given them a focus. How the feeling of pushing themselves, of setting and achieving goals, had given them a purpose. In short, how exercise had saved them.

Their conversation alternated between the Games and her life in Berggrun, but it wasn't until Cam had cleared their plates that she realised he'd given her very little insight into his own life. While he did answer some of her questions about army life, his answers were generic, giving her no insight into his personal experiences. Even his house gave no hints as to his life and the type of man he was. There were no family photographs; he'd mentioned a sister but there was no sign of her, nor was there any sign of parents or friends. No holiday snaps. No hobbies.

She would have liked to have tried again to steer the conversation back to him, but she was aware it was getting late and she still had work to do.

'Thank you for dinner. I should call Hendrik to collect me.' They had shared a bottle of wine and Viktoria assumed Cam wouldn't want to drive her home and nor did she expect him to.

'Why do you have a driver?' he asked.

She had always had a driver and didn't actually have a driver's licence. She had never had the need for one, but she knew telling him that would invite a lot more questions. 'Because we drive on the opposite side of the road in Berggrun and we thought it was safer not to drive here.'

'We do have taxis, you know.'

She would never be allowed in a taxi. Especially not unaccompanied. 'Hendrik won't mind; he'll be expecting me to call. What is your address?'

Cam told her his address and then went out onto the terrace to bring in their glasses, giving her some privacy.

'*Bonjour*, Hendrik,' Viktoria said when he answered. 'Are you able to collect me from Vaucluse? I have the address.'

'*Oui*, Your Highness, I know where you are.'

'*Comment?*'

'It is my job. I did a search on the doctor.'

'*Quoi? Pourquoi?*'

'I run a check on anyone you are alone with. I was not about to risk my job by leaving you unprotected. I am outside already.'

She should be cross. She was not even allowed that little bit of freedom. But she couldn't mind because she'd had a wonderful night. And Hendrik was right—it was his job; she couldn't argue or berate him for doing his job.

'How long did it take you to get here?'

'Twenty minutes.'

'I will meet you outside in twenty minutes.' She would delay leaving, partly because she didn't want to go, although she knew she had to, but mainly because she didn't want Cam to wonder how Hendrik had arrived so quickly.

'D'accord. Vingt minutes.'

She kissed Cam on both cheeks and thanked him again as he walked her outside to where Hendrik waited.

Hendrik held the door for her and she slid into the back seat, wishing she could have given Cam a proper kiss goodnight, but she couldn't do that in front of her bodyguard. Even if she was denying her royal background there were still rules that needed to be followed.

'Hendrik, will you be shadowing me all the time?' she asked as he pulled the car away from the kerb.

'*Oui*, Your Highness,' came his reply.

'Even when I'm with Dr Hamilton?'

'Always.'

That was not part of her newly formed plan.

Coming to Sydney had been her chance to have one last adventure. She hadn't expected to meet a man like Campbell Hamilton. She still hadn't been able to shake the feeling that they had been destined to meet. That there was a reason he had been sent to collect her, that a higher power was at work. She hadn't intended to have one last fling but if the opportunity presented itself with Cam she wanted to take advantage of it and, to do that, she needed to find a way of getting away from Hendrik's protective observation. 'Do you think, if he's trusted by the Australian government as part of their armed forces, you could trust him too?'

'He is not part of *our* armed forces.'

'We don't have an armed force. We have palace guards.'

'Well, he is not a Berggruner.'

'I understand, but you said you did a search on him. Did you find anything suspicious about him?'

'*Non.*'

'What *did* you find?'

She was curious. She wished she'd asked Cam more questions but perhaps Hendrik could shed some light on him.

'He is thirty-four years old. He was raised on a sheep station and has served in the army for four years. He has done two tours of Afghanistan and was injured during his last deployment.'

Viktoria knew Campbell carried an injury of some sort—she had noticed his limp—but he hadn't mentioned it. She wondered if Hendrik would tell her. She wondered if she should wait to see if Cam would. But she knew she didn't want to wait. She wanted to know as much about him as she could. 'Do you know what happened?'

'He was in a helicopter that was shot down. Everyone else on board was killed. He almost didn't make it. He sustained a collapsed lung, fractured ribs, leg and pelvis, and a ruptured spleen.'

'How long ago was this?'

'Two years.'

She wanted to know who was with him. Who'd nursed him back to health. Who was there for his recovery. Where was his family?

But she couldn't ask Hendrik any of that. It wouldn't

do to show that much interest. As far as Hendrik was concerned her relationship with Cam was strictly professional.

Cam swam one final lap of the pool before he hauled himself out, towelled off and padded inside. He had needed to swim after all, not to ease his muscles but to cool down. He had enjoyed the evening far more than he'd expected and it had left him energised and buoyant. He'd needed to burn off some of that energy before he'd be able to sleep.

He flicked on the light as he stepped into his bedroom and the one personal photo displayed in the house caught his eye.

On his bedside table was a photo of him with Gemma.

A familiar pang of guilt flared through him as he looked at her smiling face.

He turned his back on the photo and went to hang his towel in the en-suite bathroom.

The evening had been perfectly innocent, but he still felt as if he was cheating on Gemma. The few dates he had been on in the past twelve months hadn't gone past a drink or dinner and the occasional kiss. He'd always held back, unwilling to expose his scars, emotional and physical, and unwilling to cheat on Gemma. The evening with Viktoria had been more innocent than some but he still felt guilty and this time he knew it was because he wanted to see her again. This time he wasn't done. This time he didn't want to say goodbye.

He knew it was time he moved on—he knew he shouldn't feel guilty about enjoying himself—but the guilt had become part of him and letting it go was hard.

He stepped out of the bathroom and looked again at

the photograph, at Gemma's wide smile. He could almost hear her voice and he knew what she would say.

She would tell him to get on with his life.

She had never stopped. She'd always had a purpose, just as he always had a goal. He knew Gemma would not want him to stagnate, but that still wasn't enough to assuage his guilty conscience. He knew his world had become insular, that work and exercise were his only focus and that it wasn't healthy. He knew he needed to spend time with other people, that he was at risk of becoming a recluse, but he hadn't been very good company recently.

But maybe he could start with a small step outside his insular world. Maybe it was time.

He went over to the photo and laid it face down. He didn't want to put it away, not yet, but he found he didn't want to look at it any more tonight. Tonight, he was going to go to sleep with thoughts of Viktoria in his head.

Viktoria thanked the hotel chauffeur and hurried across the army base. She was running late after an early morning drama. Hendrik's wife and child had been involved in a car accident in Berggrun. His wife had sustained a fractured elbow and ribs and Hendrik had flown home to be with them, leaving Viktoria and Brigitta in Sydney. Viktoria didn't mind; the hotel had chauffeurs available and she knew this would give her more freedom. In her opinion that was a good thing.

She smiled as she headed for the mess hall. She was still thinking about the feel of Cam's cheek under her lips as she'd kissed him goodbye last night. Thinking about the taste of the sea on his skin and the smell of the sun in his hair.

She'd enjoyed the evening. Even if he hadn't opened up to her, he had relaxed. He'd seemed calmer in his own domain. Whether it was the glass of wine, the walk on the beach, the familiar environment or the company of his dog she wasn't sure, but she'd liked that side of him.

His house had surprised her, though. It was stunning but it hadn't felt like a home. She hadn't had a lot of experiences with regular houses, but she had expected to feel a sense of Cam within the walls. She'd expected to see something of the man he was, even if it was just a glimpse, but she'd been able to glean very little about him. It made her wonder why he was so guarded. What was he hiding?

She had no idea but at least she hadn't seen any evidence of a woman in his life and for that she was grateful. She'd been made a fool of once before and, even if she was only hoping for a fling, she didn't want to make a mistake. She'd been a poor judge of character in the past but, while she knew there was something Cam wasn't telling her, probably a great many things, she was confident that he wasn't hiding a girlfriend or a wife.

Only the dog seemed to have some personal meaning for Cam.

It felt as if only Rex tied Cam to the house, and he had been a gift from Cam's sister. Cam hadn't chosen the dog, but he had kept him and he was obviously fond of him. That had pleased her—someone who was able to form a bond with an animal had to have a kind heart, she thought as she arrived at the mess hall.

She had made arrangements to meet Lieutenant Andrews on the base this morning to begin their interview and he was waiting for her in front of the mess hall. '*Bonjour*, Mark. How are you today?'

'I'm good. Have you eaten? I thought we could grab some breakfast while we chat.'

Viktoria didn't eat breakfast—black coffee was her morning go-to—but she thought Mark might find it easier to talk if the focus was on a meal instead of directly on him. 'I do not need breakfast, but I will have a coffee,' she replied as he held the door open for her to enter the mess hall. 'How is your shoulder today?'

'The physio has told me I need to rest it from swimming,' he said as he picked up a tray and joined the queue for food. 'But I can do light exercises in the gym.'

Viktoria stood beside him as he chose his food. It didn't look particularly appetising and she was glad she didn't eat breakfast. 'What about your archery? Are you able to continue with that?'

'Yes. That's uncomfortable but the physio doesn't think I'll do any more damage.'

'Have you always done these sports?' she asked as they sat down at a table.

'No. I could swim, most Aussie kids can, but I've never swum competitively so that's new for me.'

'Which do you enjoy more?'

'Archery helps with my mental focus and balance. But, while I thought I'd like the solitary style of archery, I'm finding I enjoy swimming more. I'm swimming one individual event and also a relay and I like feeling like part of a team again. After my injury I really missed that. Comradeship is such a big part of army life and it's good to feel that again.'

'How long have you been in the army?'

'I joined straight out of school and that was twenty years ago. My dad and my grandpa both served.'

'When did you get injured?'

'Three years ago.'

'What happened?' She felt bad for asking, suddenly it felt very intrusive, but Mark had agreed to be interviewed and he knew the reason behind her quest for the stories.

'I was actually injured in a training exercise. I got tangled in a parachute and broke a lot of bones. My leg was so badly busted that even after multiple surgeries I was in constant pain. I decided in the end to have it amputated. It seemed like the best solution. And it helped. Physically I improved but mentally I was still a mess. I was angry. With the army, myself, my wife. It took me a long time to sort myself out and my marriage broke down.'

'I am sorry to hear that.'

'It happens a lot. The families put up with a lot, getting moved around every three years, having us deployed overseas, not knowing if we'll come back. It's stressful. And then we come back and we're not the same any more. Even if we haven't got physical injuries, we've got emotional scars. We've seen things no one should see. Sometimes we've also done things no one should have to do and that leaves a mark, you know? And it's not something we can talk about to anyone who hasn't been there. No one would understand. So, after everything my wife and I went through over the years, my injury was the last straw. And it wasn't even the injury. It was the black hole of depression that I fell into that finished us off.

'And then I had nothing. No marriage. No career. I was lost without my wife, without the army, without my mates. It's been a long road back. The Games have brought me back and now, here I am.'

'What made you want to compete in the Games?'

'One of my mates took part in the last Games and he

convinced me to have a go at competing in this one. Having to get out of bed to exercise really was my salvation.'

Viktoria had initially thought Mark seemed to have his life together and it surprised her to hear the level of despair that was evident in his voice. She hoped she could do his story justice.

She reminded herself that Mark and soldiers like him were the reason Freddie had started the Games. His story, while difficult to listen to, could help others who found themselves in the same predicament he had.

Mark's next words reinforced her sentiments. 'If each one of us who has been through something like this can help one other person then the cumulative effect could be enormous. Each person who finds the strength and the will to get out of bed in the morning and face another day is a triumph. I wasn't ever suicidal but some of my mates have been. That's why these Games are so important. They have given so many of us a purpose, a goal, something to aim for. I just hope I get to be a part of it.'

'You will be a part of it even if you cannot compete but what will happen if you cannot swim the relay because of your shoulder?' Would he be letting others down? What would the knock-on effect of that be? she wondered.

'We can substitute another athlete if necessary but I'm really hoping I can swim the relay—that will be my highlight, I suspect—but I guess time will tell. I'm going to continue with the modified exercises that the physio has given me. I'm heading over to the gym now to do a light cardio session with the rest of my relay team and we're having dinner together tonight. You should meet the team; they might be happy to do interviews for you too,' he said as he pushed the last bit of his scrambled eggs onto a corner of toast and finished it off. 'Why don't you come to dinner with us?'

'I would not want to intrude,' Viktoria replied as she recalled Cam's comment about being the enemy.

'You wouldn't be intruding—our wives and girl-friends are coming too; you're more than welcome. You might like to meet some of the families—they got us through the tough times.'

He was right. She had no other plans for the evening, and it would be interesting to meet the athletes' support network. *'D'accord,'* she accepted. 'That sounds good.'

Viktoria stepped into the pub and immediately saw Mark seated at a large table in the far corner. She joined the group and made sure to concentrate as Mark introduced her to his teammates. They had all suffered injuries in active service although Bud had also sustained several sporting injuries playing rugby which had also taken a toll. He was suffering from PTSD following multiple surgeries on his back, ankles and knee. Sean had a back injury and Eric had bilateral lower leg amputations.

Despite their injuries, Viktoria found them to have a positive outlook, although they made it clear that hadn't always been the case and it had been a long road for them all to get to this point.

She listened as they explained how the Legion's Games had given them all a focus but, more impor-tantly, brought them together again. They all expressed that they had experienced a sense of isolation due to their injuries and that they missed the camaraderie of belonging to a team. It was clear that their defence force family was important to them. For Bud, in particular, it was his only family.

Sean's wife, Lisa, recounted how difficult things had

been when Sean injured his back. She had been pregnant at the time and not only had Sean been unable to help physically when she was heavily pregnant, but he'd also been unable to pick up their baby when she was born. His pain had made him miserable and the whole experience of becoming parents had been marred by his moods. It had put a strain on their marriage, but they had got through that and were now expecting a second child. As Lisa was saying how she hoped they would be able to enjoy the next experience, Viktoria's gaze was drawn across the room. She couldn't have said what made her turn in that direction at that point in time, perhaps a sixth sense of some sort, because her gaze landed on Cam. She'd had no idea he was joining them and perhaps he was also unaware of her presence as she saw his slight double-take when he noticed her sitting with the group.

He greeted everyone and slid in to sit on the bench seat beside her, which was the only empty place. His thigh brushed against hers, just briefly as he sat down, and she could feel the heat of his body through the thin fabric of her skirt triggering a flurry of nerves.

'Hello, Viktoria. I didn't know you were going to be here.'

She hoped her presence didn't bother him. She thought seeing him was a pleasant surprise, but she almost felt as if she should be apologising. 'Mark invited me. He thought I would like to meet some of the families. He did not tell me you were coming.'

'I catch up with the boys when I can. I served in Afghanistan with Sean and Bud,' he said as he poured himself a drink from the jug of beer that Mark passed to him.

Viktoria sipped her wine and tried not to think about Cam sitting beside her. About the way his leg brushed against hers each time he gestured in conversation. His touch, even a brief graze, was enough to trigger a powerful reaction. Her heart rate accelerated and her breathing quickened. She had never experienced an effect like this before.

The talk moved on from their time in the army to tales of cricket, rugby and children.

'Do you have children, Viktoria?' Lisa asked.

'Non.' Viktoria shook her head.

'She's much too busy working for the Prince,' Cam said.

'The Prince? As in Prince Alfred?' Lisa asked, the excitement evident in her voice.

'Oui.'

'Do you think we could meet him?'

Viktoria was surprised. 'You want to meet him? I did not think you Australians cared about the Royal Family too much.'

'You're probably right—' Sean began, before Lisa nudged him and interrupted.

'It's not about meeting royalty—it's about meeting the man who started these Games.'

'If it wasn't for him, none of us would be here today; it's quite likely none of us would have our men in our lives still,' Eric's wife added.

'We'd like to thank him,' Lisa said.

'I will see what I can do,' Viktoria told them, thinking Freddie would be pleased to hear from the wives. 'He will be at most of the events.' She knew the events had been scheduled to avoid clashes, allowing the participants to compete across multiple sports, but it also enabled Freddie to get to as many events as possible.

'But he'll meet the competitors at the Games. Will he meet us too?'

'There are a couple of family functions that I know

Prince Alfred will be at. There is a barbecue on the first day and there is also the closing ceremony. I know there will be thousands of people there, but I will do my best.' She was determined to follow through with her promise. She knew it should be relatively easy for her to organise but she didn't divulge why.

'Okay, who's for a game of darts?' Mark asked. 'I know Viktoria would like to chat to the girls about their experiences and I don't think I want to hear all they have to say.'

Viktoria was surprised about how forthcoming the women were in sharing their stories and she was stunned to hear what they had been through. Their stories were all different, but the one common theme was how the Games had changed things for them. The Games had given their men hope and a purpose and turned things around for them mentally. Even Mark's girlfriend, who was new on the scene, had noticed a change in his self-esteem since he had begun training for the Games.

'How long have you been together?' Viktoria asked.

'Six months. What about you and Cam? Your relationship must be new.'

'We are not dating.'

'Oh, I thought—'

'Cam hasn't dated anyone since Gemma,' Lisa said.

Viktoria's immediate thought was *Who is Gemma?* And she was about to ask when Mark's girlfriend said, 'Gemma? I don't remember a Gemma. Did I meet her?'

'No. They were dating when he was in Afghanistan.'

'But that was years ago.'

Viktoria saw the look Lisa exchanged with Eric's wife, but it was fleeting and she couldn't decipher it before it was lost. She wanted to ask more but they changed the subject, leaving Viktoria to wonder about the mysterious Gemma and what she meant to Cam. Leaving her wondering about what had happened between them. Did their breakup have something to do with the helicopter incident? Was it too much for Gemma to handle? Had she not wanted to wait for Cam to recover or to nurse him back to health? Did Cam break up with her? Or did he have his heart broken? He must have if he hadn't dated for years.

Viktoria was lost in her thoughts. The conversation continued around her and she decided it was time for her to leave.

She stood up to say goodbye just as Cam returned to the table with another round of drinks.

'Thank you,' she said as he passed her a glass of wine, 'but I think I am going to say goodnight.'

'Already?'

She nodded. It was time to go. Everyone had been very welcoming, but her mind was spinning.

'Can I give you a lift?'

She hesitated only fractionally, wondering if he'd really like to stay, before deciding that he had made the offer and she wanted to accept. '*Merci*, I would like that.' It would give her a chance to spend more time with Cam and maybe even learn more about him.

'Is everything okay?' he asked her as he slid behind the wheel after helping her into his car.

Had he picked up on her sombre mood?

'I had not fully understood the impact on the families. It was a little overwhelming, if I am honest.'

She was also feeling conflicted about her own self-indulgence. She had been bemoaning the fact that she was bored of handing out trophies and attending charity functions while these men and women had suffered real hardships and still managed to smile. The only real adversity she had faced was when Luca cheated on her and she broke off their engagement. That had been a difficult period in her life, but a broken heart was not normally fatal. She had experienced nothing like the stories she'd heard tonight, and she was awed by the strength and resilience they had all shown.

'I'm not sure how they manage to stay so positive,' she added.

'They've been through a lot,' Cam agreed.

She wondered what Cam's experiences were. And she wondered about Gemma.

She was desperate to know more, for Cam to open up to her, but she knew that he might then expect her to reciprocate and she wasn't sure what she wanted to tell him. What did she want him to know about her? There was so much she wanted to keep secret and she knew that wasn't fair. She couldn't expect him to disclose his past if she wasn't prepared to do the same but she was enjoying the opportunity to be a regular person, the chance to find out who she was without a crown or a royal title, and that was enough to persuade her to continue to keep her own counsel.

Cam pulled into the hotel driveway behind a long line of taxis. There was an empty parking bay on their left and Viktoria got Cam to turn into it. 'I can get out here,' she said.

She wondered if she was brave enough to invite him to come in but then decided against it. Hearing about Gemma had confused her. What had happened between them? Was Cam in a position where he might want to explore things with her or was he still not over Gemma? His friends had said he hadn't dated for years. What reason did she have to think he would be ready now?

He was hard to read, and she didn't want to make a fool of herself.

She would err on the side of caution.

'Thank you for the lift,' she said as she leant across and kissed him on his left cheek followed by the right.

Their faces were close, their cheeks still touching, and in the dim interior of the car his eyes were dark and hard to read.

They moved simultaneously, together or apart she wasn't quite sure, but suddenly it wasn't her cheek under his lips any more but her mouth. His lips covered hers and she heard herself sigh as she closed her eyes. His lips were warm and soft, but his pressure was firm. She opened her mouth and tasted him.

She lost herself in the kiss. Oblivious to anything and everything else, completely unaware of their surroundings, forgetting who she was, where she was, as she kissed him back. She didn't care who saw her. She couldn't have stopped if she'd wanted to. The kiss was everything she had imagined.

Viktoria felt as if she was floating as she made her way into the hotel. She still wasn't sure who had kissed who, but she didn't care. It didn't matter. What mattered was that it had been a perfect kiss and that he had asked her to spend the morning with him tomorrow.

He might not want to date but that hadn't stopped him from asking her to meet him at Bondi Beach at sunrise. It had been a perfect kiss and tomorrow had the potential to be the perfect day.

CHAPTER FOUR

SUNRISE WAS CAM'S favourite time of day at the beach. Seeing the sun come up over the ocean was the best start to a day and there were still many days when he really needed to see that. It served as a reminder to him that life went on.

Bondi wasn't his favourite beach. He found it too crowded and he normally avoided it but he was prepared to make an exception today. He was prepared to make an exception after the events of last night.

He had kissed Viktoria. Or she had kissed him. He wasn't sure how that had happened and at the time he hadn't thought too much of it. He'd just enjoyed the moment and then heard himself invite her to Bondi. It was almost as if she had cast a spell over him and he knew he had to see her again. Wanted to see her again.

But once he got home the doubts began.

Was he making a mistake?

Once again, it was too late. He seemed to be going about things in the wrong order with Viktoria. Speaking first and thinking later. Inviting her out and then wondering if he should have. Kissing her and then wondering if he should have. Maybe he needed to start counting to ten. He knew he was thinking with his heart instead of his head. Somehow, she was able to make him forget his guilt. Forget Gemma. And that was where the battle began. He didn't know if forgetting was the right thing to do.

Though he couldn't deny that he'd enjoyed the kiss. That for the first time in two years he'd been left wanting more.

But he was worried. At the moment she didn't know his history. He could pretend he was undamaged. But what if she got to know him and didn't like what she saw?

He hadn't intended to let his guard down and, while it was still up to a degree, he knew there were definite cracks in his walls. He'd taken her to his house. He'd cooked her dinner. And he'd invited her to spend the morning with him.

He liked the way he felt around her, but he didn't know if she would say the same. He wanted to be the best version of himself for her. Strong and intelligent. Not grumpy and damaged.

He wanted her to like him.

So, because he wanted Viktoria's approval, because he wanted to see her smile, he found himself at Bondi at sunrise. He knew Viktoria wanted to see the famous stretch of sand and he wanted to show it to her. He particularly wanted her to experience it at this time of day, when it was peaceful, before it was invaded by hordes of tourists and families. In his opinion that was a whole other experience, iconic maybe, but not nearly as pleasant.

The Bondi lifeguards were just setting up for duty, but the beach was virtually empty. The early risers were in the water, swimming, surfing, paddling and Cam caught a wave and let it carry him back into the shore. He shook his head, spraying water across the sand, and rubbed his hair with his towel to stop the water from dripping down his back, and headed for the lifeguard tower where he'd arranged to meet her. He didn't want her to be there before him.

She was walking towards him. She had her hair pulled up into a bun today, but he was only vaguely aware of that. She was dressed in shorts and a loose top. Her shorts were very short and her legs were amazing. She was coming out of a northern hemisphere summer and her legs were slim and tanned. Cam had to force himself to keep his eyes up.

'Bonjour.' She greeted him with a kiss on each cheek. Left then right. Just like last night but this time there was nothing extra and Cam forced himself to push the disappointment to the back of his mind. Today was about showing Viktoria one of the iconic Australian sights; it was about spending time with her, not about his desires. But he couldn't deny that she had stirred something in him. Reawakened his desires. It had been years since he had felt such strong attraction and he had to admit he was actually excited to see what might develop. Would she be the one who helped him move on?

Was he ready to let go of the past?

He was tired of thinking and he was tired of feeling guilty. He wanted to feel happy and maybe, just maybe, Viktoria could help him achieve that.

Her skin was warm and soft against his cheek and she smelt incredible. 'Good morning,' he replied. 'Welcome to Bondi.'

She grasped the railing that overlooked the beach with both hands and leant over, looking up and down the beach. 'I cannot believe I am here!' She turned back to face him, a wide smile on her face, and Cam's day got even better. 'I must take a photo.'

She pulled her phone from the pocket of her shorts and turned her back to the beach, holding her phone up, ready to take a selfie with the beach behind her.

'Why don't you let me take one of you?' he offered.

'No,' she said as she grabbed hold of his hand and pulled him closer. 'You have to be in it also.' She stepped in front of him slightly, tucking herself into the curve of his shoulder, and pressed back against him. Her bottom pressed against his hip, testing his self-control. She extended her arm and looked at the screen. 'Step to your right a little,' she instructed.

He did as she asked and saw that she now had the edge of the round tower in the corner of the frame with the beach and ocean behind them. He wasn't sure that the light was right—the sun was still rising over the sea—but Viktoria snapped a photo and then adjusted the settings until she was happy with the result.

'There.' She held her phone out to him, showing him the picture.

She looked stunning. He looked a mess. He was only half smiling and he knew that was because he was trying so hard not to think about her body pressing up against his.

'*D'accord.* Are we going to swim?'

She shoved her phone back into her pocket and lifted her arms above her head, removing her top in one smooth movement to reveal a black bikini top. It was small but not skimpy, and she was probably in no danger of losing it in the notorious Bondi surf, but it was still only barely covering her, and Cam fought hard to maintain the last bit of self-control.

He definitely needed to get into the water.

'Or have you already been in without me?' she asked as she stuffed her top into the small bag she carried.

She was looking at him, taking in his damp hair, bare chest and wet shorts, and he felt himself growing warm under her scrutiny.

He nodded. 'I thought I'd get my exercise in first. The water is cool, and I didn't know how long you'd want to stay in for.'

'How cool?'

'About twenty degrees.'

'That is okay. I need to go in; I have to be able to say I went swimming at Bondi.'

She skipped down the steps and onto the sand. 'It's beautiful. I thought the beaches at home were lovely, but this is huge and the sand is so soft! Our beaches have a lot of rocks and the sand is coarse. They are nothing like this.'

Cam dropped his towel on the sand near where the lifeguards were positioning the red and yellow flags to mark the safe swimming zone.

'Are we just going to leave our things here?' Viktoria asked.

He looked up and down the almost deserted beach. 'It's safe enough,' he said. 'Anyone on the beach at this time of the day is more interested in getting their exercise done than in stealing stuff.'

She stepped out of her shorts and piled her things with his and followed him into the sea. Cam dived under a small wave and swam away from the beach, keen to get back into the cold water. He turned and looked back at Viktoria. She was wading in slowly, gradually getting in deeper, until she finally gathered her courage and pushed off the sandy bottom and swam breaststroke out to him. She was treading water to stay afloat.

'Hold on to me,' Cam told her. He was still able to touch the bottom.

She wrapped her arms around his shoulders and floated off him. He was aware of each of her ten fingertips pressing into his skin. Tiny little circles of heat. They faced the beach and the morning sun reflected off the windows of the houses. They could hear the waves breaking on the shore but otherwise it was peaceful. They didn't talk but it was a comfortable silence.

The surfers were all at the southern end of the beach and only a few lone swimmers shared their patch of the ocean. Cam watched one man whose strokes looked a little laborious. He did not look like a natural swimmer. He wasn't making a lot of headway and when he lifted his head he barely cleared the surface. Cam saw him swallow a mouthful of water before stopping and coughing. He sunk under the waves and Cam waited for him to come back up.

He did. But only briefly before he disappeared a second time.

His hand broke the surface but only momentarily and Cam knew he was in strife.

'Viktoria...there's a swimmer in trouble.' He pointed towards the spot where he'd last seen the man, knowing even as he did there was nothing for Viktoria to see. He waved his arm, signalling to the lifeguards, but it was impossible to know if they had seen him. The man had swum out wider than the red and yellow flags; he was out of the manned zone. 'He needs help. I'm going to swim over to him. Can you get out of the water and run to the lifeguard tower? Can you do that?'

'*Oui.*' She didn't question him. She let go of him and kicked away, swimming freestyle towards the beach as Cam sprinted in the opposite direction. He wasn't sure that he knew exactly where the man had been, but he would try his best to find him. Even if the lifeguards had seen him there was no certainty that they would be any more accurate.

Cam swam a dozen strokes and then dived under the water, searching for the man.

Nothing.

He swam a dozen more, faster this time, and dived again.

This time he saw him, suspended under the surface.

Cam cut through the water and grabbed the man under the armpits. He was unconscious, a heavy, dead weight even in the buoyant saltwater.

Cam hauled him to the surface and used one hand to cup the man's chin and hold his head out of the water as he kicked sideways and aimed for the beach. He was out of breath by the time he was waist deep. His feet hit the bottom and he dragged the man into the shallows, laying him on the wet sand.

He looked up. Viktoria was still running towards the lifeguards; she was on the soft sand, making hard work of the distance. She should have stuck to the firm sand, but she was too far away to hear him if he called out to her. The tower was a long way from the northern end of the beach and the smaller north tower wasn't manned unless the beach was busy, but he could see lifeguards responding now. They had seen Viktoria and were sprinting for the buggy.

Cam turned his attention back to the unconscious man. He guessed him to be in his early sixties. He was slightly overweight but not in bad shape. If you ignored the fact that he wasn't breathing.

Cam pressed his fingers to the man's neck. There was no pulse.

He rolled him onto his side to clear his airway before rolling him back onto his back so he could start CPR.

The man was in cardiac arrest and time was critical. He started compressions, counting in his head as he kept one eye on the buggy and the lifeguards.

Thirteen, fourteen.

The buggy stopped to pick up Viktoria.

Seventeen, eighteen.

It was racing along the sand now.

Twenty-nine, thirty.

He stopped compressions and gave the man two breaths.

The buggy came to a halt and two lifeguards jumped out.

Cam kept the compressions going as he counted to thirty again.

'Are you okay to continue the compressions?' one of them asked as he knelt beside Cam. 'I'll do the breaths.'

Cam nodded. The other lifeguard was readying the defibrillator.

He sat back as he got to thirty, allowing the lifeguard to attach the leads while the second one breathed air into the man's lungs.

The defibrillator charged, preparing to shock.

'All clear. Shock now.'

They waited for the result.

Nothing.

Cam continued compressions as the defibrillator prepared itself again.

'I'll take over after the next shock, if needs be,' one of the lifeguards told Cam.

Cam nodded in acknowledgement as he kept counting.

The defibrillator shocked the man again. But again, there was no response.

Cam stood up, leaving the man in the care of the lifeguards. He could hear sirens in the distance and knew the ambulance was on its way.

A crowd had gathered. Joggers, dog walkers and swimmers surrounded them, and Cam wondered where they had all come from. The beach had seemed virtually deserted ten minutes ago. He could see Viktoria at the back of the crowd, her hand pressed to her mouth, her face pale.

He went to her as the lifeguards continued to work on the man.

She was shivering. He wrapped his arms around her, trying to calm her, to warm her, to reassure her. Her skin was cold, but he knew she was probably also in shock.

'*Mon Dieu!* Is he going to be all right?'

'I don't know,' Cam said. The man's prospects were not good, but it was clear that Viktoria was already overwhelmed and he knew there was nothing to be gained by giving her more bad news. What she was witnessing was already traumatic enough.

Viktoria leaned into Cam as he wrapped his arms around her. She was shaking and Cam rubbed her arms, trying to warm her up, but she wasn't sure that it was the cold making her tremble.

His skin was warm in contrast to hers; the physical exertion of performing resuscitation had warmed him. He felt solid and safe and comforting. She needed the comfort.

'Come on. You need to get warm.'

A large crowd had gathered and she was finding the situation confronting and she was relieved when Cam led her away. She had never witnessed anything like that before and wasn't in any hurry to prolong the experience.

'What about the man?' she asked as she let Cam lead her away from the crowd.

'There's nothing more we can do.'

'Are they going to be able to revive him?'

'I really don't know. It's not looking too good.'

He picked their towels up from the sand and wrapped one around her shoulders, but he continued to hold her close as they made their way to the lifeguard tower. He left his details there in case they needed to speak to him before he bundled her into his car and turned the heating up.

'Where are we going?' she asked as he pulled out of the parking space.

'I thought I'd take you to my place. It's closer than your hotel. You'll feel better after a hot shower and something to eat.'

She didn't think she could stomach any food, but a hot shower sounded divine.

She kept her eyes averted as they drove past the ambulance.

'Are you okay?' Cam asked her.

She nodded. 'I think so. I have never seen a dead person before. I do not think it is something I will forget.'

'No,' he agreed. 'Those images can be hard to get out of your head. But, in my experience, it's easier when you don't know the person.'

'I am sorry. Being in the army, you have probably seen much worse. You have lost friends?'

'I have.'

She reached across and put her hand on his thigh, offering him comfort this time. He turned his head and gave her a brief half-smile.

He seemed lost in his thoughts and she wondered if they were solely to do with the drowning man or if there was more going through his head. Was he thinking about his friends? Who had he lost?

She would love to know more but she didn't want to pry. She knew how it felt to be the subject of gossip and speculation but that didn't stop her thinking about Gemma again.

What had happened to her? Where had she gone? Was she one of the people he'd lost? Why had she and Cam broken up?

Cam had kissed her but what if he'd been thinking about Gemma? What if he regretted the kiss? Had it reminded him of Gemma? Brought back memories? She wished, almost desperately, that she knew what he was thinking, what he was feeling, but it was impossible to tell and she could go crazy trying to figure it all out.

She knew he was making an effort for her. She would cope. She wouldn't dwell on the unknowns, about the man on the beach or Cam's exes. She'd be upbeat and lift the mood.

'So what are we going to do to cheer ourselves up?' she asked.

'I'll think of something,' he said as he turned into his driveway, 'but first a shower and some dry clothes.'

Rex greeted them at the door, his tail wagging, and Viktoria immediately felt her spirits lift as she bent down and rubbed his head.

Cam showed her to the bathroom. He handed her fresh towels and said, 'You should have everything you need in there. Take your time; I'll make a start in the kitchen.'

She was tempted to drag him into the shower with her. She thought they could possibly both benefit from the distraction, but she wasn't sure what mood he was in. He was so difficult to read, sometimes looking as if he had the weight of the world on his shoulders. She realised he was probably feeling bad about the events of the morning, but they hadn't been his doing. He probably thought she was still in shock. She knew she'd be fine.

She washed and semi-dried her hair. She could smell coffee brewing and decided her hair could finish drying while she got her caffeine fix.

Cam had laid the table outside by the pool. 'I wasn't sure what you would like. There's coffee, smashed avocado on toast and poached eggs. Take a seat and help yourself.'

She didn't normally eat breakfast and forty minutes ago she would have thought she couldn't handle any food but it felt as if she'd been up for hours and the combination of a swim and the fresh air had left her ravenous, despite the unfortunate events.

A light breeze blew across the deck and, despite the sun, she could feel goose bumps on her skin; the air was fresh after the heat of the shower.

Cam disappeared into the house and when he returned he handed her a soft, well-worn top. 'Here, put this on, or we could eat inside if you prefer?'

'*Non, merci.* This will be perfect,' she said as she took the offered jumper. She slipped it over her head and rolled up the sleeves. It was soft and well-loved and she imagined it smelt of Cam. Wearing his top was like being wrapped in his arms again.

Cam spread some avocado on a slice of toasted bread, squeezed a little lemon juice on and added some cracked pepper. 'Try this,' he said as he passed it to her. 'It's an Aussie speciality.'

She pushed the sleeves of his jumper up her arm and took the toast. She looked adorable in his jumper and all he wanted to do was take her in his arms and remove it. No matter how good she looked in it, he knew he'd prefer to see her in nothing at all. He was unsettled. Pleasantly unsettled.

He was attracted to her and he wasn't at all sure what to do about it. He hadn't felt like this in a long time. There was something different about her. Being in her company felt different to the other dates he had been on but, as yet, he hadn't been able to figure out why.

Perhaps it was because she made him remember his old self. How he'd been before the accident. He felt lighter. Freer. Maybe even happy. And it was nice to have some company, other than Rex.

And the kiss had been phenomenal. And he wanted to do it again.

That was also new.

He was fighting a battle between guilt and desire and he didn't know which would win.

'This is delicious,' Viktoria said as she finished the smashed avocado and licked her fingers clean.

Cam tried to make conversation as he also tried to ignore the way her lips curled around her fingers. 'What are your plans for this afternoon?' he asked.

'I have none.'

'I'm going to visit my sister this afternoon; she lives on a property about ninety minutes away. Would you like to come with me? It would give you a chance to see something other than the city.'

He told himself he was asking because he was worried about her being alone after the morning's events. He felt responsible for her, given the shock she'd had this morning. But he also knew he wanted her to keep him company.

'Are you sure?'

'She has horses,' he said, hoping that would convince her. She had told him she loved to ride.

'Well, then, of course I would love to come. Is this the sister who gave you Rex?'

'It is. I only have one sister.'

'And she lives so far away?'

'It's only a little more than one hundred kilometres away. That's not far in Australia.'

'If I was at home a one-hundred-kilometre drive would put me in another country!' she exclaimed. 'Either France or Spain. Berggrun is only six thousand square kilometres in size. Half the size of Sydney. Two hours' drive is about as far as you can go before you find yourself out of the country.'

'We might not get into another state, but it will feel a world away.'

The city had given way to green fields, grapevines and small country towns and Viktoria was as excited as a young child at Christmas to see kangaroos with joeys in the bush as they drove past. Eventually Cam turned off the highway and drove over a cattle grid between white wooden fence posts. Horses grazed in the paddocks on either side of the driveway, but they were a breed Viktoria didn't recognise.

'What sort of horses are they?' she asked.

'Walers,' Cam replied. 'My sister and her husband breed them.'

He drove past the stables and up to the house. It was built of stone but clearly modern, with large windows that looked over the paddocks. A steel pergola, covered in vines, jutted out from the front of the house.

A heavily pregnant woman with dark hair stepped out of the house as Cam pulled his SUV to a stop.

Cam opened Viktoria's door for her before greeting the woman with a hug.

'Hello, little brother,' she said as she let go of Cam and smiled at Viktoria.

Cam introduced them. 'This is my sister, Skye, and her husband, David.' Skye had the same blue-grey eyes as Cam. David was a tall, solidly built man with sandy hair and a pleasant face.

'Hello, Viktoria,' Skye welcomed her. 'I hear you've had rather an eventful day.'

Viktoria handed Skye the bouquet of flowers that she had bought from a roadside stall during the drive. She'd insisted that Cam stop, knowing she couldn't arrive both uninvited and empty-handed. '*Oui*, a little more stressful than I am used to, *certainement*. Thank you for including me this afternoon; I know you were not expecting me.'

'Don't be silly. Friends of Campbell's are always welcome.'

Viktoria didn't miss the sideways glance Skye gave Cam and she wondered what it was all about.

She followed Skye into the house, stepping straight into a large living room adjacent a modern kitchen.

'And I agree with Cam,' Skye said as she filled a vase with water and arranged the flowers. 'You had a nasty shock this morning; it is better not to be on your own. Although he could have postponed the visit instead of dragging you out into the countryside.'

'I was happy to come. I must admit, I might have invited myself. I wanted to see something of the country and, once Cam told me you had horses, I was not going to let him cancel his visit.'

'Do you ride?'

'*Oui.*' She had ridden almost before she could walk.

'Would you like to see the horses?'

'I would love to.'

'Perfect. I'll leave the men to sort afternoon tea and I'll take you to see the animals. The two of you can handle that, can't you?' she asked, looking from David to Cam and back again. 'Boil the kettle and cut some cake; we won't be long.'

Skye peppered Viktoria with questions as they wandered down to the paddocks. 'You're working at the Games? Is that where you met Cam?'

'*Oui*. He had to show me around the event venues. He was not too happy about that, but I hope he has forgiven me the inconvenience.'

'I imagine he has.' Skye turned her head and gave her another look that she wasn't able to decipher. 'Are you living in Australia or just here for the Games?'

'Just for the Games. I only have ten more days.'

'Ah, I see.'

Viktoria wondered what that meant. She was having trouble deciphering Skye's language. She had thought Cam was hard to read but it seemed his sister was just as difficult. Perhaps it ran in the family.

Skye reached into a plastic tub and pulled out several apples. Immediately the horses came to the fence.

'Cam said they are called Walers,' Viktoria said as she fed the apples to the horses. 'I have never heard of them. They don't look like thoroughbreds.'

'No, they're not. They are heavier. Stronger. They're an Australian horse,' Skye explained, 'A mix of thoroughbred, Arab, the Cape horse from Africa, the Timor pony and, most likely, a little bit of Clydesdale as well, but they originated here in New South Wales—hence the name. Have you ever heard of the Australian Lighthorsemen?'

'From the War, *oui*?'

'Yes. They used Walers. They were bred as stock horses initially but then used for the military because they were so tough and strong. There are some amazing stories of their efforts in both the Boer War and the First World War.'

'You have so many. What do you do with them?'

'We sell them. Mainly as stock horses but we've sold a few recently to be used as therapy animals.'

'I have heard of therapy dogs,' Viktoria said, recalling Fiona and her dog, Leroy, 'but I have not heard of therapy horses.'

'Some horses develop a good relationship with people if they have the right temperament. Walers form strong attachments. I breed them and then they go to stables around the country and people suffering from depression and PTSD and the like can spend time with them. Some ride, some just like to brush them, to talk to them. The horses don't judge.'

Viktoria was fascinated. 'And who looks after the horses? Do you need special training?'

'No. You just need to know how to look after a horse and once you get to know the horse's personality, and they know yours, you'll have a friend for life.'

'And this is something you have always done?'

'Not exactly. Cam and I grew up on a sheep station. Naturally, we learnt to ride, and I bred some horses when I was younger but nothing serious. Neither Cam nor I wanted to inherit the sheep station so when our parents sold it to retire and move into town, I spent my inheritance on this property and Cam bought his house.'

'Does he ride?' Viktoria asked. Cam hadn't mentioned riding when they'd spoken of the horses. She'd told him she rode but she hadn't gone into detail. It was another one of the things she had kept quiet.

'Not any more,' Skye said as she handed over the last apple and put the lid on the tub. She wiped her hands on her apron and said, 'We should get back for afternoon tea before the boys eat all the cake.'

Once again Viktoria had the feeling of things unspoken.

They had spent a pleasant afternoon with Skye and David, but Viktoria had been keen to be alone with Cam again. Freddie was due to arrive in Sydney tomorrow and she suspected that might curtail her freedom. She wouldn't be able to disappear on a whim. She had messaged Brigitta to let her know she was spending the afternoon with Cam but while Brigitta could track her movements through an app on her phone she wouldn't question Viktoria's decisions. Freddie might be more interested in the company she was keeping.

As Cam turned into the hotel driveway she decided she would ask if he wanted their day to continue. He would either say yes or no.

'Are you going to walk me up to my room?' she asked as the doorman approached.

She waited. There was no pretending that either of them didn't know what she was asking, and she wasn't getting out of the car until she had his answer.

He switched off the engine, stepped out of the car and handed the keys to the valet attendant.

She smiled and took his hand and led him to the private lift that would take them directly to her penthouse. If he noticed that she had her own lift, he didn't comment. They stepped out into the foyer of the penthouse and she swiped her access key again to let them into the living room. The curtains were open, and Sydney Harbour glittered in the twilight.

'Is this what working for a prince looks like?' he asked as he took in his surroundings. He wandered over to the floor-to-ceiling windows. 'Please tell me the charitable trust isn't paying for this.'

He had his back to her as he looked out to the water and she quickly messaged Brigitta to tell her that she was back but didn't want to be interrupted and she would let her know if she needed her before she replied to Cam. 'It is not. But I did not invite you up here to look at *that* view.'

As she hoped, that got his attention.

He turned to find that she had kicked off her shoes and had her fingers on the top button of her shirt.

He crossed the room in three strides as she undid the first button.

His grey eyes were dark, and his gaze was unwavering. She could see her own desire reflected in his eyes and she felt her temperature rise as a flush stole over her cheeks and anticipation burned bright inside her. She couldn't breathe; his gaze was so intense it felt as if the room lacked oxygen, as if it was being burnt up in his eyes. She parted her lips to take a breath.

Her lips felt dry, her throat parched. She licked her lips with the tip of her tongue as Cam groaned and gave in to his desire. Gave in to hers.

He wrapped one arm around her back and pulled her to him and kissed her hard. He tasted of coffee and cinnamon, of freedom and promises.

She reached one hand behind his head, holding him to her as she kissed him back. His tongue was warm in her mouth. His hands were warm on her skin. Every inch of her was on fire, consumed with desire. She felt his fingers on her arm, could feel them tracing a line up to her shoulder, across her collarbone to the sweet hollow at the base of her throat. She felt his thumb dip into the little dimple. She couldn't breathe; she'd forgotten how.

She needed to breathe.

She pulled away and he lifted his hand, releasing her from his touch. She almost begged him not to. She didn't want him to let her go.

'Are you okay?' he asked.

She nodded, unable to speak but, aware that the curtains were still open, she knew they needed to move into the privacy of her bedroom. She knew it was unlikely, but she couldn't ignore the fact that paparazzi were everywhere and, even though no one seemed to have worked out who she was, old habits died hard. She knew all about photographers with long camera lenses and she couldn't afford to take the chance.

She took his hand and led him into the bedroom. She hit the button on the remote to draw the sheer curtains across the windows, giving them some privacy without total darkness.

She wound her arms around his neck and pulled him close. His gaze ran over her face before moving lower, over her breasts. How could grey eyes hold such heat? Such intensity? She held her breath, trying to stop the rise and fall of her breasts, but still her nipples peaked in response to his gaze burning through the thin fabric of her shirt. She could feel the moisture between her legs as her body responded as his gaze devoured her. He'd scarcely laid a finger on her and yet she felt ready to self-combust. A look, a glance, a smile was all it would take for her to melt under him.

'Are you sure about this?'

Again, there was no pretending they didn't know exactly what he was asking.

'Yes.' Her voice was breathless. She wasn't going to

pretend that they hadn't been leading up to this moment all day. 'I want you to make love to me.'

She didn't need to ask twice.

His fingers found the buttons on her shirt and he undid them in seconds. He bent his head and trailed a line of kisses from her collarbone to the swell of her breast. Her legs trembled, threatening to give way, but before she could stumble he scooped her up with one arm and lifted her onto the bed.

She lay back as he eased himself over her, supporting himself on his elbows. She reached up and ran her hands over his biceps, feeling his strength, marvelling at the firmness within him. His breath was coming fast now, she could hear it and feel it as it hit the bare skin of her shoulders and neck, but he didn't move. How could he hold himself so still? He was poised to move forward, to take this to the next level, but somehow he held his position. He was in no hurry. How could he be so calm when desire threatened to consume her?

The waiting was exquisite agony. A delicious sense of anticipation battled with the desire to have him take her now, right now. She arched her hips up towards him, pushing herself against his groin, and was rewarded when she felt his matching desire, hard and firm, straining against his pants.

She breathed out on a sigh as she let her knees fall open and wrapped her legs around him, pulling him closer, pulling him down against her. She heard him groan and he lowered his body until it covered the length of her. She wanted this. She wanted to feel his weight on her; she needed to know this was real.

Every cell of her body tingled in anticipation; she could feel each one straining, reaching out to him. Her skin was on fire and every nerve ending quivered with anticipation, alive with the possibilities of what was to come. Her expectations were almost painful, her reaction intense.

He reached for her, ending her suspense. His lips were on her earlobe, soft and warm, his breath in her ear. He kissed her neck and then his lips covered hers and she melted into him and let him consume her.

His fingers skimmed over her nipples, hard and peaked. He swept the strap of her bra from her shoulder and exposed her left breast to the cool air. His thumb brushed over her nipple, teasing, tantalising. She cried out as a wave of desire washed over her and a bolt of heat scorched through her, sweeping from her nipple to her groin in a searing flash.

His hands slid behind her back and with an expert flick of his fingers he undid her bra. He bent his head and his lips left a trail of hot spots from her lips to her throat and collarbone until finally he took the tip of her breast in his mouth, rolling his tongue over the taut flesh until Viktoria thought she might come then and there. But she didn't want it to end. Not yet. Maybe not ever. She wanted to feel him, to touch him, to arouse him too.

Her hands found the bottom of his T-shirt and she pushed it up until she could run her hand over his warm skin. His skin was firm but soft under her fingertips. She pulled his shirt from his body as his mouth continued to tease her nipple, sucking and licking. He paused momentarily to let her drag his shirt over his head before he returned his attention to her and her pleasure.

He cupped her breast in his hand and ran his thumb over the peaked bud, making her moan. She arched her back, offering herself to him, and he took one peak in his mouth again, sucking hard, and she almost exploded in his arms.

She ran her index finger from his sternum down along the line separating his abdominal muscles, following the line of dark hair that led below his waistband. She concentrated on him, wanting to extend the pleasure, wanting to share the delight. She snapped open the button on his trousers, unzipping his fly and pushing his pants low on his hips. His erection strained against the fabric of his boxer shorts. She ran her hand over his shaft; it was strong and thick, and she felt it rise to meet her. He groaned and the sound of his arousal urged her on.

His hand ran up her thigh and under the hem of her shorts. She pushed against him and instructed, 'Take them off.'

She lifted her hips as he undid her shorts and slid them off. His fingers met the elastic of her underwear and slid under the lace of her undies. Viktoria let her legs fall apart again, opening herself to him, giving herself to him, and she bit back a cry of desire as his fingers slid inside her. She was slick and wet, throbbing. His thumb found her centre and she gasped as his touch took her to the edge.

But she didn't want it this way. She wanted to share the experience. She wanted all of him and she wanted him to have all of her. She let go of him and pulled her underwear off and lay naked before him. His blue-grey eyes roamed over her body, setting her on fire with his gaze.

She watched as he stood and divested himself of his pants and shoes. She didn't think she could bear to wait much longer. She was desperate to feel him inside her. Desperate for them to be joined together.

To know that he wanted her as much as she wanted him.

Cam looked at Viktoria lying on the bed, naked, waiting, and he pushed aside any reservations. He hadn't made love to anyone since Gemma, but it was too late for any doubts. He didn't want to think; he couldn't think. There was no room in his head for anything other than desire. It took all his self-control to hold back long enough to find his wallet and retrieve a condom.

She lay, propped on her elbows, naked and gorgeous, and watched him roll it on.

She reached for his hand and pulled him back onto the bed. She reached behind him, holding his hips, cupping his buttocks, to pull him close. She arched her back and let her knees fall open as she fitted him to her like pieces of a jigsaw.

She sighed as he thrust into her.

She gave herself to him and he claimed her. All of her.

He filled her, consumed her and they became one.

Cam felt himself losing control.

Everything else in his life was forgotten as Viktoria took over his senses. He wanted to go slowly, he wanted to savour the moment, he wanted time to commit it all to memory, but he couldn't resist her. He couldn't fight it. He was only a man, a powerless man, and he could feel himself being swept away. The world ceased to exist except for Viktoria.

This was what he wanted. To disappear into a world of pleasure. To escape from a world of pain.

But Viktoria came into this new world with him. He wanted, needed to escape but he also wanted her to share in this moment with him. He was choosing to let her in.

And suddenly there was nothing else that mattered.

He wasn't thinking about the incident, or his scars, or his guilt or even Gemma. For the first time in years there was no room in his head for any of those things. He was completely in the present, immersed in the moment. The only thing he was thinking about was Viktoria.

He felt her hand on his chest, felt it brush over one nipple, felt another surge of blood to his groin. He breathed her name and that was the last coherent thought he had. Her legs wrapped around his waist, pinning him to her. She pushed her hips against his and his resistance crumbled.

She tilted her hips and moved in time with him. He heard his own guttural moan as he thrust into her, filling her, claiming her for his own. He couldn't hold back, he couldn't resist and when he heard her call his name it pushed him further.

There was nothing gentle in their lovemaking. It was fuelled by pure desire. Desperate, all-consuming desire.

He thrust into her again, up and down he moved, faster and faster, harder and stronger, and she met each thrust. She arched her back and held him close with her legs, opening herself to him, offering herself to him.

He buried himself deep inside her and when he felt her shudder and come undone, he came with her. They climaxed together and when they were completely spent he gathered her to him, holding her close, reluctant to let her go as he savoured this next moment, as they lay in each other's arms, slick with sweat and breathing hard.

She had blown his mind.

She had given him a gift. She had relieved him of his trauma and stress. He felt as if she had pieced a bit of him back together. That while she held him in her embrace he was restored, renewed, revived.

For those minutes she had let him feel like the man he used to be and he wondered: Did she have the power, the ability to heal him, to restore him?

She lay curled against his side. Her fingers were

warm as they trailed over his chest, across a nipple, down his sternum and over his abdomen, coming to rest on the scar on his hip bone.

He could feel himself stirring again as her hand moved lower. Following the line of his scar.

Down the outside of his thigh.

'How did you get this scar?'

Her question brought him abruptly back to reality.

He'd been kidding himself that he could stay in the bubble she'd created. He'd thought tonight might have been different. That it could be the turning point for him. But once again he was too quickly thrust back into his reality.

But this time there was a difference. This time he had been prepared to let someone in. And if he was going to let her in then she deserved an answer.

'I was involved in an incident.'

'It is a big scar. Was it a bad incident?'

'It was.' It couldn't have been worse. Even if he'd died too, he had thought at times that that would have been a better outcome. Guilt continued to eat at him. If everyone had died, including him, he wouldn't be living with that guilt. But he didn't say that.

'Was it a long time ago?'

'Two years.'

'Will you tell me about it?'

If she'd asked him if he wanted to talk about it he would have said no, but what did it matter if he told her about the incident? If she wanted to, she could find out all the information on the internet anyway. The articles didn't talk about the personal cost of the incident. The articles didn't mention how it had destroyed his life, and he didn't need to talk about that either, but he could give her the facts. He'd repeated them often enough in various hearings and in front of various panels.

But only a handful of people heard about his guilt—the psychologists, Doug, Skye.

But he wasn't ready to leave her yet. Talking to her was a way to stay beside her for a little longer.

'I was deployed to the Middle East as a surgeon,' he said. Lying in the semi-darkness made it easier to tell his story. 'I was responsible for medical treatments and surgery at the base hospital, but I also went out into the field with the helicopter evacuation unit to retrieve injured or wounded soldiers. I was almost due to come home when a retrieval went wrong.

'The helicopter crashed. It was shot down. I thought it must have been a mistake, but I found out later it was deliberate. They ignored the medical markings and launched missiles at us. I ended up with multiple injuries, including a fractured pelvis and a shattered femur. I was put back together with plates and pins and screws, which is where that scar came from. I lost a lot of blood, but people said I was lucky.'

'That does not sound lucky. That sounds painful.'

'They meant lucky to be alive.'

'Oh.'

He hadn't felt lucky. 'The chopper crashed and then caught fire. There were six people on board. I was the only survivor.'

'Everyone else died?'

He nodded. 'I couldn't get them out.' He still felt guilty. 'I couldn't stand, I couldn't breathe. I dragged myself out of the chopper, but I couldn't save anyone else.'

He'd been told later that the others had all died on or before impact, but he didn't know if he believed that.

He still wondered if the army was telling him that to make him feel better.

He'd lain in the dirt for an hour before he'd been found.

Somehow, he'd survived. But for a long time he'd wished he'd died.

'Were they your friends?'

She had her head resting on his chest as her fingers made tiny circles over his abdominal muscles. Her breath was warm on his skin. Her deep, husky voice relaxed him, hypnotised him.

'They were more than that.'

He was aware of dampness on his cheeks. Tears. Tears for his colleagues. Tears for Gemma. He wiped them away with the back of his hand. He did not want to be sad, not tonight, and he didn't want Viktoria's pity.

He lifted her hand and kissed her fingers. He was done talking.

He wanted to forget the past. He wanted to stay in this moment in time. He was content, sated, and he wanted the feeling to last a little longer.

CHAPTER FIVE

THERE WAS NOT an empty seat in the basketball arena. Special platforms had been built to accommodate spectators in wheelchairs and every available seat and spot was taken. Wheelchair basketball was the first sport on the programme and expectations were high and nerves were taut—both for the competitors and the organising committee.

But first there was the opening welcome address from the Prince. His arrival was greeted by rousing applause, but Cam scarcely noticed. Viktoria arrived in the arena with the Prince and Cam only had eyes for her.

He hadn't seen her since he'd left her bed in the early hours of yesterday morning.

He had spent yesterday in meetings, discussing the final preparations for the games which began today. The irony of his situation wasn't lost on him. He had finally met someone he actually wanted to spend time with, and he was too busy. For once he hadn't wanted to throw himself into work. For once he had something else he'd rather be doing.

He had expected to feel some regret, but he didn't. He felt unburdened.

He'd thought he might have some reservations that he had revealed too much. But he didn't. He knew he hadn't revealed all. Fewer than a handful of people knew the whole truth.

He was standing courtside with the medical team and Viktoria came to stand by his side. He smiled at her. 'Good morning. Are you ready for this?'

'I think so. Are you?'

He nodded. He had done everything he could to prepare and now he had to hope he had covered all contingencies.

They stood in silence and listened as Doug introduced Prince Alfred.

The Prince strode to the microphone that had been assembled in the centre of the basketball court. He was tall, blond and physically fit but he had spoken previously about the effect that being part of combat missions had on him mentally and the crowd greeted and accepted him as one of their own. He was casually dressed, wearing a dark navy Legion's Games polo shirt and pressed chinos. It was the same shirt that the English competitors wore and it gave the impression that, although he was royalty, he wasn't there as the Prince but simply as one of them. A returned soldier.

Viktoria held up her phone, preparing to video the Prince's opening address. There was a large media contingent courtside as well. Cam knew the Games would get a large amount of coverage, which could only be a good thing. Hopefully, the publicity would inspire others, both soldiers and civilians, to get involved in sport. Cam knew that was the Prince's aim.

'Thank you for that warm welcome,' Prince Alfred said as the applause that greeted him eased. 'I am thrilled to be in Australia for the third Legion's Games. My vision was to encourage wounded and ill soldiers from all collegiate nations to experience the healing power of sport. I know many of you strive for perfection and love a challenge and I believed the Games would provide a platform to inspire, encourage and challenge soldiers to participate in sport. I have seen for myself how fiercely competitive most defence force personnel are, but the Legion's Games are not just about the competition; they are also about achievement, belonging and family. For many, if not most of us, our units became our family and I know what it feels like to lose that family through injury, illness or retirement and how difficult that can be when it was not by choice.

'The ideal of these Games is to bring people together. Perhaps these Games will reunite you with your defence force family or perhaps they will give you an opportunity to introduce your civilian family to your defence force family. I hope these Games give you a chance to support and embrace one another and feel part of something unifying.

'The Games are about more than medals. Whether you are a competitor or a spectator, you have all achieved something just by being here. Each and every one of you are part of these Games.

'The success of the first two Legion's Games surpassed my expectations and it is fantastic to see the Games grow in size and in recognition. This year there are one thousand competitors from twenty nations competing across a dozen different sports. I know these Games will be a great success because if there's one thing Australians do exceptionally well it is host sporting events.

'I want to wish you all good health, good luck and good times with friends old and new.

Let the Games begin.'

His speech was greeted with thunderous applause and

cheers from the crowd and Cam had to bend his head close to Viktoria's ear to make sure she could hear him. 'All right. I'm on deck now,' Cam said as the basketball teams from Australia and England took to the court. 'I'll catch up with you later?'

He wanted to stay with her but he needed to work.

He wanted to hold her, to take her hand and take her away to where it could be just the two of them. To somewhere he didn't have to worry about what to do next, to somewhere no one would expect anything of him, to somewhere with no responsibilities and no commitment. With nothing but the two of them.

He was under her spell and he had no idea how it had happened. How he'd gone so quickly from being irritated at the thought of having to chaperone her to completely enamoured.

It wasn't like him to fall so fast. He was measured. Controlled. Sensible.

They'd shared one night and two days. It was crazy but he felt transformed.

Perhaps it was a good thing that he had to work. Perhaps he needed some time for his hormones to settle. For his emotions to calm down. His heightened emotions were usually of the fight kind—tense, wound tight. He wasn't used to this feeling of peace and calm. Of happiness. It was a little disconcerting.

Viktoria took her seat beside Freddie and quickly checked and uploaded the video of his welcome speech to the various digital platforms before settling in to watch the game.

The first game of the day was Australia v England, followed by USA v Canada. The stakes were high and the competition physical. The crowd got right behind the players and the stadium was filled with family and friends along with the team members of the other competing countries.

Flags from the twenty nations were hung throughout the stadium and the crowd was vocal, none more so than the Aussies with their popular, if uninventive, chant of, 'Aussie, Aussie, Aussie, Oi, Oi, Oi!'

But Viktoria could see the attraction of it—everyone knew the words! Even the other nations were getting into the spirit of the chant. But there was equal applause for the English team whenever they shot a basket or made a good play. The spirit of the Games was off to a great start.

Viktoria had never seen wheelchair basketball before, and she was surprised by how rough it was and how often the competitors were tipped out of their chairs.

Among all the action, she was also aware of Cam. She could see him across the court in the medical tent. Even though the base medical centre was only metres away in another building, first aid facilities had been established in each venue as well. Doctors were there to treat injuries, physios were busy taping and masseurs were on hand to relieve tired, cramping muscles.

Cam was busy but occasionally he glanced up at her and smiled. She couldn't help but smile back. She had come to Sydney for an adventure, but she was getting more than she had bargained for. She hadn't counted on meeting someone like Cam, but she intended to enjoy every minute of the experience. She would soon have to return to reality, to her real life.

The crowd gasped collectively, bringing her attention back to the court in front of her. One of the Aussie competitors had fallen hard. Viktoria recognised him as one of Mark's friends, one of the swim relay team, Bud.

She held her breath as his wheelchair was righted and he was escorted from the court. She could see him undergoing a concussion test in the medical tent and he didn't re-join the game, although he was able to go back onto the court at the end of the match when Freddie went to shake hands with all the players.

Cam came to sit next to her in the break.

'Is Bud okay?' she asked.

'He has a concussion. He might miss the next basketball game.'

'What about the swimming? The relay team sounds like it might be getting quite depleted.'

'As long as he can tell the deep end of the pool from the shallow end, he'll be okay.' Cam grinned at her. 'Have you got plans for tonight? I thought I could take you out for dinner.'

'I am having dinner with Fr—Prince Alfred.' She'd almost made a mistake. 'I am going to discuss my ideas with him.'

'Tomorrow night then?'

'*Oui*, I would like that.'

Viktoria was dining with Freddie when her mobile phone pinged with a message. She glanced at it and, when she saw it was Cam, picked it up to read it.

Let me know if he's boring you and you want to be rescued.

She smiled and texted back a quick reply.

'Who was that?'

'No one.'

'Come on, Viktoria. I know you better than that. Spill.'

Viktoria knew he would persist until she gave in and

because she was more than happy to talk about Cam she filled Freddie in on the basics of the past few days.

'So, quite the adventure you're having,' her cousin said when she finished imparting the details she was happy to share. 'Are you going to tell him who you are?'

'No. That is not necessary. I will be gone in ten days. He does not need to know I am a princess. It does not matter.'

'Keeping secrets is never a good idea. I think you should tell him.'

'When I leave here I will be going home to get engaged. I will be getting married. I will not see him again so there is no need for him to know. I just want to be Viktoria for a few more days. That is all.'

'If you're sure.'

She had thought about telling Cam who she was, but she wasn't sure how he would take it. She didn't want it to change things between them. They didn't have a future together. It didn't matter that she had been picturing all sorts of alternative endings to her adventure in Australia, to what waited for her when she returned to Berggrun. Knowing that Cam was just the sort of man she could fall in love with—kind, considerate, intelligent and handsome—didn't mean anything.

He was also still guarded. She often had no idea about how he felt. She had no idea of his past. Of his plans for the future. Did he have any that could include her? She couldn't imagine him leaving everything he had here to follow her to Berggrun.

She needed to remember to treat this relationship as it was—a holiday romance—and not let herself get carried away with her dreams. She'd done that before with Luca and it had been a disaster.

The reality was that she was a reverse Cinderella.

She was a princess pretending to be ordinary and at the stroke of midnight, or in her case when she stepped onto the plane that would take her home, she would become royalty again.

She was worried that if she told him the truth, instead of Cinderella running from the ball it would be Cam.

She and Cam were from two different worlds. In her limited experience that did not get them off to a good start, no matter how intense their chemistry was. She could not imagine him anywhere but here.

His career was here. His family was here. Why would he leave all that behind for her? They barely knew each other. And it wasn't as if she could quit being a princess. No matter how much she might dream of doing exactly that, she knew it wasn't a realistic dream. It was a fantasy.

'Please don't say anything, Freddie.'

'Of course I won't. It's not my place. But I still think you should tell him.'

Dinner was at a restaurant overlooking Watson's Bay, a short walk from Cam's house. It was yet another perfect vista. Every corner she turned in Sydney seemed to bring her to another view of the water, another bay, another stretch of golden sand, more boats. Berggrun was a beautiful country, wealthy and with beautiful marinas, but it didn't have Sydney's stunning abundant natural beauty.

'Is every corner of Sydney as beautiful as the next?' she asked as the waiter took their orders.

'I haven't seen anything to compare to this view,' Cam told her, looking directly at her, his grey gaze so intense that she could feel herself blushing. 'I'm finding it hard to believe you are single.'

'I am definitely single.' For another few months at least. Until she turned thirty. 'I have been for several months. Since my ex-fiancé cheated on me.'

'You're kidding?'

'I wish I was. Or, at least, at the time I wished it was all a misunderstanding. Now I think I had a lucky escape.'

At the time she had believed Luca was the one for her but now she wondered if that was only because she was approaching her thirtieth birthday. There had always been red flags—he was charming and ambitious and selfish—but she had thought he'd loved her. She'd thought she'd loved him. But perhaps she'd been ignoring the warning signs, looking through rose-coloured glasses because in her head she knew she was expected to marry by the time she was thirty.

She wasn't sure if she'd really been in love with Luca or just in love with the idea of a fairy tale wedding.

But she'd learnt one thing from that experience—being a princess didn't guarantee a fairy tale ending.

'My brothers and Luca never got along. That should have been a warning sign for me. Next time I'll pay more attention.'

'You have brothers?'

'Two older brothers.'

For a moment she considered telling Cam who she really was, before deciding he didn't need to know. They wouldn't have a future and she didn't want to change anything between them at the moment. They only had a few more days together. 'So a holiday romance is just what I need to forget all about my disastrous love life.'

'And at the end of your holiday?'

'I have to go home. I have to be back in Berggrun for a family celebration. I leave the day after the Games.'

'So we will have to make the most of every minute,' Cam said as he signalled for the bill.

'Damn,' Cam said when they arrived home and he saw a car parked in his driveway.

'Whose car is that?'

'Skye's. I'd forgotten she was coming to stay.'

He didn't want to share this time with his sister. He didn't want family intruding. That was selfish but his thoughts were far from family. He only had one thing on his mind.

'You forgot?'

'I've been a bit preoccupied,' he said as he bent his head and kissed her. 'She hasn't come to see me; she has a doctor's appointment tomorrow. I think it must be her thirty-six-week check-up.'

'Should I get the hotel to send a car for me?'

'No.' It was late, and he hoped that Skye would have gone to bed already. Even before she'd got pregnant, she was an early to bed, early to rise person, always up at the crack of dawn with her horses. He was prepared to bet that she wouldn't be getting in their way.

He opened the door. The house was dark; just a single lamp was lit in the entry but there was a note on the kitchen bench from Skye.

Cam picked it up and breathed a sigh of relief. 'She's gone to bed.'

Viktoria stood behind him as he read the note. She pressed herself to his back and he felt her arms snake around his waist as she slid one hand under his shirt, her palm warm against his skin. He spun her around and pressed her back against the kitchen counter. He lifted her onto the benchtop. His hands cupped her buttocks.

He pulled her towards him, and she wrapped her legs around his waist.

'What if Skye gets up?' she said before he could kiss her. 'I don't want her to see us here.'

Cam scooped her off the kitchen counter, lifting her easily, but she protested, 'Wait. Put me down. I can walk.'

'I've got you.' He wasn't about to let her go.

'But what about your leg? Let me walk.'

'My leg is fine.' He hadn't even thought about his leg and he certainly didn't want to be reminded of it. His door was ajar, and he kicked it open and carried her into his room.

He pushed the door closed with his foot and leant against it, letting Viktoria slide down until her feet touched the floor, but he kept his arms around her, keeping her pressed against him.

His breath was coming fast but it wasn't from exertion.

Her breaths were short and shallow too, her pupils large, as he bent his head and kissed her again.

CHAPTER SIX

VIKTORIA RAN HER hands under his shirt. She trailed her fingernails lightly over his skin and heard him moan. The room was in darkness but the curtains were open, letting the moonlight spill in. His room faced the ocean and, for once, Viktoria didn't worry about the paparazzi. Cam's house was secluded and private. She grabbed the bottom of his shirt and pulled it over his head, exposing his flat, toned stomach.

He started to undo his belt but Viktoria stopped him.

'Let me,' she said. She undid his belt and snapped open the button on his trousers before sliding the zip down. She could feel the hard bulge of his erection pressing into her, straining to get free.

Cam stepped out of his shoes, not bothering to untie the laces, as she pushed his trousers to the floor. They joined his shoes and shirt in an untidy heap. He was naked except for his underwear. Viktoria looked him over.

He was glorious.

He grinned at her and raised one eyebrow.

In silent reply, she put one hand on his smooth, broad chest and pushed him backwards until the bed bumped the back of his knees and made him sit. It was his turn to wait for her now.

She stepped back from the bed. Out of his reach. He could watch but he couldn't touch. She wanted to tease him. She reached for the zip at the side of her dress and undid it slowly. She slipped one strap from her shoulder and then the other and let the dress fall to the floor. Cam's eyes were dark grey now, as he watched and waited for her.

She reached her hands behind her back and unhooked her bra, sliding it along her arms and dropping it to the floor. She lifted her hands to her hair, to the elastic band that fastened the end of her plait and started to pull it from her hair.

'Wait. Let me do that.' Cam's voice was husky with desire. Lust coated his words, making them so heavy they barely made it past his lips.

Viktoria dropped her hand, leaving her hair restrained.

Cam reached up and his fingers rested at the nape of her neck before he flicked her plait over her left shoulder and pulled the elastic from her hair. He wound his fingers through her hair; loosening the plait, he spread her hair out, letting it fall over her shoulders.

His touch was light as he slid her underwear from her hips. Viktoria trembled with desire as his fingers skimmed her thighs. She stood before him, completely naked, but she didn't feel exposed. She felt powerful.

He pulled her closer and kissed her belly. His lips were warm, and his touch set alight a flame that burned through her.

He lifted her off her feet and she sat on his lap, her knees spread as she straddled him.

He ran his right hand along her thigh, over her waist and her shoulder until his thumb came to rest on her jaw. It was warm and soft, his pressure gentle. He ran his thumb along the line of her jaw and then his thumb was replaced by his lips. He kissed her neck, her collarbone and the hollow at the base of her throat where her collarbones met.

His fingers blazed a trail across her body that his mouth followed. Down from her throat to her sternum, over her breast to her nipple. His fingers flicked over the nipple, already peaked and hard. His mouth followed, covering it, sucking, licking and tasting.

He flipped her onto her back, lying her on the bed.

Moonlight danced across the ocean, streaming through the uncurtained windows, and fell across the bed. Her skin shone in the pale light.

He opened a bedside drawer and retrieved a condom as Viktoria reached for his boxer shorts and pulled them from his waist.

He was lying beside her now, and his fingers were stroking the inside of her thigh. She parted her legs and his fingers slid inside her, into her warm, moist centre. His thumb rolled over her most sensitive spot, making her gasp. He kissed her breast, sucking at her nipple as his thumb teased her. She arched her back, pushing her hips and breasts towards him, wanting more, letting him take her to a peak of desire.

Still she wanted more. She needed more.

She rolled towards him and pushed him flat onto his back. She sat up and straddled his hips again. His erection rose between them, trapped between their groins. Viktoria reached for the condom, and her breasts hung above his face. He lifted his head, taking her breast into his mouth once more. She closed her eyes as she gave herself up to the sensations shooting through her as his tongue flicked over her nipple. Every part of her responded to his touch. Her body came alive under his fingers and his lips and her skin burned where their bodies met.

She lifted herself clear of Cam, pulling her breast from his lips as she opened the condom. Air flowed over her nipple, the cool temperature contrasting with the heat of his mouth as she rolled the condom onto him. Her fingers encircled his shaft as she smoothed out the sheath.

She placed her hands either side of his head and kept her eyes on his face as she lifted herself up and took him inside her. His eyelids closed and she watched him breathe in deeply as her flesh encased him, joining them together.

She filled herself with his length before lifting her weight from him and letting him take control. His thumbs were on the front of her hips, his fingers behind her pelvis as he guided her up and down, matching her rhythm to his thrusts, each movement bringing her closer to climax.

She liked this position. She liked being able to watch him, she liked being able to see him getting closer and closer to release. His eyes were closed, his lips were parted, his breathing was rapid and shallow, his thrusts getting faster.

She spread her knees, letting him in deeper inside her until she had taken all of him. Her body was flooded with heat. Every nerve ending was crying out for his touch. 'Now, Cam. Now.'

He opened his eyes and his grey gaze locked with hers as he took her to the top of the peak.

Her body started to quiver, and she watched him as he too shuddered. He closed his eyes, threw his head back and thrust into her, claiming her as they climaxed together.

When they were spent, she lay on him, covering his

body with hers. Their skin felt warm and flushed from their effort and they were both panting as he wrapped his arms around her back, holding her to him. She could feel his heart beating under her chest. She could feel it as its rhythm slowed, gradually returning to normal.

They lay in silence as Viktoria resisted the urge to drift off to sleep. She knew she should get out of bed, get ready to leave. She would have to arrange for the hotel car to pick her up soon, but she wanted to stay in Cam's bed for a little longer.

Not for the first time, she wished she could experience dating like a normal person. As Cam offered to fetch them both a drink and got out of bed she lay there and imagined what it would be like to be able to spend the night. To not have to check in with Brigitta. To not have someone having to know her whereabouts at all times.

Perhaps she should have told Cam who she was, she thought. Perhaps she should have explained herself to him. Maybe then it wouldn't seem so odd that she was almost running for the door. That she couldn't stay the night.

She rolled over and sat up and noticed a photo frame lying face down on the other bedside table. They must have knocked it over while they made love. She reached out to stand it back up, looking at the photograph out of curiosity.

It was a photo of Cam with his arm around a woman with dark hair. Viktoria initially thought it was Skye but, when she looked again, she realised it wasn't.

She felt slightly queasy, a sensation she recognised as fear and jealousy running through her veins and making her nauseous. She hadn't seen any other personal photographs or mementos on display in his house. Was this

Gemma in the photo? Why was she in the only photograph in his house and why was it beside his bed? She must be important but why hadn't he mentioned her? And why was the photograph lying down? Was he hiding something?

Viktoria was sitting up in bed when Cam returned to his room. She was bare-chested but her golden hair fell over her shoulders. The sheet was tangled around her waist and she reminded him of a mermaid perched on a rock. She looked beautiful and he wished he could ask her to stay the night, but he knew that would invite questions from Skye in the morning. Questions he wasn't ready to answer.

He put the glasses of water on the bedside table and then noticed Viktoria was holding something. A photo frame. The picture of him with Gemma.

'What are you doing?' he asked, his tone more abrupt than he'd intended.

Viktoria looked up at him. Her blue eyes were wide in her face. 'Who is this?'

'Gemma.'

'Is Gemma your girlfriend?'

'No.' He took the photo from her and put it back on the table. He turned it away from the bed. 'My fiancée.'

'*Mon Dieu!*' Viktoria sat back, putting some space between them. 'You did not think to mention that you are engaged?'

'I *was* engaged. Gemma is dead.'

He was being harsh, but he had finally stopped thinking about Gemma constantly since he'd begun spending time with Viktoria and that knowledge made him feel guilty. He didn't deserve to forget. Gemma deserved to be remembered.

'Pardon,' she said as she glanced at the back of the frame.

Cam knew the photo had been lying down. He knew she must have picked it up out of curiosity and he wasn't sure if she was apologising for prying or for his loss.

'Was it recent?' she asked.

'Two years ago.'

'Two years?' She paused and he could almost see the wheels turning in her mind. 'Your incident was two years ago, yes?'

Cam nodded. He knew what she was asking. 'Gemma was in the chopper too.'

'She was with you? She was in the army also?'

Cam could see the hurt in her eyes, and he knew he had been unnecessarily abrasive. It wasn't Viktoria's fault that he felt guilty.

'She was a pilot,' he said as he tried to make amends. He couldn't fix things for Gemma, but he had no reason to hurt Viktoria in the process. She had done nothing wrong. 'I joined the army because of her. I wanted to be with her. But I got her killed.'

'How do you figure that?'

'Gemma was one of only a handful of female pilots in the army. She loved to fly, and it was a great job. It took her all over the world but it took her away from me so I joined the medical corps so we could be together.'

'That does not make the crash your fault.'

He sat on the edge of the bed as he replied. 'On the day of the incident Gemma was on a rostered day off— she wasn't supposed to be flying—but one of the other pilots was sick. Gemma volunteered to cover his shift. She knew someone had to do it. She had a strong sense of duty and she also loved to fly. She told me there wasn't much point in having a day off if I was working. She thought she might as well work too. She wasn't supposed to be in the chopper that day.'

'If you had not been working would she have flown anyway?'

'She was rostered off. I would have been able to convince her to spend the day with me. Someone else could have taken over the roster. She volunteered because of *me*. She was only there because of me.'

'You told me the chopper was shot down. You had nothing to do with that. It was not your fault and I cannot imagine it was Gemma's either.'

'There was speculation that she was flying too high. Choppers tend to fly low, to keep out of sight, below the radar. It seemed as though the defence force were blaming Gemma. But it shouldn't have mattered. She should have been able to fly at any height. We were a medevac unit, well-marked. There was no mistaking us.'

Cam was quiet after that. Those memories were obviously hurting him, but Viktoria didn't know how to make things better.

She had been worried that he hadn't got over Gemma and was having trouble moving on, but learning that Gemma was dead, had been dead for two years, made her even more concerned. He hadn't let go. Which made her wonder what he was doing with her.

His friends had told her Cam didn't date. Had that been a warning that she'd ignored? Was she just a fling?

She couldn't be upset about that. After all, that was all she'd wanted too—one last adventure before she got married. She hadn't meant to get so invested.

She needed to stop obsessing, she thought as she let herself into the penthouse, and just enjoy the next few days. She liked him—really liked him—but they had a few days together, not a future.

'Good morning.' Cam bent down and kissed his sister's cheek. The sun was only just over the horizon, but Skye was already sitting outside by the pool nursing a cup of tea. It was a glorious morning, blue sky and not a breath of wind. Sydney had turned on spectacular weather for the Legion's Games and today was looking to be no exception. 'You're up early.'

'It's hard to sleep in when I feel like I constantly need to go to the toilet. This baby's favourite position seems to be lying on my bladder.'

'You sure you really need a cup of tea as well?'

'I need something; I'm exhausted. I can't wait for this baby to arrive.'

'You know all first-time mothers say that and then they realise that a good night's sleep is just as impossible to get after the baby is born?'

'I know, people keep warning me, but it'll be nice to stop waddling and to be able to see my toes again.'

'You won't be looking at your toes once you're cuddling your baby.'

'Fair point.' Skye laughed. 'Now, why don't you make yourself useful and bring us some breakfast? I've cut up some fruit; it's in the fridge.'

Cam made himself a coffee and carried it back to the table on a tray with fruit, bowls and yoghurt.

'So you're in a good mood,' she said as he pushed the newspaper and Skye's tablet out of the way, making room for the tray.

He was in a good mood. He had enjoyed last night and even talking about Gemma hadn't dampened his spirits. It had felt good to tell Viktoria about her. The honesty made him feel less guilty. He enjoyed Viktoria's company and that was okay. It was nothing to apologise for.

'Does it have anything to do with where you were last night?' Skye asked.

'Sorry, I forgot you were coming.'

'That's okay. I have a key. So…where were you? Are you going to give me the goss?'

'I was out with Viktoria.'

'You went out with her again?'

'Yes.' Cam hesitated. 'I thought you'd be pleased that I wanted to see someone more than once. That I'm moving forward.'

'I am,' Skye said as she speared a piece of mango with her fork. 'Is it serious?'

'Why would you ask that? I've only known her a few days.'

'You brought her to our house, Cam. You haven't introduced Dave and me to any girl in two years. Not since Gemma.'

Cam hadn't thought about Gemma constantly for several days but now that he was finally able to have a moment's peace from his thoughts, her name kept coming up. But he didn't feel quite the same intense emotion of guilt and shame.

'It's not serious.'

Viktoria was the first woman in two years that he'd wanted to spend time with but that didn't make it serious.

She was the first woman in two years who had been able to distract him for long enough to make him forget about what had happened. She was different to Gemma. Gemma was non-stop, hyperactive, a type A personality. She had challenged him and pushed him but never given him a moment's peace. Since the incident all he wanted was peace. He needed calm and Viktoria brought the calm, but she was only in Australia for another few days.

It wasn't serious. He figured he could safely spend as much time with her as he liked—as they both liked—because he knew there was a limit and that suited him perfectly. He wasn't ready to open himself up to another serious relationship.

'Oh. Okay.'

'What does that tone mean?' Cam asked.

'Nothing. I'm just not sure if that's good or bad.'

He frowned. 'Why?'

'Has she told you much about herself?' Skye asked as she reached for her tablet.

'What's going on?' His sister's behaviour was making him nervous.

'I just wondered how much you know about her.'

'Why? What have you heard?'

'I haven't heard anything, but I've read some things. Von Grasburg. That's her surname, correct?' Skye tapped on the screen.

'Yes.' His good mood was beginning to evaporate, replaced by doubts. What was Skye getting at? 'What's this all about?'

'I thought she looked familiar the other day, but it wasn't until after you left that the penny dropped.'

'What penny? You're not making any sense.'

'Did she tell you she is an internationally recognised horse rider? She's represented Berggrun in cross-country eventing and has won some major medals. That's why she looked familiar.'

Skye was horse-mad. Cam wasn't surprised that she recognised Viktoria, but he didn't see why that information was relevant. 'No, I didn't know that. What does that matter?'

'You know Berggrun is a principality, right?'

'Yes.' That he did know.

'Well, it was bugging me that she looked familiar, so I searched her on the internet, and it mentions her international eventing medals but those aren't the first articles that pops up about her. The first one that comes up is a link to the royal family of Berggrun. Apparently, her father is the Prince.' Skye paused. 'Viktoria is a princess.'

CHAPTER SEVEN

'DON'T BE RIDICULOUS. She's not a princess.'

'I beg to differ.'

'She can't be.'

'She is.' Skye turned her tablet around so the screen was facing Cam.

There were links to articles about the royal family of Berggrun, but it was the photographs that caught his eye. Official photographs of the Prince and Princess and their three adult children. Two sons and a daughter. Despite the formal style of the picture and the outfits and the tiaras on the Princesses' heads, there was no mistaking Viktoria.

Skye was right. Cam couldn't deny it and, seeing the evidence, other things began to make more sense. Viktoria's driver, her accommodation in the hotel's penthouse suite, all the charity events she attended, even working for Prince Alfred. But there was one thing that didn't make sense. 'Why wouldn't she have told me?'

'I don't know—you'd have to ask her that—but I thought you should know before you did something stupid.'

'Like what?'

'Like take her to dinner, sleep with her and then not call her again,' Skye said. 'You can't do that to a princess.'

Too late, he thought. It seemed as though he'd already done something stupid.

Cam was at the base early in order to make some changes to the day's arrangements. He had rostered himself on to staff the medical tent at the athletics stadium, but he knew he wasn't in the right headspace to cope with what could potentially be a frantic day. He made some phone calls and swapped duties with one of the other doctors, which allowed him to remain on the base, supervising the medical staff who were in attendance for the archery. He assumed two things: one, that Viktoria would most likely be attending the high-profile athletics events and two, that there would be fewer injuries at the archery, which would give him time to think.

He needed to work out what he was going to do.

Should he pretend he didn't know who she was and continue on as before? No. He couldn't do that.

So what option did that leave him? To confront her and ask her why she hadn't told him that she was royalty? But then what?

He couldn't avoid her indefinitely and he couldn't stay angry at her either. He was upset with himself for opening up to her, for sharing his feelings, only to find out there was so much she hadn't shared with him, but he knew he would have to speak to her at some point; she deserved a chance to explain and he wanted answers. But he wanted to be on the front foot for that discussion. He knew he would see her tonight at the barbecue for the athletes that was being hosted by Prince Alfred. He couldn't skip that event, so he needed to spend some time today figuring out what to say.

* * *

Viktoria was convinced that Cam was avoiding her. He had told her he would see her at the athletics stadium today, but she hadn't seen him there and had later found out that he was at the archery. And now, even though she'd seen him at the barbecue, he hadn't come near her.

She had tried several times to speak to him but every time she spotted him in the crowd he had moved elsewhere by the time she got near. He was definitely avoiding her, and she needed to know why.

She was talking to Mark, congratulating him on winning a medal in archery, when she saw Cam watching her. This was her chance to find out if there was a problem. She pinned him with her gaze, challenging him to walk away, but this time he didn't move.

'Are you avoiding me?' She waited for him to deny it, to reassure her, but he was silent, confirming her fears. 'Is this about Gemma?' she asked.

'Gemma?'

She had only come up with one reason why he would be avoiding her, and it was all to do with the photo she had seen of him with Gemma—the fact that he'd had a fiancée. That they hadn't broken up through choice but because she had died. She was convinced he felt he had made a mistake bringing her to his house.

'I wondered if you were sorry that you took me home. If you felt I was intruding on Gemma's memory.'

'No. It's not about Gemma. And she never saw my house. I bought it after the incident.'

'So, what is the matter?'

She saw him take in their surroundings. Everywhere they looked were soldiers and their families. 'Not here. Let's go somewhere quieter.'

He led her around to the side of the gym, towards the

car park, where there was less chance of their conversation being overheard. 'When were you planning on telling me?' he asked once they were alone.

'Telling you what?'

'That you're a princess.'

She had thought she had done something to upset him, or that he regretted telling her about Gemma. That their conversation last night had brought back memories that had been too much for him to handle. That he'd felt guilty about taking her home. As if perhaps he felt he was cheating on Gemma, or at least on her memory.

She had thought a lot of things, but she hadn't suspected that he knew who she really was.

She was floored. Freddie had never betrayed her trust before. He'd always had her back. She knew he'd thought her unwise to keep her identity from Cam but she had never anticipated that he'd divulge her secret. And Cam was obviously upset.

Her stomach dropped and her heart was racing. How much damage had Freddie done?

'Freddie told you?'

'Freddie? Who the hell is Freddie?'

Viktoria frowned. 'Prince Alfred. My cousin.'

'Your cousin?'

Viktoria nodded. 'You didn't know?'

'No.'

'How did you find out then?' She knew as she spoke that she sounded guilty. She sounded as if she'd been trying to hide the fact that she was royalty. Which she had. But for good reason. At least from her point of view, but, if the expression on Cam's face was any indication, it looked as though he disagreed.

'Skye told me. She thought she recognised you. It turns out she did, from cross-country eventing, but she found more than she'd bargained for. But she didn't tell me you're related to Prince Alfred.'

'What does it matter?'

'What does it *matter*? You're a *princess*! There must be some sort of protocol, some rules, for dating a princess. I'm sure it's not right to sleep with a princess on a second date. I never would have done that if I'd known who you are.'

'And that is exactly why I did not tell you. I just wanted to be treated like a normal person. I did not think you needed to know I am a princess. I like you and I wanted to know that you liked me, Viktoria. Not me, the princess.'

'I don't appreciate being lied to.'

'I never lied to you.'

'Maybe not, but you didn't tell me the truth either,' he said as he walked away.

She watched him go. She couldn't make him stay and she didn't know what else to say.

She could feel tears threatening. She shouldn't be upset. She shouldn't let him get to her, but it was too late. It hurt.

It shouldn't matter. It was never going to be a long-term possibility, but it hurt her more than she expected to be cast aside like that.

She really liked him. She enjoyed his company. He was intelligent, handsome, great in bed. A little moody and guarded, but she had seen glimpses of what he would be like if he would let his guard down, enjoy himself, and she'd been looking forward to the next week.

Would she be able to make it up to him? Would he calm down, see reason? Would she be able to explain herself to him—to make him understand why it was important to her to keep that side of her life private—or would he walk away without a backward glance?

Freddie had been right. She should have told him who she was, but all that would have done was speed up the inevitable.

He didn't want to date a princess.

She ducked into the gym and headed for the female toilets. She needed a moment to compose herself; she didn't want anyone to see her cry.

She'd thought not telling him she was a princess was the right thing to do. She'd thought it didn't matter, but she was wrong. And he was right. She had lied by omission.

She would apologise. That was the right thing to do.

She took several deep breaths and blew her nose. She touched up her make-up, grateful that Brigitta had taught her a few tricks, and steeled herself to go back outside. To find him. To apologise.

She opened the door and almost collided with a woman coming the other way.

'Pardon!'

The woman had a dog by her side and Viktoria realised it was Fiona with Leroy.

'Bonjour, Fiona. How are you?'

Fiona looked up at the sound of her name, but Viktoria could see that she didn't recognise her immediately. 'It is me, Viktoria. We met in the gymnasium the other day.'

'Oh, yes. Hi.'

Fiona looked a little pale, but her skin had a sheen that looked like she'd been sweating. She had one hand on Leroy's head and Viktoria got the sense that the dog was anchoring Fiona rather than Fiona controlling the dog.

'Are you all right?' she asked.

'I just needed to catch my breath. The crowd is bigger than I expected. I just need a quiet minute.'

Fiona lifted her other hand and steadied herself against the door jamb, but Viktoria could see her hand was shaking. Viktoria was concerned; Fiona didn't look alright.

Viktoria frowned as Leroy began whining.

Fiona didn't seem to notice the dog's distress, which concerned Viktoria even more. 'You should sit down and I will get you a drink of water,' she offered. She was reluctant to leave her alone, but she didn't know what to do. There was a chair in the vestibule just outside the bathroom door and Viktoria led Fiona to it. 'I will not be long,' she said as she went to find a water cooler.

She had taken less than three steps when Leroy's whining morphed into frantic barking. Alarmed, Viktoria turned around and saw Fiona collapsed on the tiled floor. She was shaking uncontrollably, and Viktoria recognised the signs of a seizure.

She knew what was happening, but she wasn't sure what to do. She needed to get help, but was it safe to leave her?

She moved the chair, concerned that Fiona would hit her head, before realising that she could still hit her head on the wall. Leroy was still barking furiously. Maybe someone would hear him and come to investigate, but she couldn't take that chance. She needed to get help. She didn't want to be responsible for Fiona. This was out of her area of expertise.

She knew the bathroom was empty. She had to go and find someone.

She left Fiona with Leroy. She knew the dog wouldn't leave Fiona's side.

She ran outside and scanned the crowd, looking for assistance. Looking for Cam.

He hadn't got far. He was only a few metres away, talking to Sean and Lisa.

'Campbell! *Vite! Vite!*'

Cam turned at the sound of her voice and Viktoria beckoned to him, waving her arm frantically. Fiona's seizure had distracted her from her own problems and all she felt was relief at seeing Cam. Their issues were pushed to the back of her mind; she had far more pressing concerns.

Cam took a second or two before he started moving towards her and for a moment she wondered if he would ignore her.

But he didn't. He couldn't, she supposed. It was obvious something wasn't right.

He hurried towards her, but she couldn't wait. She ran to meet him. *'Vite, vite,'* she said as she grabbed his hand. 'Hurry. Fiona is having some sort of a seizure.' She pulled him along with her, back to the gymnasium.

'Fiona?'

Viktoria didn't know her last name. She'd assumed Cam knew everyone. 'She is competing in the rowing event. She has a service dog, Leroy,' she said, giving him the only other identifying information she knew.

She could still hear Leroy barking as they entered the gym but as she pushed open the door into the ladies' toilets and the dog saw them he quietened down, emitting a soft whine instead. He was pacing around Fiona, who was still convulsing on the hard floor.

Cam brushed past Viktoria. She saw him check the time on his watch as he pulled his phone from his pocket. He swiped the password, dialled a number and handed it to her. 'There's an ambulance stationed on the base for the Games; I've just dialled them. When they answer, put them on speaker for me. Can you do that?' he asked as he thrust the phone at her and knelt on the floor.

Viktoria nodded as she took the phone. She held it to her ear as she watched Cam get to work.

He unbuttoned his shirt and ripped it off, stripping down to the khaki T-shirt that moulded to his chest and arms. He bundled his shirt up and put it under Fiona's head, protecting her from the cold, hard, unforgiving tiles.

He talked in a low, quiet voice. Viktoria wasn't sure if he was talking to Fiona or the dog, but the dog calmed down. He stopped pacing and stood at Cam's shoulder. He seemed to sense that Cam was trying to help.

Viktoria put the phone on speaker as the call was answered. She quickly explained what had happened before holding the phone towards Cam.

He sat back on his heels, keeping one eye on his watch as he spoke to the paramedics.

'This is Dr Cam Hamilton. I'm with a female soldier who is having a seizure. We're in the women's toilets at the back of the gym.'

'She sustained a serious head injury a year ago. No history of seizures that I know of, but this one has been going for several minutes.'

'What do we do now?' Viktoria asked when Cam finished his phone conversation.

'We wait for the ambulance. There's nothing else we can do.'

'And when they come?'

'She'll need to go to hospital. We'll need to run some tests to see if we can determine the cause of the seizure.'

'I don't know how you do this. This constant surge of adrenalin. Of drama.'

'It's not so dramatic when you're trained to deal with it.'

The paramedics arrived as Fiona's seizure finally abated. Within minutes they had loaded her onto a stretcher and into the ambulance. Cam had offered to take Leroy and follow them to the hospital. Viktoria wasn't sure if that was really in his job description or whether it just gave him an excuse to get away from her.

She didn't know and she wasn't about to ask.

Viktoria had spent the morning watching the road cycling event. The course was spectacular; it began and ended at the Opera House but wound its way around the harbour and through the Botanic Gardens, which gave the spectators plenty of vantage points from which to watch the race. A large number of them had spread picnic blankets on the lawns of the gardens and were sitting in the spring sunshine cheering the cyclists on as they rode past.

Viktoria had been present at the start, taking photographs to upload to the social media pages, and while she'd kept an eye out for Cam, she'd stayed clear of the medical tent. She wasn't sure if he was even working at the cycling today and, while she wanted to see him, she didn't want to talk to him. She was afraid of what he might say.

She tried to focus on her job, but it was difficult to be enthusiastic when her brain was crowded with thoughts of Cam.

She still needed to apologise.

She wondered if he'd forgive her.

At the end of the day's events, to distract herself from spending all her time thinking about Campbell and what she could have—or should have—done differently, Viktoria called in to the hospital to visit Fiona.

She was relieved, and a little surprised, to find her in her room looking perfectly well.

'You are all right?' she asked.

'Apparently so,' Fiona said.

'Do you remember what happened?'

'Not really. I was told I was lucky you were there, though. You made sure I got immediate attention, so thank you.'

'I am glad I was able to be useful. Have you had a seizure before?'

'No. Never.'

'Do you know what caused it?'

Fiona shook her head. 'I had some scans done today. The doctors think that when I had the accident in the Middle East I suffered a traumatic brain injury along with multiple fractures. The brain damage can manifest as seizures.'

'What will happen now?'

'I think the doctors will just monitor me. If it happens again or frequently, I might need medication but I'm already on several.'

'And how are you feeling?'

'I'm tired and I feel like I've got a massive hangover, but the doctors assure me that is normal,' she said.

The door opened and one of the nurses came in and ushered Viktoria out with a brisk instruction. 'The patient needs to rest.'

'Bien sûr.'

Viktoria said goodbye to Fiona and headed for the lift. The doors opened and Cam stepped out, surprising her. She felt her knees wobble. She put her hand out, reaching for the wall to steady herself. 'Campbell! Are you here to see Fiona?'

'Yes.'

'Do you have a minute?' Maybe this was her chance.

'Not really.' His eyes were guarded.

'Please. It is important,' she said, knowing she might not get another opportunity to apologise.

He sighed and took a step forward and she thought he was going to continue walking past her, but he inclined his head and said, 'Follow me.' He pushed open a door to a small lounge, which Viktoria realised was a waiting area for families of patients. She could only imagine the sorts of things they'd been told inside these four walls.

'What is it?' he asked as she followed him inside.

'I owe you an apology.'

'I don't need an apology. I need an explanation,' he said as he closed the door behind them. 'Why didn't you tell me who you are?'

'I just wanted a chance to be anonymous. To be ordinary. All my life, people have wanted a part of me. They are fascinated by royalty, by the fame and fortune they assume is associated with it. I have never known who has wanted to get to know me and who has wanted to know the Princess. I am never sure who to trust.'

'I'm not interested in fame and fortune.'

'And this wasn't about keeping a secret from you; I was keeping it from everyone.'

'I didn't think I was just anyone.'

'You are right. I should have told you, but I did not want it to change the way you felt about me. I wanted you to get to know the real me. I wanted you to see me. I wanted you to lo…to like me without knowing that I am a princess.'

'You can't pretend not to be who you are. There are two sides to you. You can't separate them.'

'I wanted some freedom to just be me, Viktoria. Being a princess is only a title. I just wanted to be the same as everyone else.'

'But, at the end of the day, you're not, are you?'

'I am still me.'

'And who is that?'

She wasn't sure any more. She had thought she'd enjoy pretending to be a commoner and, at the end of the adventure, she'd be ready to return home, back to the life of a princess. Back to her duty. She had made a promise to her parents, but she'd never imagined that she'd want to change her mind. That she might not want to return.

But what was the alternative? Could she seriously imagine staying in Australia? Giving up everything she knew?

She didn't know what to tell him, so she said nothing.

'You talk about trust,' Cam said, 'yet you didn't trust me enough to tell me who you are. You should have been honest with me. You should have trusted me like I trusted you. I confided in you, but you couldn't confide in me. Or you chose not to. I have told you things about myself that no one else knows and you've told me half-truths.'

'*Non!* Everything I have told you about myself is true. I am a daughter, a sister, an aunt. I have a marketing degree and I do spend my time at charity events and handing out trophies. I have not lied to you.'

'But you haven't been completely honest either.'

'No. But I wanted to forget I was a princess. With

you I felt like Viktoria and that was what I wanted. You made me happy. I hoped I was making you happy too.'

'I don't deserve to be happy.'

CHAPTER EIGHT

'EVERYONE DESERVES TO be happy,' Viktoria told him.

But Cam disagreed. 'No. Not me. I don't get to be happy.'

'Why not?'

'Why should I get to be happy? When Gemma is dead.'

'I realise I did not know her, but I cannot imagine she would not want you to be happy. The incident was not your fault. You didn't fire the missile. Whoever did that is the one who killed her. Who almost killed you.'

'But if it wasn't for me, she wouldn't have been there.'

'That was not your decision. That was hers. That was her job. You told me she felt it was her duty. I know what that is like and I am sure you do too. You cannot blame yourself for that.'

'Maybe not, but I should have saved her. Even if I couldn't have stopped her from flying, I was there and I should have saved her. And I couldn't. I'm a doctor. It's my job to save lives. And I let her die.'

'What about the other people who were in the chopper with you? Do you feel the same responsibility for them?'

'No.'

As a doctor, Cam knew that there was nothing he could have done for them. They'd most likely been dead before they'd hit the ground and, with no functioning equipment and with his extensive injuries, he couldn't have helped them.

'Well, is it not the same for Gemma?'

'No.' He shook his head. 'My Hippocratic Oath is to do no harm. That's different from promising to be there for her always. We were a couple, we were engaged. I promised to protect her—to look after her—and I let her down.'

'Cam, you have to forgive yourself. You have to give yourself permission to move on. You are living a half-life, afraid to let people in. That is no way to live. I should know. It is rare that I am able to be my true self. That is one of the things I have loved about spending time with you, and the reason I did not tell you everything about me. I wanted to be free to live my life, and you should do the same.'

She was most likely right but that didn't mean he was ready to change his ways. Because of Gemma, he was prepared to connect physically with people but not emotionally. His heart was hardened now. He wasn't afraid he'd get hurt, he wasn't afraid of letting people in; he was afraid of letting people down.

'Your guilt is stopping you from being happy,' she said. 'It is not my fault I am a princess. It is not your fault Gemma died. We can choose to live our lives the best we can, or we can choose to give up. It was Gemma's choice to fly that day. It was her duty. You are not to blame.'

He knew Viktoria was right. Gemma had been all about her duty. He supposed Viktoria was the same.

'I understand you have suffered trauma and a terrible loss,' she continued, 'but that does not mean you cannot care about people. I have seen you with your sister, your friends, with Rex. I have heard you talk about your work.

I know you care about these people, these things—do you think you could care about me?'

He did care about her, but he didn't want to. That was his dilemma. He knew Viktoria's sense of duty would mean the end of their relationship. He knew her sense of duty would take her away from him, just as Gemma's had done. And there was nothing he could do about it. He couldn't be a part of her life. He wasn't right for her; she didn't need someone damaged, someone disillusioned. She needed someone who could fit into her royal life, and he knew for certain that wasn't him. He didn't know how to be a royal. And she wasn't asking him to try. She knew as well as he did they didn't have a future, that he wasn't suitable.

Their relationship was never going to last. It was always going to end. It was probably better that it ended now.

'I have to go,' he said. He didn't want to go but he couldn't stay either.

Viktoria was the first person he had felt a connection to since Gemma died, but that didn't mean they could make it work.

Cam thanked the waiter as he put a plate of seared tuna in front of him.

He was one of thirty guests seated around a table at a dinner hosted by Prince Alfred. He had invited them to dinner in a private dining room in one of Sydney's five-star restaurants as a personal thank you to the Australian members of the Legion's Games Committee. There were two days of competition remaining and, while Cam appreciated the invitation, he was attending under sufferance and at Doug's insistence.

Viktoria was seated at the other end of the table, diagonally opposite him. He could see her but he couldn't have a conversation with her. He hadn't spoken to her since he'd bumped into her at the hospital. He didn't know what to say.

She looked amazing. But her eyes looked sad.

Had he done that to her?

Had he been foolish?

Should he have ignored the fact that she was a princess? Would there really have been any harm in continuing to see her for a few more days?

Maybe no harm but also no point. She couldn't leave her life. She had a duty. And what could he possibly offer her?

He couldn't fit in to her world.

She'd said they could be happy together, but he'd meant it when he said he didn't deserve to be happy.

He told himself it had never been serious, but that didn't explain why he still felt distraught at the idea that it was over.

He sighed and cut into his tuna. It looked superb and he was sure it was delicious, but he had no appetite. Prince Alfred was seated three chairs away and Cam noticed he didn't seem to be enjoying his dinner either.

A sheen of perspiration shone on the Prince's forehead.

'Are you all right, Your Highness?'

The Prince had his hand pressed to his stomach, his fingers probing. 'I've had a bit of abdominal pain today. I think I might have strained a muscle when I did that rowing challenge yesterday.'

Viktoria had organised for Prince Alfred to race against some of the rowers as a publicity and morale-boosting exercise.

Cam thought his explanation sounded plausible until

he saw the Prince wince and gasp with pain as all the colour drained from his face. That looked far too painful to be a pulled muscle. The Prince's fingers had been pressing over the right side of his stomach and Cam had a suspicion that he was suffering from something more sinister than a muscle strain.

'Would you mind if I took a look, Your Highness? Just in case it's not muscular.'

Cam was aware by now that they had the attention of most of the table. There was a small bar area adjacent the private dining room where they had gathered for pre-dinner drinks and he recalled seeing a few small couches in that space. 'Perhaps we could go to the room next door?'

Beads of sweat broke out on the Prince's forehead as he stood. He winced when he took a step, putting his weight on his right foot.

Doug had left his seat and was beside Cam. 'Can I help? What do you need?'

'Just keep everyone in here for now. I'll let you know,' Cam replied as he put one hand under the Prince's elbow to support some of his weight without making it look like the Prince was in need of his assistance.

Cam was aware that Viktoria was standing too. She ignored Doug's instructions and followed them out into the small bar area.

She stood behind Cam as he got the Prince to lie on the sofa. Cam couldn't see her, she wasn't in his way but she was in his head. He could smell her perfume and he knew the scent of gardenias would always remind him of her.

He tried to block her presence out so he could concentrate on examining the Prince.

He placed the back of one hand on the Prince's forehead, feeling for a temperature, although he could tell by looking at him that he was feverish.

'You have pain when you're walking?'

The Prince nodded.

'Any nausea?'

Another nod.

'I'm just going to press on your stomach,' Cam said. 'Is that okay?'

A third nod. The Prince was clammy, pale and in obvious distress. Cam pressed his fingers gently over the Prince's abdomen, over the lower right quadrant. As he released the pressure the Prince grimaced and complained.

Cam turned to Viktoria. 'Do you think you could ask Doug to come out here?'

'What is wrong?' Viktoria asked.

Cam turned back to the Prince, giving him his suspected diagnosis. 'I take it you have never had your appendix removed?'

The Prince shook his head.

'I think you have appendicitis. I am going to call an ambulance and take you to hospital. I think we need to investigate this.' Cam pulled his phone from his pocket as Viktoria went to fetch Doug. He dialled the ambulance; he'd get Doug to explain what had happened to the Prince's guests. He had other priorities.

'Right now?' The Prince could barely get the words out.

'Yes. I don't want to wait. If your appendix bursts, you'll be in a world of trouble. It's too big a risk.' Cam wasn't about to take a chance with a royal life.

Cam and Viktoria followed the ambulance to North Sydney Hospital. Cam made some phone calls on the way, calling in favours, getting the best surgeons on the job.

The Prince was whisked away on arrival, leaving Cam and Viktoria waiting for news.

It was not as straightforward as they had hoped.

Appendicitis was confirmed but while he was being prepped for Theatre his appendix burst, meaning he needed open abdominal surgery instead of the less invasive laparoscopic procedure. A burst appendix could be life-threatening.

'What do I tell Auntie Ingrid?'

'Who?'

'Fred's mother.'

'Tell her he has excellent surgeons operating on him and that you'll call with an update as soon as he is out of Theatre.'

'Will you wait with me?'

'Yes.' He had no intention of leaving her to wait on her own. 'Tell me about your family,' he said, hoping to distract her. 'You have spent a lot of time with your cousins?'

Viktoria nodded. 'We spent our holidays together every year. We would go skiing and usually spent summer together as well. My cousins are similar ages to my brothers and me. Freddie and I are the babies but he is eighteen months older than me. He has always been protective of me.'

'And now? You're still close, obviously.'

'We are. I think it is because it was always hard to know who to trust. To know who wanted to be friends because of the family we were born into rather than because of who we are. We could trust each other. We relied on each other. He will be okay, *oui*?'

'He's in the best place, in the best hands.'

'How long will he be in hospital?'

'A couple of days, I should think. It will be important to make sure there is no infection.'

'But there are only two days left of the Games.'

'I think it's safe to say he will miss the rest.'

She went quiet.

'He'll be fine.'

'I know. I believe you. I was just thinking about all the things Freddie is scheduled to do over the next two days. Handing out the medals, making a speech at the closing ceremony.'

'Someone else will have to take over.'

'I know,' she sighed.

'Will that be you?'

'Most likely. It is what I do. I cannot seem to get away from handing out trophies and making speeches. I have enjoyed my anonymity, but I always knew it would not last. But I had hoped I could make it through my last two days here.' She shrugged.

'Two days?' He hadn't actually confirmed exactly when she was leaving. He hadn't wanted to think about it.

'*Oui.* I leave the day after the Games.'

'So soon?'

She nodded. 'I have to go home. My father has been Prince for twenty-five years. There are big celebrations planned, starting in five days. I have to be there. You could come with me?'

'To Berggrun?'

She nodded.

'I don't think so.'

'Why not?'

'I don't think that's a world I'd be comfortable in.'

'You cannot make that decision without experiencing it.'

He shook his head. Viktoria had a duty and he didn't

begrudge that but, like Gemma, her duty was to more than her job. It was to her country.

He couldn't compete with that.

CHAPTER NINE

VIKTORIA WAS BACK at the hospital first thing the following morning. She was beginning to feel as if she was seeing more of Sydney's hospitals than anything else. But the surgeon was confident that Freddie would be fine and that was the important thing, she reminded herself as she pushed open the door to his room.

'*Bonjour!* How are you feeling today? Good?'

'I wouldn't say "good". I'm still really sore but apparently that is now from the surgery, so I suppose that's a positive.'

'And when can you get out of here?'

'Not until tomorrow at the earliest. I still have a slight temperature and the doctors want to make sure there is no infection. Which means I have a favour to ask you.'

Viktoria knew what was coming. 'You want me to hand out the medals?'

'Yes. But I also might need you to give my closing ceremony speech.'

'But that is not until tomorrow!'

'I know. But, just as a precaution, could you familiarise yourself with it?'

Viktoria nodded. 'If you will be in hospital until tomorrow will you be allowed to fly the day after that?'

Freddie was supposed to be leaving with her. He was also expected at her father's celebrations.

'No. I'll have to delay my trip by a couple of days.'

'You cannot fly back with me?'

'No. Can you stay longer? It might give you a chance to sort things out with Campbell.'

Viktoria had told Freddie the details of her latest woes. To his credit he hadn't reminded her that he'd warned her the decision to keep her identity a secret might not be the wisest choice and she knew he was trying to be supportive.

She shook her head. 'I promised my parents I would be home in time for the preparations for the celebrations. I need to go. Plus, there is nothing to sort out. It was never going to be anything more than a holiday romance.'

She had been trying to convince herself of that, but she couldn't let go of the feeling that it could have been more. But that was obviously only her perception. Cam wanted nothing to do with her.

'I'm sorry, Viktoria.'

'It is okay. I think I was kidding myself. Thinking we could have a proper relationship. It is just that I felt I could be my true self with him. Not a royal. Just Viktoria.'

'But at some point he had to know the truth.'

'I know,' she sighed. 'I just wish he could see past that.'

'Are you sure there's no way of making it work?'

'I am sure. Our timing is not right. He is not ready. And I cannot wait for him to *be* ready. That may never happen, and I do not have the luxury of time.'

'Is he worth waiting for? Do you think he could be the one?'

Was it possible? Could it be?

'I do not know. If I am honest there are so many hurdles. He will not let go of his guilt and I cannot let go of who I am. I cannot let go of my duty. You know my parents are expecting to announce my engagement on my return.'

'Would you give it up for him if he asked you to?'

'If he was the person I want him to be he would not ask me to.'

But she knew that if he told her he loved her and asked her to stay she would do everything in her power to make it happen. She felt as if she was the person she wanted to be when they were together. She felt they were meant to be.

But would she be prepared to sacrifice her title for him? She knew it was unfair of her to expect him to make sacrifices for her if she wasn't prepared to do the same.

It was complicated.

She'd thought love would be simple.

Somehow Viktoria had made it through the final day. The past two days had passed in a blur of exhaustion and despair but there was now only one final event—the four by fifty-metre swimming relay. She had one more medal presentation to get through before the closing ceremony tonight and then tomorrow she would be on a plane, going home to a life she wasn't sure she wanted.

Her life felt totally out of control. Nothing was going the way she wanted. Three weeks ago, she had never set foot in Australia and now she didn't want to leave. She could imagine a future here, with Cam. She could imagine herself with a real job, perhaps working with the veterans and therapy horses. But it was all a fantasy. There was no way she could stay.

She had fallen in love with a man who didn't want her and now she had to go home to a life that she didn't want—a life that was being planned for her. She'd mucked that up too, but she couldn't see a way out of it. Her title and her duty were a burden she had to bear.

She made her way back to her seat after the medal presentation as the next lot of competitors came out onto the pool deck. The teams were announced over the loud-speaker and she was only half listening, lost in her own thoughts, when she bumped into Mark.

'Mark! Why are you not with your team?'

'I've decided not to swim. My shoulder is still sore, and I don't want to let my team down.'

'But it is a relay! What will they do without you?'

'We have a reserve. Campbell is swimming.'

'Campbell!' Just the mention of his name made her heart race. 'Really?' she asked as she saw Skye walking towards her.

'Skye! Hello.' What was she doing there? There could be only one reason. 'Did you know Cam was swimming?'

'Of course; he called to tell me.' Skye frowned. 'Surely you knew?'

Viktoria shook her head as they kept walking towards the tiered seats. She felt as if she was the only one who was out of the loop. '*Non.* We have not been speaking. He is upset with me.'

'What? Why not? What's happened?'

'He is unhappy with me. He thought I was keeping something from him. I cannot blame him—I was. But I had my reasons.'

She wondered what he would say if he found out she

had kept more than her royal connections from him. What would he say if he knew she would be returning home to choose a fiancé?

They took their seats as the teams were being introduced and Viktoria thought the crowd noise might prevent Skye from asking further questions but she was not deterred. At least the volume of voices would make it difficult for anyone else to overhear Viktoria's summary of the past few days as she explained to Skye what had happened. She figured it didn't matter if Skye knew her story; it was likely that Cam would tell his sister what had happened at some point.

Viktoria finished bringing Skye up-to-date just as the Australians completed the third leg of the relay. Cam was swimming the final leg and the Americans were leading as he dived in. They were three metres ahead. He had fifty metres in which to catch them.

The British swimmer dived in seconds after Cam. The race was close. The crowd was deafening.

Viktoria wished she could cheer and scream from the stands along with the crowd but since she had taken over Freddie's duties everyone knew she was a princess, which meant she had to behave with decorum. She had duties and obligations to fulfil; she couldn't wear her heart on her sleeve, not when she and Cam were not officially a couple.

Her heart was pounding in her chest. She felt as if she was swimming alongside Cam.

He was making ground, but the end of the pool was only a few metres away. Would he run out of time?

He drew level.

There were two more strokes and they seemed to touch the wall simultaneously, Cam and the American.

Everyone looked to the screen to see the result.

Cam had touched point zero one of a second in front of the American. The Australians had won. The crowd erupted and Viktoria couldn't keep the smile off her face. She turned and hugged Skye as the crowd cheered.

Viktoria made her way down to the pool deck, preparing to hand out the final round of medals in Freddie's place. She managed to say the right things and to congratulate the third placed British swimmers and the American silver medallists but the closer she got to the Australians the more nervous she became. Their team was lined up in the order that they swam so Cam was the final competitor to get his medal. Her hands were shaking as she hung the medal around his neck.

She kissed him on both cheeks as she wondered if that would be the last time she would do that.

'Congratulations,' she said as she stepped back. She needed some space; she needed some room to clear her head. 'You swam a fantastic race. When did you know you were swimming?'

'Only this morning,' he replied.

She was hurt that he hadn't told her. But, then again, everything hurt at the moment and saying goodbye was going to hurt most of all.

Hordes of people, family and friends, waited to congratulate the relay team as they emerged from the changing rooms after the medal ceremony. Cam knew he should be pleased. He'd swum well, he hadn't let anyone down and they had won. They were victorious. But once again life had lost its lustre; he could feel no pleasure.

He missed Viktoria.

But there was nothing he could do about that.

He searched the faces of the crowd, knowing he was

hoping to see her, but she was nowhere to be found. Instead he saw Skye making her way towards him. She was frowning. He recognised that expression and knew she was about to reprimand him about something as only an older sister could. She certainly didn't look as if she was about to congratulate him on his race.

'What's going on with you and Viktoria?'

'What do you mean?'

'She just told me that you aren't speaking to her because of who she is.'

Cam led Skye away from the crowd, out of earshot. He was *not* going to have this conversation where anyone could hear them. 'That's not exactly true. I am speaking to her; I'm just distancing myself.'

'Why? Because she is a princess?'

'Among other things.'

'I thought you liked her?'

'I do, but it was never going to be serious. She was always going to leave.'

'You don't have to let her go.'

'I do. She's a *princess*. She has duties and obligations that I can't compete with. She's not going to give those up for me and I wouldn't ask her to.' He didn't like the idea that he was going to lose her. He'd lost Gemma because of a sense of duty and he was going to lose Viktoria too, but he couldn't stand in her way.

He understood her duty and he didn't begrudge her, but he knew he couldn't expect her to choose him over the throne. He thought he was doing the right thing by letting her go. Her sense of duty would always come first, and he didn't want her to feel torn between him and her role as a princess, but he also didn't want to play second fiddle. He couldn't see how they could make it work. He didn't know if she would want to try.

Meeting Viktoria had shown him that he was lonely. She had shown him what was missing from his life and he realised now he wanted another meaningful relationship, he was ready, but it was ridiculous to think that Viktoria was the woman for him. He'd only known her for two weeks.

He was going to miss her, but he'd get over her. But the more time he spent with her the harder that would be and the more it would hurt when she left.

And it didn't matter what he thought or what Skye thought; ultimately the decision was Viktoria's.

'She's leaving, Skye. She's not going to choose me.'

Viktoria took a deep breath as she stood up in front of one thousand athletes and their families and prepared to give Freddie's speech at the closing ceremony.

'Most of you will know by now that Prince Alfred had emergency surgery two days ago for a burst appendix.' The emergency had been heavily covered in the media. 'He is extremely disappointed that he is unable to be here tonight to share in the celebrations of what have been an amazing event, but he has entrusted me to deliver his message to you all.

'I want to commend all the athletes for your commitment, service and sacrifice for your countries. You have been brave in battle and brave also in the face of adversity, injury and illness to compete in these Games. If you have been watching these Games and thinking, *I could never do this*, know that you can. Every one of this year's competitors is willing to be a mentor to the next competitor, the next survivor. Be brave. Reach out. Together, anything is possible.

'Hopefully, these Games challenged your bodies, your minds and restored your spirit. Your resilience.

Your efforts have captured the hearts not only of the Australian public but of the world. You should be proud of what you have achieved. Hold your heads high, continue to set goals and enjoy your lives, your friends and your families.

'I want to congratulate not just the athletes but also the families for your determination, courage and pride. Together, you've shown everyone what is possible. I am so proud to be associated with these Games and I will see you again next year in Vancouver.'

Viktoria paused while the crowd applauded Freddie's words before adding her own.

'And now I would also like to add my congratulations and my thanks to all of you. I feel very privileged that I got to meet so many of you over the past few days and that you shared your stories with me. Thank you for letting me be a part of these Games. Your friendships have inspired me and I hope that by sharing your stories with the world I have been able to inspire others to strive to achieve, to persevere and to embrace opportunities. To embrace life. To dig deep. To support each other and to reach out.

'Set goals and you can achieve something amazing. Many of you started with something simple, a goal to get out of bed in the morning, have a shower, walk around the block, talk to someone in the supermarket, to connect with people, and then you set the bar higher and that eventually brought you here, to the Games. Congratulations—you should all be so proud of your efforts.'

She had been aware of Cam standing just to the left of the stage throughout her speech. She'd tried to block him out, tried to avoid looking in his direction, knowing it would be difficult to hold her emotions in check and impossible to speak if she made eye contact with him but at the end of her address she made her way down from the stage and sought him out. There was something she did need to say.

'Dr Hamilton, do you have a minute?'

She was going to be brave. She could do this.

'I wanted to say goodbye before I left.'

'You're leaving now?'

She was always going to leave. She had obligations and promises to keep but she was going to take some lessons from the Games.

'*Oui*. I have learnt a lot from this experience—mostly about myself—but I think I am stronger and more focused, which is not a bad thing. I am going to use my position as a royal to make real change. I am not going to be content with presenting ribbons and trophies; I am going to get more involved with causes. If I am going to have a life of duty, I am going to make sure it is one I am proud of.

'But I wanted to thank you too, for everything. For making time for me. I realise I made some mistakes; I realise I am complicated, difficult even, and that my situation is unusual, but I enjoyed getting to know you and I will not forget you.'

She leant forward and kissed him on each cheek before turning around quickly and walking away before he could see her tears.

She wanted to have a public and private life. A purpose and a relationship.

She knew that the Viktoria she wanted to be had to co-exist with Princess Viktoria. If Cam couldn't accept both parts of her then the fairy tale ending she dreamed of was impossible.

She had thought he might fight for her—she'd *wanted* him to fight for her—but perhaps she had built a fantasy around him. His commitment to his family and his career made her think he was a strong, dependable person and his strength appealed to her, but he didn't want the Princess.

She had enjoyed almost every minute of her adventure but now she had to leave. Just like Cinderella, it was time for her to go but she didn't think her Prince was going to come after her. Not this time.

CHAPTER TEN

VIKTORIA HAD ONE final check of her reflection in the mirror and readjusted her tiara before making her way down the palace corridors to her mother's wing. She took a deep breath and knocked on her mother's door. She ran her hands over the skirt of her ball gown, nervously smoothing out creases even though she knew Brigitta had steamed every last one out of the pale pink dress. The sleeveless floor-length gown had a fitted bodice with a silk underlay and a flowing chiffon skirt. The dress had been embroidered with hundreds of tiny flowers, each of which had a crystal stitched into its centre that shone and sparkled with every movement. It was stunning, a gown fit for a princess, but Viktoria barely noticed. She was too nervous.

Tonight was the gala ball to mark her father's twenty-five years on the throne. It was the penultimate night of a week of celebrations and Viktoria knew that Tomas, the Duke of San Fernando, would be in attendance. Tomas was her parents' choice as the man deemed worthy of their daughter's hand in marriage and Viktoria had known him since they were children; she supposed that was somewhat comforting. But less comforting was the fact that he was not who she would have chosen to marry.

A couple of months ago she had told Freddie that, of the men on her parents' shortlist, Tomas was her preference. But that had been before she'd met Campbell.

Her thoughts returned to Sydney, as they had done so often over the past week. Back to Cam.

That wasn't helpful.

That had been nothing but a holiday romance, but she hadn't been able to get him out of her head. Granted, she'd been home for less than a week, but this was not the right frame of mind to be accepting another man's proposal when her head and heart belonged to another.

But she was never going to have that opportunity again. It was best just to move on.

Marie, her mother's lady-in-waiting, opened the door and Viktoria stepped into her mother's suite, ready to be reminded of her duty.

'You look lovely, my darling,' her mother greeted her. 'Are you looking forward to seeing Tomas again?'

'*Oui.*'

'And you will accept a proposal of marriage from him?'

Viktoria fought back the feeling of dread, of missed opportunity. She was tempted to say no, but she was a dutiful daughter, a dutiful princess, and she would do her duty as she'd promised. It was not as if she had another option, she thought as she nodded her agreement.

'I am glad,' her mother said. 'Your father and I thought he would be a suitable match. You've known each other since you were children and he is a sensible, good-looking man.'

Viktoria wanted passionate, not sensible. She wanted someone who took her breath away when he smiled, who made her feel like she could dissolve when his lips brushed hers, when he took her in his arms. She wanted to be with someone who made her feel alive. She wanted to be with someone who needed her—Viktoria—to complete them and who completed her.

She didn't bother arguing her case. What was the point? That door had closed. She had made a promise and she would do her duty.

She nodded her agreement. He was a sensible choice. 'Do you know the role I will be expected to play as the Duchess?' She had given this a lot of thought over the past week, when she hadn't been thinking about Cam, and she was eager to get started on some charitable events. If she could put plans in place before she married, then she might have more autonomy. 'I do not want to just hand out trophies and cut ribbons.'

'I imagine you'll start a family.'

'I'm fifth in line to the throne now; I don't have to have children right away.' Her eldest brother had produced heirs and she didn't want to think about having a family just yet. She wanted time to get used to being a married woman. 'Philippe, Nicolas and Philippe's sons are all ahead of me.'

'Tomas will probably want children though, and what else would you do?'

She could think of so many things. 'Being part of the Legion's Games and seeing Freddie's involvement, I've been thinking about starting a charity,' she said.

'You and Tomas can work that out together. He's very involved in several charities. Perhaps you could assist him.'

She didn't want to assist Tomas; she wanted to be in charge. But she knew that wasn't how things worked. Hers would be the supporting role, not the other way around. But she wanted to be an equal. She wanted to feel that her voice was heard.

Marie came back, knocking on the door. 'His Royal Highness has asked if you are ready to join him in the ballroom.'

Viktoria pasted a smile on her face as she followed her mother downstairs and prepared to spend the evening making small talk with her father's guests—as she prepared to endure her last night of freedom before she became engaged to a man she barely knew. Although she had known Tomas since they were children, she'd seen him only a handful of times in the past fifteen years. He was virtually a stranger.

She had barely known Cam either, yet that hadn't stopped her from imagining all sorts of alternative futures.

She had to stop thinking about Campbell. About how easy and simple things had been. About how she'd felt she could be herself. She knew he would argue that she hadn't been. That she was a princess, not a commoner. But she hadn't felt common. She'd felt alive. Happy. Free.

She didn't want a life dictated by royal protocol. She'd imagined a whole other life for herself. In Australia. With Cam. But obviously that wasn't going to be her future.

Maybe she should just accept her fate and the husband her parents had chosen for her.

Perhaps she should try to imagine a future with Tomas. He deserved that chance.

She would try to be open to the possibility that he could be a good match for her, that she could grow to love him.

Viktoria knew the evening was a success. Her mother's meticulous organisational skills were at their peak arranging functions like this and she never settled for anything less than perfection. The palace ballroom was filled with royalty, celebrities, politicians and family and their tiaras, dresses, medals and jewels sparkled under the lights of dozens of chandeliers. Champagne flowed as white-coated staff seamlessly moved around the guests passing out myriad hors d'oeuvres. The band were excellent, and the dance floor was full.

Viktoria accepted each dance that was requested of her, although she made sure to stay close to the band where the music was louder and made conversation difficult. It was easier to dance than to talk.

As she thanked her dance partner at the conclusion of a song Tomas appeared beside her.

'*Bonsoir*, Your Highness.' He bowed slightly and held out a hand. 'May I have the next dance?'

'*Bonsoir*, Tomas, *comme-va?*' she said as she placed her hand in his, accepting his invitation.

He was taller than her, slightly balding. Blond, not dark. Angular, not handsome but pleasant-looking.

She knew she was comparing him to Cam and she knew that was unfair. No one was going to measure up to Cam. And she was well aware too, as Tomas placed his hand on her hip, that there was no spark, no nervous excitement, no anticipation of something bigger. She wasn't being swept off her feet, nor did she feel even remotely as if she might dissolve while he held her in his arms.

She closed her eyes and imagined she was in Cam's embrace. Imagined the warmth of his hand, the touch of his fingers on her skin. She felt disloyal but she couldn't stop herself. This was not what she wanted for herself, for her life, but she couldn't figure out how to get out of it.

Tomas was talking. It was hard to pretend she was in Cam's arms when all she could hear was the sound of another man's voice. She opened her eyes and forced herself to concentrate, to be the perfect hostess she'd been raised to be. *'Pardon?'*

'I was saying how excited I am for you to see the house I have purchased for us.'

'You have purchased a house?' she asked, dampening down her dismay that he'd done so without her approval, without her permission. Would she be allowed a say in anything?

'Yes.'

'Where is it?'

'San Fernando.'

She hadn't envisaged that. She had pictured them living in Berggrun. She'd pictured *herself* living in Berggrun, she realised. She hadn't actually pictured herself living with Tomas. She wondered if her parents had given their approval for her to move away.

Why wouldn't they? She probably wasn't expected to live in Berggrun for ever. But if that was the case why couldn't she live anywhere she liked? In Australia, for example?

'I thought you might like to visit next week,' Tomas was saying. 'Once our engagement is official. It is a blank canvas; I thought you would like to decorate it.'

She tried to picture the sort of house he might choose but all she could imagine was an airy white house perched on top of a cliff. Cam's house.

'It's a big house,' Tomas added. 'It will keep you busy for quite a while.'

She made a non-committal sound, struggling to be enthusiastic, as Tomas guided her confidently around the dance floor. She wanted more for herself than to spend her days decorating. Between the heads and shoulders of the other couples she caught a glimpse of a dark-haired man and, for a moment, she thought it was Campbell but, before she could get a proper look, Tomas had turned her around and she'd lost sight of him.

She told herself she was imagining things but that didn't stop her from searching the edges of the dance floor and the corners of the ballroom as Tomas spun her around.

On one pass she saw Freddie. She hadn't realised he was going to be back from Australia in time for the ball, but it was the man standing beside her cousin, watching her, that caused her to stumble.

He was here.

Cam was here.

'Are you all right?' Tomas asked. He held her a little more firmly and managed to keep her on her feet.

Viktoria was breathing quickly. Her heart was racing. She stood with Tomas in the middle of the dance floor as she stared across the room. Her brain had frozen.

'I think I need some water,' she managed to stammer.

'Of course. Come. Take a seat.' Tomas guided her from the floor to a seat several metres from where Freddie and Cam stood. 'I'll bring you a drink.'

She was barely aware of Tomas leaving her side. Her eyes didn't leave Cam. She held her breath as he came towards her. She didn't blink, couldn't blink. She was terrified that if she closed her eyes, even for a second, he would disappear.

She still wasn't certain if she was imagining things but now here he was, standing in front of her.

She wanted to throw herself into his arms, to feel his embrace, to make sure he was real. But while that was what she would have done if they were in Sydney it was not the way a princess behaved.

She looked from Cam to Freddie, trying to make sense of what she was seeing, and realised she wanted to cry. She wasn't sure why. She thought she was happy. She *was* happy to see him, but she wasn't sure what his appearance meant.

She stood up and kissed Freddie on both cheeks, all without taking her eyes off Cam.

Freddie stepped back and Cam reached for Viktoria's hand. Heat shot through her and she thought her knees might give way as her insides dissolved in a pool of delicious anticipation. She was overwhelmed by all the sensations that she had been longing to feel. Just one look from Cam was enough to melt her, let alone the touch of his hand.

He lifted her hand to his lips and kissed her fingers. 'Hello, Viktoria.'

Hearing her name on his lips, just her name, not *Your Highness* or *Princess*, was the sweetest sound. She'd missed being that person. She'd missed him. It had been less than a week, but it felt like a lifetime.

'Cam… What are you doing here?'

'I've come for you.'

'For me?' Her voice was husky and the room was swimming slightly. She really did need a drink but the last thing she wanted was to still be standing there, with Cam, when Tomas returned.

She swayed on her feet and Cam caught her at the elbow, steadying her. Her skin was on fire. Her head was spinning.

She looked to Freddie. She didn't know what to do.

'Go. I'll keep Tomas occupied,' he said.

Viktoria didn't argue. She took Freddie's cue and slipped through one of the glass doors that were set into the arches along one side of the ballroom. She wanted to take Cam's hand, but she knew she had to wait until she was sure no one was watching them. She probably shouldn't be leaving the ballroom with Cam; in fact she knew she *definitely* shouldn't be doing this—there were rules, lots of rules—but sometimes they just had to be broken.

The glass doors opened onto a large flagstoned patio. Potted conifers and several clusters of chairs were arranged around the space but there were also a few secluded seating areas tucked under arbours. Discreet gas heaters took the chill out of the late autumn air. She led Cam to a corner of the patio where they were out of sight of the guests in the ballroom.

She perched on a small cushioned seat and reached for his hand, pulling him down to sit beside her. The spot she had chosen overlooked the ocean and far below them the lights of hundreds of boats docked in the marina shone like handfuls of stars scattered across the water. But Viktoria wasn't interested in looking at any of that. Fairy lights strung over the arbour twinkled above them, giving her just enough light to take in Cam's features. She stared at him, recalling every feature, as if afraid something might have changed in the past few days. But he looked as gorgeous as always.

Tall, dark and still incredibly handsome. As perfect in a tuxedo as he'd been in his army fatigues.

'When did you arrive? How? Why?' Her head was still spinning, and his presence made no sense.

'About an hour ago. I came with Prince Alfred. The Palace was keen to have the services of a doctor on board the flight from Australia as a precaution following surgery. He was fine but it was a long flight and he suggested I might like to come with him. I was happy to accompany him, but I really came to see you.'

'But I cannot spend time with you. Tonight is the one night when I have obligations.'

Cam was only semi-aware of his surroundings, of the palace with its view over the marina, of the fairy lights and conifers, but it was all overshadowed by Viktoria. She was breathtakingly beautiful, outshining everything and everyone else. She tugged on his hand and pulled him down to sit beside her.

'I would have come sooner,' he said, 'but I didn't know if you'd want to see me. I didn't realise what I was losing until you had gone and then I figured I couldn't just walk up to the palace unannounced, and knock on the door asking for you. Prince Alfred offered me the opportunity to come with him and I realised I'd always regret it if I didn't take the chance to see if I could rectify the mistake I'd made.'

Cam knew Viktoria had a duty tonight as a hostess. He hadn't even planned on staying long. Prince Alfred had assured him he would get him into the ball and Cam's intention had simply been to let Viktoria know he was in Berggrun. That he had come to see her, and then he was happy to wait until tomorrow.

'I was stubborn and confused and I should not have let you leave. I needed you to know that, to know that I have come for you. But I will wait. I will wait until tomorrow. I will wait for as long as it takes for you to hear what I have to say.'

'Tell me now.'

'I came to Berggrun to tell you that I don't expect you to give your life up for me. I was foolish. I didn't want to let you down. I didn't think you needed someone like me in your life. I'm still not sure if you do, but I needed to find out one way or the other. You pushed me out of my comfort zone, and I didn't handle that well. Since the incident I prefer my life to be controlled. I don't like unexpected changes. When you arrived, you disturbed my life and my first reaction was to resist, to shut down. I wanted my life to be smooth. I didn't want the unexpected. But then I realised that my life would be boring. Your speech at the Games reminded me not to be afraid. I didn't want to think I might never see you again. If I did nothing I was being cowardly. If I did nothing I was going to miss out on life. On experiences. On you. That is why I am here.

'For you.

'I want you to come back to Australia with me. Or I will stay here. I don't mind. I just want to be with you. I want to be happy.'

'I want you to be happy too. I want us both to be happy, but you are too late.'

'Please, I'm begging you for a chance.'

'No, you do not understand. You are too late. It is too late for us. Things have changed.'

'What things? It's only been a few days.'

'Tomorrow I will be engaged to be married.'

'What did you say?' Cam was certain he had misheard her. He blamed jet lag.

'I am getting married.'

'Married? To whom?' His stomach churned as he waited for her reply. He fought back a wave of nausea.

'The Duke of San Fernando.'

Who the hell was that?

'When was this decided?' he asked as he picked up her hand. Her ring finger was bare. 'You're not engaged yet.'

'No, but it is all arranged. There is a banquet tomorrow to announce the engagement.'

'Tomorrow?' His heart sunk in his chest, coming to rest like a lump of lead in his gut. 'Are you in love with this guy?'

'I like him. I hope we could have a good life together.'

'You *like* him? What the hell does that mean?'

'It means I have an agreement with my parents, and they made the arrangements.'

'Arrangements? You're talking about an *arranged* marriage? Who in the world still does that?'

'We do. I am expected to marry by the time I am thirty. It is a Berggruner tradition. It is my duty.'

'And then what?' He was horrified. 'You'll spend your days handing out trophies and opening hospitals? I thought you said you wanted more than that.'

'I do. And I thought I could have more, but I made a promise to my parents before I went to Australia. I am running out of time.'

'I thought you were coming back to attend a party, to celebrate your father's twenty-fifth anniversary as Prince; you never said anything about a fiancé, arranged or otherwise.'

'I did not think it mattered any more. Our relationship was done.'

'I came here to see if there was a way forward for us...'

'I am sorry, Cam,' she said as his heart broke into tiny fragments. 'I made a promise. There is nothing I can do. It is my duty.'

She had healed his heart only to shatter it all over again.

The rest of the night passed in a blur for Viktoria. Cam had requested a last dance, but she turned him down. She had no choice. She was afraid she wouldn't be able to hide how she felt about him. That she wouldn't be able to conceal her love for him and she couldn't broadcast her feelings to the world. Not in front of Tomas, her parents or the press.

Cam had left the ball and Viktoria felt that she was losing her mind. She couldn't focus; her head was full of thoughts of Cam and she was consumed with dread. Was she making a mistake? She was certain she was, but she didn't know how to rectify it.

She knew she needed to see him again. She couldn't let him go without one more goodbye but there was nothing she could do tonight.

She slept fitfully, tossing and turning while she debated her options, before finally deciding she would need to enlist Freddie's help. She didn't know where Cam was staying, she hadn't thought to ask, but she was sure Freddie would. She'd need to call Cam, to ask him to come back to the palace. She would have gone to him but she was wary of the paparazzi. She knew there were rumours that her engagement was about to be announced and speculation about who she would be marrying. She couldn't lead the press to Cam, and she couldn't leave Tomas exposed. She couldn't risk bringing dishonour to him or her parents.

Freddie gave Viktoria the details of Cam's hotel and her heart was pounding as she dialled the number, only to have her hopes and dreams dashed when she was told that he had already checked out.

He was gone.

She was too late.

She couldn't believe what she'd done. She couldn't believe she'd let him go.

She felt sick. What was she going to do now?

Before she could figure that out Brigitta appeared to let her know her parents had requested her company for breakfast.

Viktoria felt as though she was sleepwalking as she returned to the patio where her parents were seated. All traces of the ball had been cleared away but she still couldn't help but think that the patio would always be the last place where she had seen Cam.

She was dimly aware of exchanging pleasantries with her parents and trying to listen to their opinions on the ball, but her mind was primarily filled with her own troubles. Until her father caught her attention. 'We want to speak to you about Tomas.'

Viktoria's heart sank like a stone. They were going to tell her the process for today's announcement.

'We are concerned that we may have been too hasty, that Tomas might not be the right choice for you,' her mother added.

Viktoria frowned as she tried to translate her mother's meaning. 'Are you giving me more time? I am almost thirty.'

'A tradition isn't set in stone,' her father replied. 'Things can change. Your mother and I thought you were happy to let us suggest a partner for you after what happened with Luca. But the choice is yours. If you're not certain, you can wait.'

'Is it true you met someone in Sydney?' her mother asked.

'How did you know that? Did Freddie tell you?'

Her mother nodded. 'Is he someone special?'

'Oui.' Viktoria couldn't keep the smile from her face at the thought of Cam, until she remembered that she had no idea where he had gone.

'We think you should discuss your situation with him. We want you to be positive you are making the right decision.'

'I do not know if it could work, *how* it could work.'

'There's no way to be certain of everything in life but

if you want something badly enough, if it's worth something to you, then you have to try. Do you love him?'

Viktoria thought of the way Cam made her feel. The way she felt when he kissed her. When he held her hand. When he made love to her. When he opened his heart to her.

How she felt when she had to say goodbye. 'I do.'

'Then you need to speak to him again before you make your decision.'

'Do I have your permission?' she asked her father.

'Of course. And our blessing. Now, go to him, talk to him.'

'I don't know where he is.' The realisation felt like a physical blow, knocking the air from her lungs and squeezing her heart in her chest.

'I'm right here.'

She spun around, thinking she must have imagined his voice, and saw Cam standing behind her.

'Cam!'

She stepped into his arms, reacting on instinct, without hesitation. 'I rang your hotel. They told me you had checked out. I thought you had gone.'

His arms enclosed her, and she was only vaguely aware of her parents leaving the patio, leaving her alone with Cam.

'I couldn't leave,' he told her. 'Not without you. Last night I had to respect the fact that you had a duty as a hostess. I wasn't about to create drama but, until you are officially engaged to someone else, I'm not prepared to accept that what we had is over. I spent the night figuring out what to do, figuring out where we go from here, and now I need to speak to you.' He took her hand and led her back to the same seat where they had sat last night.

He sat down and pulled her into his lap. 'I should

never have let you go but I didn't feel I was right for you. I didn't think I had anything to offer you. I was angry and sad at the same time and riddled with guilt. I was scarred. Although my physical wounds had healed, I still bore my emotional ones. I felt broken, cracked open, exposed and vulnerable but when I was with you I felt myself healing. You were a balm to my soul, and you showed me a path to a future where I thought I could be happy again, but I wasn't sure if I could make you happy. And I didn't think I could compete with your duty as a royal. But then I realised I didn't want to compete. I love you and I want to support you. If you'll have me. I don't want to lose you. I don't want you to marry someone else. I want you to marry me.'

She had wanted him to fight for her. To come for her. And he had.

'You want to marry me?'

'Yes. And I'm not leaving without you.'

'What if I can't leave?'

'Well, then, I'll figure out a way to stay here. I have always liked to make plans, but I stopped after Gemma died. When I met you I started thinking ahead again, planning a future, not knowing you were a princess, not knowing you had a duty to Prince and country. I didn't think I could compete against that. I thought I would lose you to your duty, just like I had lost Gemma, and I figured there was nothing I could do. But this time I can do something. And I am going to fight for what I want. And what I want is you. If there is any way to make this work, I will do it. I was never the type of person who gave up and I am not prepared to give up on us. I haven't lost you yet. There's still a chance. But that is up to you.'

He reached out and wiped a tear from her cheek. She

hadn't even realised she was crying. But they were happy tears. He hadn't left without her. He loved her.

'I understand you have a duty as a princess,' he said, 'and I can live with that. I'm not asking you to give that up for me, but I'm not prepared to lose you to another man.'

'Do you think you could live here? In Berggrun.'

'I have no idea,' he said with a smile. 'I haven't seen anything of it yet except for a palace and a hotel room. Will you show me around?'

'Yes—' she smiled in return '—I would love to.'

'I'm glad. But first there is something else I need to ask you.' He lifted her off his lap and put her on the seat. He got down on one knee. 'I didn't think I had anything to offer you, but I can offer you my love. Viktoria, I love you. Will you marry me?'

Her smile stretched even wider as she reached for his hands. 'You have plenty to offer me,' she said. 'You are also kind, loyal, intelligent and the sexiest man I have ever met, and I love you. I want to be more than a princess. I want to be your wife and, yes, I will marry you.'

It seemed that fairy tale endings were real after all, she thought as he kissed her.

* * * * *

REUNITED WITH HER HOT-SHOT SURGEON

AMY RUTTAN

MILLS & BOON

For Dianne.
Thank you for being so kind when I needed support,
especially when I was a new author.
You won't be forgotten.

PROLOGUE

"You don't have to do this."

"I have to. It was the plan." Pearl continued to pack her bags, fighting back the tears stinging her eyes. She wasn't going to cry in front of him.

"Why?" Calum asked, confused.

"We agreed to get married because of the baby. The baby is gone, so I'm going to continue with my plans. I'm going to take the job I was offered after residency." She hoped her voice didn't shake as she packed.

Calum had always said that they'd get married for the baby. After they finished their residency, around the time Pearl had gotten pregnant, he'd been offered a job here in San Francisco. Pearl hadn't, but there was a job in New York City. She'd originally turned it down because she was pregnant, but now that was a moot point.

She had always had reservations about getting married. He knew her parents, had met her mother, so he got why she didn't want to get married. Or at least understood why there was no point now the baby was gone.

When she'd fallen pregnant Pearl had been scared. Marriage had seemed like a safety net. It had seemed like the right thing to do at the time.

She loved Calum, but when they'd started this relationship over a year ago they had both made it clear from the start that their careers came first.

"Pearl, we can still stay together."

She stopped packing and stared at him. She wanted to believe Calum, but she knew how he felt about marriage, too. And it was hard to look at him, because she still loved him, so she looked away, because if she looked at him he might convince her to stay, and just prolong eventual heartbreak.

"So I stay and we do what? We still get married?" she asked.

He hesitated. "Eventually…"

Pearl sighed. "It's best I go. That job I was offered in New York City is still waiting for me."

"So that's it? You're taking that high-profile job? The one your father suggested you take?" There was derision in his voice.

She didn't give a lick about the fact it was high-profile or paid well. She needed to get away. The pain was too much. Everywhere reminded her of the baby, how she was almost happy. How she almost had her happily-ever-after and the family she wanted. The family she always longed for growing up with toxic parents. Parents she could never please. The only good times in her life had been with her late grandmother and Calum.

But she and Calum had both wanted very different career paths when they first met. She wasn't going to hold him back any longer.

"You don't have to run off and leave just because we don't have to get married," Calum said.

"Why? We both had plans for our career. You don't have to marry me now. I know that you were doing it because of some sense of duty, but there's no point now—the baby is gone. You're off the hook. Me leaving or you leaving for work was going to be the eventual and natural end to this relationship." She continued to pack and tried not to cry. She didn't want the tears that were burning her eyes to fall.

She wanted to keep those tears to herself. She'd learned to keep them to herself. They were hers and she wouldn't burden Calum with them.

She wanted a family. She wanted happiness, but that was a dream she'd learned to give up long ago.

"You really think that I wanted to marry you because of some outdated sense of duty?" he asked hotly.

"Didn't you?"

"Yes. At first, I suppose, but…" He trailed off and rubbed the back of his neck, not saying anything else.

"Why else would we eventually get married then? You told me you didn't want a family when we both got together. We agreed on that. So why else?"

His expression hardened. "Things changed this past year, Pearl."

"What changed? Nothing changed for me except the baby and that's gone. It's back to the way it was."

"Is it?"

"Yes." Only she was lying. She was giving him an out.

She was giving herself an out. She was too afraid to continue. She knew what happened when surgeons married, when one was forced to change career trajectory for another.

She knew from painful experience what happened. Calum would eventually resent her for holding him back.

And she'd resent him.

Are you sure?

"I've accepted the job, Calum. I've got to go." She zipped up her luggage.

"Fine. Then go. It's clear where your priorities lie."

He left, slamming the door, making her cringe.

This was for the best.

Although, she wasn't so sure.

CHAPTER ONE

Five years later

BREATHE.

Dr. Pearl Henderson took a deep breath, but it didn't do much to calm her nerves. She was perspiring and cursed herself inwardly for wearing a sweater. She'd forgotten that October in San Francisco was much milder than New York City.

She'd been on the East Coast for far too long. She'd grown accustomed to cooler and cold New York City falls and winters, and the humid, steamy summers. Although she had always longed for California.

It's your fault for leaving.

Pearl had been so scared about what could happen if she and Calum had stayed together that she had left. She was a damn fine surgeon and sports doctor, but she never took chances.

Except now.

She was back in California and San Francisco.

She was back to see Calum.

The grip on her briefcase was digging into her palm and she closed her eyes, trying to ground herself, trying to ease the stress she was feeling being back here in

San Francisco. At this hospital. The place where she'd started her career as a surgeon.

The place that held a piece of her broken heart.

A place that still haunted her, even after five years. She'd always wanted to come back, but she never knew how. She was one of the top sports injury doctors on the eastern seaboard, but it wasn't enough.

Because you miss him.

Pearl shook away that thought. She couldn't let herself think like that, even if there was a bit of truth in it. It wasn't Calum who had brought her back to San Francisco, it was her new job as head physician that brought her back here.

You're lying to yourself.

She took another deep breath, taking in the salty, crisp air as she straightened her back and held her head up high. It was going to be hard to see Dr. Calum Munro again—it would be brutal. Ending their relationship and walking away from the only man she cared for had broken her heart, but she'd had no choice.

When they got together Calum had made it clear that he didn't want to get married and she had agreed. They both had goals, aspirations, and marriage wasn't one of his.

He deserved to be free. It would take every ounce of strength to face him again, but she was a professional and her patient needed her to act on his behalf. Her employer, the San Francisco Bridgers, a new team part of the NFL, had hired her to do this.

To save their potential star player. To give George a fighting chance in the face of a brutal cancer diagnosis. A career-ending diagnosis.

The Bridgers' newest player had an osteosarcoma that only Dr. Calum Munro could handle. He may have turned down the team initially, without looking at the chart, but she wasn't about to let his busy schedule, his wait list, put this life in jeopardy. George had worked hard all his life and he deserved a chance at his dream. He'd only got to play a couple of games, he had his whole career ahead of him and now cancer.

Someone deserved to have a shot at their dreams. Pearl certainly hadn't had a shot at hers. That had been taken from her; she hadn't known what she had had until it was gone. She only hoped Calum had forgiven her and that he'd see her.

Pearl didn't take him for the kind of man that would hold a grudge. Not that there should be one. She certainly didn't blame him for the way their relationship had ended.

Pearl had been the one to end it. With the baby gone there was no reason to continue and she was keenly reminded that anything good in her life didn't ever work out. Except her work. And that was the only thing she could rely on. Even her own body had failed her in a way for not being able to hold on to her baby.

The thought of her loss made her eyes sting, but she couldn't cry.

"Surgeons don't cry," her mother had once said. *"Never show your weakness or let anyone walk all over you. Your tears disappoint me, Pearl. Do you ever see me cry over your father holding me back? No, because surgeons don't cry."*

Her mother's harsh words still echoed in her head. The only time she was ever allowed to be herself, where her tears were comforted, was with her grandmother.

After her mother shamed her, she didn't cry in front of anyone anymore.

Not even Calum.

Pearl took another deep calming breath and headed inside the Hospital for Special Surgery, where Calum worked, where they had both started together as residents. Where her career life had flourished, but her personal life had started to crumble.

You can do this.

She walked into the main lobby of the hospital. Nothing had changed and the moment she stepped inside, it was like she'd never left.

It felt like home. All the old memories came back. The friendships she had made, the triumphs she'd had, the lives she had saved.

This place had taught her everything she knew. This is where she'd belonged. This is where she fell in love.

She had thrived here and been welcomed, unlike the place she had grown up with parents constantly fighting.

With parents who were never pleased with her or themselves.

Only this wasn't her home. This was a hospital. It was a building. It was just like every other hospital she'd worked in since and she didn't belong here anymore.

She had to stay focused. Pearl found where Calum's office was. She'd already called ahead and knew that he wasn't on call. He didn't have any clinics and his rounds would be over by now.

He should be in his office.

He couldn't turn her down. If he was the same man that she had known five years ago he'd rise to the challenge of George's case.

She was sure of that.

Are you so sure?

Yes. She was sure. Calum liked difficult cases. Just like she did.

Which is why they had become fast friends in residency. They had both strived to tackle the challenges and save lives.

They had both worked hard.

Calum had been the only one to understand her.

Even though her mother always said surgeons couldn't be friends or lovers. And her mother should know thanks to her toxic marriage with Pearl's father.

"It's competitive," her mother had said. "It doesn't work. The only thing that works is surgery. That's all that matters—being the best at your job."

And her father had said the same. Only Calum had been different.

He was different.

Was he?

Her mother swore she'd loved her father once, but it changed. Her mother's career was put on hold when she had Pearl, and her mother loathed him and Pearl.

So who knew where Calum and she would be if she hadn't lost their baby. If they had gone through with the marriage.

She got onto the elevator and headed to the orthopedic oncology floor. The hospital hadn't changed much. She and Calum had spent a lot of time on this floor when they were residents under the late great Dr. Chin, who'd taught them everything they knew.

After getting off the elevator, she bypassed the main reception area and headed straight for the office down at the end of the hall. Each step she took down that long hall felt like an eternity. Her feet felt like lead and her pulse thundered in her ears. The door was open and she could see him at his desk, his back to her. The ginger hair she loved so much had a few grays in it and it was shorter than she remembered.

It had been slightly longer then and she remembered

brushing the curls off his face to kiss him. Her heart
skipped a beat remembering that. He hadn't changed a
bit. She had thought that time would've made this easier
and she had been wrong.

Everything came flooding back to her in that instant.
Every touch.
Every shared laugh.
Every kiss.

It overwhelmed her so much her heart hammered and
she couldn't speak.

So she just hovered in the doorway, not sure what she
should do. Calum turned around, as if sensing that someone was watching him, and his eyes widened. "Pearl?"
he asked.

"Yes," she answered nervously, finally finding her
voice. Her tongue was no longer sticking to the roof of
her mouth. She cleared her throat, keeping her emotions
in check. "It's been a long time."

The warmth that was once in those blue eyes that she
so loved dissipated quickly, his expression hardening.
"Has it?" And without asking her anything further he
returned to his work.

*Okay. So apparently he did hold something of a
grudge.*

It hurt, but what did she expect? She was used to indifference and formality. This is what her mother told
her would happen. She was prepared for this. Only…it
still hurt. She had hoped Calum was different. Apparently, she was wrong.

"Calum," she said firmly. She wasn't going to be
swayed or pushed aside. She was here for her patient.

That wasn't why she was back.

"There's nothing to say, Pearl. I don't want to talk
about the past. You're five years too late for that."

"I didn't come all this way to rehash the past. I came here to talk about a case."

"I have a wait list. I don't have time to take on cases," he said. "There are other surgeons in this hospital that I'm sure have room."

"You are seriously holding on to the past?" she asked, pulling the door closed behind her.

His eyes narrowed as he turned around. "I'm not holding on to the past. I'm stating a fact. I'm swamped and I don't have time to take on some athlete who has some injury that's preventing him from making millions as a...quarterback."

"Linebacker," Pearl said offhandedly.

"Whatever," Calum responded dryly. "There are other surgeons."

"How did you know it's for a football player? Is that why you turned the case down without looking at the chart?"

"I know you were hired as a physician for a sports team in New York. Everyone knows you're the top of your field. Congrats on that, by the way," he said dryly.

Was he jealous?

Calum had always told her he wanted a big career. That was why he had become a doctor.

She didn't want to believe it, but his apparent jealously seemed to prove otherwise.

"I'm based here in California now." She pulled out her patient's file. "And it's not some injury. I can handle any surgery for an injury. It's an osteosarcoma and a brutal one. I know that you have the best success rate for saving the leg, for saving the bone. This young man has worked so hard through college, scholarships and odd jobs just to get here, and then has had this sideline him."

He turned back to look at her. "An osteosarcoma?"

"Yes. I can't help him and you're the best, or so I've been told. This player came from nothing to become a superstar. He's young and deserves a fighting chance."

Calum's expression softened and she knew she was getting to him. Calum had worked so hard to get through medical school. He had had it harder than others and she knew that even though this young man had signed a six-figure contract, that the rough start in life, the determination the young man had put forth, might just soften Calum's heart a bit. It always had in the past.

When they'd been working on patients, he'd always take the pro bono cases.

Always.

Though she was worried he'd say no to the team again because she was working for them and because his father was an investor for the Bridgers. She knew Calum didn't have the best relationship with his father, but a young man's life was at stake. And if Calum was still the man she remembered, he would do what he could for George.

It was that softness she knew laid deep inside, that drew her to him.

He flipped open the file and leaned back in his chair, reading it.

Pearl stood there, her pulse racing, and she wondered if she really still did know Calum. Had he changed in five years? Would he help? If she believed what her parents had always told her, then no, he wouldn't. He would hold a grudge like her parents did.

Calum wasn't like that. He always wanted to help others. She knew that about him.

Did you ever really know him, though?

Pearl was confident she knew the type of surgeon he was. His compassion and his drive to be the best were what had drawn her to him in the first place.

Even though she didn't want to date or have a relationship after growing up through her parents' awful marriage, Calum was so different. He had been a breath of fresh air in her stagnant, emotionless life.

He had brought color to her dark, bleak world.

Pearl had grown up in a house where her parents fought, cheated and blamed each other for their failures.

Her parents were constantly trying to outdo one another, until finally in her last year of medical school they got divorced. Finally, there was no arguing. Although, there was really nothing anymore. There was no home to go home to during school breaks.

Her mother was bitter and angry. Her father started a new life and a new family with a younger woman.

Their hate for each other steeled Pearl's resolve to never date someone she worked with.

Until she met Calum.

He was a high achiever, and so was she, but he understood her unhappy childhood.

He got it.

And they bonded. She was drawn to his light in spite of the darkness of her past.

He was comforting.

He was home.

Then one night, one foolish drunken night, she couldn't resist that strong attraction, the need she had for Calum, and one thing led to another and another, and that had ended up in eventual heartache.

Heartache she wasn't too keen on ever experiencing again. She was going to make sure of that.

"This isn't good," he said gently, still focused on the file.

"No. It's not. Can I sit down?" she asked. He nodded and she took a seat on the other side of his desk.

Calum set down the file and scrubbed a hand over his face. "Look, I'm sorry. I didn't know that it was a cancer and I didn't know that it was this bad. I thought it was just another sports team trying to woo me to leave the hospital. I thought it was an injury and I thought any surgeon could handle it."

"I could handle an injury myself. I would've just asked the chief of surgery for special privileges to work at the hospital. This is something else. Something I can't handle. I need help."

Calum nodded. "I'm sorry for this young man—this is rough."

"Can you make time to see him? There's no one else I'd rather have on the case."

A strange expression crossed his face. "Why me?"

"You're a great surgeon, Calum, and I thought from one friend to another—"

"We're not friends, Pearl," he stated firmly. "Colleagues on this case, but if I take this patient on, he's my patient. I don't need your assistance."

It was another slap in the face. It stung, but she was prepared for that reaction. The only thing she was not prepared to do was step aside when it came to her patient. She couldn't.

Pearl straightened her spine. "He's my patient, too. I'm responsible for everyone on that team and I will be with him every step of the way. You don't know him or the treatments he's had. I won't back down when it comes to my patient. I'll treat you cordially, since you stated we're not friends, but I won't be pushed aside."

"Fine."

She was relieved, but she hid that from him. Like she hid so many other emotions. Calum could be just as stubborn as her. He never really liked to be backed into a corner, that much she remembered from their days as residents. He wouldn't step down if he felt it was the right thing to do. Something else she admired about him.

Part of her wanted to pull back, let him handle this case. That way she could keep her distance and not let him affect her. Already being near him was dredging up all these old feelings and memories she thought she'd locked away. She wasn't going to be bullied out of this. George was her patient and she had been with him right from the start. Right from when the San Francisco Bridgers had signed him from college, up to his injury after his third game, until his diagnosis.

George lived far from his home in Philadelphia and his mother was on her way out to see him, but she had other kids at home and Pearl felt bad that George was on his own. She made it her mission to take care of him and she wasn't going to be pushed aside because of Calum.

"Thank you," she said.

His expression softened. "You're welcome, but I do expect some compensation."

"The team will pay you."

"I know that, but for privileges to *my* hospital I want you to take some of my caseload." He grinned and there was a twinkle in his eye.

"What? I don't have time for that!"

A smile tugged at the corners of his mouth. "I think you can make time. I am making time for your patient."

Heat bloomed in her cheeks.

He was right.

And it honestly secretly thrilled her to do surgical work again. Most of her surgeries as a sports doctor involved knee replacements or torn ligaments. Sports type of injuries. It would be nice to do a rotation on the trauma floor. To work on a variety of different cases.

Pearl stood up, yanking up her briefcase swiftly. "You have a deal, Dr. Munro. Thank you for seeing my patient. When can I bring him in?"

"I'm glad to hear it," he said. "You can call me Calum, you know."

"Why? We're not friends, you said so yourself."

"I didn't mean to insult you before. I was just surprised to see you standing there again after all this time." He ran his hand through his ginger hair and sighed. "It's been a long time."

She smiled. "You didn't insult me. And, yes, it's been a long time."

"You don't need to be so formal. It feels weird having you call me Dr. Munro."

"You said you wanted to keep it professional."

"I know. Again, it was a shock. You haven't changed at all."

Her heart skipped a beat. "Neither have you."

And he hadn't. Not really. She thought five years apart would've been enough time to lay the ghosts of her past to rest.

She was wrong.

"So when can I bring George in?" she asked, trying to ignore all the feelings he was stirring up in her. She had to put an end to this conversation and put some distance between them.

"How about you bring him in this afternoon? Say around four? Does that work."

"It does."

"And Pearl, try to relax. I'm sorry for what I said. It was just… It was a shock to see you standing in my door."

She relaxed a bit. She understood that. It was a shock to see him, too, but she wasn't going to let him know that. She had to keep her distance, though it would be hard working with him. She was drawn to him. She'd always been.

Even though she knew she was here to see Calum, she wasn't mentally prepared to see him again. She thought she had prepared enough, but seeing him there, sitting at his desk, brought it all back.

The night she left him. It was still fresh in her mind, haunting her. She had hated herself for leaving. Though it had been the right thing to do.

Had it?

Pearl shook that memory from her mind. "I'll see you at four."

"Sounds good."

Pearl opened the door and left his office. Her hands were shaking and her pulse was racing. She wasn't quite ready for the effect that Dr. Calum Munro still had on her. And she was going to make sure that she had full control over it. She wasn't going to risk her heart for anything.

Not even if it wanted to.

Calum leaned back in his chair, trying to process what had happened. He had no idea that Dr. Pearl Henderson had come back to San Francisco. He had no idea that she worked for the San Francisco Bridgers. Maybe if he had known…

Would that have really changed your mind?

It might have.

When the Bridgers came to him he thought it was his father reaching out, trying to get a freebie. His father only wanted him when Calum could give him something.

After years of trying to please his father, he had

learned no matter what he achieved, no matter what he did, he'd never gain the attention or respect of Grayson Munro.

So he had given up trying and caring.

Calum had been approached by every major league team in San Francisco—and beyond—ever since he had won his major scientific achievement award, also known as the MSA, through his alma mater for his treatment in osteosarcoma. His practice blew up, but he just couldn't be lured by the money to be the exclusive doctor for a sports team. Not anymore.

When he first started out, Calum might have been tempted because he was sure it would have impressed his father, but when Pearl left he realized he couldn't live his life trying to impress others.

He loved the hospital. The hospital and his work were the only stable, constant things in his life.

He wanted to stay here.

He had researched and helped create that surgery so that he could help everyone with osteosarcoma, not just athletes. And, truth be told, he was a bit resentful of big teams like Bridgers.

It was a team out cast that had lured away Pearl after they'd lost their baby. Even though he knew that's what she'd always wanted—to work as a sports doctor for a professional team—he still hated it.

Work was the most important thing to his father, and apparently it was to Pearl. Still, there was a part of him that didn't think that Pearl was all about the work—she was just using that as an excuse to run away. She had a tendency to shut out everyone when things got too hard. Bottle up her emotions when she became overwhelmed, like she was ashamed of them. He couldn't even remember ever seeing her cry before.

She certainly hadn't cried when they lost their baby.

She always tried to remain calm and collected, but he saw through that charade.

Are you sure it wasn't just an act?

There were moments during their time together, he really saw her. Saw her joy, her sorrow, her compassion and her vulnerability, but never her tears, so he had always suspected it was all a front.

No, he wasn't sure. Pearl had made it clear to him when they first met that she wasn't interested in dating anyone, especially not someone she worked with, and she wasn't interested in a traditional family.

Neither had he been, to be honest. His upbringing hadn't been the most wholesome and he had never really thought about having a family.

Ever.

He should've kept away from Pearl, but she was fun to be around. She was smart and sexy and after one foolish night one thing led to another and she was pregnant. For one golden moment in his life he had thought he could have the thing he had secretly wanted when he was growing up. He had been terrified of being a father, but he had wanted to try to be better than his father ever was. He wanted roots. His outlook had changed. He had wanted that family. He had wanted that tradition.

He had wanted Pearl.

He'd always wanted Pearl.

Then his world came crashing down and it was all taken from him. Instead of he and Pearl comforting each other over the loss of their child, she had left for that high-paying job she'd always aspired to and he had been left to grieve alone.

She had left him, just as his father had. His father had left and then his mother had died. He had grieved for his mother alone and when Pearl left he had grieved alone for the child he had never known he'd wanted.

When he thought about being a husband and father, he thought he could be the man his father never was.

The kind of man his mother deserved. It's why he had never wanted a relationship. For so long he had known he couldn't commit. Until he'd met Pearl. He'd thought she was different.

It broke his heart, to carry that burden, when it had seemed like Pearl didn't care that their child was gone.

Only, he was used to being alone.

He should've known better.

No one stayed.

His sister, Sharon, left when she went to college and she never came back. His mother had to leave him alone to work and then she died.

Then Pearl left.

Pearl knew all this about him and she still left him, breaking his heart, but try as he might he couldn't let her go.

He could never get over her.

And that was his burden to bear.

He might never get over her, but he wasn't going to let her back in.

Calum had sworn that he would never forgive her, that he never wanted to see her again. But when he saw Pearl standing in that doorway, it was like time hadn't touched her. Like the last five years apart had never happened.

Her hair was still that deep, beautiful, rich color of chestnut mixed with red. Her brilliant blue eyes were just as mesmerizing as they were the day he looked up over a chart and saw her across the charge station with Dr. Chin.

And he remembered keenly the velvety softness of

her lush pink lips, the way she tasted and the way she melted in his arms.

She was just as beautiful as he remembered, and all that anger that he felt about her leaving him dissipated. And he couldn't say no to her patient.

He might not want to work for a team exclusively, but he wasn't going to turn down a young man and ruin his chances at his dream because he was still angry that Pearl had left him.

He wasn't a monster. He wasn't like his father.

His father had only thought of their pocketbook. He worked constantly and had never helped out Calum. Calum had scrimped and saved, worked for scholarships, worked several jobs just to get himself an education. His father had had the money, but he wouldn't give him a dime.

He had kept it to himself. And Calum had never known why. It had bothered him, but now he didn't care. There was no excuse for that behavior.

Even when Calum's mother was broke and needed money to buy food to feed him and his sister, their father couldn't be bothered. His father had a facade of charm and made people trust him, believe in him, but he didn't care about anyone.

A narcissist. That's who his father was.

Pearl's not a narcissist.

He knew that. She really cared for her patients. She was tender and kind.

Compassionate and passionate about her work under the ice-queen exterior. It's why he was drawn to her. She seemed real when he spent his life surrounded by fake people.

Calum got up and followed after her—there were a few things he wanted to say to her. Pearl was almost at the end of the hall, where the main reception area was, and he didn't want to call out to her in front of his receptionist, who was a bit of a gossip and and had known him from his days as a resident, when he and Pearl had worked under Dr. Chin and learned all they could.

She remembered that they had been together, that there had been a baby, but he couldn't let her get away.

"Pearl, wait!" he called out.

She turned around, shocked. "Calum? Is there something wrong?"

He wanted to talk to her. He wanted to tell her how he felt that day she left, but he just couldn't get the words out and it made him angry that he couldn't.

There was so much he wanted to say to her but couldn't.

And there were things that he only wanted to keep to himself about that horrible night. Things that he felt that she didn't deserve to hear, but he still wanted her to know how her leaving had crushed him so completely.

For the last five years he'd been thinking of these things in his head, of what he would say if he saw her again. But now that he was presented with the opportunity, he couldn't get the words out.

He just couldn't do it.

She'd hurt him so badly, he wasn't going to share his heart with anyone again. Least of all with her.

"Why don't I come with you now to see George?" Really, he didn't want to go anywhere today. He had a lot of charts and paperwork to catch up on, but he couldn't think of any other reason to have chased her down the hall.

Like a fool. And that's what he was.

He was a fool chasing after her like he'd chased after his father.

"You want to come see him now?" she asked, confused.

"He must be in pain."

"He is," she said softly.

"Then it's better I go and see him now instead of forcing him to come here. I can do an initial exam there and then schedule him for regular clinic days. I'm sure you have the facilities to accommodate me."

"I do." She smiled, that warm genuine smile that not many people had seen when they were residents, but he'd seen it.

"You have a great smile you know," he'd said one day.

"What?" she had asked, stunned, looking up from her charts.

"Your smile. You're kind with patients and you mean it, but with other doctors you're cold and you hide yourself away. You hide your feelings. Why?"

She straightened her back and her blue eyes were wide with fear. "Patients are different. They're not in competition with me."

"You think residency is a competition?"

"Isn't it?"

"I never thought of it that way," he said.

"Surgery is a competition. Surgeons are competitive by nature."

"Well, I'm not here to compete. I'm here to learn and save lives."

Her expression had softened, but only for a moment, and then she'd turned back to charting.

That had been the first time she'd sort of let him in.

He learned after that she'd been raised by two tough-as-nails surgeons and she was good at locking away her emotions, but that smile—that was the smile that he fell for. It was almost as if she was letting him inside the walls she had put up to keep people out.

"Good." He pulled out his phone. "Give me the address and I'll meet you there in thirty minutes?"

"Sure." She took his phone and punched in the address of the Bridgers' training facility. "I'll see you in half an hour. I'll call George now and have him come down to the training center."

He nodded and took a step back, as if trying to distance himself.

He didn't really know what he was doing. Why was he going there?

Because she smiled. You're a sucker for that smile. Even after all these years.

Pearl smiled. She showed her softness toward a patient and she came to him and asked for help. That's when he melted for her, and here he was falling into the old trap again.

Once again Pearl had turned his whole world upside down.

"See you then."

The elevator opened, she got in and the door shut, and it was then he frowned. Angry at himself for letting her in again.

You're a softie, Calum.

And he hated himself for that.

He knew one thing—this was as far in as he was going to let her.

He wasn't making the same mistake twice.

CHAPTER TWO

CALUM FOUND THE Bridgers' training facility quite easily.

He knew where it was. His father had repeatedly invited him here since he won his medical award. Finding the place was the easiest part of this whole situation.

What am I doing?

He couldn't believe that he was actually here. He could have waited until this patient came to the hospital, but no, he had to offer to come here instead.

He had gotten carried away with memories when he saw Pearl. The way she cared for her patients got to him every time. If he hadn't been so reckless and chased after Pearl, he wouldn't have had to come.

You're doing this for the young athlete, not her. Remember that.

And that's what he had to focus on.

When he entered the modern building near Haight-Ashbury, he was impressed by the new architecture that blended with the old. The Bridgers might be a fairly new team to the Bay area, but they were sparing no expense.

The last time he had talked to his father, he had gone on and on about the financials of the new team. Apparently it was okay to back a new professional sports team, and let his ex-wife and his children starve.

Of course, now his father saw some use in him since

he won the scientific award and the large grant that went with it. Looking around at the reception area of the Bridgers' training center, Calum started to feel that old resentment in himself rising.

That old resentment he felt when his father would put work over family.

State-of-the-art equipment and a professionally decorated reception area with expensive art and marble floors—this is what his father valued over him.

Over his mother.

His father valued possessions.

He had to get control of himself; he wouldn't let his father in here. He wouldn't let his father interfere with his job. Calum had a cool, professional relationship with his father and that was it.

That's all it would be and he wouldn't let all those old emotions throw him into a tailspin. He had worn his heart on his sleeve once and had it shattered.

There was no way that he was going to do that again.

"Calum!"

He turned and saw Pearl walking toward him. His pulse quickened seeing her and he hated that she still had this effect on him.

He hated that he lost control.

"Pearl," he responded gruffly.

"I'm so glad you agreed to come here. George is having a hard day," she said gently.

"It's no problem."

"Good." There was some tension to that smile. Her back was ramrod-straight and she stood there smiling awkwardly.

Honestly, he felt the tension, too, and he kept his hands jammed in his pockets.

"Why don't you follow me?" Pearl suggested, turning.

"Okay." He fell into step beside her. He tried to keep his distance, but being so close to her again, catching that whiff of her coconut shampoo, still felt the same as it did five years ago. It was hard not fall into old patterns.

It was hard not to reach out and take her hand like he used to.

So he walked rigidly beside her, trying not to come in close contact.

"I know this is hard," she said, breaking the silent tension.

"What's hard?" And he inwardly groaned, not wanting to talk about it.

She turned to face him. "I don't want this to be weird between us. You said you wanted to be colleagues on this case and I want that, too."

"We are."

Pearl cocked one of her finely shaped brows. "Come on, Calum. We're both adults, what happened—"

"We're not going to talk about what happened," he snapped, cutting her off. "That's in the past."

Her blue eyes widened, but only briefly. "Okay."

"Let's focus on the patient," he said stiffly. The last thing he wanted to do was talk about what happened five years ago.

The last thing he wanted to do was feel any kind of emotion that was attached to that horrible moment in his life.

Truth be told, the last thing he wanted to do was feel at all. And he was envious she seemed so detached from it all, but that's the way she had always been and why other residents, except Calum and a couple of others, had called her the ice queen.

Right now he wanted to think of her like that.

He didn't want to think about all the times the ice

queen had melted under his touch and had set fire to his blood.

He was here to do work. That—focusing on the patient—was what he intended to do. Calum followed Pearl into an exam room. The young athlete, George Vaughn, was sitting on an examination table, his bad leg outstretched and with ice.

He smiled a bright smile, his dark eyes twinkling when he saw Pearl. Not that Calum could blame him—Pearl was a beautiful woman.

"Hi, Doc!"

"Hi, George, this is my colleague Dr. Calum Munro and he's one of the best orthopedic surgeons specializing in osteosarcoma."

George grinned at him and held out his hand. Calum took his hand and shook it. The young man was strong, but wiry, which was good for a linebacker. He could run.

"It's a pleasure to meet you, Dr. Munro," George said politely.

"Same, George. How is your pain level today?" Calum asked, pulling over a rolling chair so that he could sit and examine the leg.

"It's about a seven. The ice is helping," George responded tightly.

Calum highly doubted the ice was helping. The lines in the young man's face told another story. The pain George felt was deep, bone pain. A tumor infiltrating the nerves. George was trying to put on a brave face, like most of the young men he had as patients tried to do.

He was glad George was determined to fight this cancer. You needed to remain strong to fight the disease, to beat it. You needed mental strength to keep going when your body wanted to give up.

Calum had seen it enough times. He had seen it in his mother.

"Do you mind if I have a look?" Calum asked.

"Go ahead." George winced as he leaned over and removed the ice pack. There was swelling near the knee and the moment he gently touched the area, George sucked in a deep breath.

Calum finished his examination, which included using his Doppler to listen to the blood flow in the leg.

"Do you think you can help me, Doc?" George asked hopefully.

"I'm going to look at your labs and your scans. From there I'll confer with Dr. Henderson about the best course of treatment." Calum couldn't give George an answer just yet. He didn't want to give false hope to the young man. Not until he had all the facts, but Calum was going to do his best to help him.

George smiled. "Thanks, Doc."

Calum grinned and patted the young man on the back.

"Let me help you," Pearl said, reaching out to grab George's arm as she and Calum helped him off the table. Pearl handed him his crutches. "Do you have a ride back to your place?"

George nodded. "Yeah, the coach brought me in and he's going to take me back. No doubt he wants to talk strategy."

"Strategy?" Calum asked.

Pearl laughed. "My friend George here, besides being one of the fastest linebackers I've seen in a while, is an excellent play strategist. He's been assisting the coach with that while he's on leave."

"Yeah, but that's not what I want to do for the rest

of my life," George said quickly. "I want to be back on the turf."

"We'll do everything we can to make that happen," Calum said, instantly regretting his words.

Don't make promises you can't keep.

Only he couldn't help it. He felt bad that George was missing out. How would he feel if he couldn't live his dream of becoming a surgeon?

Life was not fair.

He was keenly aware of that from when they had lost the baby and then he had lost Pearl, too. Life had dealt him a raw hand and he was going to try and make sure that the same thing didn't happen to this young man. He couldn't guarantee success. It was cancer and there was no cure. Only treatments.

"Right," Pearl said cautiously.

"Dr. Henderson and I will strategize this afternoon," Calum teased, winking.

George grinned and opened the door. "Thanks, Docs!"

Pearl helped him out of the exam room and watched to make sure that he got down the hall, before she came back into the exam room and closed to the door. She crossed her arms, her lips pursed.

"So we're going to strategize, huh?" she asked.

"Of course. Isn't that what colleagues do?"

"Yes. That's what they do," Pearl answered, a bit stunned. She was pleased that Calum seemed so optimistic about George's cancer, because she didn't feel that way. Of course, Calum was always the more optimistic one.

Not that she could really blame him. With her upbringing and dealing with her parents, anyone could be more optimistic than her, but it still always amazed her Calum was more optimistic than her. His childhood had been no better. Still, over the years she was trying to improve herself. Trying to see that brighter side of life, but it was hard to do that with her parents always reminding her she wasn't good enough.

Everything good in her life had been taken from her. Everything.

"Stop crying, Pearl. You're embarrassing me!" her mother had hissed, shaking her as she stood outside the hospital door where her grandmother had just died.

"But, Grandma... I can't... I miss her."

"You think you're the only one?" Her mother sighed, annoyed, and ran a hand through her hair frustrated. *"Who will watch you now?"*

Pearl wiped her tears. *"I can stay with you. I won't cry. I promise. I won't cry."*

Her mother sighed. *"Crying shows weakness. You can't show weakness."*

Pearl nodded. Inside she was bursting. Her heart was breaking. She wanted to cry, but if she did her mother would send her away. She swallowed the pain. It sat like a rock in her.

"I won't cry. I swear," she'd insisted.

Her grandmother had taken care of her, loved her, and then she had died.

Pearl always wanted that home back. She just didn't know how to get back there. To find something like that again.

And then she found Calum and got pregnant. She was terrified, but secretly she wanted a family. A real family. Maybe she could have and share that love she felt when she was a child and with her grandmother.

Then she had lost the baby. So it was hard to see the bright side, especially after that.

And even though it had been five years, it still stung.

It still felt as fresh as yesterday, but she swallowed that grief like she had when her grandmother died.

"So do you want to go somewhere and get a bite to eat?" he asked, pulling her out of her morose thoughts.

"What?"

"I haven't had lunch, it'll be a late lunch slash early dinner, but do you want to go out and maybe talk about how we're going to approach this case?"

She really shouldn't go out with him.

She should stay here and catch up on her work, but she didn't have a lot of work to do because the team was off today. Her team of capable physiotherapists and kinesiologists were with the athletes today. No one else was injured enough, which was great, but really her only patient was George.

And George had been seen to.

She could go out with him. They had to discuss George's file. It was work and nothing more.

Right.

And she was nervous. Her palms were sweaty as she rubbed her hands together.

"Sure." And she hoped her voice didn't shake It was just business. She had to keep telling herself that.

Calum had made it clear that they were just supposed to be colleagues. She should learn to keep her distance, but colleagues could have a meal together, couldn't they?

Maybe colleagues who didn't have a past like you have with Calum can just have a dinner together.

"Great. I do have some thoughts on George's case and I need your help on some of mine."

Pearl blinked a couple of times as she let that sink in. "Right, because I'm helping you with your caseload."

She was so nervous around him. She had to remind herself to keep calm, cool and collected.

They were here to work.

She had to stop thinking about the past.

"Exactly. We both win here and we're granting you privileges at the hospital, because I'm actually willing to take on George's case."

"And I appreciate that and I'm willing to help." Pearl crossed her arms, hoping by doing so she could hold him off, or at least hold back her emotions, which were threatening to spill out.

He grinned. "So since you're on my service, I would like you to do some time in the hospital."

"You make that sound like a prison sentence." She smiled and relaxed a bit. "I agreed. Just tell me when you want me to be there."

Honestly, she was okay with this option and she was glad that he wasn't doing something foolish, like removing her from George's case. She was quite fine with working shifts at the hospital and assisting on some pro bono cases—because of her job she didn't get to do a lot of surgery. Her practice, with the team, was small and limited to sports injuries. It would be nice to get back into the operating room and do some of the surgeries she didn't often get to do.

Surgeries that had made her want to become an orthopedic surgeon.

The surgeries she excelled at when she was working with Dr. Chin.

There were times she questioned why she had left, but her focus had always been to work with a professional team. That was her goal.

Her grandmother had loved football and they watched it every week. Any time there was a game on, her grandmother liked to take her to tailgate parties.

So working with a professional football team had always been her dream and when she lost the baby it seemed like the time to take the leap and make it happen.

And she didn't want to admit the real reason why she'd left San Francisco. She hadn't wanted to lose Calum. She had been afraid if she stayed things would become worse.

That he'd loathe her, like her parents loathed each other.

When they got together they had both had goals.

Goals that were both completely different, even if they were studying the same medical discipline.

Just like her parents. Her mother blamed her father for holding her back and vice versa.

She had never wanted that for her and Calum.

The thought of him loathing her was too much to even contemplate. So she had left.

Sure, he was cool with her, but they could work together. They were both professionals, both at the top of their fields. They hadn't lost that.

"When did you want me to report to you?" she asked tightly.

"Well, I won't be there, but show up for midnight. We get severe ortho traumas from local hospitals. Sometimes we get a bunch of cases, other nights we don't, but we're on call for them."

"Midnight is fine."

It had been a while since she did a midnight shift, but she'd weather it.

"I'm glad you're on board," Calum said. "So should we go have something to eat and talk business?"

Pearl smiled. "I'd like that."

And she would. That's all she wanted to talk about. Business.

Not the baby. That was still too raw.

Pearl had to put away George's file and make sure her office was locked and that her staff knew where she was going. She liked the idea of grabbing something to eat with Calum, because she wanted to be able to work with him again.

She didn't want there to be any tension between the two of them while they handled George's case. Some of the best times of her life had been when they worked together.

He was smart, talented and so sure of himself, but not in an arrogant way.

It would be good being colleagues again. She'd missed that these last five years.

And truth be told, she missed him. Even though it was for the best and she had given him back his freedom, she had missed him.

She'd always missed him. Always wondered what he'd been doing, so she was looking forward to having this lunch with him and talking about cases, like they used to do.

Being with him had been a bright spot in her life. Having a late lunch and discussing a case would be like the good old days, when they had been friends and worked together.

Those were the days she missed.

And even though she didn't want to admit it, she was lonely.

Loneliness is for the weak, Pearl. Remember that.

Her father's voice droned on in her head. And she felt bad for feeling that emotion. That keen pang of loneliness.

Calum was waiting in the lobby and her heart skipped a beat as she saw that he hadn't left, that it wasn't some sort of ruse, that maybe they could go back to being friends.

And that thought thrilled her. It made her happy.

It also scared her. She took a deep, calming breath before she approached him. She was so used to seeing him in just jeans, a T-shirt and beat-up old sneakers when he wasn't in his scrubs. The last five years and becoming chief of orthopedic surgery had changed him. He was still wearing jeans, but they weren't the same worn ones he always wore. These were pressed and new. They were well taken care of.

He was wearing a T-shirt, but a high-end one that complemented the relaxed sports jacket and there were no sneakers. Instead he wore nice dress shoes. He looked put-together and professional.

Calum took her breath away and she couldn't remember the last time that any man made her feel this way. Calum had been her first and, come to think of it, Calum had been her last.

She'd gone on other dates, but it was never the same.

No one else had made her swoon. Her pulse began to race and she was suddenly so nervous again. She'd forgotten. Forgotten how he made her feel. How he got through all her defenses.

And she was annoyed at herself for still reacting this way.

Get a hold of yourself.

She had to remind herself that she was just here to work. Nothing more. She wasn't here to rehash their relationship.

Calum understood her and she understood him. It

was over between them. It had been over for five years.
She was here to work.

He smiled at her and there were a few more lines at
the corners of his eyes, but he was wearing his late thir-
ties quite well.

"Everything okay?" he asked.

"I just had to make sure my assistant knew where I
was and that I'm not working with any player today and
they're all with my team of physiotherapists. I shouldn't
be paged, but I might be."

Calum nodded. "Well, the place I want to go to isn't
far. In fact, you should remember the little Italian place
near Buena Vista Park."

"It's still there?" Pearl asked, in amazement.

"Yes, Il Polpo Arrabbiato, and the wood-fired pizza
is still the same. It's a gorgeous day and I thought that
was a nice quiet spot to go to strategize. And it's not a
far walk."

"I would like that."

In fact, she liked that quite a bit. It had been one of
their favorite haunts. It was cheap and cheerful.

*"Here's to finishing residency!" She raised her glass
of wine.*

*Calum smiled and clinked his glass with her. "Thank
God!"*

*"And here's to the tackiest place in San Francisco,"
she teased.*

*"That, too." He took a sip of his wine, then set down
the glass and took her hand.*

*A rush, a thrill at his touch, made her blush. He made
her feel safe. She hadn't felt like this in a long time. She
didn't pull her hand away. She moved closer and rested
her head on his shoulder.*

Savoring it.

Savoring the feeling of being held and cared for.

Pearl sighed. She'd forgotten about Il Polpo Arrabbiato.

They spent many a happy time there and going back seemed like they were going home.

Only she wasn't home. She didn't have a home or a family.

All she had was herself.

CHAPTER THREE

IT WAS AN ugly restaurant. Even after five years, it still was an ugly restaurant. Il Polpo Arrabbiato, also known as The Angry Octopus, was an Italian restaurant that was tucked in an old Victorian home that overlooked Buena Vista Park. It was painted a bright orange color and looked a bit out of place and not as stylish as the famous Painted Ladies or the Seven Sisters that were usually featured in San Francisco postcards.

It stood out like a sore thumb, but also seemed to fit in for the street.

Locals were used to the garish home. She hadn't been here in five years, but she'd forgotten how blindingly orange it was.

Even though it was an eyesore it was a wonderful restaurant and a great place to get a piece of wood-fired pizza in the Haight-Ashbury area. She couldn't even really remember how they discovered Il Polpo Arrabbiato.

And then it came back to her, like a sweet memory she hadn't been expecting.

"You'll like this place," Calum had insisted.

"I don't know. It's orange!"

"You said you wanted pizza," he stated firmly. *"This is the best in San Francisco."*

"How? I've lived here my whole life and I've never heard of or seen this place!"

"You grew up near the Presidio. This is my stomping ground."

She cocked an eyebrow. "You grew up in the Mission District. How is Haight your stomping ground?"

"Home sucked. I wandered the city a lot."

She nodded her understanding. Her home sucked, too. "It's an orange house, though, with an octopus on it. How does this serve the best pizza?"

"Trust me."

And she had.

She had a hard time trusting anyone. Her parents' constant broken promises to her left her wary of any kind of trust in anyone, but in that moment she trusted Calum for the first time.

Walking toward the restaurant, Pearl felt like she was stepping back in time.

The last time she'd been here was when they were celebrating the end of their medical boards, the last step to becoming surgeons. It was when they knew they were going to be surgeons. They were done school. It had been her, Calum and their friends Dianne and Jerome.

It had been a great night.

Too many carbs, lots of wine and laughter.

Pearl couldn't remember the last time she let loose like that.

After that night, things got a little crazy. She was pregnant, they were planning to get married and they were trying to plan their careers. They never went back, because there was no time.

It was a bit strange to be back here now. It was a bit surreal. She stopped just before crossing the street and tried to calm all the racing thoughts in her head. All the emotions she seemed to be losing control of. She took a deep breath, trying to slow her racing heart.

"You okay?" Calum asked. He stopped and looked back at her.

"It's been a while," she whispered, hoping that her voice didn't shake and that he didn't sense her emotion. Her cheeks flushed in embarrassment, for letting her control slip in front of him.

Her mother had always told her to never let anyone see your *weak* side. Surgeons needed to be confident and if she wasn't going to be a cardiothoracic surgeon like her parents wanted, then she had to exude confidence and maintain control. She hated that old tape of her mother that played in her head.

Although, Pearl didn't necessarily think it was weakness, but it had been so ingrained in her that she couldn't shake that humiliation that her mother always made her feel when she shed a tear.

"I know. When was the last time we were here?" he asked.

"After our boards," she laughed softly. "We drank a lot of wine that night."

Calum's eyes twinkled. "We did. It was the cheap stuff, too. I had such a hangover the next day."

"I remember," she replied dryly. "You know you can overcome a lot when you hear your significant other be sick, and so loudly."

Calum groaned. "Right. Well, I seem to recall not long after you suffered from morning sickness and it was rough."

She winced. It stung to think about it. She'd thought she had a cold, but it was pregnancy. At first she didn't want any help, but Calum had been there, holding back her hair, bringing her cold cloths and water.

He had always been there. She was the one who left.

"I remember. We never did get back here after that night," she said, trying to change the subject back.

"No. I suppose we didn't," he said wistfully.

Her pulse quickened. She took a step back to center herself.

She shook her head, trying to shake away the remnants of those old times. They were in the past.

"You sure you're okay?" he asked again.

"I'm fine. I think I'm a little shocked that it hasn't changed at all."

"Well, they have a few more octopi decorations inside," Calum stated, grinning.

"So you come here often?" she asked, a bit hurt because she thought that this was *their* place and a really awful side to her couldn't help but wonder who else had been here with him.

Does it matter? You let him go.

Only, it did matter, even if she didn't want to admit it.

"Not that often, but sometimes." There was a hint of sadness in his voice, but only a hint and then it was gone. She understood. She was feeling the same way, but maybe, just maybe, they could have an enjoyable, productive lunch.

She wanted to work with him. Just like the good old days.

Even if things had changed.

"Come on."

She nodded and followed him. They crossed the street and walked inside, where she was blinded by the new octopi decorations. It wasn't just a few. It was like a kraken had come in, had a bunch of babies and left.

They were everywhere. It was tacky. It was trippy and

it seemed completely in place for the Haight-Ashbury neighborhood.

"Goodness, it's like release the kraken or what in here," she muttered under breath.

He chuckled. "Is a kraken even an octopus?"

"I have no idea. It's a mythical creature with tentacles, I think." She smiled to herself. Even though this place was tacky and ugly, she'd forgotten how much she loved this quirky, offbeat place in San Francisco.

They found their old corner booth, but it had changed. It was outfitted with vinyl that resembled tentacles. Purple tentacles, but it was just something stitched into the vinyl and thankfully not real tentacles.

Calum chuckled and as they both slid in on the opposite sides of the booth.

"What?" she asked.

"You look horrified. Don't they have tacky places like this in New York?"

Pearl laughed. "I was trying to hide it."

"Hide what?" he asked.

"My horror," she said quietly.

"You're not doing a good job," Calum whispered.

She leaned over the table, which was painted to look like an eyeball. A big angry krakenesque eyeball staring up at her. It was creepy, but fun. "This place is tackier than I remember."

"It's why they're so popular with tourists. Where else can you have pizza that's themed with angry octopi?"

"I honestly don't know and I'm not sure that I want to find out," she chuckled.

Calum's eyes were twinkling. "Fair enough."

She opened the menu, glad to see a lot of familiar items still graced the pages, and she just hoped that the food hadn't changed that much, either. She was hoping that the pizza didn't have calamari on it or something.

"I know what you're thinking," he said, closing the menu.

"Do you?" she asked.

"You're wondering if the pizza comes shaped like the decor? No, it doesn't. They haven't gone that far. Yet. Don't put it past them, though—they add more octopi stuff all the time."

Pearl laughed. "Perhaps. Actually, I was more concerned that the pizza would come with bits and pieces of the decor."

"Oh, there's one like that. It's the seafood surprise, but the food is still the same."

Pearl wrinkled her nose. "Okay, noted. So, I don't get it."

"What?" Calum asked.

Pearl set down her menu and folded her hands across the menu. "You said that this restaurant hadn't changed."

"Well, there are bits that changed, but the pizza is still good. Even the seafood surprise."

"You've had that?"

Calum shrugged. "One night I was feeling a bit adventurous."

"And?" she asked, trying not to laugh.

"It was not a great experience."

Now, she couldn't help but laugh. It was so easy with Calum. He always knew how to get through her defenses. How to make her happy.

She'd forgotten and that scared her. She couldn't get hurt again. She couldn't let herself get carried away with Calum. It was better for both of them.

She knew she'd hurt him when she left, but it was for the best.

It was for the best.

Was it?

Right now, in this moment, she couldn't remember why she had thought it was best to leave. There were times over the last five years she had thought of coming back, but she had been afraid.

Her parents always made her feel bad about her mistakes and she was afraid of facing this mistake again.

She turned back to her menu, trying to rein in her emotions, her pain. Her heartache.

"You went quiet there," Calum remarked.

"Did I?" she asked, hoping that her voice didn't crack.

"You did."

"It's nothing."

"Pearl, it's clearly something."

She didn't want him digging through her walls. She didn't want to lose control of her emotions again.

"Maybe it is, but you told me you didn't want to discuss it."

"What's that?"

"The baby. Me leaving."

"No. I haven't forgotten and you're right. I don't want to talk about it," he sighed. "I can't."

And she understood. The last thing she wanted to do was make a scene. To lose control.

"Well, I better make a decision on what to eat so we can come up with a plan for George. I have to get back to the training facility soon." Inwardly she cringed. She wanted to talk with him like old times, but he wasn't ready and she wasn't sure she was, either. She was so upset at herself for allowing herself to fall right back into old habits. She thought that the time they spent apart would be enough to cure it all, but it wasn't.

Clearly it wasn't.

* * *

Calum didn't know what had come over Pearl, but one minute it was like the good old days again and then the next, she threw up her wall. And he wasn't comfortable talking about the baby. Not right now.

She hadn't been there for him. He had grieved alone and he wasn't going to talk about it now. She was right. They were here to talk about work and not reminisce about old times. He had to keep it professional with Pearl.

And maybe that was the best thing to do. Except it was so easy to laugh with her. He swore he would keep this professional, but he still cared for her.

If he wanted to keep it professional, he shouldn't have brought her here.

He was kicking himself now for suggesting it. This had been their place. He barely came here anymore. He had once or twice over the years because they did have good pizza and it was in close proximity to his house, but being here was hard.

And it wasn't the garish decor that made it hard.

This is where they came after brutally long shifts, where they vented about the day.

This is where their relationship went from being friends to something more.

He had come here when he wanted that connection with Pearl when she had gone for all those years. It seemed natural and right. They'd discussed so many cases here. It just seemed right to discuss another one.

He lost all sense of reasoning when it came to Pearl and he was just setting himself up for heartache, but there was another part of him, one that remembered how much better life was around her. How much he'd been in love with her. She made him feel like he wasn't alone anymore. Like he could have the family he always wanted.

The memories of their time together...

Those he couldn't shake, couldn't run away from. They were always there and it was that side of his brain that had driven his decision to bring her here.

"Have you chosen?" he asked, curious if she'd choose the same thing she always did.

Hawaiian. Which he found abhorrent because pineapple on a pizza was gross.

"The Hawaiian," she said, closing her menu.

He smiled and shook his head. "Typical."

"What?" she asked.

"Always the same," he teased.

"I'm not as adventurous as you having calamari on a pizza!"

"It wasn't just calamari."

She made a face, her nose wrinkling. "I don't want to know."

He laughed. "I've missed this."

Her expression softened. "I have, too."

Calum reached out to take her hand, but pulled back when the waitress came.

They both ordered, but when the waitress left, the conversation that only moments before had been so free and easy had come to a standstill.

Pearl could barely look at him. Why was this so hard?

They could be friends again. They could work together. They had worked well together. It didn't have to be anything but that, even if, deep down, he wanted it to be.

"I want to do targeted radiation first," Calum said, finally breaking the silence. They were here, after all, to talk about a plan for George. If she wanted to keep it business, then he would keep it that way, too.

It was probably for the best.

It kept him from wanting to talk about what happened all those years ago. It kept him from talking about the baby, about their loss. He didn't want to talk about it now or he'd lose control.

If this working relationship was going to succeed, he had to keep control of his emotions.

"That sounds like a good start."

"It is," he said. "That's why you've come to see me. My protocol has a high success rate."

"But it doesn't always work," she stated.

He pursed his lips together. "Why would you say that? You're so pessimistic sometimes."

Her eyes narrowed. "I'm a realist. You're far too optimistic."

"My optimism has saved lives. People suffering from cancer need all the hope they can get."

Pearl sighed. "Fine. You're right. It does. I know that, but what I want to know is what you'll do if your protocol doesn't work. You don't need to explain the process to me. I know your process and yes, it's why I came to you, but what will you do if it doesn't work?"

Calum swallowed a lump that had formed in his throat. He hated to discuss outcomes—every patient was so different and because of that every patient responded differently. It was a fine balance of medications, of treatments and the patient's DNA, which skewed the results. He didn't like to deal in absolutes, but sometimes, unfortunately there was no other choice.

"I would have to amputate."

Pearl's expression softened. "I hope we can avoid that. I would hate to see George's life ruined."

"I understand," Calum said gently. "But sometimes it's too far gone. Sometimes it doesn't work. If it worked all the time I would have the patent to the cure for cancer and I definitely don't have that, but I try to remain optimistic. I try all that I can before I have to opt to the alternative."

"Which is amputation?" she asked.

He nodded. "Yes. The only way to get rid of osteosarcoma, but I'm trying to be positive that this protocol will work on George. There are many factors that might not make it successful."

"I understand."

"I knew you would. You're a brilliant doctor, Pearl. You did the right thing coming to me and asking for my help."

She smiled, and the hardness in her eyes, the indifference that tainted her expression when she pulled away from him, melted. She let down that wall she always seemed to throw up to keep people out.

This was the Pearl he remembered.

"Well, I hope that it doesn't come to that. I hope your protocol works."

Calum nodded. "So do I. I hope we caught it early enough. Did he say when the symptoms started?"

"Just before he was drafted by the Bridgers. His mother couldn't afford to send him to a good doctor at the time. It was all she could do to take care of his siblings and he was off in college. He was also on a scholarship, so if he did feel anything, he was ignoring it. He had to play in order to stay in college."

Calum scrubbed his hand over his face. "So he could've been ignoring the early symptoms for quite some time then?"

Pearl shrugged. "Maybe, but I'm choosing to believe

him. Although, he didn't come to me with the issues. It was an injury and that's how I found it."

Why were people so stubborn?

It was a cruel twist of fate that George probably had the symptoms for some time and was too scared to do anything about it. His own mother had done the same. She had spent all she had on him and his sister, Sharon. She had been afraid of going to the doctor to find out what she had. She had worried it would cost too much.

She had ignored her symptoms so long it had been too late when she finally did see someone.

George's leg hadn't broken yet, so Calum was hopeful that they caught it early, but he wasn't sure.

"So you were going to tell me about my other duties?" Pearl asked.

"Your other duties?"

She frowned at him. "You said because you're the chief of orthopedic surgery and because I was given special privileges and you were doing this work for the Bridgers that I now work for you. I'm helping you ease your caseload."

He grinned. "That's right. I momentarily forgot about that."

"Well, that's not surprising. Bad seafood, especially bad seafood on a pizza, can really mess with your head." She was teasing him and he couldn't help but smile.

Remember why you're here. Remember what happened last time.

Only, it was hard because of the pain she caused him when she was sitting so close to him, in one of their favorite places, and teasing him like she did five years ago.

His pulse thundered between his ears. She was so close. All he wanted to do was reach out and touch her, to pull her in his arms and kiss her.

After five years, he still wanted her, and he was annoyed that being this close to her affected him like this. So he tried to focus on her leaving.

It was difficult to remember the pain, because he didn't want to.

Because the pain was too much to bear. And he'd had enough pain to last a lifetime. All he wanted was just a bit more of the happiest time of his life. All he wanted was Pearl.

They ate their pizza and talked about George and the other surgeries that Calum had planned. There was a particular spinal surgery that he wanted her help with. She always had a knack for nerves and the regular surgeon he worked with wasn't going to be in town when the patient wanted the surgery done.

They walked back to her training facility so that he could collect his car and go home.

It was awkward walking the streets back to her office. He wanted to take her hand like he always used to, but he couldn't. So he jammed his hands in his pockets again.

"Thanks for the lunch," she said quietly.

"Thank you for helping out tonight."

"Of course. I'm looking forward to it." She smiled and then looked away, her cheeks flushed.

He didn't know what else to say to her and since their lunch was late, the streets were busy with people heading for home. It was rush hour. Thankfully, he didn't live far from the hospital, so it wouldn't take him long to get home to his dog Max, who was probably eagerly awaiting his return so they could head down to Golden Gate Park and have a walk.

"Have you found a place to stay yet?" he asked.

"Yes. I have a small house not too far from here. The

team rented it for me. It's a pretty modern house. Not as stylish as the Seven Sisters, but it's nice and an easy walking distance from the training center. I don't have a car yet." She looked like she wanted to ask him if he was still living in the same place, their old apartment, but he wasn't.

When she had left, it had been too much to bear being there alone without her and without the baby. He much preferred his new house, which happened to be just around the corner from the Seven Sisters.

"I don't live in our old place," he said quickly.

A blush tinged her cheeks and she looked embarrassed. "No, I didn't suppose that you would. That was a very small place in the Mission District."

"Right. I actually own a house, just around the corner from the Painted Ladies. It's a small house and definitely not brightly painted, but Max and I like going to Alamo Square Park."

"Max?" she asked.

"He's my dog. He's a mutt. A rescue. I think he's part sheepdog, because he's black and white, but there's something else in him because he's a big fella." Calum couldn't help but smile thinking about Max.

"I wish I had time for a dog, but I'm always on the move."

"Yes. Well, it's hard to put down roots when you're always running."

Her expression hardened and he knew then that he'd stepped too far.

"Well, I don't really have experience with roots," Pearl said stiffly.

"No. I suppose you don't."

He wasn't sure how they were going to be able to work together when he kept putting his foot in his mouth and then he realized they had made it back to the training facility.

"Well, thank you for the late lunch and again, thank you for taking on George. I should have his lab work to you in a day or so, and let me know when his scans are scheduled."

"I will. And I plan to see you tomorrow around eleven for that surgery I mentioned. The spinal surgery."

"Of course, and I'll be on call tonight. Have a good evening, Calum." She turned her back on him and walked back into the Bridgers' training facility. He just stood there, watching her walk away.

Why did he think that he could do this?

Why did he think that he could work with Pearl again?

He should've said no. He could've asked another surgeon to help with his other cases.

He should've turned her away, but when it came to her, even after five years he was a pushover.

And he was going to pay for his soft heart, and he wasn't sure he could deal with more pain.

CHAPTER FOUR

COFFEE IS GOOD.

She was tired. It had been a long time since she had done an overnight shift and now that she thought of it, it hadn't been since residency days.

She'd done long surgeries—surgeries that had to be done after a game. She'd been on the sidelines when players were taken off the field, but it had been a long time since she sat in an emergency room waiting for orthopedic injuries because the hospital was only sent severe cases. It was quiet tonight, which made the time drag on and on.

There had been some post-op patients that had been filtered through, but that was about it. Though she wouldn't comment on the quiet activity. That was a jinx waiting to happen.

"Look alive, Henderson!"

Pearl sat up and relaxed when she saw it was Calum in his scrubs. He was grinning and his eyes were twinkling mischievously.

"I thought you were off tonight?" she remarked.

"I was, but I felt bad. Your first night back and I left you on your own."

"I've done this before, you know," she teased. "But I appreciate you checking up on me."

"Solidarity and all that." He leaned over the desk. "The spinal fusion is booked for eleven. No point in going home since your done at four. You remember where the on-call rooms are?"

Warmth crept up her cheeks. She remembered vividly where they were and what happened in one. She remembered one particularly heated stolen moment. His hands on her skin.

His kisses, his caresses, the pleasure.

And just recalling the way it felt to be in his arms made her blood heat. It didn't help he was standing so close to her, wearing the same color scrubs he wore that night.

Don't think about it.

She cleared her throat, trying to break the nervous tension. "Yes. And I'll be ready for the spinal fusion. I'm looking forward to it."

"Good."

The phone rang at the desk and Calum leaned over to answer the call. His arm brushed hers and a tingle of electricity went through her. Just that simple touch made her body zing with need.

"Right. We'll be ready. How far out? Okay." He hung up the phone.

"What's up?"

"Accident. Severe crush injuries. A transport rolled over on a pickup truck."

Her eyes widened. "And the truck driver is the one with the crush injuries?"

Calum nodded. "It's his right side. Bones crushed, possible nerve damage. You think you're up for the challenge?"

"Yeah. How far out?"

"Ten minutes."

She stood. "Let's go."

Pearl followed Calum to the ambulance bay, where he helped her into a trauma gown and gloves. Her adrenaline was pumping. It had been a while since she was here, in this situation.

And a really long time since she'd worked with Calum.

The siren grew louder as the ambulance came closer, until it was in their bay and the doors of the rig opened.

"Massive trauma from that pileup. San Francisco General thinks this guy would be better off here with you, Dr. Munro," the paramedic said.

Calum nodded. "Anyone else they need to send, we'll take them."

The paramedic nodded and Pearl helped as they unloaded the patient. Pearl could see the damage to the right side of the patient's body, even just from a quick glance.

And the way the man's hand was, she wasn't sure how much could they save.

"Vitals are good," Calum said.

"CT scan was done at San Francisco General. No serious injuries to the vital organs," the paramedic said. "Kind of amazing."

"Yeah, for sure." Pearl helped push the gurney in.

"We need to get him up to the OR floor," Calum said. "Dr. Henderson, can you go over the file with the paramedic and meet me on the operating-room floor?"

Pearl nodded. "Of course."

Calum motioned to a couple of residents as they took away the trauma patient. He used to complain to her of being a control freak, but he was *just* as addicted to work as she was. He told her that work kept his mind off of things and he always kept busy.

She understood and respected that.

She worked to be the best, to please her parents, which over time she learned not to care too much about.

"Here's his file, doctor," the paramedic said. "All the information from San Francisco General."

"Thanks."

The paramedic nodded and returned to his rig.

Pearl glanced at the images. So much damage, yet his spine was intact and his major organs unharmed. She closed the file. It was going to be a long night, but it was these kind of challenges that had driven her to orthopedic surgery, much to her parents' disappointment. Neither of them felt like she should do this specialty.

Of course, she'd never been able to please them. Right now, none of that mattered.

But tonight she'd save a life. Tonight she'd do the best she could and give this patient a chance.

It had been a grueling surgery and Calum needed a few hours of sleep before his scheduled spinal decompression. He wouldn't have been able to handle that trauma without Pearl at his side.

There had been so much damage and Pearl had been right there beside him, working with him, and he didn't have to explain anything to her, like he did to the residents. He'd forgotten what it was like to work with her.

When they worked together she always knew the next move. She was a talented surgeon and he wanted this kind of talent on his staff.

They were able to save the man's arm and hand. The patient's hip needed to be replaced, but the pelvis was cracked and needed time to heal.

There would be more surgeries on their trauma patient, named John, but not tonight.

John's body had been through enough.

He stifled a yawn and closed the door quietly to the darkened on-call room. He knew Pearl was in here and he didn't want to wake her.

"You don't need to creep. I'm awake," she said in the darkness.

"Why aren't you asleep? You sound tired."

"I was wondering how John was."

"Stable. Vitals are good."

"Good." She yawned—he heard it and yawned, too.

"Don't. Yawns are contagious," he teased.

She chuckled softly. "I know. Sorry. I can't help it."

He sat on the bed across from hers. In the dim light coming through the blinds, he could sort of see her.

Barely, though.

He knew she was sitting cross-legged, her back to the wall.

And it was like that night five years ago when they locked the door and made love for the first time. His blood heated thinking of that night, of being with her.

"The beds are still uncomfortable," she remarked. "Have they changed at all since I left?"

"I doubt it."

"You should do something about that."

"I'm head of orthopedics, not chief of surgery."

"Not yet. Wasn't that your goal?" she asked.

"One day." It had been his goal to prove to his father he was a hard worker. That he deserved more than his father gave him. Except in five years, he realized it didn't matter. His father only doled out attention when it suited him.

Calum was tired of chasing after him.

After Pearl.

His stomach twisted in a knot.

"I'm going to try and get some sleep. Good work to-night, Pearl. It was good to work with you again."

"Same, Calum. Same."

Calum lay there in the dark listening to her breathing, until it went from light to deep, when he was sure she was asleep.

He rolled over on his back, still listening to her, and closed his eyes.

All he could see was that moment after they had made love. The two of them curled up on the small bed, their bodies pressed tight together, his arms around her as he listened to her sleep.

It didn't feel right to be so far away and it took every ounce of strength not to get up and go to her.

To hold her.

I've got to get out of here.

Calum got up and tiptoed to the door. He paused and watched her for a moment while she slept. He kneeled down beside her and lightly touched her face.

Her skin was so soft. Just like he remembered.

Leave now.

He left the on-call room He'd sleep in his office. He had to put some distance between himself and Pearl before he lost all sense of reason and curled up next to her.

Pearl woke up and expected to find Calum there, but he wasn't. She knew he'd left because the moment she mentioned his old desire to become chief of surgery it grew awkward. He tensed up. She knew that they were both circling around the issue. How they both still cared for each other. She thought their years apart were enough time to get over him. They weren't.

He'd remembered that night in the on-call room, too,

and she was glad she was so exhausted that she was able to fall asleep fast.

Maybe she should've tried to find another surgeon for George, but George was such a good kid and he deserved the best chance for recovery, and his best chance just happened to be Dr. Calum Munro.

Working with him on that trauma case just reaffirmed that coming to Calum was the best decision she could have made for George.

Pearl slept, but she felt like she spent the whole time in the on-call room tossing and turning. She couldn't get Calum out of her head. How good it was to work together on John and how every inch of this hospital reminded her of her heartache and her loss, but also the best times of her life.

She missed it here.

She missed those times, her friends, the companionship, the job.

The baby.

Calum.

She couldn't stop thinking about how easy it was with him. How quickly they fell back into old habits and teasing, but she also remembered the times they argued. When they'd disagree during their residency.

When they worked together it ran hot and cold. Pearl knew first-hand what that was like. She had grown up with two parents who were constantly at each other's throats. One minute they were toe-to-toe screaming at each other and the next minute they were locked in a passionate embrace.

Of course, they were also having lots of passionate embraces with other people outside of their marriage vows.

At least she'd never done that, but Pearl didn't want passion. Not like that.

That toxic volatile passion her parents had. It made her ashamed so she never talked about it. No one really asked, anyway. She said she came from a broken home and that was enough explanation.

Her parents' ridiculous marriage didn't need to be broadcast.

She wanted something else. Passion yes, but camaraderie, friendship. She wanted what she had with Calum, but she'd ruined that.

She groaned inwardly, frustrated that all she could suddenly think about was the first time they kissed, because that first time they kissed had lit some kind of spark inside her, one that had never been lit before.

And then that kiss led to a lot more.

And then, eventually, heartache, but she couldn't get Calum out of her head. And after being with him today, joking with him and talking with him, it was just so easy to fall back into those old routines.

Which she didn't want, but also she really did. Deep down.

So now, because of her restless night, she was walking into the attending lounge, tired and hoping that there was still that awful, black, strong coffee there. Dr. Chin used to refer to it as motor oil and she could use a couple of cups of that before she went into surgery with Calum. Especially before she went into a surgery that was going to take hours, which meant hours and hours of working with Calum.

Even though she was tired and worried about seeing Calum again, part of her was actually excited about the thought of performing surgery with him. That was another thing they were good at. They were good in the operating room together and she hoped that they would be again.

When she got to the doctors' lounge she was thrilled to see that Dr. Chin's motor oil was still there. She smiled and pulled a mug out of the cupboard, ready to pour herself a big coffee.

"Calum told me you were back, but I didn't quite believe it!"

Pearl turned around and smiled when she saw a familiar face standing in the doorway.

"Dianne! I didn't know you were still here! I thought you and Jerome bought a ranch outside of the city!"

Pearl was surprised to see her old friend, Dr. Dianne Lopez. She was another resident who had come up with her and Calum but worked with anesthesia. She had married Jerome before Pearl left, and the last she'd heard they had bought a ranch just outside of Sonora, California.

She gave Dianne a big hug. She was overcome with emotion. Her heart swelled and it was all she could do to contain the emotions overcoming her.

Dianne had been her first *real* girlfriend.

And though they kept in touch it was never the same as getting a hug in person. And she hadn't seen Dianne or Dianne's son Derek in a long time. Not since Derek was a little baby.

Dianne stepped back and smiled. "It's so good to see you. You haven't changed a bit in five years."

Pearl snorted. "I find that hard to believe."

Dianne laughed. "You look good."

"So do you. How is Derek?"

"Good," Dianne said, sitting down. "We're almost finished our full transition from San Francisco to Sonora.

Jerome has a practice out there. He switched specialties from being an anesthesiologist and is a family doctor."

"Wow, good for him. How long of a commute is it from your place to here?" Pearl asked as she sat next to her on the couch.

"It's two and a half hours on a good day. This is actually my last couple of days work here at this hospital and then I'm transferring to one in Sonora."

"So the move is almost permanent then?" Pearl asked, disappointed, but she knew that it had always been Dianne and Jerome's dream to own a big piece of land out in the country and raise kids. They had made it work.

And Pearl was a bit envious of that. Even though she tried to tell herself she had never wanted a family, even though her mother told her being tied down with a family ruined her career and even though Pearl was afraid it would never work out, she still wanted that.

What she would never have.

"My last day is tomorrow. I am taking some time off before I start my new position. I start that in the New Year."

"It sounds wonderful. I'm so happy for you. Sad that I move back to San Francisco and you're leaving."

Dianne smiled sadly. "I know, but you know this is what Jerome and I always wanted and we were finally able to make it happen."

"At least I get to work with you for a few more days." Pearl finished the coffee and winced.

"Yeah, it's still pretty bad. I can't believe that you and Calum drink that crap."

"Drink what?"

Pearl tried not to choke on her coffee when Calum walked in. Her heart skipped a beat when she saw him and she hoped that she wasn't blushing. He'd occupied her mind all night and she hadn't had enough coffee yet to deal with seeing him.

"That motor oil that Dr. Chin drank." Dianne shook her head. "It was awful."

Calum chuckled and poured himself a mug. He glanced at Pearl briefly, but just briefly, like she was an afterthought.

"It's fuel," he responded.

"Yeah, and I bet it could fuel a car!" Dianne stood up. "Well, I'm going to ready the patient for the surgery."

Calum nodded. "Okay. We'll be down soon. I want to catch Pearl up on the surgery."

Dianne nodded and then gave her another quick hug, which calmed her nerves. "It's so good to see you again."

"Same." Pearl hoped that her voice didn't crack and betray her nerves, but she was glad that Dianne was going to be in the operating room. She didn't have too many friends from her residency days, but Dianne and Jerome were always friendly faces.

So was Calum's.

She shook away that thought and tried to finish the coffee, but Dianne was right—it was so bitter, so awful. She was used to drinking nicer stuff in New York. Lattes and cappuccinos. Stuff with artisanal foam, not stuff that was bubbling long after it was boiling.

"I'm glad to see you haven't given up the old tradition of having coffee before a surgery," Calum said offhandedly.

"If you can call this coffee." Pearl winced again and set down the mug. "I was actually looking forward to it when I first came in here. I think I remembered it fondly with nostalgia and now…"

"Yes?" he asked.

"Yeah, nostalgia and fond memories have betrayed me."

"First the uncomfortable beds and now the coffee. New York has made you soft." He was teasing her.

"You look tired."

He had dark circles under his eyes, but he still looked good.

He nodded. "Didn't sleep well last night."

"I did." *Eventually.*

He chuckled. "I'm glad you're able to help me today. Especially after last night."

"A promise is a promise. So where did you sleep?" she asked.

His eyes widened—she'd caught him off guard. "I thought you were asleep?"

"I'm a light sleeper."

"Since when?" he asked.

"For a year or so. Also, those mattresses suck. So where did you sleep?"

He chuckled. "Which is why I slept on the couch in my office."

"Lucky."

"Not really. The couch fits two people, sitting upright. It's not long enough to lie flat. Hence the coffee."

"Great. Since when did we get too old for all-nighters?" she teased.

"I don't know. And I'm not old."

"I feel old this morning," she groused, trying to stretch.

"Hardly."

Warmth flood her cheeks and her stomach did a flip in anticipation. She cleared her throat. "So today's surgery?"

He nodded. "So today's surgery is a spinal decompression, but on a patient with achondroplasia and I remember that was one of your first solo surgeries."

Pearl smiled, secretly pleased he remembered. "That's right. I haven't done a spinal decompression in some time. Usually, my surgeries involve torn ligaments in the knee or shoulder. Anything to do with running or throwing."

"Well, this patient has had hip replacements done and knees done, but he's an actor and he slipped and fell during a stage performance. He didn't break his back, but something snapped and a disc in his cervical spine became impinged. Because of his achondroplasia the space was already narrow and now it's threatening to impinge the spinal cord. I'm hoping to do a decompression and not have to fuse the spine, but I may have to. I won't know until we get in there."

"You realize that he's going to have issues with airways and bleeding?"

Calum nodded. "Yes, and that's why I insisted that Dianne was our anesthesiologist. She's the best and she's done multiple surgeries on achondroplasia and skeletal dysplasia patients. They are difficult to get an airway and to maintain an airway. I want the best working on him, which is why I'm glad you're here. He's one of my top patients."

Warmth flooded her cheeks at his compliment. "I'm glad that I can help."

It felt nice he was complimenting her. It felt good to be appreciated by a fellow surgeon. Especially one she respected.

One she cared about.

Calum chugged back the rest of his coffee. "Well, we

better get down there. I'll show you where you can get some fresh surgical scrubs."

Pearl nodded. "Thank you."

She wouldn't mind changing out of the disheveled scrubs.

"Do you remember where the surgical floor is or do I have to walk you down there?" Calum teased as he stood up to leave. "Last night was a blur."

"I think I can find my way down to the surgical floor. I will be there in ten minutes."

Calum nodded and made his way to the door, only to turn back. "I scheduled George to have scans this evening. I'm hoping that we'll be done the surgery by then, but spinal decompressions can take a while."

"I don't need to be there while George has a scan. His mother is in town now and he has his coach. I would like to see the scans as soon as they're done, though."

Calum nodded. "I'll let our radiologist know. I'll see you down there."

Pearl breathed a sigh of relief when Calum left. She found her locker and inside was a set of scrubs. She quickly changed out of the scrubs she slept in into the familiar colored scrubs that she remembered wearing when she worked here.

"Hey," Dianne said, coming back into the doctor's lounge.

Pearl was surprised. "Hey, I thought you were with the patient?"

"He had some more questions for Calum before he would let me even put an intravenous in, so I thought I would come back here and ask you a question."

Pearl braced herself for a personal question. Dianne knew that she and Calum had planned to get married before Pearl had lost the baby. She was hoping that Dianne wouldn't try to dig any further.

Dianne had been pregnant with her first the same time that Pearl had been pregnant, and Derek was the same age her child would have been.

It was why she only kept in touch with Dianne through emails. It was sometimes hard to know Dianne and Jerome were so happy with their son while also knowing that if she hadn't lost her child, she would be a mother to a five-year-old, too.

"What do you need to know?" Pearl asked hesitantly.

"What're you doing next weekend?"

"Next weekend?" Pearl asked, confused.

"Are you going to see your parents?"

A ball of dread formed in the pit of her stomach. Her parents would want to see her, since she moved back, but she didn't want to see them. She hadn't seen them in two years and that was fine by her.

"No. I won't be going to see them. I'll be here in San Francisco. Maybe I'll catch up on some work."

"You don't have to be on call for the Bridgers?" Dianne asked.

"No," Pearl said, confused. "They're not playing that weekend. What are you trying to get at, Dianne?"

"Since I haven't seen you in forever and you're back in the area I want you to come out to the ranch next weekend. Jerome wants to show off his new practice to you."

Pearl smiled. It was a nice offer, but she wasn't sure that she wanted to spend next weekend with a happy family. Then again, she really didn't want to be alone.

"It's an awesome offer, can I think about it?"

Dianne nodded. "Of course. I know I'm springing it on you, but when I texted Jerome that you were here and I had seen you…he got so excited. The four of us used to be inseparable."

A lump formed in her throat. "I know. I'll think about it."

Dianne smiled. "Good. I'll see you down there."

Dianne left and Pearl leaned against the open door of her locker. She would love to go and spend time with Dianne and Jerome, but it was Dianne's comment about how the four of them had been inseparable.

It was true.

They'd spent a lot of time together as two couples when she and Dianne had been pregnant together.

It was sort of like a dream. That moment in her life when she was happy and she almost had it all.

One that she had never expected and one that she still mourned the loss of.

She couldn't go to Dianne and Jerome's ranch.

Why not?

The other alternative was to spend her weekend off alone. She had no desire to visit her parents. Her mother was in Los Angeles and her father was in Seattle. She could fly to one of their places. Each of them had begged her to come and see them more often, but Pearl had a hard time facing them and the toxicity both of them spewed.

Their relationship was the reason why Pearl really didn't believe in happily-ever-afters. She tried to believe in forever and happiness, but that had turned out so painful.

Of course, there were exceptions, like Dianne and Jerome, who honestly seemed to be happy and had been together for a long time. Now they were living out the dream they always talked about.

It hit her hard that she really didn't have any dreams.

She didn't know what she wanted out of life, other than being a surgeon, which she had become.

She sighed and shook her head, trying to dispel her disappointment, her grief. There was no place for those thoughts here today. Today she had to be that surgeon that she had become. That was the only good thing in her life.

She was a surgeon and she knew how to save a life.

Just not her own, apparently.

Pearl glanced up a couple of times to see Calum standing on the opposite side of the operating table. Their patient was in the prone position to access the spine.

It was always tricky with a patient who had skeletal dysplasia because it was difficult to get a proper airway, but Dianne was good at her job.

It was good to be in the operating room again and working on something that was not a sports injury.

Well, not technically a sports injury. The patient was an actor and had insisted on doing his own stunts, which was why they were trying to decompress the spine. She assisted Calum in the delicate surgery, but he was the lead surgeon.

And it had been far too long since she'd worked with him on a surgery. She had forgotten what a talented surgeon he was and it just reinforced her decision to have him work with George.

Calum was George's best chance.

As if sensing she was watching him, he briefly glanced up. His eyes crinkled at the corners and she knew he was smiling behind the mask.

"How does it feel to be doing a decompression again, Dr. Henderson?" he asked from behind his mask.

"It's great to be back." And it was, she just forgot

herself there for a moment. "It's a pleasure to be working with you again, Dr. Munro. I had forgotten what a talented surgeon you were."

And it was the truth. Coming back here and working with Calum was like coming home.

His blue eyes crinkled again and she hoped that was a smile and not a grimace behind his surgical mask.

"Ditto," he responded.

"Ditto?" she teased.

He chuckled as he continued to work. "Yes. Ditto."

Pearl smiled to herself. "Your compliments embarrass me, Dr. Munro." She did enjoy his compliments, but she also forgot how fun it was to banter with him back and forth across the table.

He cocked an eyebrow. "You haven't changed a bit. Can we focus?"

"I am focusing," she responded. "Or have you forgotten that I do idle chitchat during surgery. Especially when I think that surgery is going smoothly."

"I did forget," he responded dryly.

There were a few small laughs from the nurses and interns who were observing the surgery. Even Dianne was laughing a bit.

"I take it then you haven't changed and you still want almost absolute silence while you're working."

"I prefer that. Yes," Calum said. "Of course, being taught by Dr. Chin, I learned to work in noise."

Pearl smiled again. Dr. Chin had the propensity to blast music—in particular, Queen—especially when he was doing delicate procedures. It was when the patient wasn't doing well that the operating room fell silent, so the silence in Calum's room was making her a bit uncomfortable.

"So why don't we put some music on in here? The patient is responding well," she said.

"Do you blast music?" Calum asked.

"In fact, I do. I guess I adopted Dr. Chin's style."

Calum chuckled again. "I never really thought of a surgical playlist before."

"I've read studies that if music is playing it actually can help with blood pressure."

Calum cocked an eyebrow and looked at her in disbelief. "What?"

"I'll forward you that report." Pearl suctioned where some blood was pooling and it was then she saw that this was no longer a simple spinal decompression.

"Dammit," Calum muttered. "Do you see that?"

"Yes, it's wearing away at the spinal cord. There's no room for the decompression to go."

"I'm going to have to fuse him." Calum began to pull out the instruments and moved quickly to change his plan. "The patient didn't want a fusion, because a spinal fusion is going to take more time to heal and there will be more physiotherapy for him. He was pretty specific about not wanting a fusion because of his work."

"There's no choice in this case. Unless he wants to be a paralyzed."

Calum nodded. "Yep. No choice."

They both worked quickly, turning the spinal decompression surgery. And Pearl was glad to work with Calum. They had been trained by the same brilliant surgeon and even though they hadn't done a surgery together in five years, it was like they'd never been apart. There were no questions, there was no confusion. They worked together seamlessly.

It was like they were one.

And it felt right.

* * *

The surgery took longer than Calum planned. He knew that Pearl wanted to be there for George when he had his scan. In fact, there was a call into the operating room as they were working on the fusion. Pearl had been pulled away and he thought that she was going to walk away from their surgery for her high-paying VIP patient.

Really, she had no investment in staying and he could handle a spinal fusion on his own, but Pearl returned.

She told him that she'd explained to George's coach why she couldn't be there and George had no problem with her not accompanying him to the MRI. He'd had MRIs before. So when the surgery was finished, Pearl left before they closed up his patient, so that she could check the scans and Calum had no problem with that.

He was impressed and glad that her priorities still seemed to be the same. Saving lives.

He thought when she left for that job out east with that first sports team, that he'd been wrong about her from the beginning. He'd thought the most important thing to was her job. Pearl had always talked about her parents putting career and the almighty dollar before family. Just like his father.

He was hurt and disappointed that she ran off and did that, but perhaps he'd been wrong about. She didn't go running off to babysit George. She'd stayed and done the surgery with him and she'd been a tremendous help to him. Maybe he was wrong about her and that thought upset him, because then he was the fool for letting her go.

Calum had forgotten what it was like to work with her.

It was like coming home.

Don't think like that.

He shook away that thought.

He couldn't let himself associate Pearl with home. Not that he really knew what home was. He'd thought he'd found that once, and when she left he hadn't really associated anything with home since. Other than his dog, Max.

After the patient was taken to the intensive-care unit and he updated the family, Calum made his way down to radiology to see if Pearl was still there and he saw that she was.

She was sitting in a darkened room, in front of a computer, hunched over, and she appeared stressed. She was frowning and worrying her bottom lip and he knew that expression well. It was the same expression when she broke the news that she was pregnant to him, but it wasn't the same expression when she told him she'd lost the baby.

That expression had been without emotion. It was flat, cold and detached. Like she was lost. Only he'd been lost, too, in that moment, but he felt like he didn't have the right to feel so lost. He hadn't been the one carrying the baby, but he still grieved their loss just the same. Even when he thought about her like that, he wanted to hold her in his arms and comfort her, but he was sure that she would push him away just like she'd done all those years ago.

"Thanks for your help," he said gently from the doorway.

She tore her eyes from the computer screen and seemed momentarily surprised to see him standing there.

"What?"

"Your help with the patient and the spinal fusion."

She relaxed. "Right. No problem. It was good working with you again."

"Why are you still here? You should go home and rest."

"Can't. Stuff came up," she said, not looking at him.

"You seemed entranced by the computer. Is it George's scans?" he asked.

She nodded and he pulled up a chair beside her so that he could see the scans. The moment he saw them, a coil of dread unfurled in his belly.

It was the most extensive osteosarcoma he'd seen. And compared to the last scans done, not that long ago, it had grown. And now he was having a bad feeling that he might not be able to save the leg.

That he might fail at this and let down Pearl and George. His father had let down his mother and Calum didn't want to let down Pearl.

He didn't want to be like his father.

Aren't you? You're so focused on work.

He shook away that thought and studied the images.

"It's extensive," he said quietly.

"It's bad. I've never seen one grow this fast," Pearl whispered. "It's…awful."

"And what would you tell him?" Calum asked seriously.

"What do you mean what would I tell him?"

"If you were the surgeon?"

Pearl sighed and scrubbed a hand over her face. "I would say that amputation is the only course of treatment. If it were me, but I haven't worked on enough osteosarcomas. I haven't developed a plan, an award winning aggressive treatment of osteosarcoma like you have."

"Pearl, don't pin all your hopes on me." And he was serious. This cancer was dangerous, it was the most aggressive he'd seen in a long time.

The last time he had seen something like this was just after Pearl left, when he worked as much as he could with Dr. Chin. Work kept him busy and kept his mind off the loss of both Pearl and the baby.

It was on a teenage boy.

The osteosarcoma had been just like this. Calum had been full of hope that they could save the leg, but by the end there was no way he could. After multiple surgeries and lots of pain for the young man, they still had had to amputate.

It was then that Dr. Chin told him that sometimes the best help they could give someone, especially with a terminal diagnosis, was to do no harm.

Calum didn't want to accept that, but over the years, he has learned that Dr. Chin was right and sometimes there was nothing to be done.

Only, it was that sense of helplessness that drove him to work on his treatment plan for situations like this. And that boy might have lost his limb, but he was still alive and cancer-free.

Pearl then reached out and took his hand. It surprised him and he couldn't push away her hand, because he liked the reassurance she was giving him.

It felt good.

It felt so right.

"I have faith in you, Calum. I think you can do this."

"You're wrong." Her eyes widened and he squeezed her hand. "We can do this together."

And he couldn't believe that he was saying that.

Pearl nodded. "Okay. We'll tackle this together. I'm eager to learn from you."

She took back her hand and there was a pink blush in her cheeks, and it took every ounce of his strength not to take her in his arms and reassure her that everything was going to be okay. That they could do this together, even though he wasn't sure of that.

Working with her in the operating room had given him a false sense of hope and he thought perhaps that nothing had changed between the two of them, but he was wrong. Everything had changed between them and he had to keep reminding himself of that fact.

Maybe they could start again? That thought scared him. He wasn't sure he could take that chance.

Calum cleared his throat and stood. He wanted to put some distance between them.

"Is George still here?" he asked.

"No. He went back to his place with his mom. I figured we needed to come up with a plan and we could present it to him. I mean, we tried to strategize at The Angry Octopus, but that really didn't work out too well."

"No. It didn't. And there's lots I have to catch you up on. We can try dinner again, but somewhere that's new. Somewhere we don't have any ties to. Somewhere colleagues go all the time and we can work out a plan. Unless you're too tired after that spinal fusion."

He was feeling a bit tired from that surgery, which at six hours had taken longer than he had thought.

"That sounds good. I just want to go home and change."

"I can pick you up."

What're you doing?

Only he knew that she didn't have a vehicle and it was the gentlemanly thing to do.

"Sure." Only her tone didn't sound so sure. "I'll text you my address."

Calum nodded. "About eight? I'm sure I can find a place we can have a late dinner and I'll send you some information about the procedure, and we can go from there."

Pearl nodded. "That sounds good. I'll see you at eight."

Calum nodded and quickly left. He had gone to find Pearl, determined to keep his distance from her, but somehow had made dinner plans with her. What was wrong with him? Why was it when he was around her he forgot all sense?

She got under his skin.

Maybe that's where she'd always been.

CHAPTER FIVE

PEARL WAS STILL in shock that Calum had suggested dinner. She was nervous, but almost secretly pleased.

She didn't care what restaurant. She was just hoping to have a nice meal with a friend.

Is he just a friend?

There was a part of her that didn't think so. She still cared for Calum, but she had ended things between them, and he had made it clear they were just colleagues.

You should have said no.

Only, she had found herself agreeing. She genuinely wanted to learn from Calum and discover his procedures. He had such a high success rate and she had been feeling positive about the whole situation with George after his previous scan, but now she wasn't feeling so sure.

The new scan had terrified her to the very core.

She'd seen osteosarcomas like that and Dr. Chin always amputated, but medicine had come a long way and Calum had had so many successes.

She admired him for that.

She was envious that he was able to forge a new path. What had she done?

You ran away from your feelings, remember?

That's what she did. She'd taken the job offer her father had pressured her to take numerous times and if she was going to waste her surgical career on becoming an orthopedic surgeon over a neurosurgeon or a cardiothoracic surgeon, then she might as well become a private surgeon to a big-league team.

And that's what she'd done.

There was part of her that wanted to leave the job, even though it had been her goal when she became a doctor because she loved the sport, but she couldn't leave. She loved working with the players. They made her feel like part of the team. Their triumphs felt like hers.

When a player returned to the game after she helped them through an injury, it was so satisfying.

She clung to that because the memory of leaving Calum and losing the baby was too much.

The idea of facing Calum was too much. She'd let him down. And that was a punch to the gut. Every instinct of her was telling her to run.

She was terrified for George. What if this didn't work? What would happen?

You are pessimistic.

And she sighed. Calum was right. She was far too negative.

She had to think positively for George's sake. There was no running from this.

She didn't want to let down George. The team was relying on her. George was relying on her and so was Calum.

Pearl was going to learn from Calum.

She was going to show Calum that she was a damn fine surgeon, too, even if he thought she took the easy way out and left for the lucrative position.

Pearl took a deep calming breath and opened her email to read through the information that Calum had sent her. Tonight at dinner she didn't want to talk about the good old days, she didn't want to reminisce. He had promised her this dinner would be between two colleagues and they would be discussing George and George's care only.

Of course, they'd made promises like that before.

"We're only supposed to study for the boards!" Calum had said as he took the shot from her.

"We are studying for the boards. Look, we both have this down pat and you said that I couldn't drink you under the table, so I think that for every wrong answer we take a shot."

Calum laughed. *"You're crazy."*

"I know, but you know you're the one that was spouting off how you had an iron-clad stomach. So prove it!"

"I know that I do," Calum teased. *"You're the one who lost her cool at the board of director's dinner and got up to sing a really bad rendition of that song from... some Broadway musical."*

Pearl laughed. *"I'm a good singer."*

Calum had raised an eyebrow. *"I can assure you that no hills were alive with the sound of music that night. More like the sound of cat caught in an engine."*

Pearl smiled as that memory flitted through her mind.

That foolish drinking game had turned into something more and her blood heated as she thought of that first kiss. That first kiss had made her think of him constantly and then she kissed him again in that on-call room five years ago and that second kiss led to another and another. She closed her eyes and gingerly touched her lips, remembering the feeling of his lips against hers.

No man had ever made her feel that way before and

she knew deep down no one ever would, because she wasn't going to open her heart again.

She wasn't going to go through all that pain.

Her life was her career.

And that was it. That was what she'd been taught. Surgery, her medical degree, never let her down.

Pearl sighed and tried to read through the information. She tried to focus on anything that wasn't Calum, but he was like a ghost, haunting her. Always in her thoughts.

Her phone rang and she answered it. "Hello?"

"Pearl?" her mother asked, and Pearl groaned inwardly. Usually she screened her calls from her mother or father. She would call them back when she was able to handle them. When she was able to talk to them and could devote the emotional energy it took to have a conversation with them. But her parents were both narcissists and the conversations were usually one-sided.

"Mom, what can I do for you?" Because that was usually the thrust of the conversation—what Pearl could do for her.

"You're not even going to ask me how I am?" her mother asked indignantly. "I thought I taught you better manners than that."

"Mom, you called me, shouldn't you be asking how I am?"

There were a few moments of silence and Pearl tried not to smile, throwing her mother off on one of her tangents.

"Pearl, I know you're back on the West Coast and I want you to come see me. You have been avoiding me for years. You had the excuse that you were on the East Coast, but you're back here now."

Pearl groaned inwardly. "Mom, I thought you detested guests. They messed with your surgical schedule."

"You're going to visit your father's, aren't you? You always liked him more," she snapped, avoiding Pearl's statement.

"Mom, I'm not a child. I'm a grown woman. And a surgeon."

"I'm a surgeon, too, Pearl."

Pearl sighed. "I can't come to see you, Mom. I have an extensive case with one of my athletes and I work for a football team now. Autumn is a busy time for the team."

"Extensive case?" her mother asked, piqued.

"Osteosarcoma on a player."

"That's not extensive. You amputate," her mother stated matter-of-factly.

"Mom, you're a cardiothoracic surgeon. Amputation isn't always the solution, like a heart transplant isn't always the solution."

"Every surgeon worth their salt knows that an extensive osteosarcoma can only be truly cured by amputation."

Pearl rolled her eyes and was glad that she wasn't on a video chat with her mother. "I'm working with a surgeon who has developed an intervention. In fact, he won the MSA."

"You're working with Dr. Calum Munro?" her mother asked, impressed. "I didn't know that you knew him."

Seriously, Mom?

She was impressed by Calum's career in orthopedic surgery, but not hers. "Mom, I was engaged to him five years ago. You met him," Pearl said dryly.

"*That's* Dr. Calum Munro who won the MSA?"

"Yes," Pearl said, exasperated. "He's also the man you advised me not to marry. You were quite happy when our engagement ended."

"I never understood why you got engaged in the first place," her mother said, ignoring the obvious facts that Pearl was pointing out. "I've told you time and time again it interferes with your surgical career. If you hadn't been so focused on him five years ago you could've won the MSA by now."

Unbelievable.

This was why Pearl had never told her parents that she was pregnant and lost the child. She had planned to tell them eventually, but she knew they would have said that it was a mistake and that she was throwing away her career. Once she lost the baby, she never saw the need to tell them any different.

It was hers to bear.

She didn't want to share that with her parents. To share that with them would taint it. It would mean sharing her dreams, her longing for the baby, and they would make it something it wasn't. They would try to undermine it, undermine her grief.

Her grandmother had taught her, had given her the taste of a loving, supportive family. How her father came from such a caring woman, she had never understood, but it was because of her grandmother that she wanted a family.

A real family.

And if her mother or father knew what she wanted they would make her feel like she was a fool.

And she wasn't going to let them in. She wasn't going to do that. She wasn't a fool for wanting love and a career.

"It doesn't matter now, does it?" Pearl said, annoyed. "Mom, I have to go. I have dinner plans. A business dinner."

"Fine. Well, as long as you're not going to see your father in Seattle, then you should stay and do your work."

There was a hint of something in her voice. Something that Pearl couldn't quite put her finger on.

"Goodbye, Mom." Pearl disconnected the call and dropped her head in her hands. She suddenly had a pounding headache.

There was a buzz from the intercom and she looked at the clock.

Dammit.

That was most likely Calum and she wasn't even close to ready. How long had she actually been talking to her mother? How long had she been sitting here, lost in her own thoughts? This was not like her and she hated that she was losing control.

Control was the only thing that kept the grief at bay. Control kept emotions at bay.

She got up and went to the intercom. "Hey."

"Hey, Pearl it's me, Calum. Are you ready?"

"No," she admitted. "I got stuck on a call. Do you want to come up?"

"Sure."

"Great. I'll buzz you in. I'm in the penthouse."

She tried to make herself presentable to answer the door. She was half-undressed, so threw on a robe and ran a brush through her hair. All she had to do was finish her makeup, get dressed and grab her notes, and then she was ready to go.

There was a knock at the door and she peered out the peephole to see Calum. Her heart skipped a beat when she saw him standing there, her body reacting to his presence. She still wanted him, even after all this time. She was still attracted to him.

She might have run from her grief because she thought it was for the best, but she still cared for him.

He dressed so well. Like a professional, in a nice suit jacket, pants and a gray sweater.

The gray sweater and the blue suit made his blue eyes even more brilliant, even through the peephole. Her pulse was racing and the butterflies in her stomach were beginning to do the can-can. She was nervous and she had to get control of herself.

She opened the door and he looked her up and down, a smile quirking the corner of his mouth as he saw her in her tattered blue robe.

"Well, that's a little more casual than I expected," he teased.

"Shut up," she groaned, stepping aside to let him in. She shut the door. "I had every intention of being ready, but my mother called."

Calum winced. "Oh, and how is the ice queen of Los Angeles? Does she still hate me?"

Pearl laughed. "Well, she didn't realize that the Dr. Calum Munro of the MSA and the Dr. Calum Munro the cad who wanted to marry her daughter five years ago were the same person."

Calum blinked a couple of times. "Are you serious?"

"When it comes to Moira Henderson I'm always serious," she said sarcastically and then scrubbed a hand over her face.

"Was it that bad?" he asked.

She groaned again. "You know her."

He winced. "Yes. I'm afraid I do. 'You, sir, are a swine!'"

She laughed at him mimicking her mother.

"No one called me 'sir' before," he said.

She cocked an eyebrow. "Yet you've been called swine before?"

"My sister did once. She called me Mr. Swine."

"Why?"

"Oh, I borrowed her blanket for a fort outside, in a rainstorm. It got muddy."

"Ah, hence Mr. Swine."

"Dr. Swine is preferable." There was a twinkle in his eye and she couldn't help but smile.

"It was the semiannual call about visiting her. She just doesn't want my father to have one up her. And it's the same with him. A tug-of-war after all these years."

"I wouldn't know," he sighed. "My father couldn't be bothered with me."

She frowned. "He hasn't changed much. He's only around the team if investors are around. At least he's cordial and nice."

"Well, that's something," Calum snorted.

"Parents are the worst sometimes," she said.

"My mom was good," he admitted. "I miss her."

And she was envious of him. At least he had had one good parent.

"I miss my grandmother," she said wistfully. "She was kind to me. You had your mom longer. She made a good impact on your life."

"That she did," Calum admitted.

"See, that's why you're more optimistic than me."

"Well, then you're forgiven for making me wait," he teased again.

"Have a seat and I'll only be a few moments."

Calum nodded and made his way to her sparsely furnished rental apartment. It was a bit more modern than her taste, but it was clean and bright and would do. It was a place to rest her head at night. It wasn't home. It was just a place to stay while she passed through. Although she didn't want to pass through. Not really. She was tired of that.

* * *

Calum wandered around Pearl's apartment. This didn't feel like her place. The place she had before they were together was a bit cozier and eclectic.

Perhaps she's matured?

This apartment felt sterile. Like there was no life here.

It was cold. It reminded him of her mother's home the one time he'd been there.

Is your place any better?

His place was pretty similar. He didn't have much furniture and his house was in shambles. When he wasn't at the hospital he was working on renovations. He had bought it for a steal because it was near the Painted Ladies and in rough shape. After Pearl left him, he needed something to do when he wasn't at the hospital.

He needed to do something with his hands, to keep his mind off the grief, so he had decided to buy the house and slowly fix it up, so he could eventually sell it.

He had a small apartment in the large house where he lived, while the rest of the place was gutted and was a work in progress, but a bedroom, bathroom and kitchen was all he and Max needed. The house had a small fenced yard, but that was perfect for Max to play in and do his business.

There were enough parks nearby that he could take Max for a long walk. And when he had time they'd drive down the coast to the beach or into the redwoods and go on a long hike.

It was perfect for him, though there were days he questioned why he was renovating such a large place. What did he need it for? He didn't plan on getting married or having kids. The pain of losing Pearl and the baby had been too much to bear.

He couldn't lose anyone else. He couldn't go through that again.

So having a big house was a little foolish.

Although there was a part of him, deep down, that had always hoped one day Pearl would come back. That they could get another chance.

It was a foolish dream.

It wasn't really a home, either, but at least his furniture was a lot cozier and comfortable than this modern, white leather stuff.

Calum sat stiffly on the edge of the couch and waited.

He had been second-guessing this invitation out to dinner since he had invited her out to talk about George's case. She had looked so worried about George's scans, so devastated. And he was worried, as well.

He hadn't seen an osteosarcoma like that in a long time.

"I'm ready." Pearl walked from her bedroom and his breath was taken away when he saw her standing there. She was wearing a black dress. It was just a sheath dress and he'd seen that kind of dress before, on other women, but on Pearl it hugged all the right places. She looked sleek and professional.

And the short dress showed off her legs.

Legs that he intimately remembered wrapped around his waist.

Don't think about that now.

"You look great. Much better than the robe," he teased, trying to diffuse the situation and ignore the fact that just the sight of her made him want to take her in his arms and kiss her again.

He longed to kiss her again.

Even after all the hurt. He longed to kiss her one more

time. He was losing control again, like he had in the on-call room, when he watched her sleep.

It was hard not to lose control when she was so beautiful and he keenly remembered what it was like to have her in his arms.

When she was his.

Get a grip on yourself.

"Thanks," she said, and she blushed again. "I didn't have much time to read the information you sent me. I'm sorry, my mother monopolized my time."

"It's fine." And it was. It was a lot of information and he really didn't expect that she would have it all read by now. "I didn't really think that you would have time to read it tonight."

She pulled her coat of her closet and he took it from her, helping her with it. His fingers brushed the nape of her neck, his blood heating.

"Thanks," she said quietly and then took a step back. "Well, I pride myself on doing my due diligence and doing my research. I'm sorry if I let you down."

"You haven't let me down."

At least not in this situation.

He opened the door for her and they left her apartment. They didn't say anything else as they walked down the hall to the elevator.

They stood stiffly, side by side, still not speaking, and he stared at the elevator door.

Not sure what to say. Just listening to the sound of his pulse thundering between his ears and the whir of the elevator going down. It was awkward between them and he hated that it was. The elevator ride down was quick, and his car was out front of the building. He opened the door to his SUV and she slipped inside and sat on a squeaky toy, which let out a horrible sound like a chicken was being murdered.

She shrieked and then pulled out the rubber chicken. "What in the world?"

"I'm sorry. That's one of Max's toys. I thought I got all of them out of the vehicle—apparently I didn't." He was trying so hard not to laugh at her horrified expression.

Pearl was laughing and she gave the rubber chicken another squeeze.

"It sounds awful!"

"Reminds me of your singing," he teased.

Pearl gasped. "Are you again insinuating that I sing like this?"

"What? When?" he asked.

"When we studied for the boards and we were drinking."

He chuckled. "Right. Yeah, I suppose you do."

She tossed the chicken at him and he tossed it back, so it made that horrible sound again. Pearl rolled her eyes.

"You're so immature," she hissed, teasingly.

Calum laughed. "Perhaps. I would have to get you sing for me again though, but no Broadway music. Please. Don't ruin another one of my favorite things."

"Ha, ha." She threw the rubber chicken into the back seat and Calum shut the door, trying to stop laughing at the look on her face when she sat down on the chicken. That was one thing he always loved about her—she was able to roll with it. She wasn't embarrassed and took something that would potentially irk someone else and laugh about it.

She had a good sense of humor.

He climbed into the driver's side and started the ignition.

"So where are we going?" she asked.

"There's a new bistro down by the wharf. I thought it would be nice to check it out. The view is lovely at night on the bay."

"Sounds good. I always did like it down there."

"You mean down by the bay?" he teased.

"You really haven't changed. You still really make horrible puns," she muttered.

"Is that a pun? I thought it was more like a coincidental anecdote."

"Fine. Correct me if you want, but if you're not careful I'll sing for you."

Calum laughed. It was so easy to laugh and joke with her, but then other times she was so closed off, so frightened of her feelings. So frightened she ran away, but she was here now. She was back and she wasn't running this time. He was worried she'd leave again, and if she did his heart wouldn't be able to handle it.

This time was different. They were just friends.

Are you so sure about that?

He navigated the windy streets of San Francisco, making his way down to the waterfront and where the small Café Bistro, as it was called, was.

He found a parking spot and they made their way to the restaurant, and their table was waiting for them. They could've had their pick of any of the tables. The place was almost empty.

Pearl made a worried face as they followed the waiter to the corner booth that overlooked the water, where they could comfortably talk about George's case.

After they were seated and the maître d' had left, Pearl leaned over the table.

"Why are we the only ones here?" she whispered, her eyes sparkling in the candlelight. She was trying to hide her amusement.

Calum shrugged. "I don't know."

"This can't be a good sign."

"Don't order any seafood," he teased.

Pearl smiled and laughed under her breath. He hoped this was a good place. He was trying to find a new place that neither one of them had been to. He was trying to find a place that wouldn't bring up any painful memories, but if the food was bad, this place just might invoke some painful memories later.

"So about George," Pearl said. "Please tell me we can try something and we don't have to resort to amputation. Not when his career is just starting."

"I don't know. I really can't predict what will happen, but you know Dr. Chin's feelings on unnecessary surgery when there is no hope."

"The tumor hasn't spread, though. We didn't find any metastasizes."

"I know and that's good." He was hopeful.

"So then there is hope. I understand Dr. Chin's philosophy and I respect it. I keep to it, if there's no hope and the patient doesn't want it. Why do more harm than good? But if the tumor hasn't spread, can't we try your way?" she asked.

Calum pursed his lips together. "It will be a hard surgery and the radiation will be hard on him. You know one of the effects of radiation is deterioration of the muscles, weakness. Even if we save the leg, he might not be able to play professionally and he needs to come to that realization."

Pearl sighed. "I know and we need to have a united front on this. We have to present him with everything and we have to agree."

"We used to agree on a lot of things," Calum said softly.

Pink tinged her cheeks again. "I know…"

"When we worked together it was amazing. We were a force to be reckoned with at that hospital."

She smiled, her blue eyes twinkling in the dim light. "Yes. We were quite a team."

And she was right.

It was hard for him to talk about the baby, the grief, the loss. He didn't want to talk about it before, but he did now.

"I missed you when you left," he said.

"I missed you, too."

"Was it just the baby? Is that why you left?"

She worried her bottom lip. "We both had plans, the baby was unexpected and it was hard for me to deal with it."

"It was hard for me, too."

"I know and I'm sorry. I wish I could change the past, but…we both flourished professionally. My parents stayed together and it was awful."

He knew that. She'd told him that before.

"I'm glad you're back, Pearl."

She smiled. "I'm glad I'm back too and that we're working together again."

Calum wanted to ask her what had changed.

"Are you ready to order?" the waiter asked.

"I think so," Calum said. He was never so happy to have a waiter interrupt him before, because he was supposed to be focusing this evening on the patient. On George. Except no matter how hard he tried, when he was with Pearl he forgot everything else and that scared him. He was scared talking about his grief and he was scared of all the old feelings coming back to haunt him.

Sure, he wanted to work with her, but starting things up again? He wasn't so sure about that.

Aren't you?

* * *

The last thing that Pearl wanted to do was tell Calum that the food was atrocious and that was probably why no one came here. She didn't want to hurt his feelings when he seemed to be enjoying the dinner.

So when it came time for dessert, she had to pass.

Even though she wouldn't have minded just crossing the street and going to the chocolate store and getting a great big ice-cream sundae with hot fudge sauce. She hadn't indulged in one of those in a long, long time.

"You sure you don't want dessert?" Calum asked.

"Are you going to have some?" she asked skeptically.

"No." And he made a face, which made her chuckle. They split the bill when it came and got the heck out of the Café Bistro as fast as they could.

"I'm so glad that dinner is over," she blurted out.

"You didn't like it?"

"Sorry, no."

"That place should be called the Abysmal Café," he teased.

"So you thought it was awful, too?" she asked.

"Yes, but you seemed to be enjoying yourself."

"I was not. There was so much garlic in my food. So much garlic. It was all I could taste. It's going to take many breath mints to get rid of this. Or some strong liquor."

"My steak was tough. So tough I thought I would have to bathe it in water, like really bathe it in a hot-water bath so that it contained some semblance of moistness."

She wrinkled her nose. "You used that word on purpose."

"What word?"

"Moist. You know I hate that word."

"Why does everyone hate that word?" he asked.

"We've had this conversation too many times to get into it again."

"Fine. Do you want some ice cream then? Because I can't stop picturing a nice ice-cream sundae and we're down here by the water."

"I would love that."

It was an odd thing to go for an ice-cream sundae in late October, but it felt like old times. Joking and talking about things they used to talk about and going to get ice cream. They both found a table in the ice-cream shop located in an old factory. There were heat lamps on the patio and they sat outside, having ice cream in the autumn.

"This is so much better than that dinner," she said, taking a scoop of ice cream.

"Agreed. I haven't done this in forever."

"Same. I mean, there was a good fake frozen yogurt thing in New York City, but it was nothing compared to this."

"Fake frozen yogurt?" he asked, horrified.

"Yeah, some kind of whipped thing. Nothing like this." What was she doing? Why was she letting herself fall into this trap again? Why was it so easy with Calum? He made her feel like she was a carefree resident again. He got through all her barriers. It was fun and easy and so exciting with him.

She needed to change the subject fast.

"Shall we talk to George and his mother tomorrow?" she asked soberly. Talking about George and work was a safe, neutral buffer. A chance to keep him and the memories he evoked at bay.

Calum nodded. "The sooner we get started, the better. How about I come to the training facility first thing in the morning?"

"That sounds good." She finished up her ice cream.

"Thank you for talking me through everything and I appreciate that you're going to try and help him."

"I will do my best, Pearl, but if it gets too much and if it spreads…" Calum trailed off and he didn't say anything else. She knew what he was getting at.

She knew that George's career would be over before it started and she couldn't imagine that. To have a dream taken away from you.

Can't you?

And just that realization made a lump form in the pit of her stomach as she thought of her baby. It had never really been a dream of hers, but once she'd gotten used to the idea that she was going to be a mother it had all been taken from her.

She couldn't hold on to it.

The moment she lost the baby it was as though a knife had torn her heart into shreds. All her dreams had been shattered. She had no control over that moment, no control over her body not being able to hold on.

She had been powerless and it terrified her.

Even though she knew medically why she miscarried, there was an irrational part of her that made her think that maybe she didn't want it enough and therefore didn't deserve it. Although she knew that thought was foolish, it was there, in the darkest recesses of her inner dialogue, because the baby had been unplanned, because she wasn't ready and because her own birth had ruined her parents lives.

And she hated herself for thinking like that.

"Well, I should get back. I have to talk to George's coach and make sure that he's there at the training facility first thing."

Calum nodded and they both got up, discarded the empty plastic containers and walked back to his car.

The moon was high in the sky. Large and orange. A harvest moon. She took a moment to stare up at it, rising over the bay and the iconic Golden Gate Bridge. The lights of the city shimmered across the water and there was a low fog drifting across the surface.

It was silent, standing here right now. She'd forgotten how magical this city could be.

She forgot how many memories it brought back.

Good and bad. The good times were with her grandmother and the trips to the wharf or to a football game. The bad times were losing the baby and leaving Calum.

She was a fool.

"So did that sundae help get rid of the garlic?" he asked.

"Perhaps."

He turned and faced her, then took her hands, and her heart began to race as she stood there with him, not sure what was going to happen.

"Well, let's see." He touched her face and before she could stop herself she closed her eyes and melted into his arms kissing him, like no time had passed.

Like they hadn't changed.

And her emotions began to overtake her.

If she didn't put a stop to it, she was going to lose all control and she couldn't lose control. Pearl pushed Calum away. She panicked. She wanted that kiss, but she couldn't get caught up with him again. They were supposed to stay friends. Nothing more.

"You know what, I'll just take a cab home."

"What?" he asked, confused.

"Good night, Calum." And she turned and left him standing there.

Running again.

CHAPTER SIX

PEARL HATED BREAKING the news to George.

She hated this part of the job and seeing his face fall as she and Calum told him was so difficult, but he had to know all his options. He had to know what kind of treatment he was going to go through, what the repercussions were and the fact that they might not be able to do anything.

George looked broken and his mother held his hand. She was holding back tears.

"I'm so sorry, George," Pearl said gently. "You need to know your choices."

George stared at the table, looking lost. She knew that feeling well. She knew how it felt when your life was shattered, when all your hopes and dreams were dashed because your body, your health, failed you.

"So it's grown again. Really fast?" George asked.

"Yes," Calum said. "It's an aggressive tumor and when I get in there and do a biopsy I'll be able to determine which medication regimen to start you on, but we need to start treatment as soon as possible, if that's the course of action you wish to take."

George nodded, then was quiet for a moment. "And the other option is…"

"We amputate," Pearl said. "I'm so sorry, George."

"Would amputation cure his cancer?" George's mother asked.

"Yes, it would remove the cancer. So far the cancer hasn't spread, but even if we amputate we need to do a round of chemotherapy to make sure that it doesn't return."

"Baby, why don't we do the amputation?" George's mother asked, but it was more like she was pleading with him.

"Mom, I'm not getting the amputation. I want to fight this," George said fiercely.

Calum leaned forward. "Very well, George, but you do understand that I have never done my treatment on someone with such an advanced osteosarcoma. If the treatment fails, you will still need the amputation and you'll be much weaker. Even if the treatment works, you could be left very weak."

George nodded. "I understand, Doc, but I have to try."

Calum nodded. "Okay. Well, then I want to start treatment right away. I will contact the hospital and have you admitted. We're going to start with a biopsy so that I know how to target it."

George nodded and then looked at his mom. "It'll be okay, Mom. You can go back to Philly."

"I'm not going anywhere. Your brothers and sister are old enough now and they're being taken care of. Don't you worry. My place is here with you."

Pearl felt a pang of jealously. She certainly didn't have that kind of relationship with her own parents. The only person who had loved her like that was her grandmother.

And Calum.

She tried not to think of their kiss last night and how she had fled. It was the only way she could get control of herself. That kiss had thrown her off-kilter. It brought back everything and she was scared what Calum stirred in her.

"Come on, let's get to the hospital so I can beat this cancer's ass!" George said brightly.

"George! Don't swear in front of the doctors," his mother admonished.

Calum laughed and walked over to hold open the door so that George's mother could wheel him out of the boardroom where they were meeting.

"I've heard worse," Calum teased. "I'll see you in a couple of hours. No more eating or drinking okay?"

"Will do, Doc." George shook Calum's hand and was wheeled out of the room. Calum shut the door behind him.

"That was hard," Pearl sighed.

"No harder than last night?"

Pearl bit her lip. "Calum, about last night…we're supposed to be colleagues. It caught me off guard."

His expression softened. "I'm sorry about what happened. I didn't mean to kiss you…it threw me off guard, too."

"It's okay. What's done is done."

"So I take it you're coming to watch me do a biopsy?" he asked.

"Of course," Pearl said quickly. "If you're all right with that."

"It's okay. Are you okay?"

"I'm fine," she said, although she wasn't too sure. "You don't have to keep asking me if I'm okay."

The truth was, she wasn't okay. After their horrible dinner and then ice-cream date, she had once again been tossing and turning all night, berating herself for allowing herself to fall into old patterns with Calum.

She was worried that she was falling for him again.

Who was she kidding? She'd never stopped caring for him.

Why was it that she couldn't control herself when she was around him?

Why did she allow herself to slip into these old habits? Why had she let him kiss her?

The thing was she wanted that kiss and when it came to Calum she had no self-control. She got swept up in good memories, happy times, even love.

"Okay, I'll stop," Calum said. "We have a plan in place and we can do this, but you look tired."

"Right," Pearl said quickly. "I am tired. I just didn't have a good night's sleep. I was worried about breaking the news to George."

Not a complete lie—she was worried about that—but she didn't want him to know that he was the reason she was a bit off. That she was feeling tense being alone with him, that he was getting through her barriers and that's because she really didn't want to keep him out, but she was afraid of letting him in. She was afraid of getting hurt, of hurting him. It was easier for her to keep this as she intended, as friends.

One thing was for certain is that she had to get out of San Francisco for a bit and that's why when she got home after her dinner with Calum she texted Dianne and accepted her invitation to the ranch for the weekend. She just needed to get away for a couple of days.

She needed to put some space between her and Calum.

And be in a place that her parents couldn't find her and manipulate her with their toxic one-upmanship and their perpetual disappointment that she didn't follow in their respective specialties.

That her life was not the life they wanted or expected of her.

Truth be told, her life wasn't exactly how she pictured it. She just needed to get away from it all. She needed to put things in perspective.

Running again.

She shook away that thought.

"He's informed, he's an adult and he's made his decision. It will be good to have you at the biopsy," Calum said, interrupting her thoughts.

"Do you want to get some air?" Pearl asked.

"Sure."

"Let's go. I have to go down to the field and check a couple of players, anyway. They're not playing right now, but the coach wants them on the roster. I have to see a couple of them before they go out on the road."

"Sure."

Calum, ever the gentleman, held open the door for her and they walked out of the boardroom. Pearl led him through the facility and then down to the field, where the Bridgers were out running drills.

The players she wanted to see were on the sidelines.

"Do you want me to come down on the field?" he asked.

"Sure. Why not? You can help."

He nodded. "Okay. I don't know how much help I can be, though. You've dealt with orthopedic injuries."

"You can help, come on."

They headed down onto the field and over to the sidelines, where the players were waiting.

They waved as she approached them.

And she was met with greetings of "hey, Doc" and "what's up, Doc."

"Dr. Calum Munro, this is the lead quarterback, Jose

Fernandez. He's taken one too many blows recently and broken a few ribs."

"Pleasure to meet you, Dr. Munro," Jose said as he held out his hand, which was taped. Pearl frowned when she saw that and gingerly took his hand.

"What have you been doing?" she demanded.

Jose shrugged. "I got tackled pretty bad in the last game. I'm still recovering from that concussion from last month. Anyways, I lost my balance and was open for the tackle. I bent a couple of fingers back."

"Concussions can take weeks to heal, Jose." She looked at his hand.

"I know, Doc. I thought I was fine, though."

"Have you gone to get this X-rayed?" she asked.

Jose sighed. "Not yet, Doc. I swear I was on my way up."

Pearl gave him a stern look and then stepped aside for Calum to look. "What do you think, Dr. Munro?"

Calum took Jose's hand. "Definitely dislocated a joint. There's swelling. You did a good job taping though, Jose. I should've benched you, but it didn't look this bad last night."

"Thanks, Doc!" Jose said brightly. "It was fine during the game, but I finished practice today and it's worse. It's a bit tender."

"You need to get up and see Marta in X-ray. I want to see how badly you've dislocated your joints and I want to make sure there isn't any tendon damage in your arm. Your *good* throwing arm."

"Yes, Doc." Jose made his way off the field.

"You talk to them like you're their mother," Calum teased.

"I guess I am in a way, but they need to take care of their injuries and not play through the pain, but no matter how much I talk about that, they do. They're professional athletes."

"I get that," Calum said.

"Do you?" she asked, crossing her arms.

"Sure. Aren't surgeons like that in some way? We work grueling long hours, sometimes ignoring what our body is telling us. We don't eat, we don't sleep as we fight for our patients' lives."

"You're right, although my parents wouldn't agree with you."

He was confused. "Aren't they surgeons, too?"

"Yes, but they see their surgery is something legitimate. Orthopedic surgeons aren't as important as a cardiothoracic surgeon or a neurosurgeon as far as they are concerned. You can live without a leg, but you can't live without a heart or a brain…though my parents seem to be doing a good job of that."

"Are you serious?" he asked.

"I think I have told you this before."

"Right. I tend to block out memories of your mother," he teased.

She laughed. "Can't blame you for that."

"I don't understand why they hated your choice in surgery."

"Because it's not theirs. Although, my father respects my job working with the Bridgers."

"Why?" Calum asked.

"Money." She regretted it instantly the moment she said it. Like her answer was confirming something.

"I guess that's something," he said firmly. "My father, who was absent most of my childhood, felt like I should become an investor like him. Of course, that's only when I grew older and showed an aptitude for figures. When I was a kid, he couldn't be bothered with me."

"I'm sorry that I've forced you to come here. I forgot about your relationship with your dad momentarily."

"What relationship?" Calum shrugged. "It doesn't matter that Grayson Munro, one of the major investors of this team, is my father."

She knew Grayson Munro, he was very persuasive— Calum's father had encouraged her to do whatever it took to save George's career because he had personally invested so much in George's career with the Bridgers.

Had Grayson worked some deal with Calum? Perhaps Calum really didn't want to help her because he cared about George and about the case. Maybe he had no choice.

"Is that why you're helping me?" she asked.

Calum cocked an eyebrow. "What're you talking about?"

"Your father is an investor for the Bridgers. Is he the one that forced you to take on my case?"

Calum was stunned that that was the first thing she would think about. Did she really think so little of him? His father might have invested in the Bridgers, but he hadn't come to Calum and asked him for help. Why was she always looking for something to push him away?

Why were you?

"Pearl, I don't talk to my father. He had nothing to do with this."

She pursed her lips together. "I believe you."

"I've never lied to you, Pearl. You know I don't talk to him."

"I know. I'm sorry."

He knew she had trust issues, but he was glad she believed him. He had never lied to her.

Of course, he wasn't telling her everything. He wasn't

telling her that kiss last night scared him, that her walking away hurt him, but was also a relief.

Being with her made him lose all control. It was like no time had passed between them. He forgot who he was when he had her in his arms.

And suddenly, he was very thankful that he was getting out the city for the weekend. Max was going his to favorite doggy day-care place and he was going to just get away, into the mountains for some peace and quiet.

Away from this.

All of these emotions. He had been overcome when he kissed her. He'd forgotten everything. When he was with Pearl he forgot what happened. The pain when she left.

Kissing her, he lost all control.

He still cared for her.

He still loved her, but he couldn't open up to her. When she left him last night, he remembered why he guarded his heart.

"I really am thankful that you're assisting me. There's no one I would rather have."

He nodded, but he wasn't so sure about that, not really. If she really wanted him why had she left all those years ago?

"Well, I think I'm going to head back to the hospital," he said, because he didn't really have much more to say. Not at this time.

Not without saying something that he would regret.

Would you regret it, though?

"Sure. I will be there as soon as I check up on Jose's hand."

"Make sure there isn't a crush injury," he added.

She gave him a look that said "please" and then he chuckled softly. He'd forgotten who he was talking to.

"I'll see you later," she said over her shoulder, heading back into the facility.

Calum headed in the opposite direction, watching the players on the field, taking his time as he processed everything. All the emotions he was feeling, how it was so easy to get wrapped back up in Pearl's life and why he was a lost man when it came to Pearl Henderson.

"Calum!"

Hearing his name, Calum spun around and his stomach twisted as he saw his father up in the stands, not far from him.

It had been a long time since he had seen Grayson Munro, at least as long as he and Pearl had split up. And honestly, although it felt like an eternity that he and Pearl had been apart, it didn't quite feel long enough since he had last seen his father.

"Father," Calum said stiffly.

His father was still decked out in one of his expensive tailored suits and when he saw those suits all he could think about is how his mother barely scraped by and sometimes didn't have food for herself to feed them.

His father's dark hair was almost white and Calum was thankful that he took after his mother and her ginger coloring.

There weren't many ways he resembled his father. A few traits, but there was nothing but a name connecting Dr. Calum Munro with Grayson Munro.

"What're you doing here, son?"

Grayson never called him "son" unless there were people around and his father was putting on a show. As Calum scanned the bleachers, he saw there were a group of people farther up, sitting politely, so that was why his father was putting on a performance. He had no doubt that they were a group of investors.

"Laying it on thick, eh, Father?"

Grayson was not amused with that, but he didn't let the saccharine act slip. "I'm surprised to see you here, son. Why don't you come up and say hi to some people? I've been telling them all about my son who won the most prestigious medical award."

"Another time." Calum waved to the group, all of whom were looking at him. "I'm wanted back at the hospital."

"Surely that can wait? What kind of emergency case is an orthopedic surgeon needed for?"

Calum narrowed his eyes. "Actually, it's for one of your star players. George Vaughn. He has a pretty bad osteosarcoma and your team's surgeon contacted me to help him out with that ground-breaking surgery that I won the award for. He's waiting for me at the hospital."

Grayson was stunned. "I had no idea it was that bad."

"It is. So when I say another time, I mean another time," he said tightly.

"I'll call you later, son. Take care of our star player." Grayson turned and headed up the bleachers to the investors, and Calum watched him kowtowing and kissing ass in disgust.

His father only let him go without fighting because there was a crowd watching and because the patient was someone he was personally invested in.

And by invested in, Calum meant financially invested in.

If it had been anyone else and they had been alone, Calum knew that his father would have raised more of a stink. Calum and his mother were always supposed to jump whenever Grayson Munro graced them with his presence. His mother had been so in love with Grayson, even after he left, that she had always hoped he'd come back.

Right up until her death. She had held out hope he'd return. Only he hadn't.

And Grayson certainly liked to throw it in Calum's face that he had paid for his education and that Calum owed him.

Even though Calum had told Pearl the truth, that his father hadn't put him up to this, he hoped that taking care of George would repay the supposed debt that he owed his father.

This was why Calum had never really wanted a family.

Never wanted to get married.

He didn't have a good role model, but when Pearl had told him he was pregnant, he had been willing to give it a shot, because he loved Pearl that much. He wanted Pearl and he wanted their child. He thought maybe he could have happiness, and the longer they were together, the more hopeful he had become for a family life he'd never had.

Pearl had made his life better.

Calum had sworn from the moment that Pearl told him that she was pregnant that he was never going to be like his father and he was going to strive to do better.

He would do better.

Of that he was certain, only that chance had been taken away from him when they lost the baby, and Calum was too worried about the pain of ever trying again.

One thing was for certain, one thing he knew—he would never prioritize a patient because of money.

He was not that coldhearted.

* * *

"Can you feel that, George?" Calum asked as he tested the skin around where he was going to make the biopsy incision. He'd given George an epidural, because he couldn't wait the full six hours for George to have a completely empty stomach and put him under general anesthesia.

So he and Pearl had decided that it would be best if George had an epidural.

"I can't feel anything, Doc," George said from behind the surgical drape.

"Good." Calum looked over at Pearl, who was standing on the opposite side of the table. She was there for moral support for George, who was trembling, but that was the effect of the epidural.

"You're doing great, George," Pearl encouraged.

"Yeah, but I'm the only player going through all this junk and surgery."

"Jose crushed a couple of fingers. I admitted him just before I came in here."

"What?" George asked, staring up at Pearl.

Calum chuckled because he knew that Pearl, who usually didn't talk about patient-confidentially stuff, was trying to take George's mind off the fact that he was starting a rough journey treating his cancer.

And he also knew that Jose had given Pearl permission to talk to George about it because Jose also wanted to ease George's mind off the fact he was going to have his leg, the thing that helped carry him to the very cusp of his dream, be put through the ringer.

"How did he crush his hand?" George asked.

"During the game yesterday. What we thought was a sprain was a lot worse. He's still recovering from that concussion, so he's a bit out of it. He's benched for a while. I have to tell you your coach is not happy having you out this season and Jose out for a couple months, at least. He needs surgery."

"No, I suppose he's not happy." George relaxed, which was the best thing for him. Pearl was keeping George's mind off the leg. She might have been called an ice queen when they were residents, but that was the furthest thing from the truth.

She was kind to her patients and he understood why she liked her job. The players relied on her and she treated them like they were her kids.

She was concerned about them. She cared for them.

Although she tried to hide it, there was a soft side to Dr. Pearl Henderson.

He knew first-hand what it was like to have her melt in his arms and under his touch.

Calum was handed the scalpel so that he could start his incision, so he could take a piece of the tumor that was invading George's bone.

And he wanted to get a good look at it close up, under his microscopes. He wanted to know what he was up against so that he could help George.

"Hey, Doc Munro, have you started?" George asked.

"He has," Pearl said. "But if you bug him too much he might slip!"

"I never slip," Calum muttered and then winked at George.

George was laughing. "It's kind of quiet in here. Don't you have some music or something? I'm going stir-crazy."

"Well, our teacher used to like to listen to Queen when he was doing surgery," Pearl said. "It annoyed Calum and he likes it quiet."

"Why?" George asked. "Doc, that's seriously boring."

"Sure, get the patient on your side, Dr. Henderson," Calum teased.

Pearl's eyes were twinkling. He loved being here in the operating room with her. This felt right. This felt like they belonged together. They worked well together. She anticipated his moves. She knew what he needed done before he had to ask. They moved and thought like one. They were partners. They were equals and he missed this.

"I'll always side with the lady, Dr. Munro. Sorry about that."

Calum laughed softly as he dissected down to where he needed to take a sample from. "In this case, I don't blame you. Dr. Henderson is not bad on the eyes."

"No, indeed." George's eyes rolled back into his head.

"George?" Pearl asked, her voice rising. "George, stay with me."

"His blood pressure is bottoming out," Dr. Knox, the anesthesiologist, stated. "I'll hang some more fluid. It's common with an epidural."

Pearl nodded, but Calum could tell she was a bit worried.

"Surely, this isn't your first patient that's had a reaction to an epidural?" Calum asked.

"Usually my patients are under general anesthesia. I have yet to do a knee replacement under an epidural," she said.

"I have," Calum said. "Not the most pleasant thing for the patient. I do prefer general anesthesia, but a couple of years ago we had a patient who was allergic to the medication and an epidural was our only option."

"I'm envious," Pearl said.

"Of what?" Calum asked.

"You have a bigger scope of cases here. More than I do."

"Well, I didn't leave," he said tersely.

He knew that he had hurt her, and he hadn't meant for that to slip out, but it was the truth. She had left for a higher-paying job, but one that was so stifled in the scope of cases. He saw everything an orthopedic surgeon could see here in the hospital, which is why he had been so successful developing his treatment plan.

Pearl didn't say anything else as George came to.

"Whoa, is it over?" he asked weakly.

"Almost," Calum said. "Just a few more minutes."

He glanced up at Pearl, but she was focused on George, her back to him. He knew that he had hurt her, but she had hurt him, too.

Still, he hated himself right in this moment.

He hated himself for hurting her, which was the last thing he wanted to do.

CHAPTER SEVEN

PEARL TOOK A deep breath when she got off the last train in downtown Sonora. It had been a long day, but the train journey gave her time to catch up on work and to think about everything. She'd been hurt when Calum had said what he did during George's biopsy, but she couldn't blame him.

He was right. She'd run away. She'd hurt him. Every day she regretted that decision from five years ago.

After George was stabilized, she went to check on Jose and talk over the surgery she wanted to do on him and then she prepped for that, while avoiding Calum.

She performed Jose's surgery and George started his targeted radiation on Thursday, and she got on the train on Friday.

Calum had been avoiding her and she was okay with that.

She'd been avoiding him, too. After that kiss. She knew she had to put distance between them and going away to Dianne's was the perfect escape from all the ghosts of San Francisco.

She made sure that everything back in San Francisco was wrapped up and taken care of before she boarded her first, of several, trains to Sonora, California, where she was looking forward to the time out in the country, away from the city, away from her parents and most especially away from Calum.

Sonora was a six-hour train ride, but it didn't feel far enough.

"Pearl!"

Pearl turned and saw that Dianne was waiting in the parking lot of the train station. Pearl sighed in relief and made her way through the crowd and over to Dianne, where she got a big hug. It made her feel welcome and at home, like it always did. She'd forgotten.

"I'm so glad you decided to come and that you survived the train ride. You seriously need to get a car!" Dianne teased.

"I like traveling by train. I could work, but I'm glad to be here. I'm looking forward to a hot shower and a change of clothes."

"Of course. And Jerome is barbecuing."

"In late October?" Pearl asked, stunned.

"You forget you're on the West Coast. It's not freezing as New York City is."

"It's October. It's not *that* cold."

Although they had the odd strange snowfall.

She would miss New York in the snow. She always did like seeing Central Park covered in snow, but she definitely wouldn't miss the crowds and the bone-chilling cold of a New York winter. She much preferred California.

"Thanks again for having me. You saved me from having to spend another weekend alone."

"No problem. I've missed you and video chatting or texting isn't the same as being together."

They climbed into Dianne's Jeep. Dianne drove away from the train station and through the small California town, although Dianne and Jerome didn't really live in

Sonora proper—it was just the closest town that Pearl could get to. Their little village Mountain Spring was part of the greater Sonora area, but not in the city limits.

Dianne and Jerome's ranch was closer to the hills. It was nestled in the foothills with lots of trees and Pearl couldn't wait to go for a nice long walk out on their trails, just to clear her head and not think about Calum.

She was so glad that he was back in San Francisco and she was here. Ever since she'd returned to San Francisco, all she thought about was Calum and it was driving her crazy. She could not stop thinking about the kiss and everywhere in San Francisco brought back memories of their time together.

So many ghosts in San Francisco. She needed a ghost-free weekend to collect her thoughts.

"So your mom was bugging you again?" Dianne asked, breaking through Pearl's thoughts.

"She always is."

"You know, you're an adult. You don't have to deal with her."

"I know, but both my parents find a way to annoy me."

"You're too nice," Dianne said softly. "You're an excellent surgeon and you don't put up with a lot of crap, but you're too nice to them."

"I know. They couldn't give a crap about each other or anyone else. They're both so selfish. In retrospect, I should've ended up that way. But, honestly, they embarrassed me so much when I was a kid, I just didn't want to be like that."

"I understand. Family has a way of pulling on you, from different directions. It's all well and good to dump those toxic members from your life, but they make up the fabric of your existence and it's hard to pull away one thread."

Pearl nodded. It was true.

There were some people in your life that just became a part of you and no matter how much you tried to pull away, they were there, binding you to them. Pearl was just going to have deal with the fact that Calum was an important part of her past and that she'd always be drawn to him.

She would just have to cope with that, and as much as she wanted him to be a part of her life, he couldn't. She was too afraid of what would happen.

The rest of the drive out to Dianne's ranch was enjoyable. Dianne talked about her new job and Jerome's practice and what Derek was up to as a rambunctious five-year-old.

As they pulled up to the log house at the end of the long winding drive, Pearl's heart skipped a beat when she recognized a familiar SUV in the drive, one with San Francisco plates. Her stomach knotted and dropped to the soles of her feet.

"Dianne?" she asked, hoping her voice didn't shake.

Dianne worried her bottom lip, her big brown eyes wide. "I know. I'm sorry, but he comes every couple of months."

"I wish you would've have told me."

"You wouldn't have come and you would've been miserable in San Francisco. Besides, I saw the two of you in that surgery a few days ago and you were both fine. I didn't think you'd mind."

Dianne got out of the car and Pearl just sat there for a moment letting it all sink in. Yes, she and Calum had got along fine during that surgery that Dianne had assisted on, but she hadn't been there for George's biopsy. Or for that kiss and the way she had run from Calum again.

Dianne didn't know how he'd embarrassed her with that comment, not that she could blame him.

It was just the fact it was in front of other hospital staff.

You can handle this. This ranch is big enough for the both of you.

Only she wasn't too sure about that. She got out of the car and picked up her suitcase. The front door opened and Jerome came out.

"I didn't quite believe it when she told me you were coming!" Jerome came over to her and enfolded her in a big bear hug, giving her a kiss on the cheek. "I've missed you, *chica*. It's been way too long."

"It has." Pearl gave him a kiss back. "Where's Derek? I have something for him from New York."

"He's asleep. He got tired of waiting." Jerome took her suitcase and Pearl followed him and Dianne up the steps into the main foyer of their beautiful log cabin.

Pearl was taken aback by the high ceilings and the rustic feeling of the place, but also impressed with the modern amenities she could see as the space was open concept.

"Pearl?"

Pearl spun around and saw that Calum was on the stairs. He'd been coming down the main staircase and paused on the landing when he saw her.

"Hi, Calum," she said, hoping that Jerome and Dianne didn't notice the tension.

"I didn't know you were coming," Calum said, coming down the stairs. He had a strange expression on his face and she knew that he was trying to make sure that Jerome and Dianne didn't know that he was just as shocked and uncomfortable as she was.

"I didn't know you'd be here, either," she said quietly.

"I come every year around this time," Calum stated.

"He helped with a lot of the construction on this place over the last few years," Jerome said. "He is an amazing woodworker."

Pearl raised her eyebrows. "Wow. I had no idea."

"No, why would you?" Calum asked quietly.

"Come on," Dianne said, stepping between them, and from her really large smile, Pearl knew that Dianne was sensing some of the tension. "Let me show you to your room, Pearl. You probably want to freshen yourself up before Jerome tries to poison you with his homemade beer."

Dianne took the suitcase from Jerome.

"Hey!" Jerome teased and Calum was laughing.

Pearl followed Dianne up the stairs. She turned to look over her shoulder briefly and saw that Calum was watching her go up the stairs.

This was going to be a *long* weekend indeed.

When Pearl had cleaned up and changed her clothes, she headed downstairs. She was tired from her train trip and it was late, but she was hungry. Train food was okay, but when she got out of the shower she could smell Jerome's barbecue all the way from her room and her stomach was growling.

Everyone was in the kitchen area around the main island. There were wineglasses out and Calum was laughing and talking with Dianne and Jerome. And suddenly, she felt out of place with her friends. Like she didn't belong.

Like she was the interloper. She was so unnerved she almost turned around and went back upstairs.

You were invited.

Dianne wanted her here and she wanted to see Derek again. She walked into the kitchen, feeling awkward.

"Hey," she said brightly.

"Pearl, would you like a glass of wine?" Dianne asked.

"Yes. As long as Jerome didn't make it," Pearl teased.

Dianne laughed and pulled out a glass, pouring her a glass of red.

"I have to say, Pearl, I'm quite hurt that you don't trust my ability to brew beer or make wine. I mean, I have a kit and everything," Jerome stated.

Dianne raised her eyebrows and shook her head subtly as she took a sip. Pearl tried not to laugh.

"Maybe some other time, Jerome. I've been on a train all day and I don't want to risk anything after eating train food," Pearl said.

"Fair enough." Jerome headed out to the back deck, where she could see smoke rising from the large built-in gas barbecue.

"I'm going to see if he needs help," Dianne said, quickly scurrying after her husband and leaving Pearl and Calum alone.

"I'm sorry if I'm ruining your plans," Pearl said quickly. "If I had known you were coming I wouldn't have intruded."

Calum sighed. "No, I'm sorry. I didn't mean to say what I said the other day in the biopsy."

"Apology accepted. Your kiss threw me off and I panicked."

Calum sighed. "It threw me off, too. Pearl, I'm okay that you're here. You and Dianne are best friends. We can be adults—I mean, we are working together on George's case and this place is definitely big enough for the both of us."

She wanted to believe him, but she somehow doubted that this place was big enough for both of them. San Francisco didn't seem to be a big enough expanse for the two of them, but if he was willing to make this work, she was willing to make this work.

"Do you think this was a setup?" she asked.

Calum nodded. "I don't know what she's playing at. I think she's longing for the good old days."

"You mean when we were all broke and tired, making our way through residency?"

Calum smiled. "Yeah, that."

"Life seemed simpler then, from this perspective, anyway."

"Yes. That's for sure. So you avoided visiting your mother, huh?"

"Of course, I'm the master of that," she teased.

"You know, I have met your father."

"When?" she asked.

Calum chuckled. "I have. I met your father when I won the award, actually. He's not the most… He's not very warm and personable."

"That's a polite way of putting it," she said dryly.

"You never told him about me, did you?" he asked.

"I did, but he couldn't care less. It was just my mother who said I was throwing my life away, but now you're a catch." Heat bloomed in her cheeks as she said that. She hadn't meant to, even if it was the truth.

There was a twinkle in his eye as he leaned over the island. "So I'm a catch, eh?"

Pearl rolled her eyes and tried not to laugh. "You're only a catch to my mother because you won that prestigious award and are a brilliant surgeon. Of course, when I wanted to marry you, you weren't worth my time and would ruin my life."

"Did you?"

"Did I what?" Pearl asked.

"Did you want to marry me?" he asked gently.

Pearl's face bloomed pink again and his own pulse was thundering in his ears. When she blushed like that, it made his heart skip a beat.

Why did he still want her? He just couldn't resist her. He had never gotten over her and he doubted he ever could.

He waited for an answer. Not that he really expected to hear what he really wanted and he wasn't sure what that was. She was the one who had left him.

She had left him, like so many people in his life had done before. His dad, his sister and even his mom left him, in a way, when she died. But Pearl made him feel alive again. She always had. He had only ever wanted her. He still wanted a life with her.

"Calum…" She blushed again. "I…"

He reached over and took her hand. It was small and delicate, just like he remembered. He'd admired her hands many times when they were doing work. She had surgeon hands, but they were still soft and fit so well in his.

Her breath hitched in her throat and he took a step closer to her. He didn't know what he was expecting in this moment. She hadn't answered his question and he didn't care. He just wanted to be close to her again.

She looked up at him, her lips parted, and he ran his thumb over her cheek.

God, he wanted to kiss her again. He couldn't resist her. Why couldn't he resist her?

"You don't have to say anything," he whispered.

"It's not that, it's…"

"It's what?"

"I think the ribs are finally done," Dianne said, coming back into the kitchen.

Pearl pulled her hand away and took another sip of her wine, and Calum stepped back. Dianne paused and looked at them both.

"Is everything okay?" Dianne asked, confused.

"Perfectly fine." It was a lie—there was something unfinished here and he'd been so close to her. So close to finally getting through to her after all these years.

"We were just discussing our case back in San Francisco. The young linebacker for the Bridgers," Pearl said.

"No work talk," Dianne moaned. "This is supposed to be a fun weekend."

"Can I help you with anything?" Pearl asked, following Dianne from the kitchen into the dining room.

Calum tried not to sigh in regret. He was annoyed they had been interrupted. He just wanted to kiss her again. He hadn't stopped thinking about the kiss.

Maybe it was good Dianne had come in before he got too carried away.

Calum abandoned his glass of wine and headed out on the deck, where Jerome was finishing up with the cooking.

"You okay?" Jerome asked as Calum wandered out onto the deck.

"I'm fine."

Which was a lie.

He stood at the edge of the deck and stared up at the sky. The stars were out and the night was clear and crisp.

It was cooler here than in San Francisco. It was kind of perfect and he understood why this had been Dianne and Jerome's dream.

"You're clearly not fine," Jerome said.

"And how do you figure that?"

Jerome shook his head. "I've known you more than a decade. You try to hide stuff, you try to bottle up your emotions, but I know something is bothering you. You surgeons think you're made of steel, and that you're emotionless automatons that can deal with whatever, but every surgeon I've met is moody, with a capital moo."

Calum cocked an eyebrow. "What?"

"I can say that because I'm not a surgeon. I was an anesthesiologist and now I'm a family doctor. I'm not a surgeon, therefore I can express myself a lot better."

Calum snorted. "Oh, yeah? And when are you going to tell Dianne about that big-screen television that you bought, the one that's as big as her living room wall?"

Jerome shot him a look. "That's neither here nor there."

"You're hiding it from her."

"I'll eventually tell her. Are you going to tell Pearl about how you feel?"

Calum frowned. His stomach twisted in a knot, because Jerome had hit the nail on the head. He wasn't sure that he was going to ever tell Pearl how he felt. Too much time had passed. Maybe it was too late for them.

"Exactly my point," Jerome stated. "Calum, why don't you just talk to her?"

"I will…soon. Right now we have to work on an important case together and we just have to keep it professional. That's the best we can do right now."

Calum knew by Jerome's face that he didn't believe him, but Jerome was a good enough friend that he wasn't going to push Calum. Jerome had been here when Calum was grieving—not only the loss of the baby, but also the loss of Pearl.

"Okay, man. I won't say anything else. Let's go eat some ribs!"

Calum nodded. "Sounds good."

He held open the door for Jerome and followed him inside.

He couldn't let himself slip like that, but when he was around Pearl he lost all sense of reason.

CHAPTER EIGHT

CALUM CAME DOWN later than he intended to, but he had had a horrible night's sleep. Usually, he slept pretty well at Dianne and Jerome's place, but he couldn't get Pearl out of his head. All he could think about was her, how close he'd been and how it felt to touch her. How it felt to kiss her again.

And how she was down the hall. He thought he'd left her safely behind in San Francisco, but here she was at Dianne and Jerome's and so close to him.

When he finally decided to give up and get up for the day, he had a cold shower to wake himself up and try to shake the remnants of his dreams about Pearl. His thoughts about taking her in his arms and showing her how much he missed her.

How much he wanted her.

How much he needed her.

You need to get a grip.

He shook his head and headed downstairs to get a cup of coffee. The moment he hit the landing, he could hear Derek laughing. He glanced over the banister and saw that Derek was sitting with Pearl on the large sectional couch, in front of the fireplace.

It made his heart skip a beat.

Derek was curled up beside Pearl and she was so cozy

with him. She looked happy as Derek was building a three-dimensional puzzle of the Empire State Building.

It looked totally natural for Pearl and Derek to be sitting on the couch together, building a puzzle, and Calum couldn't help but think of the child they'd lost.

"I'm totally freaked out, Calum. How are you not more freaked out?" Pearl had demanded.

"I am freaked out," he said, *but really he couldn't stop smiling.*

"You don't look freaked out." She ran her hands through her hair. *"I can't be a mother!"*

"Why not?" he asked.

"I don't know anything about kids or babies or anything. I mean, I guess I could treat a sick child or a baby, but... I'm not the maternal kind of person."

He held her close. "You totally can be."

"My mother is insane."

"I hardly think she's insane."

Pearl laughed nervously. "Okay, but...this is not what I wanted."

"I'm okay with whatever decision you decide, but I'll help you. I'm here and I'm sure we can do this together."

"I think so, too," she whispered. *"Still, I'm not sure I'll be the best mother."*

"You'll be great."

And it was clear from the way that Pearl was with Derek that she would've been great. It made him sad to think that they didn't have a chance to experience it with their own child. He never had a chance to prove that his instincts about Pearl were right.

Their baby would be around the same age as Derek and he couldn't help but ponder what their child would have been like. He often thought about that when he saw Derek, but he tried not to think about it too much.

Don't think about it.

He had almost had everything he wanted, and then it was taken away. And what did he know about having a family? He didn't have any kind of home life growing up. How could he be a good father?

All his life he had worked hard to get his father's attention and it had gotten him nowhere.

He had no role models and that's what got him through his grief.

That he would never be a good father and maybe it was for the best.

Was it?

He came down the rest of the way and sidestepped the living area, where Derek was busy with Pearl, and headed straight for the kitchen, where Jerome was leaning over the island, holding a cup of coffee.

"Where's Dianne?" Calum asked, pulling down a mug and helping himself to coffee.

"She had to run into town. There was a landslide last night—there's been so much rain in the foothills and they called in everyone they could. She should be back soon."

"You look exhausted," Calum said, taking a sip of coffee.

"Look who's talking," Jerome remarked.

Calum snorted in response. "I tossed and turned all night, but I didn't hear Dianne leave."

"She left about three."

"Do you think the hospital needs help?" Calum asked. He wouldn't mind driving into town and helping out.

"No, Dianne texted about ten minutes ago and she'll be home in a couple of hours. You know, we may be smaller than San Francisco, but we do have coldhearted surgeons out here."

Calum laughed. "Really? I had no idea."

"Smart-ass," Jerome mumbled.

Calum finished his coffee and then headed outside. He needed to take a walk, but when he stepped outside there was a thick layer of fog and it was misting. He didn't really feel like getting soaked if it started to rain, and the temperature had dropped.

So he took a seat in a chair under the covered deck.

"Hey, I thought I saw that you were up."

He looked over his shoulder and saw Pearl standing in the doorway. She pulled the door closed and stepped outside. She had an oversize sweater and a wrap on, but was barefoot as she padded across the deck and took a seat beside him.

"Aren't you cold?" he asked, staring at her feet.

"No. It's warmer here than New York." She tucked her feet up under her. "I was hoping to go for a walk."

"Me, too, but I don't fancy getting caught in a cold November rain."

"It's not November," she stated. "And it's warm."

"I know, but I don't know a song about rain in the autumn other than that one."

She grinned and her eyes lit up. "I loved that song."

"I remember. It's also one of the songs you like to sing when you've imbibed too much. The rubber chicken would sing it better."

She groaned and buried her head in her hand. "You're never going to let me live that down, are you?"

"Probably not." He then proceeded to yowl, in a really bad impression of her that got her laughing.

"I do not sound that bad."

"I'm afraid you do. You're an excellent surgeon, but a terrible singer."

"You're not that great yourself. And you're a terrible dancer. You have no rhythm."

"What're you talking about?" He got up and started dancing, which made her reach over and hit him.

"Stop that! You'll scare Derek." Then she pulled out her phone, which was buzzing, and frowned when she saw it. "Oh, no."

"What's wrong?" Calum asked.

"It's George. I know Dianne didn't want me talking about work, that it's supposed to be a holiday, but George isn't tolerating the chemotherapy well. His mother is texting me." Pearl texted George's worried mother back.

"Tell her I'll call the oncologist, we'll do a blood draw and I'll get his dosage changed."

Pearl nodded and Calum pulled out his phone and sent a message to the oncology team at the hospital. His oncologist, as if expecting this, already had done the blood draw. Calum went over the lab report and sent a message back about how to proceed.

Their oncology team was one of the best in San Francisco, but there was a certain procedure to the treatment plan that he'd developed and Calum was the one that had to do the adjustments.

"There, that should help George," Calum said, finishing up his text. "The oncology team is going to keep me posted, but you can tell George's mother that we'll get it under control."

Truth be told it, was worrying him that George wasn't handling the protocol well, but he wasn't going to say that out loud and he didn't really need to—he could see the worry in Pearl's face.

"So Dianne told me that you've helped build this house," Pearl said, changing the subject.

"Yeah, I found I like renovating. My place in San

Francisco is an old Victorian home, but she was pretty much condemned when I bought her. I've been slowly fixing it up. Most of the house is inhabitable, but I have a small apartment in the top of the house where I live comfortably."

"What're you going to do with it when it's done?" she asked. "Are you going to stay there or flip it?"

"I don't know. I like living near the hospital, but I also like it out here. I really enjoyed my time here with Jerome as we worked on this place. Still, I like where I work, and I took over Dr. Chin's practice. I'm not sure I could give it all up to move out here."

And, really, who did he have to give it all up for?

No one.

"It's beautiful out here," Pearl said. "I've always loved log cabins and the forest, but my parents aren't exactly nature lovers."

"You don't say?" he teased.

"My dad thinks he's rustic living on a big piece of land that overlooks Puget Sound. He has some trees, but the house is a modern eyesore in the middle of nature and he's never there, but he has a new wife and they have a couple of kids."

"I didn't know that you had half siblings."

"I do, but I'm not really welcome."

"Then why do your parents argue over who you're going to visit every holiday?" he asked.

"My father does it to annoy my mother and for control. He likes to be in control and he likes all the attention on him. That's the only reason. My father's new wife doesn't like me and, trust me, the feeling is mutual."

"So they both fight over you, a grown woman, in order to make each other miserable."

"You got it," she said.

"That's messed up."

Pearl laughed. "You have no idea."

"I think I have an idea. You are aware who my father is, right?"

"I am aware and that is true." She stood up. "Looks like the rain and the fog is letting up. I think I'm going to go for a walk, after all."

"Would you mind some company?"

What're you doing? That's not keeping away from her.

"Sure."

"All right, I'll grab my jacket and we'll take a hike through the woods. I know where all the trails are."

They got their jackets and Pearl's shoes and headed outside, leaving Derek and Jerome behind to watch cartoons. Derek was excited about going to Mountain View's Founder's Day parade that evening, though Pearl did not share his excitement.

She really detested parades, but it was nice hanging out with Derek.

If her baby had survived, she'd probably be taking him or her out to different holiday parades and just the thought of never being able to experience that made her sad.

Don't think about it.

She didn't want to get lost in those kind of thoughts. Not today. She was just trying to make it through this weekend without things being too weird.

She knew that she probably shouldn't be going on this walk with Calum, but it would be nice to have company, especially company that knew their way around Dianne and Jerome's property. Calum was waiting out front for her. He was wearing a leather jacket and hiking boots. She was glad that she had brought a pair of boots, too. Her sneakers or heels weren't going to cut it in the woods.

"You ready?" he asked.

"As ready as I'll ever be. Hopefully this hike isn't up the side of a mountain or anything."

"Hardly. It's easy, I promise. And besides, you're used to climbing mountains in heels in San Francisco."

"True."

They fell into step and Calum led her down the drive, where there was a small dirt trail off the driveway that disappeared into the woods. She hadn't noticed it last night because it had been too dark, but it looked like a fairly easy, groomed trail and was wide enough for a horse.

"Don't tell me Dianne goes horseback riding?" she asked.

"No, but she lets other riders from around the area use her trail system, so you might have to watch for horse patties."

"Fun." And she really hoped she didn't find a present from a horse.

It was a beautiful day and the sun was starting to come out and melt the last remnants of the fog and mist.

It was nice to walk with Calum. It felt so right. She wished that she could hold on to this. She still wanted him. She loved being with him, here.

Even after all this time.

When he reached out and took her hand, touched her face, it had reignited something deep inside her. Something she thought was long gone, but she'd been kidding herself to think that it was gone. It would never be gone. Not where Calum was concerned.

"About last night," she said, stopping.

He paused. "What about last night?"

"You asked me if I wanted to marry you when I was…" She trailed off, because she couldn't even bring herself to say that she was pregnant once. It was hard to even admit something so painful. "The answer is…yes. I wanted to marry you."

His expression softened and he took a step closer to her. "You did?"

"Well, I didn't want to marry anyone ever, but… I wanted you, Calum."

And she still did.

She still wanted him. She still loved him. Even after all this time. Even though she wasn't really sure what love was.

He didn't respond to that. Instead he closed the gap between them. His hands were in her hair and she was pulled into a deep kiss. The moment his lips touched hers, it ignited that burning passion that was always simmering below the surface.

Her body remembered him and she pressed herself against him, holding on to him, afraid to let him go. This time she didn't want to run.

She was so enraptured by the kiss, his lips against hers, hungrily claiming her, that even the ground was shaking beneath her feet.

Wait. The ground is shaking.

Calum broke off the kiss and held her tight. "It's a quake."

"Right."

Calum held her—there was nowhere for them to go in that moment. They just stood there, on ground that suddenly didn't feel so solid. It felt like they were standing on a big bowl of Jell-O, but as quickly as the shaking started, it was over.

Calum let go of his hold on her and they just stared at each. She was not really expecting the earth to move quite that much.

"That wasn't too bad. I just hope it's not a foreshock," Calum said, but she could hear that his voice was shaking.

"I forgot about earthquakes and I hope it's not a foreshock, either." Pearl couldn't look at him. She was embarrassed she had let down her guard, but also, she was still a bit rattled by the quake.

"We'd better get back and see if Jerome and Derek are okay."

"Right," she said nervously.

He took her hand without thinking and they walked quickly off the trail and back up to the house. Everything seemed to be fine, but Jerome was standing on his deck holding Derek, who looked a bit shaken, too.

"Thank God. I was worried about you two," Jerome said, setting down Derek, who still stuck close to his father.

"We're okay," Calum said.

"I turned on the police scanner. There doesn't seem to be too much damage yet and Dianne texted that she's on her way home."

"Can I go back inside, Dad?" Derek asked.

Jerome nodded and Derek ran back into the house.

"We were wondering if it was a foreshock. It was strong, but didn't feel that deep like a real quake," Pearl said. She had grown up in California and was used to some real doozy earthquakes.

"Let's hope not. Let's hope it was just a tremor," Calum said.

"Fingers crossed," Jerome said.

It was then a car came up the drive and Jerome let

out a sigh when they saw it was Dianne's car. Pearl felt a surge of relief, too.

Jerome greeted his wife and they hugged and kissed. Pearl was envious and she couldn't help but think about the kiss in the forest with Calum. It had come out of nowhere and though she shouldn't have let it happen, because they were only supposed to be friends, she had wanted it, too.

In fact, she wanted more, and it terrified her. It thrilled her, but scared her, too, how much she still wanted him. How she lost all control around him. She pulled back her hand, realizing that she was still holding his hand. He looked at her.

"You okay?" he whispered.

"I'm fine."

"Look, about what happened…"

She shook her head. "You don't have to explain anything else. I'm okay. It's all good and we don't have to talk about it anymore."

A strange expression crossed his face. "Right. We don't have to talk about it."

And he walked away, up the stairs into the house, and Pearl sighed.

When was she ever going to learn?

Just as Pearl expected, the nighttime Founder's Day parade in Mountain View was crowded and she hated it, but what she liked was seeing Derek's excitement and she liked watching Calum with Derek.

He had Derek on his shoulders most of the night and they were laughing and following the parade, with Dianne and Jerome.

Calum was so good with Derek and she couldn't help but wonder what he would've been like with their own child. A lump formed in her throat as she thought about it. About how her life could've been so different.

So much better.

She also couldn't stop thinking about that kiss. Even after the parade ended and they all went back to the ranch. She just couldn't stop thinking about how good it was to be in his arms. How his lips felt against hers. The way he made her blood heat with need. She loved when he held her. When he kissed her. Calum made her feel safe when his arms were around her and how she wanted to be there again, even if just for a night.

They never had their breakup sex.

Can you really just have one night with Calum?

And she knew she couldn't. So it was good that it was just one kiss and they didn't have to talk about it again.

Only she had to stop worrying and thinking about Calum, because when she woke up the next morning it was all hands to the kitchen to prep for a big Founder's Day dinner. It seemed to be a weekend affair in Mountain View. Dianne's parents were driving in, so there would be seven people for dinner and Dianne was not the niftiest in the kitchen.

Not that Pearl was, either.

She was on the sweet-potato-pie duty, which meant mashing the sweet potatoes and adding the most important ingredient—the mini marshmallows—and she took her job seriously.

"You're doing that awfully slow," Calum teased as he was mixing something in a bowl.

"It's got to be just right."

"Just dump them on," he said.

Pearl picked up a mini marshmallow and threw it at him. "Just stick to your assigned tasks."

"I am," he teased, continuing to mix whatever was in the bowl.

"What're you making?" she asked, wrinkling her nose, because whatever was in the bowl smelled awful.

"I think it's pastry, but it doesn't smell right." Calum frowned. "I think I did something wrong. I thought pastry was supposed to be like dough, not like…"

"It looks like wallpaper paste. You better go back to the drawing board on that one."

He winced. "Well, you need to move faster or that sweet-potato pie will never get done."

She tossed another marshmallow at him as he retreated to the other side of the kitchen. She wanted to make sure that everything looked okay. Jerome was outside barbecuing the turkey, or smoking it—Pearl couldn't really tell. She continued placing marshmallows on the sweet-potato pie. She wasn't the best cook, so she really hoped she didn't make someone sick and that the pie tasted good.

There was a rumble and she froze. "What was that?"

"What was what?" Calum asked as he bent over a recipe book.

And then the rumble came again—this time there was clattering of dishes and then the big shake came.

"Oh, my God." She froze, terrified.

Calum was beside her in a second and grabbed her, dragging her under a door frame. They braced themselves as the house heaved. This was more than just the tremor that they experienced when they were in the woods.

This was the real deal. She was hoping that the previous tremor was just that—a tremor—and not a prelude to what was happening now. Even though she grew up in California, she could never get used to the quakes and still remembered the big quake in San Francisco.

Calum's arms were around her and she felt safe. She snuggled closer, holding on to him as the floor beneath them shook. She buried her head against his shoulder.

It felt like it went on for an eternity, but it ended. Her pulse was thundering and she still clung to him. It felt right to hold him and to be held by him.

"Pearl," he whispered. "Are you okay? I didn't mean to grab you so forcefully."

"I'm okay and that's fine. I'm glad you did."

Of course, it was a bit of a fib. She wasn't okay and she didn't want to let go of her hold on Calum. She just clung to him as if he was her safety net and though she never really wanted to ever rely on someone, she liked being here with him. His arms were so strong and she had never felt this safe before. His arms were tight around her, holding her close, and she closed her eyes as she listened to his heart.

She could stay here forever.

"Derek!"

The blood-curdling scream from Dianne sent a chill down her spine and she was off running outside. She'd forgotten that Jerome, Dianne and Derek were outside when the earthquake hit.

Calum was behind her and they couldn't see any of them.

The barbecue was on its side, the turkey on the ground.

Calum shut off the gas line with a wrench from the meter that ran alongside the pipe outside.

"Dianne?" Pearl shouted.

Jerome came running around the corner of the house—he was bleeding. "This way!"

Pearl and Calum followed him around to the side of the barn, and back behind the barn they found Dianne crouched beside rubble, and it looked like a piece of the barn had collapsed. Pearl's stomach twisted in a knot as she got closer and saw it wasn't only rubble that Dianne was crouched beside.

She saw a small arm from underneath.

It was Derek.

He was trapped.

CHAPTER NINE

THE AMBULANCE WAS on the way and Calum was thankful that Pearl had her phone on her. He helped Jerome move the rubble away as Pearl held Dianne.

As soon as they got visualization and Calum knew it was safe, he got beside Derek and assessed his ABCs without trying to disturb him. If there was a crush injury, a spinal injury, he didn't want to move Derek, who was bent over a barrel. Calum was really worried that there was damage to Derek's spine, as the barn collapsing had stretched him in an odd way over the side of the barrel.

A curl of dread uncoiled in the pit of his stomach and he hoped Derek would come through this. He'd known Derek the boy's whole life. He was terrified, seeing Derek there, but he compartmentalized it and got to work. He wouldn't let Derek die.

Jerome, even though he was a doctor, tried to take Derek's hand, but Calum stilled him.

"Don't move him. Not until we get a backboard. There could be damage to his spine."

"Oh, God," Jerome said.

"It's okay. I've got this. Get the paramedics here and send Pearl over."

Jerome nodded and left.

Pearl crouched down beside Calum.

"Derek," she whispered, her voice shaking.

"I'm worried about his spine," Calum said. "See how he's bent."

Pearl craned her neck. "Yes. We can get him on a backboard and get him to the hospital."

"We're going to the hospital," Calum stated. "I'm not letting just anyone touch his spine and I need you in there with me."

Pearl nodded and he could see that glint of determination in her eyes. He only wanted her by his side when he operated on Derek. Together, they could save Derek's life. He was certain of that.

"Of course. I agree, we should be the only surgeons working on him."

Pearl stood to let in the paramedics. Calum directed them with easing Derek to the backboard, not shaking Derek and protecting the spine. Once Calum felt he was secure, he let the paramedics do the rest of their work, to make sure Derek was stabilized.

"Calum," Dianne said, tears running down her face as she clung to Jerome.

"He's breathing. I'm going with the paramedics to the hospital and I'm going to make sure that I'm consulted if there's a single bone broken."

"I'm going, too," Pearl stated.

Dianne nodded. "We'll follow."

Calum stood by Derek's side and helped the paramedics wheel the stretcher back to the ambulance. Pearl was on the other side and they climbed into the back of the ambulance after Derek was loaded.

Calum's pulse was racing. He was so worried about the little broken human in front of him, and he prayed that the spinal cord wasn't severed; that he could save

Derek from paralysis. He looked up at Pearl and she met his gaze.

She didn't smile, but he could see the concern in her eyes, too.

He could see her worry and pain as the ambulance raced down the hill, down into town.

"It'll be tricky," one of the paramedics said. "There are power lines down and trees. The hospital is bombarded after the quake."

"We're both surgeons from San Francisco and we'll help any way we can, but after we make sure Derek is okay."

The paramedic nodded.

There wasn't much to say. He'd work for days on end, straight, if it meant he could use hospital privileges and save Derek's life. He would've done the same for his own child.

He would do the same for Pearl.

Once they got to the hospital, there was mass confusion in the emergency department, but he had to focus on Derek.

"What do we have here?" a trauma doctor asked, meeting them at the door.

"Male, age five, suspected break to the spine. GCS score in the field was five, but improved upon arrival to nine," the paramedic stated.

"And who are you?" the trauma doctor asked, looking at the both of them. "Are you the parents?"

"No. I'm Dr. Munro, orthopedic surgeon, and this is Dr. Henderson, also an orthopedic surgeon, and we'll be leading this case."

"This is my ER," the trauma doctor shouted.

"And we're specialists in spines," Pearl snapped. "The parents will be arriving soon and have given us permission to take care of their son. This is Dr. Dianne Lopez's child."

The trauma surgeon nodded. "You can use trauma pod three. We're slammed."

"I promise, we'll help you after we make sure that Derek is stable," Calum offered. He hadn't asked Pearl if she was willing to help, but he knew that she would. She might shirk other duties, but she never shirked her medical duties.

The patient always came first.

The paramedics wheeled Derek into trauma pod three and the trauma team helped Calum get into a yellow trauma gown.

"I'll go speak with the chief of surgery," Pearl said, tying the back of her gown.

"Okay, he may have a break in his spine. We need to move him carefully, make sure he's stable and then I need a CT scan stat. We could be looking at crush injuries." Calum helped the team move Derek's backboard onto the bed so the paramedics could have back their stretcher.

Calum leaned over Derek and checked the vitals again.

There was reaction to the pupils, so he had hope that there wasn't a head trauma and that Derek wasn't bleeding in his brain.

Pearl returned. "Shall we get him down to the CT? We have clearance. The chief was very accommodating."

"Yes. He's breathing, intubated, but he's as stable as he's going to be and we need to find out what's going on in there."

Pearl nodded and they worked together to make sure that all the lines and all the bags were secured. Then they wheeled him out of the trauma pod, following one of the nurses to where the MRI was and where they jumped the line.

Together, Pearl and Calum lifted the backboard and secured Derek so that he was able to have his scans.

He had to drag Pearl away into the other room so they could do the scan. Truth be told, he had to drag himself away. It was hard to leave Derek alone and vulnerable, even though the child wasn't aware what was going on.

The radiologist had come down so that he could interpret the scans, but Calum had seen enough scans to know what he was looking for. Pearl worried her lip, her arms crossed, and kept her eyes on Derek.

"He's so little," she whispered.

"I know."

"This shouldn't have happened to him."

"I know."

She glanced at him—there were tears in her eyes, and he'd never seen her like this before. So close to crying. "I can do this, it's just…when you have a moment to feel…"

Calum sighed. "I know."

"I'm scared, Calum. Scared for Derek."

He took her in his arms and held her. She clung to him and he held her close while they waited for the scans to come up.

"Scans are up, Dr. Munro," the radiologist, Dr. Redding, said.

He let go of her then.

Calum leaned over and winced when he saw that there was a fracture, but the cord appeared to be intact. Derek was going to need a fusion. There were a couple of ribs that were broken, but they were hairline fractures and didn't appear to be infiltrating his lungs.

"There appears to be a bit of internal bleeding near the spleen, but it doesn't appear to be excessive and is quite normal for a crush injury. We can monitor it and see if it gets any worse," Dr. Redding said.

"Thank you, Dr. Redding." Calum turned to Pearl. "We need to get him into the OR and we need to know where to go."

Pearl nodded. "You stay with Derek and I'll fill in Dianne and Jerome what's happening and speak to the chief of surgery again. We'll have him in the operating room as soon as possible, I'm sure."

"Thank you."

Pearl nodded. "Just keep our boy stable."

It stunned him when she said that. *Our* boy. He wasn't their boy, but it felt like he could've been. Their child would've been the same age.

Derek swallowed a lump that had formed in his throat. He had to be strong, he had to clear his head to be able to do this.

He was going to make sure Derek was taken care of. He wasn't going to let down Derek, Dianne or Jerome.

Pearl looked down through her microscope at the spinal cord of her godson. Really, they shouldn't be working on him, but there were no specialists like them in this hospital. They were Derek's only chance.

Dianne and Jerome had given their permission and the chief of surgery graciously was assisting on Derek. They had everything they needed and it was hard to keep Dianne and Jerome out of the operating room.

Especially Dianne, who wanted to do the anesthesiology on her son, but that was against every oath they took. She couldn't work on her son. She couldn't be present in the operating room and Pearl couldn't even imagine the pain of being so helpless.

Can't you?

And just that thought made her recall in vivid detail the absolute agony of losing her baby. Of losing Calum and her baby. How she had felt so helpless and there was nothing she could do to stop it. Her medical degree had been useless in that moment when her baby passed.

It was extreme, agonizing helplessness.

"The T4 and T5 are crushed. We're going to have fuse here and place rods," Calum muttered.

"I agree," Pearl said, hoping that her voice didn't shake.

Calum glanced up at her briefly. "Pearl?"

"I'm okay," she said. "I can do this."

"Good, because I need you," Calum said.

It caught her off guard. She knew that he meant he needed her for this surgery. He needed her expertise and assistance, just like he had needed her when they were working on their patient with skeletal dysplasia. They were a team. Right in this moment they needed each other.

He was staring at her, his blue eyes intense across the operating-room table.

"I need you, too," she said. "We got this."

The corners of his eyes crinkled and she knew that he was smiling under his mask. "Right. We do."

Pearl nodded and went back to work. She was going to make sure that Derek wasn't paralyzed. She was going to take care of Dianne and Jerome's little boy.

This is why she became a surgeon.

You walked away from it, remember?

She found her work rewarding, but there was something different about being in an operating room and working on a patient's spine after an accident compared to a busted knee or a torn rotator cuff after a sports injury.

This was saving a life. The deep-rooted part of her emotions wanted to run because she wanted to cry seeing Derek like this. She was losing control of herself seeing Derek on this table, but she couldn't run from Derek. Derek needed her. Dianne and Jerome needed her and Calum needed her.

Right here.

Her control over her emotions had to wait and she'd lose control if it meant Derek would be saved. She'd do anything to save him.

This was what she'd been born to do as a surgeon. This was what she missed, and she was angry that she walked away from it, and she wished she could go back.

You can.

Only she wasn't sure that she was strong enough to do that. She wasn't sure that she could turn back the clock and walk back into her old life.

She was too terrified, but she had to try.

Pearl walked with Calum down to the small waiting room. Dianne and Jerome were there, on their own. Pearl saw that Jerome's head had been bandaged and she was glad someone had taken care of his superficial laceration.

She felt bad for ignoring it, but their main focus was Derek.

When they walked in, Dianne's eyes were wide, she was pale, and Jerome put his arm around her. The surgery had taken hours and when Pearl checked the clock, it was six in the morning. They'd been working all night. She was beat.

"He made it through the surgery," Calum said. "We had to fuse his spine. He had a couple of crushed vertebrae. He has a long recovery, but I feel confident that he will walk again."

Dianne started sobbing and then hugged Calum and then her.

"I don't know what would've happened if you two weren't there," Dianne sobbed.

Tears were stinging Pearl's eyes. "Well, we were, and Derek is stable. He's going to be okay, but he's in the intensive-care unit. He's under the care of the paediatric surgeon on duty."

"And that surgeon has my pager if something else happens," Calum said. "I will be here in a heartbeat."

Dianne hugged him. "Thank you. Thank you both. Can we go see him?"

"I don't think the ICU doctor on duty is going to stop Dr. Lopez from seeing her son," Pearl teased.

Dianne nodded and left with Jerome.

Pearl sighed. "So much for a relaxing weekend, huh?"

Calum chuckled and sank down in a chair, scrubbing his hand over his face. "What a day."

"Not exactly how I thought it would go." She sat down in the chair next to him. "I was going to take an early morning train to get back to San Francisco. I missed it."

"I'll take you home. I drove here and it'll be faster than the train."

"Thanks. I appreciate that."

"Well, if I had known that you were coming to the ranch I could have driven you here."

Pearl cocked an eyebrow. "Would you? Especially with how things were a bit awkward before we came?"

"Okay, maybe not when I was in that frame of mind. You're right, but I can give you a ride back to San Francisco today. I just need some strong, strong coffee and then we can head back. I haven't checked the extent of the damage from the quake."

"We've been busy." Pearl stood up. "I think we'd better check with the chief of surgery and make sure that we're not needed, as we did promise to help out if we got privileges."

Calum yawned. "Right."

"Come on. You can do a few more hours' work and we'll head back."

"Point me in the direction of caffeine and I can spend some time setting bones or putting shoulders back into place."

"That's the spirit."

They left the waiting room. She was completely and utterly exhausted. Not just physically, but emotionally just done.

She was burnt out. Burnt out from all the emotions that she was trying so hard to control, burnt out from trying to keep everyone out, but she didn't know how to go back.

There was no way to turn back time, but she knew one thing—she had to figure out how to get back. She was tired of running.

CHAPTER TEN

"I'M SORRY, BUT the road is closed."

Pearl groaned inwardly as the state trooper talked to Calum. They had left Dianne and Jerome's ranch. Dianne's parents had got in and were updated on the situation. They were going to take shifts going to the hospital.

Pearl helped Dianne's mother clean up what they could and make sure that there was food and everything was okay. Then she packed up her bags. They had hit the road back to San Francisco in the late afternoon. Both of them were wiped out and now there was a washout from the rainstorm that had picked up.

They were stuck and they were too tired to drive back up into the foothills two hours behind them and they were too tired to try and find a detour to get to San Francisco. They were stuck.

"Do you know of any hotels around here?" Calum asked the trooper. Things seemed to be conspiring against them to get back to San Francisco.

"Sure. About three miles back into Catfish Canyon, there's a small motel that would be able to accommodate you. Follow this road back, take the first exit into town and follow Main Street until you find the Golden Corral Motel."

"Thank you, officer."

The state trooper stepped back and Calum did a U-turn and headed back into the last small town they had blasted through on their way back to San Francisco.

She didn't really want to stop for the night, especially with Calum, but at least at a motel she could get her own room. They had used their exhaustion as an excuse not to talk about what happened the day in the woods, or how she had clung to him during the quake.

Or the fact that in the surgery he had said that he always wanted her and she had admitted to the same. It wasn't a lie. She missed him.

She wanted him and she wanted to talk to him. She was overwhelmed and Calum made her feel safe.

It was no problem finding the motel, and despite its name, it actually looked kind of cute and cheerful, which was hard to pull off in a downpour. Calum ran inside to see if there were any rooms.

Pearl hoped there were, because she was exhausted. She wanted a hot shower and bed.

And Calum?

She shook away that thought.

Yes. She wanted Calum again, but there was no way she was going to let that happen. Although, she couldn't get that kiss out of her head. It's all she could think about. It wasn't long before he came back to the car.

"Were there any rooms?" she asked.

"Yes. There was one."

She raised her eyebrows. "One?"

"Yes. So I took it."

"Calum!"

"Pearl, we're adults and we're both tired. I think we can share a room. It has a queen-size bed and a pullout couch. I think we can make do."

She sighed. It wasn't ideal, especially when she

needed to put space between the two of them. Not that she was expecting him to do anything—she was worried about hurting him, about not being able to resist him. She was worried that she would want his kisses again, to be held by him. She was worried about how much she wanted it.

"Come on. We can't sit here in the car all night."

"You're right." She reached into the back and grabbed her suitcase, and Calum grabbed his bag. They ran to their room and Calum opened the door.

It was a clean room and there was a sofa bed, a queen bed, a tiny kitchenette and a tiny bathroom. It wasn't perfect, but it would do for one night and she could manage that.

"You take the bed and I'm good on the pullout."

"I can sleep on the pullout," she said. "You've been driving and—"

"What kind of gentleman would I be if I didn't let you have the bed?"

She blushed. "Okay, but no complaining about a bad back tomorrow."

"I don't have a bad back. I slept on these all the time when I was in college."

"That was a very long time ago," she teased.

"Ha, ha." There was a twinkle in his eye. "Do you want a shower first or should I?"

"You go first, since I'm getting the better bed and I'll see if I can order in some pizza or something."

"Sounds good."

Pearl kicked off her shoes and sat down on the bed, which was surprisingly comfortable, and flipped open the book with all the amenities while Calum grabbed his bag and headed into the bathroom.

It wasn't long before she could hear the water running and she tried not to think about the fact that he was in there, naked.

You need to order pizza and not fantasize about your ex-fiancé who is in the shower.

She found what looked like a good pizza place and ordered a pepperoni pizza. Once she'd finished ordering, Calum came out of the bathroom, only wrapped in a towel. She tried not to stare at him.

"You'd better get dressed," she said.

"I will."

"The pizza guy will be here soon and I'm going to have my shower."

"Once you go in for your shower, I'll get dressed."

Pearl left the money for the pizza on the bed and then grabbed what she needed for a shower, including a change of clothes. She wasn't coming out in a skimpy motel towel. It was bad enough that Calum had.

When her shower was done and she was dressed in a fresh set of comfy clothes, she left the bathroom and hoped that Calum had gotten dressed. She was relieved to see that he had and that the pizza had arrived.

"You came out just in time," Calum said. "It just got here."

"Good. I'm starving. I was hoping for a Founder's Day dinner or some leftovers, but the earthquake had had something else in mind." She put away her stuff and walked over to the kitchenette and took a seat at the little table, hoping her towel holding her wet hair up didn't slip over her face.

"I was watching the television and the earthquake's epicenter was in the Sierra mountain range. We weren't far from it."

"I can believe that. Was there much damage?"

"Yes, and a few deaths."

"We're lucky Derek wasn't one of them."

"I know," he said. "I got an update from Dr. Knowles, the paediatrician attending, and Derek is doing well. He's still in the ICU, but they're thinking of waking him soon from his medicated coma. He's stable and there have been motor responses from his lower limbs."

Pearl sighed in relief. "Thank goodness."

"Do you ever think about our child?"

The question caught her off guard. Of course she did. All the time, but she tried not to. Work kept her busy, kept her distracted, so that she didn't have to think about their baby. And the fact that the question came from Calum shocked her.

She couldn't think about it when she ran off to New York. It was a foolish thing to do, but Pearl realized that when it came to matters of the heart, when it came close to her fear of losing something she wanted so badly, she fled.

It was easier to manage that pain.

"I do," she said quietly. "I do all the time."

"I'm surprised."

"Why would you be surprised by that?"

"Because you left, because I tried to talk to you about it and you left," he said.

"I left because I… Because I failed, Calum. I failed you. I failed our child. I'm the reason the baby was lost. My incompetent cervix. I failed you." She couldn't stop the tears then and she couldn't believe that she had let that out. She'd never cried in front of him before and there was no way she could stop them now.

She was struggling to accept that she had told him; that she was vulnerable to him.

She was never vulnerable to anyone. She'd been taught that vulnerability was a weakness, by both her parents, but she couldn't hold it back anymore. She was tired keeping everything in, and she wasn't less of a person for feeling something.

"You didn't fail me. Your body failed us, but not really. Why didn't you tell me this before?"

Tears slid down her cheeks and the dam burst. There was no more holding back. "I shouldn't be crying."

"Why?"

"I was told tears were a weakness. Tears meant failure, and failure was a weakness. You think I'm a strong person, cold and detached, but I'm not. I'm not."

"You're the strongest person I know, Pearl."

Calum couldn't believe she was crying. That she blamed herself.

He knew that's why the baby had been lost, but not that she carried the blame. She thought she'd let him down.

He didn't feel that she had let him down because she lost the baby; she'd let him down because she left. But now she was crying and he hated to see her cry.

When he'd held her in his arms during the earthquake, he had wanted to keep her there. He had wanted to comfort her, because she had never let him comfort her before. Even when they were together, there had always been barriers between them. She had never let him in.

He closed the gap between them and took her in his arms. Tipping her chin, he kissed her on the lips, wanting her to know he didn't blame her for the loss of their child, but he was unable to say that he was still hurt she had left him.

All he wanted to do was hold her, to kiss her and just

be with her. Even if it was only one more time. He just wanted her. He'd always wanted her.

"Calum," she murmured against his lips.

"Pearl, I've missed you."

Her lips were so soft, he wanted to savor them. He so wanted to savor every second with her. He wanted her so badly.

He broke the kiss and stepped away, unsure of what to do. Unsure of everything. Pearl was standing so close to him. Just a few feet away. That's all that separated them. Maybe that's all that ever had. Maybe they were closer than he thought.

"Calum?" she asked, and her breath hitched. Her face was flush with desire and her eyes were still moist with tears.

Their first time together they'd been intoxicated. This time the only thing impeding him was his heart and the only thing he was drunk on was her.

Only her.

It had always been only her.

"I want you, Pearl. I've always wanted you."

"I meant what I said in that operating room, Calum. I've only ever wanted you, too."

Then why did you leave?

Only he didn't say that out loud. He just stared at her, his pulse thundering in his ears, his blood burning with need to have her again. To never let her go.

"You really mean that?" he asked.

"I want tonight, Calum. I want you. Please. Even if it's just for one night."

There was no other answer needed. He closed the gap between them, reaching down to cup her face and kiss her again. Gently at first and then possessively, letting her know how much he wanted her. How much he only wanted her.

There had never been a time when he hadn't wanted her. There would never be time when he wouldn't desire her. Pearl was everywhere. She was in every dream, every memory of the best times of his life. She was like a ghost haunting him. She was everything.

Pearl melted under his lips, her arms around his neck and her fingers tangling in the hair at the nape. He pushed her over to the bed. He knew he shouldn't, but he missed her, and she wanted it as much as he did.

Calum wanted to chase away the memories of their loss, her leaving, by making love to her. Even if it was just for one night.

"Are you sure, Pearl?" he asked again. "I don't have protection."

"I'm sure," she murmured against his ear. "I'm on the pill. It's okay."

"Pearl…"

She silenced him with a kiss, then undid his belt. "I want you, Calum. I've always wanted you."

The moment her hands slipped under the waist of his jeans, he moaned. He knew he was a lost man and he had to have her.

"You're all I've ever wanted, Pearl." He cupped her breasts and kissed that spot below her collarbone that he remembered so well. She moaned with pleasure. This is what he'd been dreaming of since she'd left.

Calum lowered her to the mattress, running his hands over her body, but pressing himself against her so he could feel her against him, feel every inch of her. He desperately wanted to be skin-to-skin.

Nothing separating them.

"Touch me," she whispered, wrapping her legs around his waist.

"Pearl, you're driving me crazy."

"I don't care. I want you. Now."

Her urgency really drove him wild with desire.

With hurried fingers they undressed so that nothing was between them. She ran her hand over his skin, causing gooseflesh to break out. He loved the softness of her touch.

"Yes. Touch me," he said.

"With pleasure." She teased him with the tips of her fingers, running a finger lightly down his chest, over his nipples, along his ribs, lower and lower until she gripped him in the palm of her hand, stroking him.

"Oh, God," he groaned.

"I love it when you moan," she said huskily, still holding him. She leaned forward to kiss his neck, and her eyes were glittering the darkness of the room as she continued to stroke him, holding him captive to her touch.

Every nerve was burning under her touch. It was driving him wild. He didn't want her to stop, but he didn't want to come. Not this way, but it felt so good.

"Don't stop."

"I don't plan on it." And then her kisses trailed down his body until her mouth was on him, then his hand slipped into her hair. He wanted to be inside her, bring her pleasure.

The same pleasure she was giving him.

Growling, he pulled her away and then pushed her back against the mattress. She wrapped her legs around him and he moved them, pulling her legs open.

"Calum, I want you."

"I know, but now it's my time. I want to taste you."

"Your turn...oh, my God." She cried out as he did exactly what he said he would do. He was using his tongue to taste her, running his tongue around the most sensitive part of her, making her thighs quiver as he brought her close to the edge of ecstasy. Just like she had done to him.

"Calum!" she cried out.

"What?" he asked, knowing what she wanted. He wanted it, too. Badly.

He just wanted her to beg for it. To ask for it.

"You know."

"No, I don't." And he went back to his ministrations, her hands in his hair, her back arched.

"Calum!"

"Tell me what you want, Pearl. Tell me."

"I want you."

He moved over her and entered her with one quick thrust.

Oh, God.

She was so tight, so hot, and it took every ounce of control he had not to take her hard and fast, like his body was screaming for him to do. He wanted to make this last.

He wanted to savor this moment, if it was to only be one night.

He wanted this one night to last forever.

Only he knew that it wouldn't.

So he thrust slowly, agonizingly so, making her cry out, and he didn't have long to wait. She began to meet his thrusts, urging him to go faster. They moved in sync like no time had passed between them, like they had done this so many times before. Like it was yesterday. He sank deeper, lost to her. He held her tight, his hand cupping her bottom as he let her ride him.

It was frenzied, fast and hot. It was everything to be

that connected with her again and when he thought he couldn't take much more she cried out, tightening around as she came, her nails digging into his back.

Only then did he let go of his control and join her. It had been so long.

Far too long.

He rolled away when it was over, trying to catch his breath and process what had happened. How powerful it had been. How deep their connection was, but there was no trust and there was nothing keeping her here. Just a job and she could leave him again.

They had made no promises to each other.

Don't think about it now.

Only it was hard not to think about right here. She curled up next to him and he put his arm around her. They didn't say anything to each other and he didn't want to say anything. He didn't want to ruin this moment. He just held her, listening to the sound of their breathing and the sound of the rain on the roof.

He wanted her again.

He was lost and he realized that, no matter how much he wanted to deny it.

He would always be lost.

Always.

CHAPTER ELEVEN

One month later, end of November

"I DON'T KNOW how much longer I can go on, Doc."

Pearl worried her lip and looked at George. He didn't look well. The port in his leg that was feeding chemotherapy straight to the tumor was doing a number on him, but Calum had been insistent that they needed to do a month of the targeted chemo to shrink the osteosarcoma before he even thought of operating.

The chemo that Calum's oncologists were using was very potent and George was no longer that robust athlete—he was wasting away to nothing and the first thing on Pearl's mind was that he had an infection.

Calum was sympathetic. "You're almost done. One more session and I'll determine when I can go in and do the surgery. Hang in there."

George nodded and laid back down. He was now an inpatient. Two days after he'd started the chemotherapy he began to get constant fevers, and since his mom had to travel back and forth, Pearl and his coach had thought it best that he stay in the hospital to be monitored.

Pearl knew that George wanted to go back to Philadelphia for Christmas and it was hard to be stuck in the hospital, even being an adult. George wasn't the only one in the hospital. Poor Derek still was and Pearl wanted to go see him, but George needed her and Mountain View was too far for just a quick visit.

And she was also fighting something. It was hitting her hard today. Some kind of bug she just couldn't shake.

Derek was doing well and there was no paralysis thanks to her and Calum. He was still in the hospital getting physiotherapy, but he was doing brilliantly. Pearl and Calum were planning to go up there and visit soon, but right now they both needed to be in San Francisco with their patients.

They left George's room. Which she was thankful for, because the room was hot. George was always cold.

"You're sweating. Are you okay?" Calum asked.

"Yeah. It was hot in there."

Calum frowned. "Not especially. I hope you're not getting sick."

"I hope not, either." The last thing she needed was a bug. "I'm fighting something, but I don't have a fever. I checked before I went into George's room."

George looked as awful as Pearl felt. And she'd been feeling poorly since the end of October. Just after she and Calum had spent that incredible night together. Their one night. The next day they made it back to San Francisco and agreed that they would go back to being friends and work together. She had been busy traveling with the team and she hadn't seen him or George in a couple of weeks. She wanted to talk to Calum about their night together, but with this sickness and work she hadn't had a chance to talk to him.

It was fine for the first week and then Pearl had caught this bug, probably from the rain and getting wet that night, but she just couldn't shake it. Calum had been inviting her out, but she was just feeling awful.

"You know, you've been feeling run-down for a couple of weeks. Maybe you are getting sick," Calum suggested.

"I can't get sick. If I get sick, then I can't help George. I haven't had a sick day in years! I get my flu shots regularly, I do everything right. The only thing I can think of was it was that night in the motel. We were both soaked to the bone when we got into the room."

Just thinking about that night made her flush with heat.

They had both agreed that was a one-time thing, but there was a part of her that didn't want it to be. Especially while they worked on the case. She had thought that spending one night with Calum would be enough. That it would get him out of her system, but it hadn't.

It made her crave his touch again.

She'd forgotten what it was like to be in his arms. How he made her feel.

No one had ever made her feel the way that Calum did.

It just made her want more and she didn't deserve to have more.

She was glad she had told Calum how she felt about the loss of their baby, and he'd said that he didn't blame her, but she had a hard time believing it. Other than asking her to come out with him, he didn't seem all that interested in starting anything up.

It hurt her, but she couldn't blame him.

And it was for the best.

"That could've done it. Why don't we do a blood test and see if you have infection or something?" he asked.

"That's a good idea." She'd been thinking about doing it herself, but she'd been so drained of energy that all she was trying to do was keep it together to get through work. Her patients needed her.

She didn't have time for this nonsense.

And if she had an infection she couldn't go see Derek, either.

She followed Calum into a small exam room and he washed his hands, then pulled out everything needed for a blood draw.

"If I'm sick, you're still going up to see Derek, right?" she asked.

"Yes. I will," he said. "My father wanted me to come see him. Said he had something important to tell me, but honestly I don't really care what he has to say."

"Are you sure you don't want to hear it? He's never reached out before. My parents reach out all the time and they have nothing new to tell me."

"That may be so, but he put work before me and my mom. He left her and even though he made all this money, he barely gave her alimony. Mom gave everything she had for me and my sister. So really, there's nothing I have to say to someone who runs away."

That last comment caught her off guard. She didn't think it was directed at her, but she wasn't sure. Isn't that what she'd done? She'd run away.

"I'm sorry for bringing it up."

"It's okay. Now, stop moving for a few moments and I'll do this blood draw."

"Yes." She winced when the needle pricked her. She had a medical degree, but hated needles, especially when they came near her.

"There. All done." Calum pulled out the needle and placed a cotton swab on her arm. "Now apply pressure."

"I know."

He chuckled. "I'll run this down to the lab and put

a rush on it. No sense in dallying around if you're sick. Might as well treat it."

"What about George?" she asked.

Calum sighed. "I know. He's going for a repeat scan so I can see if the cancer has shrunk, but honestly I don't think that the chemo is touching it. I've never done my surgical procedure on someone with such a large tumor. I don't have a lot of faith that he'll play again and if he continues this way, I'm worried that he won't make it."

"Me, too," she sighed.

"We'll worry about that after his scan and then we'll talk to him and his mother about the options. I don't think he'll be happy."

"You mean about amputation?"

"It would save his life."

"Would it, though?" she asked. "His dream has been to play in the NFL—your procedure could save his leg."

"*Could* is the key word, Pearl. *Could.* There's no guarantee. Medicine is not infallible. Things don't always turn out the way you want." He left the exam room and Pearl leaned back against the chair.

Boy, did she ever know that feeling.

She knew that things didn't always turn out the way you wanted. If they did, she'd never have left San Francisco and she'd have a kid Derek's age.

Then another part of her worried whether she'd still be with Calum. Just a small part because her heart still believed it would've worked out. She could've had a happily-ever-after.

Pearl was called down to the CT room and her heart sank when she saw that Calum was sitting next to Dr. Knox and the tension in the room was palpable.

"What's wrong?"

"Come see," Calum said grimly.

Pearl leaned over and her stomach churned. The osteosarcoma wasn't being shrunk by the chemotherapy. It was invading further. It was like the poison that was used to kill cancer was doing nothing.

The radiation that George had endured was doing nothing.

Immunotherapy was doing nothing.

Nothing was working and there was only one option.

"It's a beast," Calum said.

"Oh, God." Tears were welling up in her eyes. "This is going to…devastate him."

And she didn't want to cry in front of Calum and Dr. Knox. Pearl left the CT room and stood in the hall, trying to breathe. What had come over her? What was wrong with her?

She'd had other patients who had had their careers stalled or ended because of cancer or injuries. She'd always managed to keep her emotions in check.

"Pearl?" Calum asked, following her.

"I'm sorry. I don't know what came over me. I know there's no other option."

Calum nodded. "I'm sorry, but he hid his symptoms too long and I get why. My mother did the same. She hid them, ignored them, until it was too late."

Pearl nodded, but she couldn't control her tears. "I don't know what I'm going to tell the owners."

"You're worried about the owners of the Bridgers?" Calum asked sardonically. "You think that you'll lose your job over this?"

"No, I'm worried about George's future," she stated. "They knew it was a long shot, but still…this whole thing. It's going to ruin a lot of his plans, his career in football."

"Well, cancer has a way of doing that."

"I'm sorry. I'm having a hard time explaining what I want to say. It's all a big mess."

"You need to pull yourself together," Calum stated.

She glared at him. "You're being unkind."

"I'm not being unkind. I know you and I know that you don't like appearing this way. I know that you don't like to lose control."

She sighed. "I can't remember the last time I lost control."

And then it hit her.

Yes, she did remember the last time she was a bundle of nerves. She recalled in vivid detail the last time she'd cried at the drop of a hat. The last time she felt so ill, so sweaty and uncomfortable.

Oh, God.

"Have my lab results come in?" she asked, hoping her voice wasn't shaking.

"I don't know." Calum pulled out his phone and then checked his messages. "Yeah. They have."

He handed her the phone so she could open the file. She glanced through it all, showing normal blood work, except one thing.

One thing that could be detected in the blood but was too early to detect in a urine test and was too early to detect because her period was not yet late.

The hCG in her bloodstream didn't lie.

The lab result didn't lie.

She was pregnant.

Again.

"Pearl, what's wrong?" Calum asked. "You've gone pale. You look like you're going to faint."

She handed him back the phone, because he had the right to know. He was the father, after all. He took the phone from her and went through the report and his eyes widened when he saw what she saw.

"You're pregnant?"

She nodded. "It appears so."

"I thought you were on the pill?"

"I was, but apparently that didn't work. You know that no form of contraception is perfect. We had protection the first time we got pregnant."

Calum scrubbed a hand over his face. "It seems like the fates *want* us to have a baby as we seem to get pregnant in spite of using the proper protection."

"Right?" She laughed nervously.

She didn't know what she was going to do. Her job involved traveling. She sometimes had to leave San Francisco and travel to other states to be there when the team played. And she had offers from other teams who wanted her. Offers she'd been seriously considering so that she could put distance between her and Calum since their night together.

Running away again.

"Well, I think I know the best solution to this whole mess."

Pearl cocked an eyebrow, intrigued. "You do?"

"I think we need to do what we were going to do the first time."

"Are you serious?" she snapped. "You think that's the best course of action? Look what happened last time."

"I know what happened last time," Calum stated quietly. "You lost the baby and left. I distinctly remember what happened last time."

"So if you remember what happened last time, why do think that repeating that mistake is a good idea?"

He took a step back, shocked. "Mistake?"

"We didn't plan it. And we didn't plan this one. Do

you really think that marrying me is the best course of action?"

"I do. I think a family should be together. And that's why I want you to marry me."

"Because of duty? That's why you want to marry me. That's the only reason. I can't marry you because of your sense of outdated duty, Calum. Look how that turned out for my parents and look at your parents. A family can't be forced together."

His expression hardened. "Your parents are hardly a good example."

"Exactly."

"And my parents..." He trailed off. "It wouldn't be like that. We're not like them."

"How do you know?" she asked.

"We're better than them, Pearl."

"Are we? Are we really?" she asked.

"Pearl, I'm asking you. Marry me."

"And I'm saying no, Calum. I can't marry you. Our lives are so different..." She was terrified of losing the baby again, of losing Calum.

She was losing control and she felt like she was going to be sick. She was scared of reaching out and taking her happily-ever-after.

"Right, and you'll leave again if a job comes up. Your career means more to you because for whatever reason you're trying to please parents who will never be pleased with you. Why can't you see that?" He asked that with such anger, it caught her off guard.

"It's my career. And look who's talking. You worked hard to gain your father's attention."

"You complain about their toxicity and how they were narcissistic, how they only put their careers first, and that's what you're doing. You'll take my baby away from me if I don't marry you."

Those words sunk in.

They hurt.

And there it was. He was only marrying her because he was afraid of her leaving. He didn't love her. He just didn't want her to leave.

She should've known. She should've trusted her instinct. She should've kept her distance, but she was in love with him.

She'd never stopped loving him, but she wasn't going to marry him because of a sense of duty. She wasn't going to marry him because she was pregnant with their baby.

And she wasn't going to marry a man who, deep down, didn't trust her. Who didn't love her.

Tears stung her eyes. "I can't marry you, Calum. I won't marry you."

"You can't leave. Why do you want to leave?"

"And you just want to marry me to make me stay so that I won't leave you like your father left you!"

He took a step back, like she'd slapped him. She'd gone too far, but so had he.

She turned to leave. She had to get away from him. She couldn't be around him. As she walked to the door, there was a panic in the CT room.

Dr. Knox ran out. "George is crashing!"

She spun around on her heel and dashed for George. A resident had intubated and was doing chest compressions. She took over and Calum followed behind her.

Right now, she didn't have time to talk about the past. She didn't have time to think about her feelings, about her hurt, or the fact that she'd turned down the man she loved and always had loved.

She had a life to save.

* * *

Calum was crushed that Pearl had turned him down and he was so mad at himself for what he said. He regretted it the moment he said it, but she was going to leave again. She wasn't going to stay in San Francisco, and she was going to take their baby with her. He loved her. Why couldn't he say that?

He didn't want to lose either of them. And he was shocked Pearl was pregnant again. With his child.

He was still processing it all. He couldn't quite believe it when he saw the lab report. He couldn't quite believe that Pearl was pregnant again.

And then the world came crashing down. She said no, he lashed out and George crashed.

He was angry at himself for saying those things to Pearl and he was angry that she had said those things to him, but she wasn't wrong.

He was terrified of losing her again.

He was terrified of her losing the baby and losing her.

Calum was ecstatic about the baby, but he wanted Pearl. It had always been Pearl and now he'd ruined it. He'd gotten so hotheaded and had wanted to stop her from leaving. He had tried to cage her and that was foolish.

And then George almost died.

Calum had just spent the last hour consulting the oncology team and the outlook was grim. Pearl was standing next to him as they observed George through the glass window of the intensive-care unit, but they hadn't said a word to each other. The tension between them was palpable. George's mother was by his bedside and George was coming to. The ICU attendant had pulled out the breathing tube and George's vitals were stable.

For now.

So he and Pearl stood there, side by side.

He could sense that she was angry at him and he couldn't blame her.

He was angry at himself. Right now, though, they had to work together to save a life.

"So there's no choice," she said.

"No. He'll die if we continue this. It's too far gone."

Pearl nodded. "I'll break the news to him."

"I can do it."

She glared at him. "He's my patient. I will break the news to him. It's his dream that's being shattered. If anyone understands that, it's me."

"Really?" he asked. "How was your dream shattered?"

"I wanted our baby, too, you know. I was devastated when I lost it."

"So was I."

"I was grieving," she said.

"I was grieving, too, and you left me. Just like everyone else has. For that, I do blame you."

Her expression softened for a moment and then hardened again. "I have to talk to George."

Calum watched her walking into the ICU room, where George was. He looked away—he couldn't watch her do it.

It was killing him. His heart was breaking all over again and he didn't know how to change it. He was afraid of her leaving again, of the loss again, and didn't know what to do.

You do, you know.

He walked away and pulled out his phone. There was one person he had to talk to. If he was ever going to figure this out, there was one person that he had to make things right with and that was Grayson Munro.

"Calum, I'm surprised to hear from you," his father said on the line.

"I'm wondering if you had a few minutes to spare for me. We need to talk."

There was a pause on the other end. "Of course. Can you meet me in thirty minutes? There's a coffee shop not far from the hospital, the Café au Lait."

"I know the place. Sure. I can meet you there."

"Good. I'll see you soon, Calum."

Calum ended the phone call. He looked back once at Pearl speaking with George and he felt a pang of guilt. He wished he could've helped him more, but as Dr. Chin used to say, sometimes there was nothing more to do.

Sometimes things ended to stop the pain.

CHAPTER TWELVE

"I DON'T UNDERSTAND," George said quietly. "I thought this was a new, cutting-edge treatment."

"It is," Pearl stated. "Unfortunately, your cancer is highly aggressive and isn't responding to either chemotherapy or radiation. We have no other choice. To save your life, we have to take your leg."

"Then take it," George's mother said through tears holding hand.

"No, Mom!" George snapped. "I'm a grown man. You can't take my leg. I just got to the NFL. This can't be the end of my career!"

Pearl swallowed the lump in her throat. She was trying not to cry. "I'm sorry, George. There are no other alternatives. The cancer has infiltrated too far. You'll die if we don't take the leg. There are good options for prosthetics. Prosthetics that will help you run again."

"No. No, Doc. I'm sorry, but no." He shook his head, angry, not that she could blame him. She was angry for him.

She was angry that she had to deliver this news to him.

She was angry at herself for being too scared to try and make a life with Calum work.

She was angry at herself for running away five years ago. She was angry that she had hurt and left Calum.

She was a fool.

"Baby, please see sense," George's mother said.

"No." George wouldn't look at them. "I won't do it."

"Can I talk to him alone?" Pearl asked.

George's mom nodded and left the intensive-care unit. It was just her and George now.

"George, you understand that you will die. This will kill you. You'll still have your leg, but you won't be able to play, the chemo will make you so ill and the surgery to take away the tumor will destroy your muscles. It'll make a mess of your leg."

George glanced at her.

She was getting through to him.

"I can't lose my leg, Doc."

"You'll lose your life if you don't," she said gently. "You're young. Your whole life is ahead of you. The cancer hasn't spread above the knee. It hasn't spread anywhere else, but it will sooner rather than later, and the strongest chemo isn't stopping its progression. If you let Dr. Munro take the leg, you'll have your knee still and there are athletes that still play professional sports with a prosthetic. It'll take some time, some physiotherapy, but you can still run. You can still play and in the meantime, I know that your coach offered you a job as assistant coach. The Bridgers still want you, George. Even if it's just for your brains instead of your speed."

A half smile appeared on George's face. "It's been my dream, Doc. It's been my dream for as long as I can remember."

"It can still be your dream. Sure, it looks a bit different, but you can still have what you want. You can still do what you love."

And just those simple words, which were supposed to help ease George's mind, hit her like a ton of bricks and tears welled up in her eyes.

"Whoa, Doc, are you okay?" George asked.

"I'm fine. Actually, I'm pregnant so I'm slightly over-emotional."

George grinned. "That's wonderful."

"It is, but here's the thing… I lost a baby five years ago. I swore I never wanted a family. I didn't have the best childhood, but then I got pregnant, and when I lost that baby I was terrified of this happening again, but it has and with the same man."

"It's Dr. Munro, isn't it?" George asked.

"How do you know?" Pearl asked, shocked.

"I know when people are in love. I don't just have strategizing smarts. I have to say I'm a bit jealous, Doc. You're a beautiful woman and I'm sorry that you were my doctor and that someone else got there first."

Pearl smiled. "I'm very flattered."

"You've been in love with him a long time."

"I have. I thought he blamed me for the loss of our baby, and I thought he was better off without me, but I was wrong."

George sighed. "Well, I guess I have no choice then."

"No choice?" she asked.

"I'll have the surgery, Doc. It's not how I planned it, but I want a chance to live and I want a chance to find a woman like you and fall in love, have a family. I'd be throwing an awful lot away because I was afraid of a change of plans, because I was afraid to take a chance."

She nodded. "Good. I'm glad, George. You almost died and you're too young. We take care of this and you go through physio, we can have you back in fighting form in a year or so."

"I'm tired of feeling like shit," George sighed. "Book the operating room and can you call my coach to come in. I want to strategize with him."

Pearl smiled. "Of course. I'll let Dr. Munro know your decision."

"Thanks, Doc."

Pearl nodded and left. She found George's mother in the hallway and she told her his decision. The woman thanked her for talking sense into George and gave her a hug, then headed back into George's room.

Pearl sighed. She had to find Calum. She had to let him know what was going on. She headed to the ICU charging station.

"Can you page Dr. Munro for me?" Pearl asked.

"I'm sorry, Dr. Henderson, he left for the day."

Pearl was stunned. "He left for the day?"

"Quite suddenly," the nurse said, like it was strange for Calum to leave abruptly.

"Thank you." Pearl frowned and walked away. It was unlike Calum to do something like that, not that she could blame him really.

She'd hurt him, but she was going to change that. She was tired of running. She was tired of hiding and worrying about how life changed in an instance. Even though she was scared she might lose this baby, even though she was scared that she would be a terrible mother and worried that a marriage would end up like her parents, she was done running.

She didn't know what the future held, but for the first time in her life, she knew that if he'd have her, her future included Calum.

And only Calum.

* * *

Calum found his father sitting alone in a corner table. He looked a bit tired and worn out, but that really didn't surprise him too much. His father was in his sixties and was still trying to burn the candle at both ends.

He perked up when Calum came in. Calum made an order at the counter and then went to sit down with his father.

"I'm glad you called, Calum," Grayson said.

"Are you?"

"I am."

"It's just…you never seemed to really care in the past."

Grayson frowned. "I know. I was too busy some of the time."

"All of the time," Calum stated. "You were busy all of the time, Father."

"Well, I'm glad you called me because I've been wanting to talk to you, as you know."

"And I wanted to speak with you, since you're an investor with the Bridgers."

"Oh?" his father asked, which of course made sense that as soon as Calum mentioned one of his father's investments, his interest piqued.

"Your linebacker, George. I can't save the leg. The cancer is too far gone and I have to amputate or he'll die."

His father didn't seem shocked. "That's awful to hear, but I'm aware that the coach made contingency plans, and the Bridgers are willing to pay for his recovery and prosthetic."

Calum was taken aback. "But you invested a lot in this young man. Don't you just want to get rid of him? Isn't he a drain?"

"He's smart," Grayson stated. "The coach feels like he's an asset and wants to keep him on the team. I support the rest of the owners and the coach on this."

Calum was shocked. "I'm impressed you're backing this."

"Of course. Sometimes you can't stop cancer. I hoped you would for the sake of the young man."

"Amputation will save his life."

"And that's good, because sometimes there are circumstances where the cancer is too far gone and there's no hope and you've realized that you've wasted your life being angry, chasing something so foolish that you really have nothing to show for it. You have money and power, but you really have nothing, especially when no one cares."

Calum's stomach twisted in a knot. "What're you saying?"

"I had a heart attack last year and I almost died. It made me realize how wrong I've been my whole life about my priorities. It's why I wanted to talk to you."

Calum couldn't believe what he was hearing.

He had a heart attack?

And as he looked closer at his father he started to see how his father had thinned out and aged a bit more. He saw the signs that he had ignored before, because he'd brushed his father away so many times because his father had run from him.

Pearl had come back and he was trying to force her into an uncomfortable situation. All he could think about was his own grief, his own hurt. Yes, he'd been alone, but he never followed Pearl. He had never fought for what he wanted.

He had never fought for their love.

Calum had assumed Pearl was like everyone else in his life that left him.

He'd forgotten that his mom had tried to fight for his dad.

His mom had tried to fight until the end. Even though it was useless and his dad never came back, she had always hoped he would. Calum had always thought she was foolish for doing that, but he had done the same with Pearl. He waited for her, hoping she'd come back.

The only difference was Pearl came back, and in his own way he was trying to push her away, too.

"How are you doing now?" Calum asked calmly.

"I'm good. I'm taking care of myself and putting things right. I'm making amends."

"So you wanted to tell me this to seek sympathy?"

His father shook his head. "No. Just to say, I'm sorry. I loved your mother, but I didn't like to be pinned down. I didn't like the responsibility of you and your sister—I didn't want that job."

"It's too late to take up that job."

"I know, but I wanted you to know that I didn't fight hard enough for you. I don't want you to make my mistakes. Career isn't everything, money isn't everything, and I wish I had found that out sooner. I'm sorry, Calum. I'm sorry for what I did. I don't have to have your forgiveness, but I wanted you to know just the same."

Calum really didn't know how to take that, but he understood his father for the first time, probably in his entire life.

"I appreciate you telling me this. Have you told Sharon?" Calum asked, wondering about his sister, whom he hadn't heard from in years.

"I have. She thanked me and that was the end of that. I want you to know, you don't owe me anything for schooling. I held that over you because I didn't know any better. I thought it meant I could control you and keep you in my life, but I was wrong."

"Thank you." He was having a hard time processing all this information. "I don't think I can forgive you for what you did to Mom, but for me, you have my forgiveness. I'm just sorry that this didn't happen sooner and for that, it's my fault. I was so wrapped up in my career and you were reaching out to me. I hope you can accept my apology."

Grayson smiled. "Yes. Thank you. I do."

Calum finished his coffee and stood. "You can call me. You don't have to do this alone."

His dad smiled up at him weakly. "I will."

Calum nodded and left.

He had to find Pearl and talk to her. If she didn't want to marry him, then that was fine, but he was going to make things right. He wasn't going to let her leave again. The two of them were in this together and he was going to make it work however she needed it to work.

He loved Pearl.

He had never stopped loving her.

He was never going to stop loving her. No matter what happened next.

No matter how uncertain the future was.

CHAPTER THIRTEEN

CALUM FOUND PEARL in the intensive-care unit. She was sitting at the nursing station, her head in her hands.

"Hi. Sorry, I heard you were looking for me," he said breathlessly.

He'd run all the way back.

He wanted to see her and he wanted to take care of George. The cancer had to come out today. Both physically and metaphorically.

Pearl glanced up, her eyes full of tears. "Where were you?"

"What happened?" he asked.

"Nothing, I just...you know I get overemotional and I was thinking about what happened and how foolish I was."

"No. I was the foolish one." He glanced over his shoulder because he really didn't want an audience listening in. "Come on, let's go talk. There's an empty meeting room down the hall."

Pearl followed him and he shut the door.

Once they were alone, he turned around.

"I love you, Pearl."

She blinked a couple of times.

"What?"

"I love you. If you don't want to marry me, that's

fine. You're right. I was trying to keep you with me by having you marry me. I was not willing to change and move with you. I didn't go after you. I was stubborn and hurt that you left me, like everyone else has done. I love you so much. I always have and if staying in your life means that we don't get married or I have to leave here, I will. I just want to be with you."

A tear slid down her cheek. "What if I lose this baby?"

"What if you don't?"

"I—I don't know. I guess, I'm too afraid of going through that pain again." She sighed. "I know why I lost our baby and I can take precautions this time, but there's no guarantee. I don't want to let you down again. I've let so many people down…"

"Who? Your parents? I think they let you down, just like my parents did, too. My mother spent her whole life pining after a man who didn't want to be pinned down and my father has spent his whole life trying to earn more money, but ultimately that didn't get them the happiness they sought. I'm happy when I'm with you. You coming back into my life gave me back my life."

"Yes. The same. I love you, Calum. I always have. There's been no one else in my life. I felt like I let you down the way that I've let my parents down. I blamed myself for losing the baby, for leaving you…"

Calum closed the gap between them. "You can never be a burden. You are my life and I haven't been living that life these past five years."

"I'm so sorry that I left you. I was in so much pain I felt I had to hide it. I'm so sorry. I wanted our baby so much. It broke me when I lost it and I didn't know how to let you in. I didn't know how to share the grief."

He brushed away the tears with his thumb. "When *we* lost it. We're in this together."

She smiled and nodded. "Right."

"I don't ever want to lose you again. If this doesn't work out, we'll adopt—or not. I don't care, I just want to be with you. I want a life with you."

There was a knock at the door.

Calum stepped back and opened it. A nurse was standing outside. "Dr. Henderson?"

"Yes," Pearl said, stepping forward and wiping her eyes.

"The patient is in the operating room, prepped and ready."

"We'll be down shortly."

The nurse nodded and Calum shut the door. "What's this all about?"

"No one knew where you went, other than you apparently left for the day. I paged you, but you didn't respond. George agreed to the amputation, but only if we do it today. His vitals are good and we need to get rid of that cancer."

"I'm glad he decided to proceed. I thought he was against it."

"He was, but we had a good talk and he helped me understand some things."

"What's that?"

"Life isn't always as planned, and dreams don't always pan out, but strength and resilience and adaptability are what matters." She walked past him. "Come on, let's go give George a second chance."

The surgery went smoothly and though Pearl was sad that Calum's new procedure couldn't save George's leg,

George would still have a life. The chemotherapy and radiation was killing him as much as the cancer was.

And she remembered Dr. Chin's words, too, which Calum reminded her of, and that was that sometimes doing good could cause more harm and sometimes it was better to let things go. She used to think that applied to her dream of a family. Even though she swore she never wanted that, she really did.

Deep down, she did.

She wanted roots and she wanted a safe place.

She wanted a place to call home.

She wanted Calum and she wanted a family with him, whatever that consisted of. She wasn't terrified of having a toxic relationship with Calum. She was afraid of having a toxic existence without him.

George was getting a second chance at life and as Pearl worked with Calum to ensure that George had that chance, she realized that she was being given a second chance at life, too, and she wasn't going to squander it.

She was done running.

"George?" Pearl asked.

George was coming to in the postanesthesia recovery unit.

It had been a long surgery, but Pearl was glad that they were able to take his leg and leave a good enough stump, that when it healed, he would be able to get a prosthetic. With physiotherapy and training, George had a chance to run again.

For now, he would could use that keen eye and mind of his to strategize and train. On some level she wished

that a relationship could work between two people who worked together, but being here in this hospital again, it reminded me of everything I gave up. The most important piece of that was you."

Calum smiled, his expression softening. "So what are you saying?"

"The chief of surgery said I had to clear it with the head of orthopedic surgery, but I would like to work here. If you could use another attending?"

"This is what you want?" he asked.

She grinned, nodding. "Yes. It is. I want to come home."

Calum stood up and took her in his arms. "I think that can be arranged."

"I want to stay in San Francisco. My life is here and I was a fool to think that I could run from it. I love you, Calum, and I'm glad that I get a second chance with you and I'm sorry that I wasn't there when you needed me most, when I needed you the most. I was just too lost in my own darkness to realize that."

"I love you, too, but I will say as your superior the moment the obstetrician puts you on bedrest you're done. No more surgeries!"

"I'm seeing the OB in the morning and we'll talk about what happened last time. There's no guarantee this one will stick. It's all risky." And it terrified her still. She was nervous.

"It's worth the risk." He tipped her chin and kissed her gently. "It's worth the risk to have you in my life. To have you stay with me."

"I love you." She kissed him again, deeper this time. "And in answer to your other question, yes."

He looked confused. "What other question?"

"Yes. I'll marry you. If you still want to get married?"

His eyes twinkled and he smiled. "I still want to marry you. How about Saturday?"

She laughed nervously. "The courts won't be open."

"Yeah, but Las Vegas is always open. We can fly down, get married. What do you say?"

"I think it's insane."

"Insanely good, right?" he teased. "So, what do you say?"

She kissed him again. "I say yes."

And he answered her, by kissing her and never letting her go.

EPILOGUE

One year later

"DID YOU TIE the bolt down?" Pearl asked.

"Yes," Calum answered, stuck under the pine tree they had purchased at the lot and trying to adjust the tree in a very rickety stand. Max the sheepdog was under the tree, watching what Calum was doing and wagging his tail nonstop.

"It looks crooked."

He frowned at her briefly from under the tree. "That's not helpful."

She chuckled. "Well, I don't know... There was nothing wrong with a fake tree."

"Those are awful. This is Aidan's first Christmas and we're going to have a proper real tree."

"Did you grow up with real trees? I grew up with fake ones," she teased.

"Well, no. This is my first real tree, but I learned all about them before I decided on this."

"You educated yourself?" she asked.

"Of course."

Pearl rolled her eyes as Calum went back to work under the tree, cursing and muttering to himself. What he needed was a better tree stand, but he was happy with the one he had bought himself.

He'd just underestimated the size of the tree he'd purchased.

It was cute that he thought they needed a real tree for Aidan's first Christmas when Aidan was only three months old. Pearl glanced at him, sleeping soundly in his portable bassinet, totally unaware of the ministrations that his father was going through to make his first Christmas magical.

When it was already magical.

Aidan had been their miracle baby. The pregnancy had been a breeze. She'd gone into labor and Aidan was born on his due date, promptly and quickly.

She had a feeling that if she ever had another baby she wouldn't be so lucky. And he was the best baby there was, sleeping through the night, no colic. Calum liked to tease that he was an alien baby because he was just so perfect.

Pearl didn't know about the alien thing, but she couldn't help but agree that he was perfect. Everyone doted on him and Derek, her godson, called himself honorary big brother. Derek was walking so well. He couldn't climb as well as he used to, but he was still active and Pearl was glad to have Derek in Aidan's life.

He was going to be a good influence. Although, Dianne still like to bring up that she thought it was a sore spot that she didn't get to go to their impromptu wedding in Vegas. However, Dianne and Jerome being Aidan's godparents more than made up for it.

After the wedding she moved into Calum's home and together, when she was feeling up to it, they finished off renovations. His little apartment inside the home was good enough for him, but Pearl had other plans for the large home.

The Bridgers had sent over a team onesie, personally delivered by George, who was managing so well with his prosthetic. When he had come over to see the baby, he was talking to her about training in the spring and that he was getting married to his old college sweetheart.

They'd gone their separate ways when he was drafted to the Bridgers because she didn't want to go to San Francisco and he had shut her out because of his cancer. George had been inspired by what Pearl and Calum had gone through, the moment he could travel again, he went to Philadelphia, found Reese and proposed right there and then.

Max barked and the sharp sound startled Aidan so he began to fuss.

Pearl scooped him up and held him close. He instantly stopped fussing and her heart soared with happiness. Aidan George Munro was the perfect child and she was so lucky to have him.

Her parents were distant and Calum's mother was gone, but Grayson was involved in his grandson's life, though Calum was still sorting through his emotions for his estranged father. Still, he didn't deny his son is grandfather. Aidan had enough people who weren't blood-related to make up a family and that was all that mattered.

Blood didn't make a family. Love did.

Max barked again.

"Max, you're not helping matters, buddy." Calum slid out from the tree. It was still leaning heavily on its side. He frowned. "I can do a surgery so intricate on delicate, brittle bones, surgeries that deal with nerves, and yet that blasted tree…"

Pearl laughed. "You need a bigger stand. Your eyeballs were bigger than the stand you had."

Calum nodded. "Yes. You may be right."

"What do you mean I may be right? I am right. Look at that thing."

He stood up and stretched. "Fine. You're right."

Calum put his arm around her and stared down at his son.

"I'll get a bigger stand in the morning," he said.

"Good." And as she said good Max stood up from under the tree and they both watched in amusement as the tree fell to its side again.

"You know, this reminds me of one of those cheesy Christmas movies where the dad overestimates the ratio of tree and house."

Calum chuckled. "I will not be that dad."

"You have a blinding amount of lights outside the house. You are so that dad and trying to make a good old-fashioned, fun family Christmas."

"Fine. I am. We both haven't had really traditional Christmases. I wanted something Aidan would remember…even if he won't remember this." Calum picked up the tree and set it in a corner until he could get a new stand.

Pearl headed over to the large bay window, to look out over the street and all the lights. Aidan was sleeping in her arms, but it didn't matter.

This time of year had never really mattered to her, until now.

Calum came up behind her. "I love you. Thank you for being my family."

"I love you, too. Thank you for being my family."

He kissed the top of her head, his arms around her and her arms around their son.

Now she understood what these holidays meant, because she had finally found her family. Even if it had been under her nose all this time.

She had found her family.

She had finally come home.

* * * * *

COMING SOON!

We really hope you enjoyed reading this book.
If you're looking for more romance, be sure to
head to the shops when new books are
available on

Thursday 20th August

To see which titles are coming soon, please visit

millsandboon.co.uk/nextmonth

MILLS & BOON

MILLS & BOON

Coming next month

THE VET'S SECRET SON
Annie O'Neil

Lucas threw Ellie a confused look and caught a flare of guilt lance through her green eyes. She looked pale, her hands shaking as she feebly tried to wave away her white lie. He looked back at the little boy, registered his hair colour, his eye colour, the way they sloped a bit, like his mother's…and his. Almond shaped, he called them. Sleepy sexy, Ellie had called them. He had the strangest feeling of déjà vu. As if he was looking at a photo of himself from when he had been a little boy.

He tried to estimate the little boy's age and then, with the power of a lightning strike, he got it.

Maverick was his son.

His heart crashed against his ribcage with a ferocity he wouldn't have believed possible.

One look at Ellie, eyes bright with a sheen of tears, and he knew he was right.

Trying his best not to frighten the boy, who quite clearly did not know Lucas his father, he knelt down in front of him, took the paper and signed it, drawing in his signature pawprint at the end of the 's' in Williams.

This was not the way he'd expected to meet his son. Not even close.

He felt Ellie's eye boring into him throughout the short interlude.

When he looked up at her, she was shaking her head, No, no, no—don't you dare tell him.

So what was he meant to do? Leave?

Not a chance.

Emotions assaulted him like knife wounds. Elation. Pride. Loss at having missed so many precious moments. His birth. His first word. His first tooth. Disbelief that Ellie had kept Maverick a secret all these years.

He knew things hadn't ended with any sort of grace between them but hiding a child? His child? What the hell had she been thinking? This gorgeous little boy was his flesh and blood. More than any of their shared hopes and dreams, Ellie knew he'd wanted a family of his own. With her! But life had ripped that possibility away from him.

And now, thanks to her, he'd missed the first five years of his son's life.

He forced his raging thoughts into a cage as he reminded himself, thanks to Ellie, he had a son. A beautiful, healthy, happy little boy. But at this moment? The gratitude ended there. She should have told him.

He rose and looked her straight in the eye. 'You and I need to talk.'

Continue reading
THE VET'S SECRET SON
Annie O'Neil

Available next month
www.millsandboon.co.uk

Copyright © 2020 Annie O'Neil

WE'RE LOOKING FOR NEW AUTHORS FOR THE MILLS & BOON MEDICAL SERIES!

Whether you're a published author or an aspiring one, our editors would love to read your story.

You can submit the synopsis and first three chapters of your novel online, and find out more about the series, at **harlequin.submittable.com/submit**

We read all submissions and you do not need to have an agent to submit.

IF YOU'RE INTERESTED, WHY NOT HAVE A GO?

Submit your story at:
harlequin.submittable.com/submit

MILLS & BOON

LET'S TALK

For exclusive extracts, competitions
and special offers, find us online:

 facebook.com/millsandboon

@MillsandBoon

@MillsandBoonUK

Get in touch on 01413 063232

For all the latest titles coming soon, visit
millsandboon.co.uk/nextmonth